THE VAMPIRES OF GREENWICH VILLAGE

NYPD WIZARD DETECTIVE BOOK 2

ARJAY LEWIS

MIND
BENDER
PRESS

The Vampires of Greenwich Village: NYPD Wizard Detective Book 2

Cover Design: Marianne Nowicki, PremadeEbookCoverShop.com
Editing: Brandi Aquino; www.editingdonewrite.com
Editing: Libby Broadbent

ISBN-13: 978-1734229103
ISBN-10: 1734229101

Published by:
Mindbender Press
474 South Main Street
Phillipsburg NJ 08865
www.mindbenderpress.com

DEDICATION

To a very big fan
Ramona
May you ride again

"It's almost as if we each have a vampire inside us. Controlling that beast, that dark side, is what fascinates me. "

—*Sheryl Lee*

"I have never met a vampire personally, but I don't know what might happen tomorrow. "

—*Bela Lugosi*

PROLOGUE

It was well past midnight as a tall Caucasian man with strong Roman features and a pointed nose walked past the huge marble arch that bordered the north end of Washington Square Park.

He was clean-shaven, and his gray-black hair was long but stylish and well-cut. His fingernails gleamed from a recent manicure, and he wore a suit that easily cost a thousand dollars.

Another man accompanied him, almost as tall and immaculately dressed in a gray suit with a subtly matching silk tie. His gray hair was thinning, and he wore a haughty look as he trailed a few feet behind the first man.

The leader pulled a pocket watch from his vest, keeping it in his hand as he passed to the left of the huge marble archway. The pair avoided the silent fountain in the center, advancing instead to the left path and into a tree-covered gloom.

The first man glanced back at his companion. "Is everything in order, Howell?"

"Oh yes, sir. At least they didn't request this meeting during the full moon."

"I am annoyed that they asked for this meeting at all," he snorted in reply. "I am not some errand boy you call when you want to send a message."

"Of course not, sir," Howell agreed.

They strolled along the path dimly lit by old-fashioned cast iron street lamps that allowed darkness to pool along the walkway.

To their right, there was a darkened playground behind a metal fence—the swings silent, the slides empty, and the climbing bars unoccupied. They turned left into a small oval-shaped area lined with benches.

There was no electrical fixture in this alcove, with the only light coming from a lamp ten feet away, leaving the area in shadows.

The pair stood as a man and woman approached. The man was thin with dark hair and pale skin. He wore a black T-shirt with no sleeves and black leather pants. His skin was inked with tattoos, and multiple piercings marked his face.

The woman was different. She was statuesque and sultry, in a black dress that showed off the pale skin of her fantastic legs. She was taller than the man, and her raven hair hung down her back in curls.

The woman spoke first. "Have the time?"

The man with the good suit held out the watch in his hand. "I have some time. Perhaps that can help."

The thin, nervous man with the tattoos glanced around, his eyes fixed on Howell. "You dare bring this thing with you?"

"Hush, Strix," the woman ordered. "We speak of nothing until protections are in place."

The thin man glared at his companion, but nodded, annoyed.

The first man held the pocket watch aloft, and a dome of bluish light rose over the oval area where they stood, then faded so only the shadows of the park remained.

"We are now protected. No mortal—" he gave a disgusted look at the tattooed man "—or any other creature can hear or see anything we say or do."

With that, he held the watch as it shifted into a long wooden staff over six feet tall. His clothing shifted also, changing into dark-blue robes and tall boots. "I meet you as the Wizard Greywacke. This is my companion, Howell—"

"He is *Wolfen*," Strix spat in disgust. "We did not invite him."

"I would be a fool to meet with your kind alone," Drusilicus Greywacke announced, as he watched the woman like a hawk. "Lysandra, I have come at your request. Please keep the child controlled."

"Child?" Strix said. His fangs grew longer, and his fingernails sharpened to points as his eyes began to glow with a reddish hue. "I will not be insulted in this way—"

"Hush, Strix," Lysandra cautioned. "If the wizard wished it, he could turn you to ash with but a gesture."

Strix bared his elongated canines but kept his peace.

"It was good of you to heed my call, Drusilicus," Lysandra observed. "I only requested it to save both of our worlds."

Drusilicus nodded, unperturbed by this statement. "Your message said it was urgent."

"If you bring news, will the coven listen?"

Drusilicus stood a little straighter. "I am one of the Five, and I carry the staff of the element water. Trust me, I have sway in the coven, and the ear of the coven master."

"I'd prefer his heart," Strix scoffed. "To dine upon."

Drusilicus stared down his nose at the young man. "At least *my* associate knows to speak when appropriate."

Howell nodded at Strix smugly.

"I did not wish to come," Strix hissed. "Lysandra insisted. She can be most persuasive."

Drusilicus arched an eyebrow, and a smug smile appeared on his face. "I am familiar with just how persuasive she can be."

Lysandra curtsied and a wide, hungry smile appeared on her face. "You honor me, wizard."

Howell cleared his throat. "Sir, if I may be so bold…"

Drusilicus set his jaw and glanced at his companion. "Of course Howell, you are right, as always. My spell of containment will not last long. We must to business."

Lysandra's face fell into a pout. "You are right. Pity."

"Why have you asked me here?"

Lysandra turned to her companion and slapped him on the back of his head. "Speak, fool."

He eyed her with a look that could kill and cleared his throat. "I was at a meeting where they made announcements."

Drusilicus stared at him with disdain. "How scintillating. What was the announcement, pray tell?"

Strix glanced about, then spoke quietly, "The Drakula is coming to New York."

Drusilicus leaned back in shock. "The Drakula! Here?" He glanced about nervously, then leaned in and whispered, "Why? What does he want in New York?"

Strix leaned in close to the other three and said ominously, "He seeks a papyrus."

Drusilicus frowned. "What papyrus?"

Strix shrugged. "How the hell should I know? That's what they said."

Drusilicus grew angry. "How did you hear these things? Didn't you ask what they meant?"

Lysandra spoke, "Strix was guarding the door at a meeting of the council."

"If I'd gone in and started asking questions, they would've ripped my throat out," Strix whined.

"You're lucky I don't rip your throat out right now," Drusilicus threatened in a low voice.

Strix appeared confused. "I didn't know wizards did that."

"Metaphorically," Drusilicus muttered.

Howell spoke up, "If you come around during the full moon, I shall gladly rip it out for you."

Strix growled at the older man.

"Enough!" Drusilicus snarled, and turned to Strix. "This is important. Did they say anything about this papyrus, anything at all?"

"Something about a prophecy of 'everlasting life' and 'everlasting contempt'."

"Not very useful," Drusilicus complained.

"Oh yeah, they made a big deal about, 'he shall scatter the power of the holy people,' and 'all things shall be finished'."

Drusilicus went pale. "I see." He glanced to Howell. "We must go."

Lysandra commented, "I thought you should know."

"You were quite correct. Thank you, Lysandra, this was helpful."

Strix cleared his throat loudly. "I was told I would be taken care of?"

Drusilicus peered at Strix as if he were a worm. "Of course." He turned and snapped his fingers. "Howell!"

The manservant stepped forward, pulling several hundred-dollar bills from his pocket and handing them to the young man.

"I was thinkin' it would be more than this," the black-clothed man complained.

"At least I didn't rip your throat out," Drusilicus hissed. He took Lysandra's hand and bowed as he brought it to his lips. "Thank you, good lady."

"This will make a great deal of trouble," Lysandra told him. "The Drakula in New York does not bode well."

"None of it bodes well. Now go. I will hold the charm for a few moments as you leave to keep away any prying eyes."

Lysandra waved and her body shrank, sprouted wings, and a bat flew away into the darkness of the park.

"I'll just walk," Strix announced and turned to leave.

"Haven't mastered transformation yet?" Howell asked quietly.

The young man looked over his shoulder. "At least I have a choice. Not like you. Enjoy the next full moon, old guy. It might be your last."

"Old guy?" Howell growled. "I shall thrash you here and now, you young raggabrash."

With speed much faster than any human could accomplish, the young man ran off.

"Don't let that fool bother you, Howell. He is inconsequential," Drusilicus stated, as his blue robes melted back into his expensive suit and the large staff in his hands once again became a pocket watch which he slipped into his waistcoat.

"I beg your pardon, sir. I do not enjoy disrespectful youth these days," Howell apologized.

"Understandable, Howell," Drusilicus said. "But that young fool may prove useful. If the arrival of the Drakula doesn't get us all killed, first."

ONE

E ddie Berman and Luis Vasquez proceeded quietly down the sidewalk to the small series of buildings next to the roadway in Central Park. Cars zipped by, although traffic was light at this time of night. The buildings were brick with slate roofs and fanciful pillars rising between windows covered with crisscrossed steel that protected the glass.

The bigger man was tall, wide, and as sturdy as a tree with a light-brown complexion. He turned to the thin man next to him, who was African-American, though he had a fairly light complexion, only a shade or two darker than his companion.

"Do you think they're in there?" the bigger man whispered with a slight Spanish accent.

"That's what our witness said," his companion muttered back.

"They gotta be pullin' down a lot of money, and they come *here*?" he responded. "I mean, Mind-Blo is the biggest thing in years. I don't see why they would work out of these moldy old buildings, Eddie."

Lieutenant Berman looked up at his large partner and smiled. "We won't know unless we go in there, Luis."

"You got that," Luis said, reaching into his coat to pull out his service weapon. The Glock 19 fit easily into his big hand. Meanwhile, his partner pulled out his own handgun, a SIG Sauer.

Luis reached out to the doorknob and quietly turned it.

"It's open," he hissed.

Eddie nodded. "One… two… three."

The two men burst through the door with practiced ease, Eddie going low as his massive partner went high.

"NYPD! Hands in the air."

They cleared the doorway. The room was dirty, the plaster on the walls damaged, and there was the smell of mildew in the air. Five feet in front of them was another open doorway revealing two men seated at a card table on rickety chairs. One man wore denim, had long hair, a pale complexion, and big eyes that glared at the sudden interruption. Next to him was a bigger rat-like man with slicked-back dark hair, dressed in a dark suit.

On the table was a bright battery-powered lantern that shone down on a dozen small vials filled with a blue liquid, carefully measured out in doses.

The two men raised their hands, and Luis stepped forward. Eddie paused as the staging of the scene bothered him, as well as the small smile he observed on the face of the well-dressed man.

Luis pushed through the open doorway, just as there was the click-clack of a pump-action shotgun.

A voice growled, "Drop it or I drop you."

Luis slowly raised his hands. "You don' wanna do this—we're cops."

"Tell your partner to come in here, or I'll blow your damn head off," the unseen man ordered.

Eddie sighed and stepped forward, his pistol pointed at the floor. The long-haired guy stood, lifting a gun that had been sitting on the card table. "Put the guns on the floor, nice and easy."

Eddie crouched and placed his weapon on the dirty tile floor. Luis bent at the waist to do the same, both of them standing upright with their hands raised.

The man in the suit leaned back in his chair, relaxed, the smug smile still on his face.

Luis glanced over at the person who'd been lying in wait for them. He was average height and rail thin, probably both a user and a dealer. He appeared nervous, but held the rifle in a firm grip.

"You know, a sawed-off shotgun is illegal in this state."

"Shut up!" the man barked and turned to his companions as the long-haired man picked up Eddie and Luis' guns.

"You got no way out of this," Eddie spoke in a firm tone. "We have backup coming, and if you kill police officers, it's the death penalty."

The man in the suit laughed. "As if I care about death!"

The nervous guy pressed the barrel of his shotgun against Luis' head. "Besides, we got hostages now."

With remarkable speed for a man his size, Luis grabbed the barrel of the shotgun and lifted it to the ceiling, to the shock of the man holding it. The thug pulled the trigger, and the weapon resounded in the small room as the muzzle flash went well over

Luis' head. The shot hit the ceiling, causing plaster and dust to rain down and instantly filling the room with a fog of powder.

The long-haired man raised Eddie's gun to find that the detective gestured and a six-foot-tall staff of wood appeared in his right hand. Eddie easily swatted the gun from the man's grasp and brought the gnarled top of the staff against his head, knocking him to the ground.

The man behind the table stood up and, with inhuman speed, leapt over the table toward Luis to pull him off his associate.

"*Oppressio!*" Eddie yelled. With a gesture, an invisible force lifted the man and threw him across the room, slamming him against the wall. Eddie turned to the man struggling with Luis, just in time to see his partner smack the man in the face with the butt of his own rifle.

"You are *he*! The Newling!" the dark-haired man said as he rose from the floor, his suit now covered with fine powder. As the dust settled, it revealed Eddie. His inexpensive suit had morphed into a short red robe with full sleeves that ended in decorative cuffs at his wrists. No longer trousers and shoes, but loose, full red pantaloons embroidered with shining gold thread and tall black boots. The wooden staff in his hand crested with a halo of fiery-red light.

Eddie glared at the man. "What are *you* doing, dealing drugs with these guys?"

Luis leveled the shotgun at the man. "Is this guy one of yours?"

Eddie's mouth was a tight line. "He's a vampire. Speak—who is your master?"

"I have no master, save the Drakula himself," the man spat. "And I have no fear of a new wizard, still wet behind the ears."

With that, there was a puff of expanding air, and in place of the man in the suit there was only a dark mist that flew toward the door.

"*Coerceo!*" Eddie said, making a tiny circle with his stick. It caught the dark mist in a small tornado that pulled it into a shape the size of a basketball floating at eye level.

"*Transfiguro!*" Eddie commanded, and the ball of mist spun, lowered to the ground, and in an instant, the man in the suit knelt on the floor in its place.

The man panted and glared at Eddie's face with his dark eyes. "You have learned your lessons well, Wizard."

"Thanks for noticing. You're going nowhere until you tell me why a vampire is working with some two-bit drug dealers in my park! And what about this new drug you guys are putting out on the street? People have died from it."

The smug smile appeared again on his face, and a red glow filled his eyes. "You may have learned your lessons well, but I have millennia of practice, fool."

In an instant, the man disappeared, and a small bat streaked past Luis' face, out the doorway and into the night. It was so quick, Eddie barely had time to move to the door to watch the creature fly out and into the night sky.

"Damn," Luis said, just as red and blue lights appeared on the roadway.

Eddie shook his head, and with a gesture his red robes transformed into his suit and his wooden staff vanished.

An hour later, Eddie was finishing up his report on the bust. Since the men had both drugs and weapons, it had been easy. Eddie also listed the escaped man—that was the part where he had a few problems. Since he and Luis were between the man and the door, how did he get past them?

Luis peered over Eddie's shoulder. "I'm calling it a night, partner."

"Did our perps get booked and given a nice cell?"

"Yeah, heading to Rikers in the morning." Luis slipped his large body into the chair next to the desk so he could look his partner in the eye. "You're getting good with this stuff, man."

Eddie nodded. "Three nights a week for nine months. But I told Marlowe I gotta cut back."

"Oh yeah—Marlowe, your old wizard-guru guy. How's he doing?"

"As mysterious as ever. Still won't tell me anything plain out—he has to let me know slowly."

"How's Cerise?" Luis asked.

Eddie responded with a proud smile. "Good, but as huge as she is, I'm figuring she's either having twins or a horse."

Luis shook his head. "Man, you finally get to go to Aruba, and she comes back pregnant. Who knew?"

"Not us. Believe me, we were both surprised."

Luis nudged him in the ribs with his elbow. "Forgot to pack the birth control, eh?"

"We haven't needed it for years! After Douglas was born, we tried for a girl, with no luck. Doctor said it was my sperm count and Cerise had a blockage in one of her tubes, so we stopped worrying about it."

Luis smiled knowingly. "Well, something worked. For once you're having the new kid instead of Maria and me."

"Maria's been nice to keep tabs on Cerise."

"*No problemo*," Luis said and rose to his feet. "Can we work a regular shift tomorrow? I haven't seen my wife awake in a week."

"I am afraid not yet, partner. You saw that vampire. We can look for him all day, but without a clue about where he sleeps, we won't find him. Plus, that new drug, Mind-Blo? It's out there, and we still don't know how it's made or what they make it from. We have to keep hitting the nights until we bring him down."

"You gonna alert your wizard crew? If we had some magical backup, we'd be able to take him down faster."

"You're going home, and I'm going to see Marlowe about that very idea."

"Good. We should have uniforms check on those old buildings during the day though, make sure no one else moves in."

"I'll include that recommendation in our report."

Luis waved and headed for the door.

Eddie smiled after his partner, grateful that he'd revealed the secret of his strange abilities to him. On a case ten months earlier, Eddie was at a murder scene when a decapitated head informed him he'd been 'summoned'. Gifted with a staff of power, he joined a group of wizards, some of them centuries old, to take on the obligation of bearing the mystical staff of the element fire.

He rapidly learned skills so they could bring down an ancient demon and find the murderer of the wizard he'd replaced.

Now, months later, he had improved his skills, but with his wife pregnant and Eddie's job as a detective lieutenant for the Central Park Precinct, he would have to focus on family and work.

He already had two sons: William, fifteen, and Douglas, twelve. Eddie could remember just how much work babies were. He would need all his reserves to handle diapers, sleepless nights, and the unending work that a new baby created.

He vowed it wouldn't all fall on Cerise's shoulders.

Nine months earlier, they'd enjoyed a second honeymoon in Aruba, courtesy of Marlowe. A month later, Cerise had missed her period and discovered she was pregnant. They were shocked but elated.

Their doctor was very concerned, as Cerise was almost forty, but Eddie couldn't be happier. Unlike his partner, who had six children, this would be the Berman's third. Also, his mother was in the house, and recently healed of cancer by the wizard Drusilicus. Because of that, she was feeling more energized than she had in years and helped Cerise run the household.

Although Eddie had been training hard with his mentor, the last nine months had been quiet. The Central Park Precinct was not the busiest for a pair of homicide detectives. Eddie and Luis had been doing boring cases, following up on purse snatchings and nuisance crimes, but Captain Jacobs got a line on a gang of drug pushers that had made Central Park their home base, and tonight Eddie and Luis brought down some of that gang.

Except for the vampire.

Eddie needed to learn just who that character was.

TWO

"So," Marlowe said, sipping tea as he sat across from Eddie in the large open space of what Marlowe referred to as the breakfast room. "A vampire led your gang of evildoers?"

Marlowe was a short man with a long white beard and long hair, resembling a skinny Santa Claus. He was in a white shirt and slacks with a red smoking jacket with black lapels. He carried a thin walking stick with an ornate handle that was black and glowed with many layers of stain and varnish.

"You got it," Eddie told him as he took a sip of the aromatic tea. Eddie wasn't really a tea drinker, but in his months studying with the old wizard, he developed a liking for the brew, though he had to improve it with cream and multiple sugars. "I was hoping to talk to Daniel, see if he could track down any information."

Daniel Kraft was a tall vampire with movie-star looks who stayed at Marlowe's spacious townhouse on fashionable Central Park West and did odd jobs for the old man. He had connections with the darker side of New York City's occult world, and could go places a wizard would not be welcome.

"I am afraid that Daniel is out this evening," Marlowe said. "But if you can give me a description, perhaps I can ask him in the morning."

Eddie nodded. "You got pen and paper?"

Marlowe raised his slim stick, and a drawer opened on a nearby breakfront. A scroll of parchment rose gently out of it, unrolling as it flew to the table. A small glass inkwell and a large feathered quill followed this. All three objects landed on the table close to Eddie.

Eddie gazed at the jar of ink and feathered writing implement. "You're kidding, right?"

"Have we not trained with quill and ink?" Marlowe asked innocently.

"Hasn't been high on the priority list," Eddie replied as he pulled a ballpoint pen from his pocket and gawked at the scroll before him. "You don't have any sticky notes, do you? You know, small squares of paper you stick on things?"

"I am afraid not, Eddie."

Eddie shrugged, clicked the top of the pen, and wrote on the parchment. "There's been something I've been meaning to ask you."

"Of course, Eddie." Marlowe sat back in the chair with his tea and saucer in hand.

"Well, you know my wife is pregnant—"

"As you've mentioned several times," Marlowe sighed.

"Yeah, well, my question is—how did this happen? After Douglas was born, we did some tests, and the diagnosis was secondary infertility and a low sperm count."

"Ah yes! Well, the explanation is quite simple," Marlowe said, and held up his cane. "When you received your staff, it filled you with the energy of life. That is why wizards live so much longer than ordinary people."

"Okay, well, that explains my... um... success, but how did it help Cerise?"

"To explain without being too graphic, I would say your abundance of energy flowed into your wife, and affected her anatomy as well as your own."

"You could've warned a guy." Eddie smiled. "I've been firing blanks for years."

"If you wish to prevent this in the future, I would recommend simple birth control, Eddie."

"No, it's good. I'm hoping for a girl."

"I was under the impression that modern science allowed one to know the sex of the child before birth."

Eddie shook his head. "Cerise thinks it's bad luck."

Marlowe frowned. "She believes in bad luck?"

"After the things we saw in Central Park, she believes in a lot of things she didn't before," Eddie pointed out. He put his pen away and slid the parchment across the table to Marlowe. "Here is the description of the guy for Daniel."

Marlowe glanced at the paper. "I'll see if he can find out anything."

"Luis and I are working nights until we catch the perp, so Daniel can call me, or use a mirror."

Wizards often used mirrors as a fast and easy way to communicate. Eddie had done it once with Daniel Kraft, except since he was a vampire and cast no reflection in the glass, Eddie had spoken to an empty room.

"Daniel doesn't like to use the mirror, and phones are a technology he is not yet comfortable with."

"Yeah, they've only been around about a hundred and fifty years," Eddie snorted.

"Daniel—like my fellow wizards—is not very adept with modern technology, Eddie."

"Hey, I finally got you to use a computer," Eddie said. "Even though you fought me every step of the way."

"True. Now I must learn to stop checking the Book of Face all the time."

"Facebook, Marlowe. It's called Facebook."

There was a knock at the door that reverberated through the rooms. Eddie rose.

"Oh my, who could that be?" Marlowe said. "Shall I call Wraith?"

Marlowe referred to his dreary ghostly manservant who haunted the house and did tasks for the old man.

"Or you could just answer the door," Eddie told him as he headed for the foyer. He had to walk out of the large breakfast room and through the enormous living room that was more like an auditorium or ballroom than a place to relax. As he made his way to the front of the house, his eye wandered to the huge circular staircase in the corner. It was a tall structure that went up the equivalent of several stories before it reached the high second floor. In the center of the spiral was an inner caged area that contained a cylindrical elevator car. Surrounding this elevator shaft were not walls, but decorative wrought-iron metalwork that resembled spears.

He stepped from the living room to the front lobby. The house had an enormous interior that went up multiple stories. Even though it was as large as a football field on the inside, the outside was a modest four-story building with a circular turret that towered high above the street. Marlowe had told Eddie that this was because of fourth-dimensional physics. Eddie didn't know what that meant, other than it was bigger on the inside than on the outside.

He glanced quickly through the peephole, a recent addition Eddie had insisted on. Drusilicus stood at the top of the stairs. Eddie quickly unlatched the door and opened it.

"Oh good, you're here," Drusilicus said as he pushed his way in. "That will save time."

"The question is why are you here at this time of night?" Eddie asked with a glance at his watch. "It's after midnight."

"Which bears the question—what are *you* doing here, lieutenant?" Drusilicus huffed. "Shouldn't you be home? I heard your wife was expecting."

"That she is, Drew."

"My congratulations. Boy or girl?"

"We don't know yet."

His eyebrows went up. "Really? Hasn't Marlowe taught you the basics of divination? Even midwives can predict the sex of a child—"

"We don't want to know," Eddie blurted. "I'm here because I've been working nights for a couple weeks on a case to stop a drug gang."

"I guess you're enjoying the benefits of needing less sleep," Drusilicus told him as the two men walked through the cavernous living room.

Eddie stopped walking. "Hey, yeah, I've noticed that. Is that part of all this, like the living longer thing?"

"Indeed," Drusilicus snapped, and headed into the living room. "Isn't Marlowe going over all this with you? It's not my job to teach you basic information you should have learned before you ever gained a staff."

"There's the Drew I know and love. You scared me for a second —I thought you were becoming *nice*."

"I was being polite, and I am *always* polite. I'm here on urgent business and I have no time to dilly-dally."

"Dilly-dally?" Eddie repeated as they headed into the breakfast room. Marlowe was staring at something in his small crystal ball filled with purple mist. He quickly slipped it into his pocket as the two men entered.

"Drusilicus?" Marlowe said, not getting up.

"I came straight from a worrisome meeting in Washington Square Park."

"Is that another wizard hangout? Like Central Park?" Eddie wondered.

"Actually, that is territory claimed by the vampires," Marlowe explained.

Drusilicus grimaced. "Although some of them are moving out to Brooklyn because the rents are cheaper."

"They don't grab people down there, do they?" Eddie worried.

"Hunting is limited within the entire city," Drusilicus stated blithely. "Most of the vampires have followers who give themselves for feeding."

"Wait—people *allow* themselves to be killed?"

"Hardly!" Drusilicus argued. "They allow their vampire to drink some of their blood to sustain them, but not so much as to cause personal harm."

"That's terrible!" Eddie said. "Feeding on people like that!"

"It's been a tradition for centuries," Marlowe explained. "People do it by their own choice. It's not coerced."

"You feed on animals yourself, lieutenant," Drusilicus pointed out.

"Why would their followers do it?" Eddie demanded, choosing to ignore him.

Marlowe cleared his throat. "An allure surrounds each vampire, a glamour that attracts humans. It's the ability that manifests once a person has transformed. That glamour attracts weaker minds, and some followers become quite devoted to their vampire. Add to that, the vampire's saliva not only contains elements that allow the blood to flow, but it possesses a venom that gives a euphoric feeling to the victim. Therefore, they do not resist."

Drusilicus broke in before Marlowe could continue. "Vampire lore aside—I had a meeting with a vampire who worked as a guard for a meeting of the council."

"What council?" Eddie asked.

"The vampire council," Marlowe said. "They have regular monthly meetings, third Wednesday of the month."

"You're kidding," Eddie gasped.

"Or is it the third Thursday?" Marlowe considered.

"I don't care if it is alternate Sundays, Marlowe," Drusilicus snapped. "This informant told me that the Drakulea is coming to New York."

"The who?" Eddie said.

"You would know him as Dracula, Eddie," Marlowe explained.

"Dracula? *The* Dracula? There really is a Dracula?"

"The Drakulea or the Drakula," Drusilicus offered, "is the name given to the Lord of the Vampires. The first person to claim this title was Vlad the Impaler, a fifteenth century nobleman who ruled part of what is now Romania. He was a barbaric leader who impaled his enemies, as well as peace envoys sent by the Ottoman Empire."

"A fine, upstanding guy," Eddie said. "Is he the one who started all the vampire legends?"

"There have been stories of vampires throughout history," Marlowe reassured. "Since ancient times, even in Egypt and Babylon. As far as we can tell, vampires have existed almost as long as there have been humans." Marlowe rose from his chair and went to pour himself more tea. This was odd to Eddie, since the teapot and its enchanted accessories responded to spoken commands.

Marlowe went on. "I have heard rumors about the being who currently bears the name, but I am not sure of his true identity."

"He informed me of more than that," Drusilicus recounted. "It would appear the Drakula is seeking some papyrus here in New York."

Marlowe turned suddenly, his blue eyes blazing. "A papyrus? What kind of papyrus?"

Drusilicus sighed. "The informant did not know, but said the papyrus will, and I quote, 'scatter the holy people' and 'all will be finished'."

Marlowe turned pale as he finished pouring his tea. "I see. Was there anything else?"

Drusilicus stood up straighter. "No, but that prophecy sounded familiar to me, so I thought I should bring it to you at once."

"Sounds like a bunch of BS to me," Eddie announced, and looked at the two wizards carefully. "What does it mean to you, Marlowe?"

"Nothing good, I'm afraid," Marlowe related with anxiety. "I must do some research, see if I can find the exact references." He took a sip of the tea and gazed at his two companions. "It is late, and I think it best if we speak on the morrow."

"Okay," Eddie said, and took his cup and saucer to place them on the tea trolley. "But you guys know I got a pregnant wife, so don't pull me into anything big like the last time."

"We didn't 'pull you in,' lieutenant," Drusilicus challenged. "You were *summoned*, and we had nothing to do with that."

"Well, this time, you guys are the ones getting us into a battle, not some big-ass demon."

Marlowe spoke up. "If a battle is even necessary at all, Eddie. But if the Drakula is coming here, looking for trouble, there is naught we can do but fight."

"It has always been a strained relationship between the vampires and the wizards," Drusilicus put in.

"I'm just saying I have other priorities right now. My wife and baby are number one on the list."

"We understand, Eddie," Marlowe intoned with a sigh. "It is late and we are all tired. Let's call it a night. I shall do some study on the morrow and see if I can figure out this reference to a papyrus. More importantly, see if I can locate it before our foe can."

Eddie headed out of the townhouse, down the long steps and across the street to Central Park, smiling that he had a fast way home. By car, the trip to Teaneck, New Jersey, even late at night, would take at least twenty minutes, but Eddie seldom used his car for the trek. It was currently parked in the lot reserved for police off the transverse road across from his precinct.

Instead of driving home, he merely stepped within the park, and into the shadows. He extended his hand, so that his wizard staff flew into it, entered a grove of trees, and instantly exited from a small park in Teaneck, two blocks from his house.

Marlowe's explanation of this ability was that it was an act of sympathetic magick. The concept was that all the forests in the world were one forest, just as all the air in the atmosphere was the same air. When he entered the grove of trees, all he needed to do was hold his destination in mind and walk out of the forest in another location.

Although this explanation was odd to Eddie, it was an easy way to teleport to any place on the planet, provided there were trees.

Coming out of the wooded area in a blink of an eye, his staff — the bearer of his mystical abilities—turned into a simple credit card that he placed into his wallet.

The street lamps made scattered pools of light as he walked briskly towards his home, still energized but winding down from his day.

An odd feeling crept up his spine, and he paused.

He was being watched.

Facing the empty street, he whispered, "*Ostendo.*"

A circle of red light slid away from his body in all directions, making little sparks of white as it revealed leaves of trees, overhanging wires on poles, and a sleeping bird in a nest.

Eddie thought he noticed a quick movement to his left and turned to face it, but saw nothing. The circle of red light extended out and away from him, and then finally faded into the darkness.

He had seen movement, but whatever watched him preferred to run rather than confront him. Eddie nodded triumphantly and couldn't help but smile.

The learning of Latin words that he could use to empower simple spells were rapidly becoming second nature to him, after months of practice. It was useful. It was a real pain to pull out his staff if he wanted to do something small, or with no one noticing. His red robes and the tall staff were impressive, and as he proved tonight, very useful in a life-and-death struggle, but he had learned that most of what he wanted to do was fairly mundane, like the spell he'd just cast to reveal a hidden observer.

When he'd first started training with Marlowe, he was preparing for a battle with an ancient demon determined to bring Armageddon. Marlowe started with techniques that pushed his abilities to their fullest extent, fighting mythological creatures and monsters in practice sessions. Once the emergency had passed, the training became more focused on basic skills and spells that were more useful on a daily basis.

Making his way up his lawn and to the back door of his house, a motion sensitive floodlight blinked on. He unlocked the door, let himself in, not worrying if someone had been following him. Over the months, he and Marlowe put magical protections around the house that kept out otherworldly beings. No mystical creature could enter without an invitation.

Eddie took off his shoes by the door and tiptoed quietly through the living room and upstairs to the bedroom where his wife was sleeping. He undressed in the bathroom and, in T-shirt and boxers, carefully lifted the covers and slipped in next to her.

She was snoring quietly and slept on her side—her protruding belly making almost any other position impossible. Eddie reached around and stroked the bump through the covers and felt a small kick that his wife slept through.

Eddie smiled and wondered how you could sleep when something inside you was kicking you? He was once again in awe of the miracle that was happening within his wife's body. He knew that he could never fully comprehend what she went through, and it made him adore her even more.

Two figures sat on thick branches of a large tree just outside the magical boundary that protected the Berman house.

"He don't look that tough," the short, stout man said as he sat firmly on his branch.

"It is said he stopped a demon and a warlock by himself, and after carrying the staff for only two weeks," Lysandra replied. She easily held onto the trunk of the tree from her branch. "He also chased you away easily enough, Tuck."

"How come we always get the crummy jobs?" Tuck muttered.

"We only have to watch until he's asleep, learn his schedule, find out when he is home and when he is not."

"Yes, but why?"

"Because the orders from the Drakula told us so."

Tuck smiled. "I hope this means war."

THREE

E ddie's cell phone rang at 7:00 AM the following morning. He had put it on a charger in the bathroom, but the noise still woke him, and he stumbled his way into the bathroom to grab it.

"H-Hello," Eddie said, as he tried to think his way past the cobwebs in his brain.

"Lieutenant Berman? It's Captain Jacobs," the big voice said over the phone.

"Yes, sir," Eddie responded, waking up instantly.

"I'm sorry to bother you, but we have a murder in the park."

"A murder, sir?"

"Yes, and you and Sergeant Vasquez are my only experienced homicide detectives. Sorry to pull you in after working last night, but I need you on the scene."

Eddie took the phone into the bedroom and grabbed a pen off the top of the dresser. "What's the address, sir?"

"The body is in the Springbanks Arch under the 102nd Street crossing, near Central Park Driveway."

"That's the low arch, right, sir?" Eddie asked as he scribbled the information on a notepad he kept on the dresser.

"Yes, only about six feet high. Will you and the sergeant be all right?"

"We'll make do, sir."

"How fast can you get there, lieutenant?"

"Twenty minutes, sir. Should I call Sergeant Vasquez?"

"No, I'll do it. Better if he's annoyed with me instead of his partner for waking him."

"Thank you, sir," Eddie said, and ended the call.

"So, twenty minutes, huh?" a sultry voice said from the bed. "That ruins my plans."

Eddie saw his wife's eyes sparkling in the dim light of the bedroom. "I woke you, I'm sorry."

"All I do is sleep and eat," Cerise complained with the slight African accent that colored her words. Her parents emigrated from that continent before her birth, but speaking two languages at home always made some words sound foreign. "This pregnancy has been so different from Douglas and William."

"Not surprising, since Douglas was over a decade ago," Eddie said as he knelt at the bed and kissed her. She returned the kiss with passion.

Eddie pulled back. "Oh, you had *that* in mind?"

"I am entitled." She grinned. "After all, you won't make me *more* pregnant."

"I have to hit the shower, honey. And you're beautiful."

"I expect some action tonight," she sighed. "Get home at a reasonable hour."

"Boy, work, work, work," Eddie kidded.

"If I'm the one who has to go into labor, so you have to do your work as well!" she quipped. She rose and groaned.

"You okay?" Eddie worried.

"It's my back, and it aches."

Eddie sat next to her on the bed and rubbed the lower part of her spine with his fist.

She groaned. "Oh, that feels good."

"Honey, I know you didn't want to know the baby's sex, but they would tell us if you have more than one in there, wouldn't they?"

"I would hope so," Cerise said with a glance to her engorged belly. "Mm. You better stop. This is turning me on."

"You *are* in a mood."

"Damn right. Get home early and take care of your woman!"

Eddie kissed her and headed from the bedroom for a quick shower.

She shouted after him, "And you be careful, my big, black man."

In a few brief minutes, Eddie showered, shaved, dressed, and headed out the door. He entered the small grove of trees in the park near his house and used his abilities to transport himself to Central Park near the Springbanks Arch.

By focusing his mind and his intention on the arch, he stepped out of the woods just north of it. He casually strolled down the

North Woods Walking Path toward the opening under the roadway.

He was grateful it had rained little in recent days, because this one arch flooded in a rainstorm. The arch was one of the more hidden decorative arches that filled Central Park, and the reason for its location was to allow runoff of the North Meadow to flow easily into the Harlem Meer.

Eddie was now familiar with the fact that each arch was not merely a clever way to move traffic throughout the park, but each was a monument to a great wizard. Riftstone was the name of an arch and also the wizard who died to give Eddie his staff. He had lived disguised as a homeless man in the park.

Eddie drew near the semicircular arch, segmented with rough-cut stone and a wrought iron ornamental railing on the far side of the roadway that snaked on the top of the stone opening.

A uniformed officer was standing outside. He raised a hand in greeting, familiar with the detective.

"Officer Young, isn't it?" Eddie said to the blond man.

"Yes, sir, here with Officer Taylor," he reported. "She's at the other end of the tunnel."

"You look a lot better than your first homicide."

The young man flushed red. "Yes, sir, but this one is a lot less messy. Oddly, there's hardly any blood."

"Did you see the body?"

"Yes, sir. Taylor and I were first on the scene. We came straight up after 9-1-1 got the call."

"Who reported it?"

"Anonymous call, sir. From a payphone, no less."

"A payphone? Those still exist?"

"Yes, sir, one about two blocks from here."

Eddie pulled on a pair of latex gloves from his pocket. "Any idea of the COD?"

Young nodded. "Pretty obvious in this case. The cause of death is a wooden stake inserted into the man's chest."

Eddie paused. "Did I just hear you right? A wooden stake?"

Young shook his head. "Just like an old vampire movie, sir. The weird part was, he wore all black, kinda Goth, like those guys who play at being a vampire."

Eddie pulled out his notebook and pen and wrote with his gloved hands. "You think someone thought he really *was* a vampire?"

"Could be, sir. But like I told you, there was very little blood. That suggests they killed him elsewhere and dropped the body here."

Eddie pointed with his pen. "Good eye, Young. I can see you're noticing little details."

"Trying to, sir," Young answered with a smile.

"When my partner gets here, send him in."

"You got it, LT."

Eddie ducked a little and stepped into the tunnel. It was good to see that Young was more relaxed with the job now that he'd been doing it for a while. That was the way it was—you either learned the job or you left it along the way. Being a cop wasn't easy, but it was the life Eddie had chosen.

What he hadn't chosen was all this wizard stuff.

Springbanks Arch was one of the longer tunnels in a place where there were many arches and roadways. About halfway down the tunnel, he located the dead body. He crouched to look at the corpse.

The young man lay out on the ground wearing a black T-shirt with no sleeves, black pants, and heavy boots. Tattoos snaked their way up his arms and metal piercings decorated his face.

A large, carved rectangle of wood stuck out from his chest.

The victim had notably pale skin. Eddie shot a look to both ends of the tunnel, then gently lifted the corpse's upper lip to gaze at the deceased's canine teeth.

"That's what I thought to do as well," a female voice said behind him.

Eddie leapt to his feet, hands up and the words of a spell on his lips, his right hand glowing red in the dim light of the tunnel.

Facing him was a woman in a long orange dress, shiny like silk and wrapped around her lithe body in an Indian style. A simple scarf covered her head, and her skin was ruddy, but her features were attractive for a woman that Eddie guessed was in her late forties or early fifties. She carried a wooden staff in her right hand.

The stranger lifted her left hand in a gesture of peace. "I am sorry to have startled you. Are you not the Wizard Riftstone, bearer of the Staff of Fire?"

Eddie lowered his hand, and the glow faded. "No, I'm Lieutenant Berman with the police."

She frowned, surprised by this. "But—you are indeed a wizard?"

"I carry the Staff of Fire once owned by Riftstone. The real question is: who are you?"

She gestured at the surrounding tunnel. "I am the Wizard Vasantbainkon and this fair tunnel is my arch. I sensed your presence and came at once."

"Your name is Vasant—what was it?"

"That will do. Merely call me Vasant," the woman replied with a friendly smile, her bright teeth in contrast to the color of her skin. Eddie glimpsed the glint of gold in her mouth.

Eddie studied the woman's clothing. "Were you in India?"

"Yes," she answered simply. "I sensed a wizard within my arch, and felt I should investigate."

"Know anything about this DB?"

The lady's frown grew. "DB?"

"Sorry, dead body. I have a hunch this guy was a vampire."

Vasant gazed at the inert form, stepped closer and with her finger and thumb opened one eye. "You are quite correct. This unfortunate one is… or, was… a member of the undead."

"And now quite dead. Why didn't he turn to dust?" Eddie glanced back at the end of the tunnel to make sure no one else was coming in.

Vasant stood up to her full height, easily filling the tunnel. "I see you have limited knowledge of the vampire. This person would only fall to ashes if exposed to sunlight, burnt in a fire, or injected with an unusual poison."

"Great," Eddie muttered in disgust. "Look, you really need to get outta here. My partner is coming, and a forensics team. If we

put him in a body bag, he won't turn to ash if they take him out
in the sun, right?"

The lady smiled sweetly. "Forgive me, but you use many words
that I do not understand."

"Really?"

She shrugged. "I have been living in solitude for a hundred
years as I studied the mysteries of the *Atman*." Her face
brightened. "It is good to see my English is still quite acceptable."

"At least it's not 'Oldspeak,'" Eddie said, referring to a type of
English wizards often used filled with "thees" and "thous."

Vasant shook her lovely head. "I never got the gist of that
method of communication. Good wizard, it was a pleasure to
meet you. What did you say was your name?"

"Eddie Berman."

"That is an odd name for a wizard."

"I'll work on that. Does Marlowe know how to find you if I
need to ask you questions?"

She brightened immediately. "Marlowe! Ah yes, he will know
how to find me. I shall plan to make myself available. This is all
very exciting."

"Sure, if you've been living in solitude. You should get out, see
New York. You'll find things are pretty different from a hundred
years ago."

"Very well. I believe I shall see you again, Wizard Berman."
Vasant smiled, gestured at the far wall, and an opening appeared
with a room behind it. With a nod, the woman passed through
the space into the room, as the red bricks immediately
reassembled into their original position, sealing the doorway.

Eddie watched her go, his head still lowered because of the height of the tunnel.

"Yoo hoo, anyone in there?" another female voice echoed down the passage.

"Here!" Eddie said, and the beam of a flashlight struck his face. Eddie shielded his eyes as the silhouette of Doctor Beverly Warren approached, the assistant medical examiner for the City of New York.

She was a tall woman, with pale white skin and stunning green eyes, her long chestnut-brown hair wrapped around her head to get it out of the way. She wore blue scrubs and had gloves on her hands as she entered the tunnel.

"Hey, Berman!" she said joyfully. "I thought you guys were on nights these days."

"Yeah, we've been hunting down that drug gang that's been using the park. Any word on the chemical breakdown of Mind-Blo yet?"

"There is an entire team analyzing it, and the mayor put out a bunch of print and TV ads warning people just how dangerous it is."

"I arrested a couple of people who had psychotic breaks, and I've heard there have been, like, six deaths."

Beverly shook her head in disgust. "I'm sure there have been more than that. The chemical mixture is similar to Ecstasy, but it has some kind of organic compound we haven't figured out yet. Finding an antidote for anyone who ODs is a problem."

"Let us know, okay?"

"Sure. If you're on nights, what are you doing here at this time of day?"

"The captain called us in special for this case." Eddie shrugged. "Luis and I are the most experienced at working a homicide."

"No rest for the weary." Warren flashed the light down on the body and grimaced at the wood protruding from his chest. "Well, that's one way to take someone out."

"May I ask what you are doing at a crime scene? I thought you stayed in the autopsy bay."

"Your captain called me as well, asked me to take it. You don't get a lot of DBs in the park, and Jacobs knows you like me to handle a case when you're involved. I have a team on the way."

"I'm glad it's you," Eddie said, drawing close and lowering his voice. "There might be weird forensics on this one."

Beverly sighed. "Don't tell me, gold teeth, organs in good shape?"

"How about no blood and a problem of burning up if exposed to sunlight?"

Beverly shone the flashlight down on the body, then up to her own face. "You gotta be shitting me." She surveyed both ends of the tunnel with the light and then returned her attention to Eddie, her voice a whisper. "You mean, like a *vampire?*"

"I don't know where your autopsy will take you, but I want to be the one you talk to first."

Warren put her free hand on her hip. "You know I don't work for you, Berman. I work for the medical examiner."

"How would he react to the idea it might be a dead vampire?"

Beverly returned the light to the prone figure. "Not well."

"Then I guess you should talk to me first."

"I am not enjoying this, Berman. You still didn't explain everything the last time I helped you out when things got weird."

"Beverly, I'll tell you as much as I can."

"That's not very reassuring." She peered down at the body again.

"*Hola?*" a deep voice called from the end of the tunnel.

A second flashlight beam came into the dark tunnel, and Luis Vasquez, his head low, made his way toward them.

"Hey, Doc Beverly," he said joyfully. "It's been a while."

"Luis, how are the kids?"

"A handful, but Maria is supermom! You know Eddie's going to have another, right?"

Beverly turned to Eddie, one eyebrow cocked. "Another medical miracle?"

"No miracle. Cerise is in her third trimester."

"Not bad for an old guy." Beverly grinned. "I am going to have to do that one of these days."

"Kids are great," Luis said. "They really give your life meaning."

"You have six, right?" Beverly chuckled. "Your life must have a helluva lot of meaning."

"You got it," Luis said, and flashed the light on the body. "Whoa! Talk about your horror movie murder."

"Okay, well, if you gentlemen have seen what you need to see, clear out. I have to get my team in place, and I don't want you contaminating my crime scene."

"Yes, ma'am," Eddie said. "Let me do one thing first." He pulled out his phone and took two quick flash photos, illuminating the tunnel. He then returned the device to his pocket. "You have my number?"

"Yes, lieutenant. I'll let you know once I know something."

Eddie nodded, and he and Luis headed toward the south end of the tunnel, just in time to see a forensic van pull up. Two technicians wearing white coveralls hopped out of the van carrying an empty body bag. They put on face masks as they headed for the tunnel.

Standing nearby was Officer Taylor in full uniform. She was a short African-American woman with a sturdy body and a no-nonsense style.

"Hey, Taylor," Eddie said, waving to the woman.

"Lieutenant, sergeant. Surprised to see you two here. Thought you guys were working nights."

"We are," Luis griped. "See the bags under my eyes?"

Eddie smiled. "Captain called us in. I heard *you* had some excitement the other day. You tackled a suspect who tried to flee?"

"The perp called me a black bitch," Taylor claimed. "I figured it was a good time to teach him some manners."

"Good job, Anita," Luis praised her.

"You do what you have to," she answered, nodding.

The pair headed toward the nearby roadway. "You have your car?" Eddie asked his partner.

"Yeah. I take it you used your 'special' way to get here?"

"You got it."

As they headed toward Luis' car that was pulled off the roadway, they heard a small voice call Eddie's name.

"Is that your phone?" Luis asked.

Eddie pulled a small, circular black compact from his pocket. "Let me get this."

He stopped walking and opened the small makeup mirror.

Instead of his own reflection, the face in the circular glass was Marlowe. His face showed relief. "Oh, thank goodness you heard me!"

"Yeah, I carry a mirror all the time like you suggested. What's up?"

"Eddie, I was contacted by Bankrock this morning—"

Eddie sighed. Bankrock was a thin, prissy wizard, who ensured that all the wizards in New York followed an arcane set of guidelines. With his round glasses and pinched features, he was often an annoying little man.

"What's ruffling Bankrock's feathers today?" Eddie sighed.

"Feathers?" Marlowe replied, puzzled. "Eddie, I do not approve. If you cast a spell and gave him feathers—"

"It's just an expression, Marlowe. What's bothering Bankrock?"

"Could you come by? It might be best if you spoke to him, and I called in some other people as well."

"Fine, fine," Eddie grumbled, annoyed that once again his mentor couldn't get to the point. Eddie closed the mirror and slipped it back into his pocket.

"Why doesn't your old wizard guy use a phone?" Luis asked as they got into the car.

"He knows how, he just doesn't like to," Eddie explained. "Besides, using the mirror there is less chance of any regular people tracing or recording the call."

"Thanks for letting me know," Luis said as they got into his car.

"Officially, you are my apprentice, so I am allowed to divulge any and all secrets to you."

"Is that official now?" Luis asked.

"I even filled out a paper, signed it in blood."

"What?" Luis said, eyes wide.

"I'm kidding. I signed with a pen."

FOUR

E ddie looked up at the four-story brick edifice at the corner of Central Park West and 85th Street with the huge turret that jutted from the facade like a fairy-tale tower. It seemed odd to Eddie that no one noticed this unusual structure, placed as it was in the middle of the city.

He crossed the street, stepped up to the front door, and knocked. Bankrock opened it a moment later.

"It's about time!" Bankrock said, adjusting the round glasses on his pinched nose. "Come in, come in."

Eddie was at least five inches taller than the thin, nervous little man, and attempted a friendly greeting. "How are you, Bankrock?"

"Worried, that's how I am," he complained.

They strolled into the expansive living room where Marlowe had gathered the padded comfortable chairs into a circle. He sat in one near the enormous fireplace.

In one chair sat Drusilicus, dressed in a very expensive suit. In the next chair was a man Eddie didn't know, in a white shirt with a bright-yellow tie. He had gray hair, a round face, and a bit of a gut. On the arm of his chair there was a police-style hat, except with a yellow brim and some kind of emblem where a police badge would be.

Next to him sat a woman in a simple but stylish dress who wore a small pillbox hat with a veil that covered one-half of her pretty face. She possessed long brown hair that was wrapped in several twists under the hat.

Marlowe stood. "Eddie, glad you could join us. I believe you know the Wizard Claremont?"

The man in the white shirt rose.

"Not really," Eddie said, trying to place the man.

"Sure," he said with a heavy Brooklyn accent. "You met me in da park da night the Great Evil tried to take down New Yawk. I was one of da wizards that helped clean up at da end."

Eddie nodded with recognition. "Oh yeah, sure. Nice to see you again, Claremont."

"Hey, just call me Rusty," the man replied with a big smile.

Eddie turned to the woman, who remained seated.

Marlowe spoke, "This is the Wizard Dalehead. She was not in New York during our battle last year."

"You must *pardonnez-moi*," she said with a French accent. "I was in France, *s'il vous plaît.*"

"*Enchanté, Mademoiselle,*" Eddie tried. She smiled at his attempt and offered her hand to be kissed. Eddie, unsure what to do, shook it.

Eddie went to one of the remaining seats, and Bankrock sat as well.

"I have asked you here because of some information passed to me by Drusilicus Greywacke. I have been able to do some research, and it has led to a very disturbing conclusion."

"Is it about the Drakula coming to New York?" Eddie asked, and stared at the others. "I assume you told them that before I got here."

"Indeed, we did, lieutenant," Drusilicus snorted. "I also told them the warning about the papyrus."

"What did you find, Marlowe?" Eddie asked.

Marlowe exhaled heavily. "The phrase Drusilicus quoted last night was part of an ancient prophecy, written in the Book of Daniel."

"From the Bible?" Eddie frowned.

"Exactly," Marlowe replied. "Chapter twelve, to be precise. It speaks of a noble prince, that there will be a time of trouble, and they shall write things in a book."

"I don't see how that could be right. That's talkin' about a book, not a papyrus," Eddie pointed out.

"In ancient times, a 'book' could easily refer to a papyrus , a parchment, or even a scroll," Bankrock clucked.

"Okay, but we still don't know which book, parchment, papyrus or whatever Drak is looking for," Eddie said.

"We shall get to that, may I continue?" Marlowe grumbled. "The next line says that many who sleep in the dust of the earth shall awake—some to everlasting life, and some to shame and everlasting contempt."

"People rising from the dust?" Eddie frowned. "Like from... graves?"

"It is possible, lieutenant," Drusilicus stated plainly. "And the ones who rise to contempt could be vampires."

"That would go against the Magical Restoration Act of 1916," Bankrock interjected at this point.

"Yeah," Rusty quipped, "like da freakin' Drakula gives a damn about wizard law."

"May I please go on?" Marlowe interrupted. "The prophecy states: 'And they that be wise shall shine as the brightness of the firmament—'"

"Zat is encouraging," Dalehead said. "Ze wise could be us— ze wizards."

"Yes," Marlowe warned, "but in the next few verses, it claims what Drusilicus was told, that the power of the holy people is completely shattered, and that all things shall be finished."

"Wait a minute," Eddie said. "*All* things? What things?"

"The prophecy says that the wicked shall do wickedly, and none of the wicked shall understand, but the wise shall understand."

"I don't understand nuthin'," Rusty ranted. "Jeez, like most prophecies, dis one don't tell us nothin' we can use."

"Was there any more to it, Marlowe?" Drusilicus insisted.

"The prophecy ends with the admonition that Daniel shall stand in his lot at the end of days."

"What?" Claremont demanded. "A parking lot?"

"I doubt it," Drusilicus huffed.

"The prophecy claims that this will be a time of trouble such as there never was," Marlowe sighed.

"What about the book, or papyrus, or whatever it is?" Eddie asked, leaning forward in his chair.

Marlowe shrugged. "I am still not sure, but I have a few theories."

"Do share," Drusilicus said with an imperious look.

Marlowe exhaled in frustration. "According to some texts, vampirism has its roots in Egypt, from Sekhmet, an ancient deity known for drinking blood. Some have suggested that she was the first vampire."

Rusty leaned back and folded his arms. "Everybody knows dat!"

Eddie raised an eyebrow. "Really?"

Marlowe went on. "My concern is that what Drakula is pursuing is an ancient papyrus that is part of a collection of spells known as the Egyptian Book of the Dead."

"The Book Of The Dead?" Bankrock repeated.

Dalehead snorted in a very unladylike way. "Zey have published zat book for years. What of it?"

"That was merely one collection of some ancient writings translated and published." Bankrock grimaced. "In fact, the wizards made sure that it was only simple spells that could do little harm."

"Wait, you're telling us that there are *more* of these spells?" Eddie inquired.

"Indeed, Eddie," Marlowe noted. "Many people believed when the published book was first printed that it was the equivalent to an Egyptian bible. These were ancient spells written on papyrus and placed with the bodies of the deceased. Each papyrus was handmade and often customized with incantations for individuals or families, usually the royalty or priests. These were located in tombs, collected, and only a select few were translated."

"Very interesting from a scholarly point of view, Marlowe," Drusilicus intoned. "Can we get to the point?"

"There are ancient prophecies that the children of Sekhmet—if not pacified—could rise up and destroy humanity. I once found an antediluvian papyrus, buried in the tomb of a high priest, that contains the spell to bring that about."

"What happened to it?" Eddie asked.

Marlowe sighed. "I am not sure. But if it is here, in New York —."

"That's a problem," Bankrock complained. "We cannot allow ancient Egyptian deities just showing up in New York without the proper paperwork—"

"Wait a minute," Eddie challenged. "*Another* world-ending event? We just saved the world last year."

"It is part of the job, Eddie," Marlowe sighed.

"So, you think the Drakula is looking for dat papyrus here?" Rusty added. "What does he get out of it?"

"A world in chaos?" Drusilicus reasoned. "It would be the perfect feeding ground for vampires."

"And if ze writings of Daniel are correct, and new vampires rise, zere will be many mouths to feed," Dalehead fretted.

"Yeah, and a whole lotta blood gettin' sucked," Rusty moaned.

"Wait a minute," Eddie said. "If any of this is right, and there is some kind of spell on an old paper, can the Drakula do it?"

Marlowe gazed at Eddie blankly.

Eddie went on. "Wouldn't he have to possess a talisman or a wizard's staff to activate the spell?"

A murmur of agreement went through the group.

"The lieutenant has a point," Drusilicus conceded. "A vampire, even the Lord of the Undead, cannot bring such a spell to fruition without a magickal implement."

Marlowe shook his head. "I do not know who currently wears the mantle of the Drakula. Bankrock?"

"Don't look at me," Bankrock claimed in an annoyed tone. "I don't associate with vampires."

"Hey, how about you, Marlowe?" Rusty suggested. "You got a vampire living here. Can he look into it?"

"I have asked, and I am sure he will do his best," Marlowe vowed. "But there are those who know of his association with me and avoid him."

"We need a plan of action, Marlowe," Drusilicus snapped. "If the Drakula is indeed coming—"

"Wait a minute, everybody calm down!" Eddie said, rising to his feet. "The first thing we have to do is investigate. We need to know just how much is actually happening and how much is theory. First, why come to New York to find this papyrus? If it is here, we need to figure out where it might be."

"I hope there is not a warlock working against us," Bankrock admitted. "It did not bode well at the last conflict."

"But we can check museums and historic places where such a papyrus could be hidden," Eddie said. "The point is, you guys all know magickal beings who might know something. Marlowe, you have prophetic abilities. Can you try to figure this out?"

Marlowe shrugged. "Well, I am a bit out of practice, but I do know many methods of divination…"

"Well, pick one that works," Eddie said. "Anyone else?"

"In France, we have *petite peuple* known as Lutins and Lutines who have knowledge, as not much gets past zeir attention," Dalehead suggested. "Could you not ask your little people 'ere?"

"In America, the small folk in this part of the country are called *Pukwudgies*," Bankrock stated. "I worry about involving them in any of this."

"What is wrong with zem?" Dalehead demanded, apparently insulted.

Bankrock blanched. "They are reclusive and remain hidden in small groups that are highly—uncooperative."

"We should take any help from anywhere we can," Eddie insisted.

"Good, good," Marlowe approved. "Let us all reach out to whatever magickal beings are against the vampires."

"We also have another problem," Eddie announced. "My partner and I discovered a gang of drug dealers who set up operation in my park."

"*Your* park?" Drusilicus sneered.

"We busted them last night, but the leader got away. He was a vampire."

"Really?" Bankrock exclaimed. "How odd."

"Anything you could find out would be helpful," Eddie insisted. "I'm stuck working nights until I bring this guy down."

Bankrock frowned. "A vampire selling drugs? I was unaware that vampires had taken up professions."

"I guess blood-sucking don't pay good," Rusty quipped.

Eddie went on, "This morning Luis and I reported to a crime scene. Best as we can tell, the victim might be a vampire. Someone had stabbed him through the heart with a wooden stake."

Drusilicus furrowed his brow. "Can you describe him?"

Eddie pulled his phone from his pocket as he spoke. "Sure. Average height, skinny, pale skin, black hair. He was all 'goth' in a black T-shirt with no sleeves, tattoos, face piercings." Eddie pulled up the photograph he had taken earlier and turned the phone to Drusilicus. "Do you know him?"

Drusilicus turned pale and then attempted to regain his composure. "I do. This is Strix. He *was* the vampire who gave me the information last night."

The room fell silent.

"It would appear," Marlowe volunteered, "that we must be very careful with any informants we might pursue."

This drew nods from the other people in the room just as Eddie's phone rang. Eddie rose to his feet to step away from the others. "Berman."

"I need you to get your ass down here," snapped a very annoyed Doctor Beverly Warren.

"Beverly, what's wrong?"

"Wrong? *Wrong?* Your freaking dead body almost *killed* me!"

"You're not making any sense."

"Just get down here, now!"

She ended the call.

"Anything wrong, lieutenant?" Drusilicus inquired.

Eddie glanced back at the group as he held the phone in his hand. "That was the assistant medical examiner. She was doing the autopsy on that dead vampire."

Everyone got to their feet.

Drusilicus asked, "She didn't remove the stake from his heart, did she?"

"I guess. I told you, she was doing an autopsy."

Murmurs ran through the room.

"Zat is bad," Dalehead muttered.

"Yes," Bankrock added. "You see, a stake only paralyzes a vampire until you can remove his head."

"Remove his head?" Eddie asked.

"That, or burn him," Bankrock said, nodding.

"Eddie," Marlowe explained, "when you remove a stake from the vampire's heart, he returns to his undead existence."

"Yeah," Rusty added. "And he's hungry."

"Oh Jeez," Eddie said, "I gotta get downtown *fast*."

Rusty's eyes lit up. "You need a ride? My cab is right out front."

Eddie stared at the man. "Cab? You have a cab?"

"It's what I do," he announced, and took the yellow cap from the arm of his chair and placed it on his head.

"You're a *cab* driver? *And* a wizard?"

Rusty glared at him as if he were crazy. "You're a policeman *and* a wizard. Now, you want that ride or what?"

Rusty drove Eddie quickly through the tangled midtown Manhattan traffic as if they were riding on a magic carpet.

When they stepped outside of Marlowe's townhouse, Eddie sent a quick text to Luis to meet him at the medical examiner's building ASAP. It wasn't until he reached the bottom of the stairs that he saw the vehicle Rusty was moving toward.

It wasn't just any car, but a big old-fashioned Checker cab, the kind with a huge back seat that could easily seat five adults, as well as their luggage. It was bright yellow, but boxy, and the styling was from the 50s or 60s.

Eddie gawked at the classic car.

"I thought you was in a hurry," Rusty complained to the unmoving Eddie.

Eddie peered into the car. "I didn't think there were any Checker cabs still on the road."

"There's still dis one. Now get in," Rusty boasted.

Eddie got into the back of the immaculate cab with smooth leather seats, with not a speck of dirt on the floor. Eddie marveled at the amount of leg room and the fact that the roof of the back seat was so high Eddie could have worn a hat like Abraham Lincoln and still had headroom.

Rusty got into the driver's seat and glanced back at Eddie. There was no glass separating the driver from the passenger like in most cabs. "I believe you was headin' downtown?"

"That's right, downtown." Eddie considered this for a moment. "Are you a prophet?"

"Yeah, well, somewhat," the cabbie said as he started the car, activated the meter by pulling a metal flag downward, and pulled into traffic. "I mean, it's limited. I know whenever a wizard needs to get somewhere and needs an alternate method of transportation. I can sense traffic and roads even with my eyes closed, and I'm aware of hidden roads when I get near 'em."

"I didn't think wizards had regular jobs. I mean, Marlowe keeps saying that money is the easiest thing to manifest."

"He's right," Rusty told him. "Check the meter."

Although they'd gone at least ten blocks, the meter only registered: $.50.

"I don' do it for da money. I like it. I mean, I been a cabbie for over four hundred years."

"Four hundred years!" Eddie said, and his mouth fell open. "Marlowe told me wizards age slow, but damn!"

"Yeah, I used to drive a horse and carriage in dem days, then a rig, and now a cab."

"But, if you don't need the money, why do you do it?"

The driver shrugged. "Money don't mean much, you come right down to it. Bein' useful means more. My guess is dat's the reason you stay a cop."

"That and my mortgage and bills," Eddie sighed.

"Nah, you like to solve crimes. It makes you feel you're doin' somethin' important, somethin' good. We need more wizards dat are just plain folk. Too many of 'em think they're all high and mighty."

The cab pulled up to a six-story structure on First Avenue and 30th Street, a rectangular building that contained the morgue for the City of New York. Within that building, more cases were processed in a single week than most morgues could handle in a year. The facility contained state-of-the-art computers, X-rays, and medical equipment taking up entire floors. The autopsy rooms numbered into the dozens, and there was enough refrigerated storage to hold hundreds of the deceased.

The building's most striking feature was that the side that faced the East River was windowless. Otherwise, it blended into the neighborhood and contained the office of Doctor Beverly Warren.

"We've made good progress," Eddie said with a glance out the window. "We didn't hit one red light."

"Course not," Rusty grinned. "Another one of my little gifts. Problem is, it messes wid the lights for everybody else."

"Really? I always wondered why the traffic patterns in Manhattan made little sense."

"Probably my fault," Rusty said with a shrug. "What can ya do?"

He slid the large vehicle to the curb, and Eddie stared at the meter.

It read: $2.00

He took a five from his wallet and handed it to Rusty. "Keep the change."

"Thanks, Mac," Rusty said. "You need a ride, just yell out my name. I'll be there."

"Really?"

"Sure! I mean, providing I don't got anudder fare."

The cab pulled away as he strode into the building. He went to a security desk and showed his shield and signed his name on the visitor clipboard, just as his out-of-breath partner ran up to join him.

"Wow!" Eddie said as Luis panted. "You made good time."

"Yeah," his partner answered through his gasps. "I followed a cab."

Eddie smiled. "That was me. I was riding with a—" He glanced at the security officer behind the desk. "A friend."

Luis nodded in acknowledgement and quickly showed his shield and signed in. They received adhesive paper passes that they stuck to their jackets and headed down the hall.

As they stepped out of the guard's hearing range, Luis asked, "Why did you catch a cab? I could have picked you up."

"The driver was a wizard," Eddie murmured. "He was at the meeting this morning."

"No kidding? I thought those guys didn't have jobs."

Eddie shrugged. "He says he likes it. He's been a cabbie for four hundred years."

Luis shook his head. "Man, you would think he might retire at some point."

They reached Doctor Warren's office, and Eddie knocked politely on the door.

The door flew open and a wild-eyed Beverly Warren stared daggers at the two detectives. Her hair was down and curly and hung past her shoulders and was mussed as if she had recently removed it from a surgical cap. She still wore scrubs but had a white lab coat on and a surgical mask hung from its ties around her neck.

"Did you *know*?" she demanded of Eddie, and then turned to Luis. "Were *you* in on it?"

Eddie held up his hands in what he hoped was a calming gesture. "Whoa, Beverly, we don't know what you're talking about."

She gesticulated wildly toward a room down the hall. "That corpse. I mean, that guy— whatever that was! If this was some kind of practical joke, I swear I'll kill you two—"

"Slow down," Eddie soothed her.

Luis appeared stricken. "Beverly, we wouldn't do anything to scare you. We like you!"

Eddie nodded in agreement. "Tell us what happened."

She glanced in both directions down the hallway and gestured the detectives to come into her office. They went in and she shut the door.

"That corpse from this morning—"

Luis brightened. "Oh yeah, the one from that arch uptown."

Eddie grunted. "Damn, I forgot to ask about Vasant!" He saw Beverly and Luis stare at him blankly. "Sorry, please go on."

"Okay," Beverly huffed and seemed to calm down a bit. "I got ready for the autopsy. One of the forensic technicians set up the suite, and I got a good one this time, with all the first-class equipment. Do you know that sometimes, I get the worst rooms —"

"Beverly," Eddie suggested, "please get to the point?" He had never seen the calm Doctor Warren act like this before.

"The point, right," she grimaced. "We were pretty busy. So, I fetched the gurney with that John Doe—"

"The guy from the arch?" Luis put in.

"Right, and I'm in there alone with the body and that goddamn stake in his chest." She motioned at her desk, as if she stood above the body. "First, I cut off his clothes and removed them. Next, I have to remove that wooden stake. I mean, I couldn't make my cut-Y with that thing in the way…"

"Uh-oh," Eddie mumbled, aware of the implications.

"I wanted to pull it out, and if that didn't work, I could cut around it and pull it out that way." She mimed the motion and gazed at Eddie and then Luis. "I mean, that makes sense, right?"

"Sure, sure," Eddie agreed.

"Were you able to pull it out?" asked Luis.

Beverly stared at Luis for a moment until the question seemed to register. "Oh, yeah. Actually, it came out pretty easily, and there wasn't even any blood on it."

Luis and Eddie exchanged a look.

Eddie touched Beverly's arm. "So what happened, Beverly?"

"It was the stake," Beverly continued. "There was a… a foreign substance on it, like a glob of something—"

"A glob?" Eddie asked.

"Like… like… mucous. I wanted to examine it under ultraviolet light, see if it luminesced so I could figure out what it was—" She fell silent.

Eddie tried to encourage her. "You wanted to examine it?"

This got Beverly's attention. "Yes, so I went over to a cabinet and got a handheld ultraviolet light we use. It's a compact unit, but it's powerful, because we often have to use Luminol—"

"What did you find?" Luis queried, trying to keep Beverly on track.

"So, I turn out the overhead lights, and I'm standing there, my eyes watching the stick through my goggles, and I flash the light on it, and this mucous glows. But… more than that, it *burns*."

Eddie frowned. "Burns?"

"Or dissolves, like completely," Beverly reported, mystified. "It just turns to smoke, and it's gone."

"That's pretty weird," Luis surmised.

Eddie spoke up, "But I don't see what freaked you out so much."

"It freaked me out because that's when the hand grabbed me," Beverly bleated, wide-eyed.

"What?" Eddie gasped.

"I know, I know," she babbled. "I've worked the morgue for years, and now— this!"

Luis crossed himself. "Madre de Dios, what did you do?"

"Do? I turned around, thinking it was a lab technician trying to be funny—but it wasn't!" Beverly became more upset. "It was the guy from the table!"

Luis and Eddie exchanged another look.

Beverly raised her arms for emphasis. "The *dead guy*, with fangs growing out of his freakin' mouth!"

Eddie's face was stern. "Are you all right? Did he—bite you?"

"All right? How can I be all right? A dead guy attacked me!"

"What did you do, lock him in the room or something?" Luis worried.

"No, I just turned around with that light in my hand." She mimed as if she was still holding the light. "As the light flashed on him, he started screaming and smoke flew off him, and he... just... fell apart."

"Fell apart?" Eddie repeated.

"Yes, right there on the floor," Beverly responded. "He fell, smoking and screaming!" She pulled a key from her pocket. "Come on, I'll show you!"

The trio exited the office and headed down the hall, Beverly in the lead and still visibly agitated.

They reached the first room, and she opened it with the key. "I locked it so that no one else could go in," she explained.

They went into a well-supplied autopsy suite with an empty metal gurney near a large sink. Cameras were overhead, and so was a water sprayer, an overlarge shower head with a control to spray the water. The room had a metal cabinet connected to the wall opposite the gurney. The UV light and Beverly's hastily abandoned notebook sat on the counter.

On the floor was a desiccated corpse, shriveled like a mummy. The flesh had collapsed on itself and dried tightly against the skeletal structure. Around the face and hands the bone underneath lay exposed. Fine ash lay in an outline around the remains.

"See! *See!*" Beverly shouted, hysterical.

"A UV light did this?" Luis frowned, looking at the mess on the floor.

Eddie grabbed the handle of the compact lamp with a pair of dark-purple tubes in it. He turned it over to find the switch on the back. "Is this the light?"

"Yes," she chirped, her eyes on the heap of ashes. "You don't get it! This is the body! His body! Bodies don't just disintegrate when you shine a UV light on them."

Eddie hit the switch and the light popped on. He crouched low and waved the dark-blue light over the remains laying on the floor. Smoked streamed off the body.

"What are you doing?" Beverly demanded and grabbed his hand to pull the light away from the smoldering remains.

Eddie met her eyes. "Look Beverly, do you have any explanation for what happened?"

She glared at him, but released his arm. "No."

"Then the best course of action is to get rid of the evidence," Eddie told her, and waved the dark light over the shrunken corpse on the floor. Smoke rose again, and it gave off a scent like burning sulphur. Every place he shined the light the parts that remained simply dissolved away. After a couple of minutes, it was all gone.

Beverly stood over Eddie with her hands on her hips. "Okay, tell me what is going on!"

Eddie shut off the light. "Simple. You get rid of the clothes and the stake. Then, you report that a body got misplaced, and you don't know where it ended up."

He placed the light on the table.

"And tell me where I can get one of these."

FIVE

E ddie rode in Luis's car back up to the Central Park Precinct. Using his smart phone, he searched online to find portable ultraviolet lights.

It had taken close to an hour to calm Beverly down, and the more they tried to relax her, the angrier she became, demanding an explanation for her experience.

She soon caught on that she couldn't very well report that they had disintegrated a corpse with a UV light, so she saw the wisdom of Eddie's suggestion of reporting that the body got lost.

The two detectives made slow progress in the snarled traffic. Luis spoke as Eddie continued to look at his phone. "Any luck on those lights?"

Eddie sighed. "I want to bring this to Marlowe because there are several handheld lights that might work. You know what this means?"

Luis made a wry smile. "That you got a way to kill a vampire."

Eddie sat back in the seat. "Which would come in very handy if we ran into our drug dealer again."

"I would love to knock the smile off his face," Luis mused. "But, I don't know, killing him— isn't that going too far?"

"Technically, the guy is already dead. If what happened in the morgue is any indication, he won't even leave behind a body. We can't put supernatural bad guys in the same league as ordinary ones. After all, a street dealer can't become mist or turn into a bat."

"There is that," Luis muttered.

"They don't need a gun to kill us, and they heal from a bullet in moments. We need something to give us an advantage."

"I guess. Beverly was pretty freaked out."

"I would imagine it is a medical examiner's worst nightmare when a dead body gets up—"

"And attacks," Luis finished the thought and sighed. "Can we finish out today in daylight and let me spend the evening with my wife?"

Eddie nodded. "I think, since they called us in early, that we might just work a half day and call it quits. That is, after we write up the report."

"Is there any way we can keep Beverly from getting in trouble because of the lost body?" Luis worried. "I mean, she led the team on site. Is she gonna say it got lost on the way to the morgue?"

Eddie sighed. "I can't think of everything, Luis."

"Could you conjure a body?"

"Conjure a body?" Eddie repeated as he stared at his partner in disbelief.

"Sure! Make one out of, I don't know, tofu or something?"

Eddie blinked in amazement, then chuckled. "Tofu?"

Luis seemed hurt by Eddie's laughter. "I don't know, they make a lot of things out of it."

Eddie laughed harder.

"It was just a suggestion."

Eddie calmed down, wiping his eyes. "I'll ask Marlowe, but I don't think there's a spell for that." He chuckled again. "Tofu."

Luis pulled into the lot just off the 86th Street Transverse Road and pulled the car into his usual spot. The older vehicle gave a pop and stalled as a puff of black smoke came out of the tailpipe.

"Excuse me for trying to help!" Luis huffed, and got out of the car. He glared at his partner as Eddie exited the vehicle. "You think maybe you can do some of that voodoo to my car at least?"

Eddie headed toward the end of the lot and the wooden stairs that would take them down to street level. "I haven't done cars yet, Luis, or fake bodies. But if it will help, I'll ask Marlowe. Maybe you should talk to a mechanic?"

They descended to the sidewalk on the transverse road. The precinct was originally a collection of Victorian Gothic cottage-style buildings constructed from brick and stone as stables and storage sheds for park staff.

The police took over the buildings in 1936, but over the years, they had become more and more dilapidated. That led to building the steel structure the precinct cops referred to as the '22.

With the help of the Central Park Conservatory and an ambitious plan, not only were the older buildings rebuilt and restored, but they added a magnificent atrium to link the individual smaller buildings. It was a large, open two-story structure fronted by bulletproof glass with the words "Central Park Precinct" etched in bold white letters on the glass.

Eddie and Luis turned onto the pathway that took them into the courtyard around the building and passed through the double glass doors, nodding to the officers who manned the huge lobby desk that could easily seat six. As usual, there were people milling about, some to report a pick-pocketing or a purse snatching, and some were merely visitors who wanted advice about which subway they should take or what bus might get them where they wanted to go.

Eddie and Luis took a turn through an open doorway and into the detective's bullpen. A man at one desk glanced up. He was heavyset with jowls, large bags under his eyes, and exaggerated eyebrows one could imagine would hide his eyes completely in an emergency.

"Hey, Dominic," Eddie greeted him, and Luis just raised a hand.

"Hey, the hotshots," Dominic chuckled. "Heard you caught a dead guy with a stake through his heart."

"Yeah, we just got back from the ME," Luis said as he flopped in the chair by his desk. "The body went missing."

Eddie glanced at his partner and knew from experience that the fastest way to pass information around the precinct was to tell detective Rocco Dominic. The man was harmless enough and a good cop, having spent most of his career at the '22.

"Missing?" Dominic replied. "Maybe the vampires got him, huh?"

"Vampires?" Eddie scoffed.

"He had a stake in his heart, right?"

"It was a piece of wood in his chest," Luis corrected. "Might've been a stake. Coulda been a table leg for all I know!"

Dominic shook his head. "You guys always catch the weird stuff. Give me a plain old pickpocket any day."

"We've certainly busted enough of those," Luis agreed.

"I see you guys arrested the dealers pushing Mind-Blo in the park," Dominic said, his eyes going to his computer screen. "I was there when they loaded them for court and Rikers this morning."

"Didn't catch the ringleader," Eddie lamented. "He slipped out on us."

"I can see that," Dominic conceded. "He would have been the brains of the group. The two perps this morning weren't the brightest bulbs on the shelf. Heard they pulled guns on you."

"Stupid move, pulling a gun on a cop," Luis growled. "Don't they teach these criminals manners no more?"

Dominic chuckled. "When they took them out, one of them kept insisting the black guy made a stick appear and then beat him with it."

Eddie shook his head. "Next time he shouldn't sample his own product, then he won't see things."

Eddie sat in front of his computer at his desk and pulled up the report that Luis had started when he was meeting with the wizards that morning. As he reviewed the paperwork, he thought about the Indian lady wizard, Vasant, and how he wanted to ask Marlowe about her.

Eddie sighed. He needed to write up the information about that morning's body, as well as complete his account of the previous evening's bust.

"Luis," Eddie said across his desk to his partner, "go over the report of the DB from this morning, while I finish our statement from last night. Then we need to get out of here and see our families."

Luis was inputting information into the computer with only two fingers, and slowly. "I'm all for that, man."

By 3:00 in the afternoon, Eddie picked up his car that he'd left days earlier in the police lot. He felt wide awake, despite the limited amount of sleep. Getting behind the wheel, he wished to avoid the dreaded rush hour that started at 3:30 and ended at 7:00. After working the four-to-midnight shift for the previous few weeks, he was looking forward to seeing his sons. He hoped that Cerise would still be in the same lustful mood as that morning.

He would get home before she returned from the hospital where she worked as a nurse.

At 3:30, he pulled into his driveway, glad there had been little traffic. Glancing at his reflection in the rearview mirror, he waved his hand in front of it and whispered, "Marlowe."

The thin glass became bright silver until, a moment later, Marlowe's blue eyes showed in the rectangle.

"Eddie, is that you?" Marlowe said and tilted his head left and right, trying to get a good view of Eddie. "You know I hate it when you use the mirror in your car."

"Sorry, but I gotta make this quick," Eddie told him. "I wanted you to know that the medical examiner removed the stake from the body we recovered this morning. It came back to whatever life it had and attacked her."

"My goodness! Is Doctor Warren all right?"

"A little shook up, but she was holding a portable ultraviolet light. It killed the guy."

"Really?" Marlowe said. Although Eddie could see little of the old man's face, his eyebrows rose in surprise.

"Yes. I'm getting us an ultraviolet light to use against vampires. It might be a good thing to have if the Drakula is coming to town."

The old man nodded. "Sound thinking."

"Also, when I went to the crime scene this morning, a wizard showed up. She told me her name was Vasant, and she was aware of the dead person in the arch."

"Vasantbainkon?"

"Yeah, that's the name."

"It is Hindi, and the closest translation is 'spring banks'."

"Like the arch?"

"Correct. We named it for her. Last I understood, she'd taken up a life of solitude. If she has returned from her self-imposed exile, she could prove most useful right now."

"Anything I should know about her?"

"In her day, she was a famed philosopher, equal to any man."

"Wow, I thought they repressed women in places like India."

"In the Vedic period, things were quite different. They considered women equals. In fact, some women married several men in those times."

"So the woman could have a harem?" Eddie wondered.

"As easily as a man, if she could afford it. But Vasant—no one has seen her for a hundred years, after a... certain situation... but I am sure that is all but forgotten at this point."

"Well, if you could run a background check or whatever you guys do. We don't want an unexpected warlock showing up."

"Agreed. Will you be training with me this night?"

"No, I'm with my wife tonight. Tomorrow, Luis and I are going back to the night shift to catch this vampire drug dealer."

"Very good, Eddie. I'll be here if you need me."

"Later," Eddie said, and with a wave of his hand, the mirror again reflected Eddie's own eyes and—

Standing on the back seat was a man about eighteen inches tall, dressed in simple buckskin pants with a band and feather on his head. Although perfectly proportioned, the small man had pointed ears and a gray tint to his skin.

"Jeez!" Eddie bellowed, surprised. He twisted around in his seat to stare at the invader. "You can't just do that to me!"

"Walker of the Path of the Wise, I have need of your skills," the small man said solemnly. "Our protector, *Misinghalikun*, sent me to you."

Eddie gave a heartfelt sigh. Couldn't he get *one* night off?

"Look, uh, sir, I don't know any Miso... whatever... and you need to call me in the morning!"

The small man placed his hands on his hips and glared at Eddie.

Eddie paused, remembering what Marlowe had instructed him concerning magickal beings, whether they be leprechauns or some other species. Such beings had powerful magic at their fingertips, perhaps equal to his own wizardly powers. The most important thing was to show respect.

Eddie cleared his throat and centered himself, trying to think of the right words. "Forgive me, I spoke in haste. I am a weary traveler whose needs must take him to home and rest."

This went over better, and the tiny man relaxed and sat down on the seat. "My needs cannot wait, Walker. He who bears your staff swore to help my people. *Misinghalikun* has assured me of this."

Eddie felt his temper rise, but controlled himself. "I don't recall swearing to anything."

"It is an ancient vow," the tiny man insisted, obviously displeased by Eddie's denial.

Eddie hung his head and sighed a second time. "Okay. Who are you?"

"I am Skysoarer of the *Pukwudgie* people."

Eddie brightened. "Oh yeah, we were just talking about you today—"

"We have not time to argue—we must make haste."

"Okay, okay. I'll do it, but only on the promise that you'll bring me home!"

"Agreed," Skysoarer said and clapped his hands.

They were instantly on the top of a mountain. Eddie was still in the sitting position he'd been in and had to shift quickly to not fall backward off the hilltop.

He stood upright, contemplated the little man. With a gesture, his staff slammed into his hand and his suit transformed into his red robes with tall boots.

Skysoarer smiled at him, approving.

"So," Eddie said and gazed down at the valley below him, nervously. "Where to?"

"You must follow me. Our lady needs healing."

With that, as sure-footed as a mountain goat, Skysoarer leapt from ledge to ledge on his way down the side of the mountain.

"Why didn't we just materialize down there?" Eddie muttered and did his best to follow. It was treacherous going, and more than once Eddie needed to use the power of his staff to levitate so he didn't fall. He panted as he attempted to keep up with the quick little man. "Where are we?"

"We call it Wach Unks," responded Skysoarer. "Your people refer to this land as the Watchung Reservation."

Eddie had limited knowledge of the area, but knew he was still in New Jersey. He recalled that the Watchung Reservation was a nature preserve that took up something like two-thousand acres, and was once the home of the Lenape Indians.

It seemed logical that what appeared to be a forest-dwelling being would reside in one of the few remaining untouched wildernesses in the state.

Finally reaching level ground, the *Pukwudgie* pointed to the large opening of a cave hidden by brush from curious onlookers.

"You want me... to go in there?" Eddie asked.

"Truly, Walker, you must," Skysoarer said.

Eddie was suspicious, but decided good manners would be his best choice. "After you."

Skysoarer nodded and strode confidently into the cave. Eddie followed, ducking his head to make it through the entrance. He engaged the slightest bit of power, and a red light appeared at the tip of his staff, illuminating the way.

He went on for about twenty feet when the claustrophobic tunnel opened up into a huge and spacious cavern that rose high above his head. Around him were a multitude of the tiny people, each one more perfect and beautiful than the last, with pointed ears and buckskin garb that reflected a Native American way of life, unspoiled by centuries of change in the outer world.

There were wigwams, or small houses, throughout the cavern. Each one appeared to be made of a wooden frame and covered with woven mats or peeled bark from trees. Each one was shaped like a dome with an arched roof. Eddie stared in amazement at the brightly colored sigils that glowed on the outside of the structures. Most of them were only a little taller than Eddie himself, except for one in the middle that rose at least fifteen feet into the air.

Skysoarer pointed at the large wigwam in the center of the room. "That is where we must go. You must help Granny."

"Granny?" Eddie asked. "What's wrong with Granny?"

"The blood poison. You shall see," Skysoarer responded ominously.

The little man stepped forward, ahead of Eddie, who noticed that the cave floor was very smooth, almost like poured cement. All the little people had stopped working on their individual tasks and watched him. Eddie was nervous to have so many eyes focused on him as he passed.

The *Pukwudgie* reached the center wigwam and pulled a flap aside, but Eddie put out a hand to stop him. He went down on one knee, and whispered, "Look, I really don't do healings."

"Do you not?" Skysoarer gasped.

"No, I'm pretty new at all this," Eddie fretted. "I might not be able to help her."

"You *shall*. You *must* be able or *Misinghalikun* would not have sent me to you," Skysoarer declared, and pulled the flap aside. "Go, you must help Granny."

It was dark inside the structure, and Eddie made the little red light at the top of his staff grow brighter so he could see. Several sticks in a triangular shape were suspended from the ceiling by a rope. In the center of the poles was a basket suspended off the ground— in it was a small woman. She wore a buckskin dress that was heavily decorated with hundreds of colorful beads. Her white hair hung around her head, and her face was a collection of wrinkles.

She may have been taller when she was young, but age and infirmity had shrunk her, so she was only a foot tall.

Next to her a small female *Pukwudgie* touched a damp cloth to the old woman's head. The young woman saw Eddie, rose, nodded respectfully, and stepped away.

Eddie knelt before the old woman, put his head down, cleared his throat, and said, "Granny, Skysoarer has asked me to look in on you. Can you understand my words?"

She gave a tired nod. "You are a Walker of the Wise," she croaked barely above a whisper.

Eddie smiled. "Yes, I am one who walks the path. Tell me, Granny, where does it hurt?"

The tiny old woman raised a hand and dabbed her shoulder.

"May I examine you, Granny? Touch you?"

She nodded feebly. Eddie lifted his hands gently to her head. He was nervous because the old woman seemed so very fragile, and the last thing he wanted to do was to hurt her.

If she dies, will I be able to leave? No one even knows that I'm here.

Eddie pushed the thought away and brushed the woman's white hair from the shoulder she had touched. He lifted the buckskin at the shoulder and Eddie examined the dry and wrinkled skin underneath. He couldn't see any mark, bruise, or discoloration, but gently lifting her head to get a better look— he froze.

On her neck were two tiny dots, red with blood. Eddie saw the marks and exhaled heavily—a vampire had attacked the elderly *Pukwudgie*. He checked again and from the small even marks, he surmised the bites came from a small animal, possibly a tiny bat.

Vampires could transform into bats of almost any size.

He didn't understand why they had gone to the trouble to attack this old woman. Was there something special about her that made a vampire seek her out?

Eddie gently returned the woman's head to her litter and rose, trying to think of what he could do. He stuck his head out of the flap in the structure to see Skysoarer waiting patiently.

"Skysoarer, are your people okay with sunlight?"

The little man frowned, as if this was an odd question. "We are the dwellers of this forest but we hide from those who hike these woods. It is our preference to come out at night."

"Will it hurt your granny to be out in the sunlight?" Eddie asked with an eye to the cave tunnel and the light coming in from the setting sun.

"It will not, Walker."

Eddie nodded as he decided. "Then clear a path for me to the tunnel entrance."

He let the flap fall closed. The young *Pukwudgie* maiden was still in the room, hidden in the shadows. Eddie smiled at the tiny girl. "I'm going to bring her outside. You may come if you wish."

She stared blankly at Eddie, and he thought maybe she didn't understand him, but as he stepped close to the makeshift bed, the young woman rose to her feet.

"Granny," Eddie said in a calming voice, "I think I can help you, but I need to take you outside and into the light."

The old woman's eyes were barely open, but she nodded.

Eddie summoned his power, allowing it to rise in him, surrounding his body with a red glow as radiant strings of light surrounded his staff.

With a gesture, the strings coalesced and wrapped gently around the old woman. On nothing more than strands of bright-red light, she rose into the air.

Eddie pulled the flap aside and Granny slowly floated out of the wigwam and toward the cave entrance. Eddie followed carefully as he thought through his plan. Marlowe had guided his training, and the old wizard was always there to fix any significant errors or misbegotten creations.

This time, he would have to do this on his own.

He only had a rough idea of what to do, with no assurance it would succeed. The use of his abilities required two things: will and intent. He needed to set his concentration on a cure with the intention that his actions would not hurt the old woman.

If it were indeed a vampire bite, Eddie hoped the sunlight would aid him.

They proceeded through the village of the small folk, Eddie being careful where he stepped to not harm any of their belongings.

He needed to duck as he made his way to the entrance, the small woman still floating before him.

At the mouth of the cave, Eddie moved in front to make sure there were no witnesses around, even in the middle of the wilderness.

He stepped into the sunlight and allowed its warmth to wash over him. He took a moment and focused, smelling the fresh air and listening to the nearby birds as they chirped and called.

Setting his mind to the task, he brought the old woman toward the light.

The woman raised a hand to cover her eyes and cried, "It burns, it burns!"

Had she been made into a vampire? Was exposing her to sunlight going to kill her?

Hundreds of the little people filled the mouth of the cave, all with their eyes fixed worriedly on the old woman as he brought her into the light.

As her tiny body slid into the sunlight, she did not burn, merely shook a bit as if there was a battle going on inside of her.

Eddie closed his eyes and tried to reach out to the old lady, trying to feel what was inside her. He murmured, "Cleanse your body, remove the darkness," over and over.

All at once, he sensed the shadow within her, focused on the area around her neck but traveling through her blood, infecting her with an energy that was hidden and evil.

With the strings of red light all over her, he drew out what he'd sensed, using his will to remove the taint within her body that fought to corrupt her.

Skysoarer stepped away from the cave mouth and closer to the floating woman watching the energy strings.

Eddie focused on the negative energy and felt a ball of destructive power move down the strings toward his hand.

A ball of dark mist swirled over the palm of the hand not holding his staff, and Eddie was suddenly aware that he did not want to touch it. With a cry, he threw the energy ball as far as he could and turned away as he raised a dome of protection around himself and the old woman.

The air seemed to explode as the energy dissipated with a flash of shadows that knocked the unprotected Skysoarer off his feet.

Eddie dropped the protective charm and carefully lowered the woman to the ground. She gave the impression of being better— her skin had taken on a healthier color, though still quite gray. After a moment, she sat up and rubbed her neck.

The puncture wounds were gone.

Eddie lowered himself to one knee and asked, "Do you feel better, Granny?"

"Muchly, I thank you," she responded, and pushed herself up to her feet. Eddie offered a hand to help her, but she seemed steady, and a light now shone in her eyes.

Skysoarer had also gotten back to his feet and ran over to the old woman to fall on his knees before her. "Granny, you are up and well!"

She turned to him and bid him rise. Even though Skysoarer was so much shorter than Eddie, he towered over the tiny old woman.

"You have done well, and brought me a Walker of the Path," she said.

Skysoarer bowed his head with respect. "It is the wisdom of *Misinghalikun* that has saved you. I was merely the feet that needed to walk."

Granny turned to Eddie, who had remained on one knee. "Walker of the Wise, we are grateful."

Eddie bowed his head. "I am worried, as I believe an enemy of my people attacked you. A vampire."

"Vam-pire?" the old woman said with a frown. "We know not this word."

Eddie nodded. "They prey upon the blood of others. You had the mark of one on your neck."

"I have heard of creatures like these, Granny," Skysoarer told her. "The *Wabanaki* people call them *Skadegamutc*."

Granny's frown grew deeper. "Creatures that look like corpses but come out at night?"

"Close enough," Eddie said. "They can also change into other forms, like a bat."

"I had a dream that a bat came to visit me." She rubbed her neck. "Perhaps it was not a dream after all."

Eddie peered at the setting sun. "With your permission, I would ask Skysoarer to return me to my home."

"We would like to honor you with a feast," said Granny, a smile on her face.

Eddie bowed again, trying to think fast. "It... um... would honor me to break bread with you, but my wife... uh... is great with child." He mimed an enormous belly in front of himself for added effect.

Granny nodded and chuckled. "Ah! So you wish to be with her. I wish to give you a gift."

Eddie nodded. He had very limited knowledge of Native American culture, but from what Marlowe had told him of the little folk in Europe, he knew that to not take a gift for doing a task would be a great insult.

Granny turned to Skysoarer and gestured to Eddie. Skysoarer reached into a leather bag at his side and pulled out a beautiful wooden tube with intricate symbols carved into it and a hole near the top. "This is a whistle. If you are ever in need, blow upon it, and I shall come to your aid."

Eddie took the carved wooden totem and bowed again. "It was my honor to serve you, Granny."

"We shall not forget, Walker of the Wise," she said and turned to Skysoarer. "Guide him home."

Eddie took a deep breath, not looking forward to climbing back up the mountain. To his surprise, Skysoarer merely said a word, and with a clap of his hands, the cave and the *Pukwudgie* all transformed into his house.

Eddie was standing at his own front door of his house. He inspected his clothes, frightened that the neighbors would see him in his wizard robes, but he only wore his suit, with regular shoes on his feet.

Eddie noticed his staff was no longer in his hands and worried that it had not traveled with him. He quickly opened his wallet and found the small wooden card that was the form of the staff when he wasn't using it. Since the large stick was so ungainly, it was much easier to keep it as a small object in his wallet.

He stood near his car which was still running. Pulling the handle, he found it tightly locked. With a glance to make sure he was alone, he whispered, "*Patentibus.*"

The window on the driver's side lowered.

Eddie had expected the door to open, but this was good enough. He got in, rolled the window up, and shut the car off. He got out and locked it with the fob.

"How long was I gone?" Eddie wondered aloud, as he ogled up at the sun still high above the horizon. It had been setting when he left the tribe in Watchung. He glanced at his watch and in shock saw it was only a few minutes after 4:00.

Eddie leaned against his car. How was it possible to have traveled that far and still be back only a few minutes after he left? Had it all been some kind of hallucination?

He reached into his jacket pocket, and there he discovered the small, hand-carved whistle.

"So, the other answer," Eddie said aloud, "is that the *Pukwudgie* can do magic I haven't even thought was possible."

SIX

E ddie's mother came to the front door to greet him.

Eleanor Berman was only about five feet five, with silver-white hair, thick glasses, and a trim figure. In the last ten months, she had blossomed, going from a woman who had three months to live to being able to face life with renewed energy and vigor.

In the last few months, Cerise's doctors advised her to cut back on chores, due to her being forty and pregnant. Cerise claimed she felt fine, but the doctors insisted that she was an "at-risk" pregnancy and needed to get off her feet, whether she wanted to or not.

Fortunately, Eleanor took care of the housework with joy. Since her health scare almost a year earlier, she was pleased because her body had grown so much stronger, and at sixty-seven, she was a powerhouse. She had very much become the person in charge of the house, and was a great help for the entire family.

Eddie leaned down to kiss his mother's cheek. "How's it goin', Momma?"

"I'm doin' fine, Eddie. I worried about you staying in your car out front for so long. Then I looked out a window, and you weren't even in it."

Though sworn to secrecy in the normal world, Eddie's wife and mother knew about the unusual occurrences that had involved Eddie since he'd gained his abilities. So far they had shielded his sons from most of the weirdness, and Eddie was thankful that they didn't notice the odd comings and goings.

"I had to take care of something," Eddie offered. He was still unsure if the events he'd just experienced with Skysoarer and Granny were real, but it was better not to bother his mother with it.

"Did you help someone, son?" Eleanor asked.

Eddie smiled and nodded his head. "I think I did, Momma."

"Good! Cerise is getting home in about an hour. Do you want to help me get dinner ready?"

"I don't *want* to," Eddie teased, "but I will be happy to help. I haven't been home for dinner in weeks and I've missed it."

Eleanor took Eddie's arm and escorted him toward the kitchen. "We missed you, too. Especially your sons. It's good for them to have a man in the house. They always act better."

Eddie stopped walking. "What? Are they acting out?"

Eleanor patted his arm. "Only a little. And some of it is because of the new baby coming. You know that has to affect them both."

Eddie nodded. Life in the Berman house had undergone a lot of changes. Douglas and William had to share a bedroom as they prepared a nursery for the new baby.

William was now fifteen, tall and lanky. He had shot up three inches over the last summer to five foot ten. His round face had become thinner, and because he had inherited his mother's striking good looks, he worried about looking good and longed for nice clothes and expensive sneakers. Douglas, who preferred Doug, now twelve and dark-skinned like Cerise, had begun his own growth spurt that would probably put him at his brother's height or taller.

Eddie understood how the arrival of a newcomer might annoy both young men, just as they were working on stretching their wings and becoming their own people.

They went into the kitchen, where Eleanor was preparing several saucepans of food. Potatoes were cooking in one, red sauce in another, and a third that was heating water for pasta.

"Spaghetti and potatoes?" Eddie wondered. "Are we carb loading for a marathon or something?"

"It's what your wife wanted—pasta and potatoes. She has a craving, and if that is what she wants, she gets it."

Eddie stirred the sauce. "Are those your homemade meatballs?"

"Nothing but!"

"Then who am I to complain? What can I do?"

"Make garlic bread," Eleanor told him as she stirred the sauce. "Your wife thinks it tastes better when you make it."

"I will do my best to keep that legend going. Anything else?"

"Just that, but it would be nice if you showered and got dressed up."

Eddie examined his suit and tie. "What's wrong with this?"

"You need to make Cerise feel special. You going off and practicing after work all these months has been hard on her. And I know that she's feeling pretty unattractive right now."

"You're right, Momma." Eddie sighed as he took off his jacket and rolled up his sleeves.

"Of course I am," she stated, as if it were an accepted fact.

Eddie could have used his abilities to clean himself and had done so after many a tough training session with Marlowe fighting off re-creations of dragons or learning potions that sometimes filled a room with noxious smoke. Instead, he did it the normal way, going into the shower and washing himself, then dressing up nicely for his wife.

Eddie also called out to his sons to "dress up for your mother" on his way to the shower and waited until he heard a response. It surprised him when he got downstairs to find his sons had indeed put on better clothes and made themselves look good.

Eddie had to stop and admire the two young men, shaking his head in pride and amazement. "You guys look great!"

William glanced up from the smart phone in his hand. "You said you wanted us to look good for Mom."

Douglas focused on his own tiny screen in his hand. "Yeah."

"Okay, well, put the phones away. I just saw your mother pull her car in the driveway."

The two boys grunted a reply and slipped the phones into their pockets, just as Eleanor stepped from the kitchen to the dining room. "Stand up straight," she muttered to Doug, who did.

The front door opened, and Cerise waddled in wearing her hospital scrubs. She had her purse in one hand and the other supported her stomach, pushed out before her almost as a challenge.

She stopped at the door, overwhelmed by the tableau in front of her, and her eyes grew wet. "What a beautiful family I have."

"Mom, don't get all weepy," William complained as his mother came close and touched both of her sons' faces.

"I can't help it," she said with her slight accent. Despite her distended belly, Cerise's face was still thin, and her arms were strong but lithe. She stepped to her husband and had to turn her head to kiss him.

"Yuck," Doug said, and turned away.

This made Cerise laugh, and she bent to kiss Doug's head, and then William's cheek.

"We are having a proper dinner tonight, with everyone home!" she announced.

"Can we eat now?" William whined, and with a laugh, they all made their way to the table.

"I'm only in scrubs, and you all look so nice," Cerise pointed out.

Eddie held out her chair for her. "You're beautiful."

Her hand went to her kinky hair, pulled back in a bun. "I'm just glad you're home, sugar."

She sat and Eddie slid the chair in with a little difficulty. For a moment he considered using his magick to move it but quickly quashed the idea.

Eddie went with Eleanor to the kitchen to help serve the food, carrying large dishes out to the table. He served Cerise first, before anyone else.

"You could spoil a girl this way, Mr. Berman," Cerise said as her eyes sparkled.

"Any way I can, Mrs. Berman," Eddie replied, as his eyes bore into her.

"Hey, we're trying to eat," Doug whined. "Can you save the lovey-dovey stuff for later?"

This made both Eddie and Cerise smile. Eddie knew she was still in a charged mood like in the morning, and his little signs of appreciation helped fuel it.

Eddie had learned that marriage was a deep and loving friendship. His love for his wife was so strong that he would sacrifice anything for her, as she would for him. But there were also times lasciviousness sparked anew, and your best friend was suddenly an attractive partner in the ancient dance.

Both Eddie and Cerise snickered at each other, knowing what they both wanted but keeping it a secret joke between themselves.

They ate and talked about William going out for basketball and Doug spoke of a new magic trick he was working on. Soon, the young men were done and left the table, back to staring at their phones, which left the adults to talk.

Eleanor spoke up. "So you caught the dealers you were after, Eddie? Will you be coming home at a reasonable hour now?"

"I had to go in early because we caught a homicide. But, with the drug gang the ringleader got away. Luis and I will work nights to solve both cases."

"But you will be home more soon, won't you?" Eleanor worried.

Eddie nodded. "I'm taking time after the baby is born, and I've told everyone that I have less time for them, once it's here."

Cerise and Eleanor understood the meaning of the word "everyone." They knew the training schedule Eddie had been on and the many missed dinners and events as he learned to control his strange powers.

Eleanor rose. "Tell you what, I'll clean up. You two go relax."

Cerise frowned. "That's too much to ask, Momma."

"It's okay, you're still in scrubs and probably want a shower," Eleanor told her, her eyes glinting with awareness. "And y'know, I think both of you could use a nap."

"A nap might be nice." Eddie winked at his wife.

"I could use a… rest," Cerise agreed. "Thank you, Momma."

Eddie got behind Cerise's chair and pulled it out, then offered his hand to help her up.

Halfway to her feet, Cerise gave an involuntary, "Oof!"

Eddie panicked. "You okay?"

She stood up the rest of the way. "The baby kicked." She took his hand and placed it on her belly, covered by the fabric of her top. "Here, feel."

Eddie felt her flesh jump under his fingers. "She's strong."

"Or he is," Cerise agreed. "With the kick of a mule."

He helped her up the stairs and they were soon in the bedroom, and Eddie shut and latched the lock. He pulled his wife as near as he could and kissed her deeply. Cerise moaned in the back of her throat as their tongues played and awoke senses.

"Can I ask you to do something?" she requested as they parted.

"Anything," Eddie replied.

"Could you rub my back again?" she begged, and turned away from him.

Eddie's powerful hands started at the base of her spine, the spot he knew always ached, and she leaned forward to place her hands on the nearby desk.

Eddie reached under the loose garment and caressed her spine with his thumbs. He gently removed her top and her bra so her breasts hung free. One hand reached around to cup her dark bosom.

"That's not my back," Cerise chuckled.

"I got lost," Eddie said, as his hand located her other breast and he cupped it as he pressed himself against his wife.

"Oh, yessss," she hissed. "We have to be quiet. I don't want the boys to know what we're doing."

Eddie leaned close to her ear. "You mean the *lovely-dovey* stuff?"

Cerise giggled, straightened up, and turned to her husband to unbutton his shirt. "Shall I focus on the 'lovey' or the 'dovey?'"

"I just don't want to hurt you or the baby."

She smiled. "Then let me take charge."

Soon they were both naked, and hands and lips were everywhere, touching and tasting in the ways each preferred. It was difficult to arrange themselves where both were comfortable, but they finally shifted into a position that was effective and each of them enjoyed.

Afterwards, they lay side-by-side in bed as their breathing returned to normal.

"Now I really need a shower," Cerise complained good-naturedly.

"After that, me too," Eddie smiled.

"I'd offer to take one together, but there isn't room for you, me, and my belly. Oh!"

"What's wrong?" Eddie asked with alarm.

"Just another kick," Cerise said, and pulled Eddie's hand to the spot. "I swear, this child will be a soccer player."

Eddie again felt the life pulsing just under her skin. "Well, then we'll have two children interested in sports."

"Doug is getting serious about his magic tricks. He wants to do shows."

"Shows?" Eddie reflected on it. "Might not be a bad idea. He can find out if he really likes it or not."

"Then he has your permission?" Cerise cajoled.

"Wait—did you wait until after we had sex to bring that up so I would be in a good mood?"

"First, it was my idea to have sex," Cerise insisted. "You have been away too much and I have needs."

"Glad we cleared that up."

"Second, I was not sure how you felt about it because of your own 'activities'."

Eddie thought about it a little more. "You know, it's a great idea. If Doug is working on magic tricks, we can use that to explain any weird things to the neighbors. We can tell them it's part of a trick Doug is working on."

"I hadn't considered that, but I think you're right," Cerise said and pulled away to the other side of the bed to get up. "Now I have to get cleaned up. I smell of sex."

"Very good sex," Eddie insisted.

"I cannot argue with that," Cerise said, grabbed a robe, and went into their bathroom.

Eddie lay back in the bed. This was what he needed. A night away from his job, dinner with his family, and a chance to make love to his wife. He sighed in contentment.

"Psst! Eddie," a voice called from somewhere in the room.

"Crap," Eddie muttered, then spoke aloud to the empty air. "Who is that?"

Even in the dark room, he saw movement at his wife's dressing table on a small makeup mirror. Eddie pulled on a robe, keeping to the shadows.

"It's Marlowe, Eddie. I can't see you."

Eddie turned on a small light and sat at the dressing table. In the mirror was the image of Marlowe with his white beard and hair.

"Glad you didn't call ten minutes sooner," Eddie muttered wryly.

Marlowe frowned. "What?" He then gazed past Eddie. "Oh dear, is that your bedroom?"

"Nothing but."

Marlowe's cheeks flushed. "Oh, I'm sorry if I… interrupted anything."

"I don't wanna be rude, Marlowe, but I have the night off. What is it?"

Marlowe blanched but quickly recovered himself. "I'm afraid we have an emergency, Eddie."

"No," Eddie moaned. "I am staying home and sleeping with my wife!"

"Eddie, it's the Drakula," Marlowe said. "He arrives in New York this very night!"

SEVEN

It was after dark when Eddie climbed the steps to Marlowe's townhouse. He hadn't bothered to use his car, choosing instead to transport himself from the nearby park to appear in Central Park just across the street from the building.

The hard part had been rousing himself from his bed when the only thing he wanted to do was to fall asleep holding his wife.

As he reached the top step, the door was flung open by Daniel Kraft. The tall vampire had fine features and a face that could make angels weep. His fashionably barbered hair was as black as a raven, in contrast to his alabaster skin.

"So glad you're here, lieutenant," Daniel said, and his eyes seemed to glitter in the darkness of the entryway. "We appreciate your aid."

"Yeah, yeah," Eddie muttered. "Here to do my mystical duty, protect and serve, and all that."

Daniel frowned. "You seem a bit put out."

Eddie sighed. "I'm just tired. I wanted to spend a night at home instead of chasing ghouls or whatever." He came into the front hall and Daniel shut the door.

"You are not chasing ghouls, and for that you should be grateful," Daniel told him and shuddered. "You never forget your first ghoul."

Eddie glared at him but said nothing as Daniel led him into the living room. Scattered about the room were the large chairs, no longer in the neat circle as earlier. There was a large table in the center of the room, covered with various implements and weapons. Eddie spotted a crossbow, a spear, several knotted ropes, and multiple stakes of different sizes and sharpness, mostly wood, but one seemed to be cast from silver. There were bottles of potions, all carefully labeled to explain their contents.

Eddie leaned over to read one bottle that had a flexible rubber top like a medicine dropper: Sasquatch Blood.

He looked at Daniel. "He's got Sasquatch blood?"

Daniel peered over Eddie's shoulder. "Oh, so he does. Quite fatal for a vampire."

"*Sasquatch* blood?" Eddie repeated.

Daniel nodded. "They are powerful beings, possessed of ancient magic. If you were to inject a vampire with it, it would prove most deleterious."

Eddie frowned. "I thought you guys had very hard skin. Wouldn't a needle just break on you?"

"You would need to use one made of silver," Daniel explained. He pointed at a ring that glowed in the light from the sconces on the walls. "See this ring? That would do the trick."

Eddie picked up the large ring. He attempted to place it on his fingers, but it only fit on the middle finger of his right hand.

The ring bore a strange family crest: a heralding shield with a medieval helmet on the top. There was a line through the middle separating the top half of the shield from the bottom. He turned his hand over to gaze at it from all angles. "Kinda big. How do you inject the vampire?"

Daniel smirked and touched a small catch on the side. A tiny needle, only an inch long, sprung up from the top of the ring, and the point glinted sharply in the light.

"Oh, that's how." Eddie carefully folded the needle back into the ring where it disappeared into the design.

"Yes, but there is another button on the other side," Daniel went on, and touched the other hidden catch. The entire top of the ring folded over to expose a small space.

"What's that for?"

Daniel lifted the bottle of Sasquatch blood and squeezed the rubber top of the eyedropper, then carefully unscrewed it loose from the bottle.

"Hey, be careful!" Eddie warned. "You said that was fatal for vampires."

"I *am* being careful, and I have a very steady hand," Daniel explained patiently, then lifted the dropper, with about a half-inch of dark-red liquid. "You would fill the reservoir with a few drops of holy water or, in this case, Sasquatch blood, or whatever poison you prefer."

He dripped several drops into the opening of the ring, returned the stopper to the bottle, and sealed it. He put the bottle down and gently closed the lid of the ring, being careful not to spill any. "There! Now the ring is an armed weapon."

"Pretty neat," Eddie nodded, and surveyed the room. "Where's Marlowe, and who else is coming?"

He reached his left hand to the ring, being careful not to touch either of the catches. He didn't want to stab himself or drip Sasquatch blood on the floor. He tugged at the ring to pull it off.

Daniel was speaking, not looking at Eddie. "I have no knowledge of who is going to help, but Marlowe is upstairs talking on the mirror to see who he can reach."

"Did he tell you about the vampire we tried to catch? He's been running a gang of drug dealers in the park," Eddie said, trying to pull the ring off a second time, unsuccessfully.

Daniel nodded. "Marlowe gave me the description you wrote. I will look into it over the next few nights."

"Good. Is this something that's happened before? I mean, vampires dealing drugs?" Eddie attempted once more to remove the ring, then gave up and instead focused on Daniel.

Daniel's expression hardened. "The criminal element attracts vampires. They like to be around people who have no compunction to kill, and they can use that opportunity to feed without worry. Also, a vampire bite contains a venom that is like a drug."

"Like a drug, huh?"

Daniel shrugged. "It's why people become infatuated with a vampire and offer themselves."

"Eddie, I am so glad you made it!" Marlowe announced as he came hurriedly into the room.

"Well, if the Drakula is coming…" Eddie said, then looked at Marlowe and Daniel. "Is it just the three of us, then?"

Marlowe sputtered. "No, no, Drusilicus is on his way, as well as Rusty."

"Rusty?" Eddie asked. "The cabbie?"

Marlowe spread his arms in a gesture of helplessness. "Someone needs to drive out to Teterboro Airport."

"The Teterboro in New Jersey?" Eddie questioned. "That's a small municipal airport. Is it even open this time of night?"

"Open and operating, it would appear," Marlowe proclaimed. "And apparently it does international flights."

"Only private planes for the international flights," Daniel commented.

"It makes sense, Eddie. A small airport where the Drakula can land unseen, with perhaps less security than a large airport like JFK or LaGuardia."

"I see," Eddie said. "Us five against the Drakula?"

"I am afraid it would just be the four of you," Daniel asserted. "The vampires are already suspicious of me. If they saw me fighting by your side they would shun me, and my usefulness as a source of information would be lost."

"I must agree," Marlowe conceded. "I hope this does not upset you, Eddie."

Eddie shook his head. "Not at all. I've worked undercover. You can't afford to blow your cover."

Daniel exhaled. "Thank you for understanding, lieutenant. Others have not been so sensitive to my position."

"I take it you're the one who got us this intel?" Eddie asked.

"Yes. The word has been going around the community that the Drakula will arrive this very night on a midnight flight."

Eddie shook his head wearily. "Why is everything at midnight with you guys? Can't you do stuff at 10:00 PM and let a guy go home and get some sleep?"

Daniel and Marlowe exchanged a glance, just as a knock came at the door.

"I'll get it," Eddie offered, just to get away from his companions. He didn't mean to be annoyed with them, but he had his evening planned, and although Cerise was understanding, she would have preferred her husband home. He opened the door to let in Drusilicus and Rusty.

"Hey, Eddie, how ya doin'?" Rusty asked as he stepped across the threshold and into the house. "Ain't dis a hoot? We gonna go kill the Drakula!"

Drusilicus was right behind him. "If he doesn't kill us first."

The three men joined Marlowe and Daniel at the table laden with weapons.

Upon seeing it, Rusty whistled. "Whoa, you got some nice stuff here, Marlowe." He picked up a crossbow fitted with a wooden shaft and a silver arrowhead.

Drusilicus put his hand on top of the bow in Rusty's hands. "We must travel light and be unobtrusive. I think entering an airport, even a small one, with a crossbow might get us some... unwarranted attention."

"It'll certainly make someone call the police," Eddie added. "And if they have any TSA agents, they'll come out with guns. Whatever we bring is going to have to be discreet. We can't stay there until 5:00 AM adjusting everybody's memory."

Rusty spoke up. "If we gonna make da airport by midnight, we haveta go pretty soon."

Eddie smiled. In his old life, he'd have to glance at his watch to make such a determination. Marlowe had informed him that wizards knew what hour it was all the time, as one part of their abilities. Eddie noticed in the last month or so that he had an unerring awareness of what time it was as well, but he wasn't ready to give up the comfort of his watch.

Rusty examined the group. "Is dis everyone?"

"Bankrock was otherwise engaged," Marlowe sighed.

"Good. He would merely be in the way," Drusilicus snorted.

"Talk about someone I'd be happy to put a stake in," Rusty muttered.

"There is another on her way, whom I expect any moment. I must remain here," Marlowe insisted.

"You can't—" Eddie said.

"You da coven master—" Rusty added.

"Our strongest combatant—" Drusilicus worried.

Marlowe raised his hand, silencing the others. "I have uncovered some clues about this papyrus that the Drakula seeks. I must continue to search for it or everything is for naught."

The group muttered, but agreed. The men inspected the choices on the table, and each picked up one or two items. Rusty took several vials marked "Holy Water," while Drusilicus slipped the silver stake into the inner pocket of his fashionable suit, where it didn't even produce a noticeable bulge. Marlowe set aside several bottles of potions and a wooden stake.

Eddie didn't know what he could use to fight a vampire, but he possessed his staff, and with that, he knew what he was doing. Soon, there was a knock at the door, and Daniel dutifully went to open it.

"Too many choices for ya, Eddie?" Rusty asked.

"I have no idea about fighting vampires. The only one I've really dealt with is Daniel."

The last guest walked in. She was a tall and sturdy African-American woman, her hair covered in a turban, and she wore a simple blouse and skirt with a colorful shawl on her shoulders.

Her eyes took in the group, she nodded and said, "Bonswa."

"Gentlemen," Marlowe said, "this is the Wizard Willowdell. She has traveled up from New Orleans to assist us."

"Oh, Marlowe, you make it sound like I had to take a carriage," she said with an accent that suggested Haiti. "I transported to the woods across the street."

"It's a pleasure," Eddie said, and offered his hand. "You seem familiar to me."

"Ah, I get t'at a lot," Willowdell offered. She took his hand and turned it palm up, then ran her long fingernails down the lines. "Ooh, you lead a most interestin' life, do you not?"

"Um, I guess," Eddie confessed.

Drusilicus stepped forward. "I am familiar with your work—and your legend—good lady. I am Drusilicus Greywacke, and this is Rusty Claremont."

"Charmed, I'm sure," Rusty said.

She scrutinized the men and released Eddie's hand. "I can see why you called me, Marlowe. A group of fighters and not one prophet among them."

"You see through me so easily, Madam. I have selected some weapons for you," Marlowe offered.

Willowdell walked over to the table, scanned the selections, and placed several bottles of potions into various hidden pockets of her skirt.

"With five of us, we should be able to stop the dark forces," Willowdell said as she hid away the final bottle.

"Marlowe ain't comin'," reported Rusty.

Willowdell raised her head. "Ah? T'will be a challenge."

"Odd to tell that to a prophet," Drusilicus wondered.

"Did I say I was a prophet, you silly man?" Willowdell snapped.

Taken aback, Drusilicus said, "No, I guess— you did not."

"There is a difference between a prophet and a seer," she confirmed.

Rusty interrupted. "We gotta get goin'."

With no further comments, the three men and Willowdell headed for the door, down the outside steps, and into the large yellow cab that waited for them. Rusty got into the driver's seat and the group was off, heading uptown to catch the George Washington Bridge. It impressed Eddie that even with three people in the back there was still plenty of leg room.

Rusty hummed as he drove, and Eddie tried to take it in stride, though it was annoying. He had ridden in New York cabs where the driver had played loud music or had terrible body odor so humming wasn't that big of a deal.

"Madam, did Marlowe give you a plan of attack?" Drusilicus asked.

"Not that he mentioned," Willowdell replied. "Now you must excuse me— I have to prepare." She shut her eyes and placed her hands on her knees.

"How about we surround the plane and give old Drakky a permanent send-off?" Eddie suggested.

Drusilicus jeered. "It's so comforting that the law enforcement officer comes up with such a blatantly idiotic strategy."

"Well, it's not like we can arrest him," Eddie pointed out.

Rusty spoke from up front. "I figure we go into da plane, stake him, and we're done."

"I appreciate your enthusiasm, Rusty," Drusilicus answered. "But I believe that there will be other vampires there to meet and escort him. We must approach with stealth, gauge the strength of our opposition. Open warfare might not be a wise choice."

Eddie remarked, "Well, if it's a skeleton crew—"

"Hey, you think dere'll be skeletons, too?" Rusty worried.

"Just an expression, Rusty" Drusilicus huffed. "The lieutenant believes the workers at the airfield might be small in number."

"Right," Eddie agreed. "And if it is just a few people, we can alter their memories, make them forget the whole thing, right?"

Drusilicus considered it. "I guess not all of your plan is idiotic."

Rusty spoke up. "If I knew we was gonna do dat, I woulda brought dat crossbow. I once killed a vampire from 100 yards with one of dem things."

"Stealth," Drusilicus repeated. "We must pull into an unobtrusive place and move in carefully."

"You know there are cameras on every inch of that airfield, right?" Eddie suggested.

"We can easily dispatch them," Drusilicus replied. "Though I suspect the Drakula's minions will have already done so."

"Dat makes sense," Rusty bantered. "Dey don't want no video either. Plus, we ain't sure how da Drakula is arriving."

"I assume—in a plane?" Eddie said.

"Yes, of course, but more likely in a coffin," Drusilicus replied with a raised eyebrow.

"What?" Eddie said.

"Dat sounds like what he'd do," Rusty reasoned. "He coulda had his coffin picked up during da day and taken to da airport until da flight leaves. I mean, it's safer to wait inside da coffin until da plane lands and you're sure it's night."

Drusilicus continued. "Which again suggests that he has vampires waiting to escort the coffin to a safe location. Undoubtably, the Drakula planned for a midnight arrival to assure that vampires—and not merely humans held in sway— would meet his coffin."

"Humans held in sway?" Eddie repeated. "I mean, you told me that there are humans who offer themselves to vampires for blood —"

"The vampires call such mortals 'Skivvies'," Drusilicus muttered. "I suppose the term is better than 'cattle'."

"But not much," Eddie objected.

Drusilicus sighed. "It's an old term—very derogatory—for servant. You cannot trust such humans with complex tasks. The vampire's control is through the euphoric effects of his venom, and it leaves the human in a state where they find it hard to focus."

"Didja ever see da movie *Dracula*, Eddie?" Rusty asked.

"The old black-and-white one? Sure."

"Okay! Think of Renfield."

"The guy who ate spiders?"

"You got it."

"Ew," Eddie said.

"Don't mean dey ain't dangerous," Rusty quipped from the front seat. "I remember I was after dis guy livin' in a castle out on Long Island. So, I goes during da day, figurin' da vampire is asleep and vulnerable. He had like ten guys guarding da place dat I had to blast through to get to his coffin. By den it was almost dark. But, in de end, I took him out."

"How did you stop the—skivvies?" Eddie asked.

"Stunned 'em, mostly. They ain't got de strength of a vampire. One guy had a sword and was pretty good with it. Him I had to take out."

"Wait," Eddie said. "You killed him?"

"Didn't have no choice," Rusty replied in a conversational tone. "It was him or me."

Eddie sat back in the chair, disturbed by this idea. For all his bluster about just going and killing the Drakula, at least he wasn't *human*. To use his powers to kill a person—a mortal human being —did not sit well with him.

As a uniformed officer, he had used his gun only when necessary, and he only had to shoot to kill one time.

Years earlier, Eddie was a rookie and his strongest influence had been his own father, who worked a beat in Harlem for many years. He partnered with an older white guy named Greg Martin, a good guy, salt-of-the-earth cop, and optimistic as they worked their beat.

The day had started like any other. They were working the four-to-midnight shift, keeping a focus on the theatergoers that were the lifeblood for Broadway and the NYC tourist industry.

It was about 11:00 PM, most of the shows had let out, and he and Greg were watching people at the corner of Eighth Avenue and 49th Street when shots rang out.

Eddie and his partner ran up 49th Street and toward the open space behind One Worldwide Plaza, a towering office building that faced the avenue.

Eddie had pulled his police radio and spoke into it as he ran. "10-34S, 10-34S." The code meant for shots fired, and he followed it with the address.

Eddie caught up to his partner at the corner of the Starbucks, right before the public space, where the older man pressed up against a wall and tried to peer through the darkness.

"NYPD," shouted Greg, whose hand was on his weapon, though it was still in its holster. Eddie pulled his SIG Sauer P226 and held it in a two-handed grip pointed toward the ground.

"Back me up," Greg hissed. "NYPD," he shouted a second time as he stepped into the plaza.

A woman's scream split the air, and Greg was on the move with Eddie right behind him.

A man was just past the fountain with his arm around a woman. He was a tall, powerful man with a short beard and a wild mane of hair. The woman was an average-height brunette with panic in her bright eyes. He held her in a neck lock in front of him as a shield with a revolver pointed at Eddie and Greg.

The two officers ducked at the corner of the fountain, and Eddie tried to focus to keep his hands from shaking, sweat made his fingers slippery.

Greg yelled, "NYPD, put the weapon down and let the woman go."

"No," the man screamed. "She wants to take my kids!"

"Think it through. You'll be no good for your kids if you're in jail," Greg announced in a calm voice.

"No, she took everything from me! Just because I went to prison."

Greg slowly stood up.

"Partner, what are you doing?" Eddie hissed.

But Greg held up his empty hands, his gun still holstered. "How about we just talk? Maybe there's a way out of this that doesn't involve anybody getting hurt. How about that?"

Confusion clouded the man's face as he considered Greg's words.

"In about two minutes there are going to be a hundred cops in this plaza," Greg said simply. "You can walk out with me, and no one will shoot you. But, while you hold that gun, you are a threat."

In the moment of confusion, the woman, who had been playing possum the whole time, smacked the man in the chin with a sudden strike of her elbow, and kicked his leg.

He loosened his grip, she pushed free, and the gunman raised the weapon at Greg who had stepped closer.

One shot rang out as the woman screamed.

The gunman fell to the ground as Eddie watched the smoke float out of the barrel of his police service weapon. Greg gave him an angry look, but took a deep breath and went to the woman. "You all right, Ma'am?"

"Yeah, yeah," the woman said, and sat on one of the concrete benches.

Eddie approached the fallen man and kicked the gun away from his lifeless hands. The shot had made a round hole in the center of the man's forehead.

Greg was talking to the woman. Her eyes were dry, and she glared over at the fallen man. "I always pick bums. The bastard told me he had money for me, like he ever had a dime in his life."

Two pairs of uniformed officers ran into the plaza, guns drawn.

"Shooter's down," Eddie yelled out so the other officers would know and he holstered his own weapon.

Greg came over to Eddie. "You okay?"

"You almost talked him down," Eddie said, feeling as if he were no longer in his own body.

"Yeah, almost. But you did the right thing."

"Did I?" Eddie said as grief washed over him.

"We're almost there," Rusty said as he pulled onto a dark dirt road.

The bumpy car ride shook Eddie out of his own reverie. Looking forward, he could see little in front of the vehicle. "Are your headlights on?"

"No, I turned 'em off when we got close. Dis is a service road only workers know about," Rusty replied in low tones.

"How does he know such t'ings?" Willowdell wondered aloud to the others. The road was bumpy and Willowdell had been roused from her meditation.

"Wizard Claremont has a very select skill set," Drusilicus explained to the newcomer. "One of those abilities is, when he gets close to a location, he can see every road that exists, even those that are no longer in use."

Eddie leaned forward. "You keep impressing me, Rusty."

Rusty shrugged and focused on the road in front of him, having slowed the car to about fifteen miles per hour.

Eddie leaned back and turned to Drusilicus. "Can he see in the dark?"

Drusilicus considered this. "A little, but more accurately, he *senses* the road ahead of him."

Rusty pulled the car over and shut it off. The engine cooled and made quiet clicking noises.

"Dis is as close as we dare," Rusty said.

"Well done, Rusty," Eddie said.

Willowdell took a deep breath. "So, here we are."

"Indeed, Madam," Drusilicus said. "As our seer, are you aware of when the plane shall arrive?"

"T'e plane has not yet landed," Willowdell said as she peered out a nearby window.

"How do you know?" Eddie queried.

"I foresee the emanations of events, if I am involved. T'at was what I was doing as we drove," Willowdell reported. "I am aware of a group of at least ten vampires, no doubt here to meet the plane."

"How far away?" Eddie asked.

Willowdell considered for a moment. "In a terminal about a hundred feet from here. But I am unsure."

"About what?" Rusty asked.

"I believe more are hiding nearby."

Eddie nodded, but he felt a bit off-kilter. The memory of his one fatal shooting was like a message to remind him that there is always another way to solve things other than attacking.

Then again, sometimes there isn't.

They stepped out of the cab, closing the doors almost silently. The spring night had grown cooler, and Eddie pulled his jacket around him to fight the chill.

Willowdell gestured in the air and then spoke. "I have us hidden from all eyes, magickal and otherwise. I also t'ink if we are to do battle, we should select more appropriate clothing."

Drusilicus gestured first, his staff appearing and growing to full length in his hands, as his suit melted into flowing blue robes. Eddie's clothes became the red tunic and pants with the tall boots he was most comfortable working in as his staff slapped into his right hand. Willowdell's clothing shifted into floor-length robes as black as the night, but her turban stayed untouched, her staff at the ready. Finally, Rusty's cabbie uniform melted into robes of a very subdued yellow tint, as his hat became short and pointed with a broad brim, and a gnarled stick grew from the car keys he'd been holding.

"You two'd better bring your colors down a bit," Rusty whispered to Eddie and Drusilicus.

Drusilicus nodded, and the blue of his robes became much darker. Eddie made a small circle with his staff, and the red faded into a dark maroon.

"Okay," Eddie announced quietly. "Let's go kick some vampire ass."

EIGHT

T he team approached the terminal warily, their eyes looking in all directions for any movement.

"The plane will arrive soon," Willowdell said as they crept through the darkened parking lot toward the terminal. "I shall hold the spell so they can't see or hear us until we reach that building. Then, we must use the shadows to hide ourselves."

"I wish I'd brought the crossbow," Rusty muttered.

"Will you please let it go," Drusilicus snapped. "We have but a few scant minutes until the plane is here and we must face the most powerful vampire on earth."

"Thanks, Drew," Eddie muttered. "Good pep talk."

They reached the large steel building with a brick and tile foundation and metal siding up to the flat roof marked "PRIVATE AIRLINE."

A flat roof—perfect place for vampires to wait to attack.

The four of them moved silently under the overhang of the building, and Willowdell closed her eyes again for a moment. Then she pointed into the sky.

In the distance, a small aircraft was coming down slowly from the night sky. Eddie glanced over and saw that Rusty was pouring a vial of holy water into something he held.

"What are you doing?" Eddie whispered to Rusty.

"Getting ready for combat." Rusty smiled and held up what he'd been filling.

It was a water pistol.

"I put some garlic juice in it before I got to Marlowe's," Rusty gushed. "Dis oughta stop any vampires, you know what I mean?"

Eddie nodded. It was certainly an inventive idea. He'd brought little more than his staff with the thought that it was more than enough to take on the vampires. He had trained for months, learning every kind of defensive and attack spell his head could hold. He'd drilled again and again, believing that if he knew enough, he could take on any adversary.

The experience of combatting the Great Evil, an extremely ancient and powerful demon a little over nine months earlier, had made him take the lessons to heart. His job as a detective in Central Park was not nearly as demanding as when he was a homicide detective with the Manhattan Midtown North Precinct.

Why did he think of the one time he had shot a man tonight? Why, of all nights, did he bring up a memory that made him feel he wasn't worthy?

The aftermath of that shooting years ago was that Eddie was off active duty while Internal Affairs examined the reports and Eddie had to have a psychological review. In the end, it was a justified use of his weapon, as the man was a threat and Eddie saved his partner's life. He just wished it had ended the way Greg wanted—peacefully.

The plane touched down on the runway hundreds of yards away and slowed as it approached, finally coming to a stop. Then it turned toward the terminal.

"In the plane, can you tell who is human and who isn't?" Eddie whispered in Willowdell's ear.

Willowdell spoke up. "The pilot is human, surely controlled by the vampires."

"Dat makes sense," Rusty put in. "If da flight got delayed or anything and da sun rose, you'd want da pilot to be human."

Willowdell nodded. "I will tell you for certain when t'ey come out of the plane."

"In this light it will be hard to recognize the pale flesh of a vampire," Drusilicus added.

"Then let's keep it nonlethal until we're sure," Eddie told the other wizards.

Willowdell grasped her staff and hissed, "My spell is fading, we must move."

The others separated in different directions, and for a moment, Eddie was unsure of what to do. His cop instincts kicked in, and he held his staff, crouched low, and made his way to the cover of a nearby empty luggage cart.

The plane stopped about fifty feet from the terminal. It was a mid-size jet, necessary for the distance that it had traveled. There could only be a few people on the inside.

The door on the side of the plane lowered to reveal steps, and a man in a blue suit came from the terminal with a small set of stairs that joined with the ones from the jet to reach the ground and locked them together in place.

Eddie observed the man, but Drusilicus was correct. In the dim light, he couldn't tell if the man was a vampire or not.

The pilot stood at the top of the stairs and gazed down at the tarmac. He then stepped back into the plane and two people came out. One was a woman in a black dress that hung past her knees with a veil that covered her face. She held onto the railing built into the stairs and started walking down the steps in impossibly high heels.

Right on those heels was a superb-looking man. He was tall and dark-haired, with a thin face and features that appeared as if someone had chiseled them out of marble. He wore a long black shirt and black pants—simple but elegant.

"Now *that's* a vampire," Eddie muttered to himself as he watched the pair descend the stairs. The man couldn't be the Drakula—he was far too young. Even if he had not aged for a thousand years, he didn't carry himself with the gravitas that the Lord of the Undead should have.

Several men in coveralls came out of the terminal carrying what resembled a hospital gurney, only it lacked a mattress. When they arrived under the plane, two of the men pulled it and it extended until it was large enough to carry a body.

Or a coffin.

A door opened in the aircraft's bottom, and Eddie understood. It would lower the coffin that contained the Drakula from that hatch onto the cart and they could wheel it to a waiting vehicle, probably a hearse.

Eddie's eye kept being drawn to the two vampires. Why had these two been in the cabin of the aircraft while the Drakula rode in a coffin?

He thought for a moment, reaching into his magical mental clock that allowed wizards to know the time everywhere they went. London was five hours ahead of New York. If it were a six or seven hour flight that arrived at midnight, and considering the time difference, that meant it could have left at eight or nine o'clock local time in London.

Which was after dark.

Why did the Drakula ride in a coffin instead of in the cabin? The most logical answer was that he didn't. This was something to lure the wizards into revealing themselves.

It's a trap.

Eddie reached into his robes and pulled out a mirror. He quickly made a small circle with his staff and his reflection silvered over. "Drusilicus," he gasped, "can you hear me? This is a trap—"

Eddie heard the yell from above and glanced up to see a full-sized man falling toward him from the roof.

"*Oppressio!*" Eddie shouted, and with a gesture of his staff, he swatted aside the falling man as easily as a bug. Eddie slid out of the shadows and allowed the red light of his staff to surround him. He needed a distraction, something that would take everyone's attention. If this was a trap, the best way to deal with it was to force the vampires to spring it so that his allies might stop them.

Or save him, if he'd guessed wrong.

Eddie ran for the plane, the bright glow around him. He screamed, "It's a trap!" as he ran.

From various hidden spots around the terminal roof, dark figures leapt down. They were in humanoid form, but even in shadow they had elongated fingernails and teeth. Dozens of bats shrieked as they flew, the dark shapes moving with purpose to the ground to transform into men and women as they landed.

Eddie planted his stick on the ground and reached into the earth to draw his power: the energy of the element fire. There was one weakness he could exploit— all vampires had a fear of fire. It could destroy them, or injure them in ways that their superhuman healing couldn't fix quickly.

Marlowe had been teaching him Latin words and phrases when he used his magick, and the Latin word for fire was "Flamma." What had worked better in his practice sessions was his own version, and he called it out now.

"Flamma-Lamma-Ding-Dong," he announced in a deep voice as the army of pale-skinned attackers grew near.

A ring of fire shot up around Eddie, with him as the epicenter. The horde of monsters drew back—some all but turned and ran. The pilot, who had come down the stairs and stood near the two vampires, covered them with his own body to protect them from the fiery assault.

The ring of fire pitched away from Eddie with flames at least five feet tall. It struck the pilot, and his coat flared up. He shrieked, but just as he did, the fire fell away and went out, and he turned, surprised that he was uninjured.

Eddie turned to the large group of vampires that had stopped, dumbfounded, and yelled, *"Oppressio!"* This threw them backward through the air as a wall of magical force washed over them.

The fire Eddie sent out had been little more than a display, about as dangerous as sparklers on the Fourth of July. Eddie used the vampire's fear to put them off-guard—and to make a point.

"I am the Wizard Riftstone," Eddie bellowed, using the name of the wizard from whom he'd received his staff. "I can conjure flames that would burn you all, but I chose not to! Leave this place in peace, and I shall do likewise. I will not stop your travels if you do not impede mine."

The red glow around his body increased and the group all backed away, crouching and hissing. All of them wore human form at this point, but their faces appeared animalistic, the desire for blood upon them all. They clawed the air with their long fingers and several had extended their fangs past their chins, ready and eager to attack.

They possessed strength and speed, but Eddie knew they mostly hunted alone. As a group, without a leader, they were unsure what to do, and backed away whimpering and cursing.

The young pale vampire from the plane stepped forward and yelled out in a clear voice with a slight English accent, "You are but one wizard. How can you stand against an army?"

"Buddy," Eddie growled, his eyes still on the crowd and his back to the accuser, "you ain't the first army I've faced." Eddie raised his voice to shout to the crowd. "For those of you who know what happened in Central Park nine months ago, let it be known that I was the wizard who took down the Great Evil while fighting a warlock. If you doubt my abilities, I shall prove them to you. That ring of fire was a warning. I suggest you heed it."

"He does not stand alone," Drusilicus announced as he drew near Eddie, his staff at the ready. "I am the Wizard Greywacke. We are two of the Five."

Drusilicus referred to the wizards who bore the staves of fire, air, water, earth, and spirit—the Five, considered the most powerful wizards on the planet. Soon after Eddie received the Staff of Fire, Drusilicus had claimed the staff of the element water.

As if to support his assertion, blue light surrounded his body.

"What are you doing?" whispered Eddie.

"Following your lead, lieutenant," Drusilicus muttered back.

Rusty stepped into the glow of his companion's staves, and a yellow light grew around him as well. "And I be the Wizard Claremont," he said with a deep growl in his voice. "If thou shalt stay, we shall have no choice but to smite thee!"

He stepped close and Eddie asked, "Smite thee?"

He shrugged and raised his staff.

"And I am the Wizard Willowdell. You would do well to respect our words," the black-draped woman said as she came into view and held her own staff aloft, magenta light flashing around her.

It surprised Eddie how impressive the newcomer appeared, and he exchanged a glance with Drusilicus.

The four of them stood close, and all shifted to face outward, each with their backs to one another to fend off an attack from any direction.

Eddie was now facing the plane and the people who had come off it. "Shall we call off this battle? Maybe we can avoid some unnecessary smiting?"

The woman raised the veil from her face. For a moment, Eddie thought she was Lysandra, a vampire he'd met briefly months earlier, because of her pale skin, chiseled features, and black hair. But at second glance, he realized she simply appeared similar.

She faced Eddie. "Are you saying you shall let us leave with the casket?" She gestured at the box within the hold of the plane.

Eddie smiled. "Sure will."

"Does that not defeat your purpose here this night?" she challenged, a smug smile on her face.

"Not at all." Eddie smiled. "Because it's empty."

This elicited another gasp, this time from his fellow wizards, as well as the many vampires that stood staring, but not from the woman whose eyes never left Eddie's. Eddie kept his mind focused, in case she was trying to use her glamour to influence him.

Her mouth was a tight line. "Very well. Let us pass, and then you may go in peace."

"That is agreeable," Eddie responded, not taking his eyes from her.

"Are you sure, lieutenant?" Drusilicus hissed under his breath.

"You're gonna have to trust me on this one, Drew," Eddie muttered.

"Willowdell, what do you sense from the coffin?" Drusilicus demanded.

"I can sense not'ing, ominous or not," she replied.

The tall, thin man next to the vampire woman and the pilot became angry. He bellowed "No, these fools shall not order us about!"

"Lycius, let it be," the woman said, and reached out to grab his arm.

Lycius wasn't there.

He had launched himself into the air, and with a speed that dazzled the eye, he leapt past the glow of the wizard's staves and grabbed Eddie in one fast move.

In mere seconds, he had an iron grip on Eddie's head, jerking Eddie off his feet and Eddie saw the bared fangs ready to plunge into his neck. On instinct, Eddie lashed out and hit the vampire in the face with his right hand.

To Eddie's surprise, the vampire released him, and Eddie fell to the ground. He watched as the vampire reached up to his face, stumbled back a step or two, and then let out a wail of agony. His hand came away with a chunk of his face, revealing the skull beneath.

Eddie crab-crawled away, grabbing his staff to protect himself as the attacker's face shredded like tiny pieces of paper falling away. His body within his clothes shifted into impossible angles as the man made horrible gurgling screams and fell to his knees.

Drusilicus pulled Eddie to his feet, as the skin on the vampire's face melted away to a white, leering skull. And then in moments, the flesh on the hands was gone, and the clothes fell as the flesh of the body simply disintegrated.

The skull fell off of the neck, and even that just turned to powder, leaving nothing but the empty clothes that lay on the ground within a heap of white powder that blew away in the gentle wind.

The vampire was gone.

Eddie peered at his right hand, and realized he had struck the vampire with the hand that bore the ring, and the needle was sticking out.

He must have accidentally hit the catch when the vampire attacked. He carefully folded it back into place and held his head up.

The gathered vampires shouted and cursed the wizards, and the four of them pressed their backs closer together, each staff at the ready.

"Will that be enough?" Eddie accused loudly, fighting to regain his composure after the sudden, brutal attack. "I told you I didn't want any unnecessary killing, but you struck first!"

The woman raised her hand, and the others became silent. She gazed down at the empty clothes. The look on her face showed she wasn't at all upset about the fate of her companion.

"Wizard, please forgive Lycius' lack of manners," the woman conceded with a bow of her head. "We did not prepare him for a warrior of your stature. He has paid for it dearly."

"Shall we call a truce, then?" Eddie yelled out. "We announced ourselves. Could I have your name?"

"I am known as Selene, and I am the consort of the Drakula. If you allow us to depart with what is ours, then we shall leave with no further hostilities."

This caused a cacophony of angry voices from the rooftop of the terminal as well as from the group facing the wizards.

Selene held up her hand again and screamed, "Silence! The Drakula has given me the authority."

The noise stopped, and a heavy stillness filled the night. She nodded to the men in the overalls, and they lowered the overlarge coffin from the plane. It was ornate, with carvings of intricate shapes, demons, fauns, and even gargoyles and trimmed in places with gold. The two attendants grabbed the large box by two of the six shiny brass handles, and with far more strength than any human, placed it on the carrier.

As they carefully brought it out of the plane, Selene approached with her hands raised to show she had no weapon. Eddie gripped his staff tighter, just in case.

She strode to three feet from Eddie and spoke. "What gave us away?"

Eddie set his jaw. "The fact that you and lover boy were on the plane. That meant it took off after night had fallen. If that was the case, then there was no reason for the Drakula to fly here in a coffin. Plus the waiting party you had here. It was obviously a trap."

She nodded, pleased by this answer. "I shall have to be more wary of you, Wizard Riftstone. Oh, and Lycius was not my lover. He was a young soul that I was training." She surveyed the empty clothing on the ground and kicked the shirt with her high-heeled foot. "Some learn faster than others."

"So tell me," Eddie asked dryly, "where did the Drakula arrive?"

"JFK," she smiled sweetly. "I suppose that's too far for you to get over there quickly enough?" She glanced at the diamond-encrusted watch on her slim wrist. "Oh, and by now they have escorted him to a safe location."

"I have no doubt," Eddie replied. "And all of our attention was here."

Selene glanced back to see that they loaded the coffin onto the carrier, and they were now wheeling it toward the front of the terminal.

"I have your word you will not follow our hearse?"

Eddie glanced over to Drusilicus, who nodded curtly. "I don't chase empty coffins." Eddie scanned the top of the terminal and saw the many pale faces in the shadows. "You'll take your friends when you go?"

"Of course," she told him as she strode away. The carrier rattled as the coffin disappeared around the corner.

"Stay on guard, all of you," Willowdell whispered. "I sense there is disquiet among the ranks."

The four wizards kept watching all around for any movement.

There was the sound of a large vehicle starting up, and after a minute or two, they heard it pull away.

With a frightful cry, the vampires launched into the air. Eddie, Drusilicus, Rusty, and Willowdell all raised their staffs to repel an attack.

As they moved, all of them man and woman alike, transformed into bats. The air filled with an entire cloud of the dark creatures as they passed over the wizards' heads, then rose and headed off into the night in different directions, each group a collection of individual colonies.

Eddie was the first to pull back the glow of his staff and lower the protective enchantment he'd placed around himself. He would have to work on getting that charm up faster.

Soon the other wizards' lights faded. Rusty maintained a small, subdued light atop his staff so they could find their way back to his cab.

"That was a big chance you took, Eddie," Drusilicus chided him.

"Yeah, but you sure took out dat dumb vampire," Rusty exulted, his Brooklyn accent having returned. "Man, talk about fast and dirty!"

Eddie muttered. "I was lucky that I had this stupid ring stuck on my finger. It's got a silver needle, and it's loaded with Sasquatch blood."

"I wondered what was so venomous to a vampire," Willowdell considered as they trooped along. "Sasquatch blood is most difficult to get. Leave it to Marlowe to have some."

Rusty pulled out his squirt gun. "I didn't get a chance to use dis! I think da holy water and garlic will melt 'em like hot wax."

Eddie stopped and turned to the others. "Look, is there any way we can stop this confrontation from happening?"

Drusilicus, Willowdell, and Rusty all stared at Eddie, puzzled.

Eddie went on. "I mean, wizards and vampires have been able to get along in the past. Why can't we do that now?"

Drusilicus sighed. "None of us want open warfare between their kind and ours, but if the Drakula is in New York and can find this lost papyrus, what choice do we have but to confront him?"

"Dey want to bring down New Yawk," Rusty declared. "We gotta face 'em and stop 'em."

They walked the rest of the way to the cab in silence. Eddie transmuted his robes back to his suit and made his staff into the credit card as he returned it to his wallet.

The others changed their clothing as they got into Rusty's cab. The cabdriver started the engine and pulled the car out of the lot, using the main road instead of the hidden dirt road this time.

"We coulda taken a bunch of 'em out tonight," Rusty muttered as he drove.

"T'ere was a strong probability that they could've 'taken out' all of us," Willowdell chastised him.

"And what would New York do then?" Eddie replied solemnly as the car rolled steadily back toward Manhattan.

NINE

The next morning, Eddie woke up late in his own bed. Rusty had been kind enough to drop Eddie off at home in Teaneck as he returned Willowdell and Drusilicus to the city.

He rolled over to find a note on the pillow next to him in the place where his wife slept. In her neat, round hand it read:

> *Didn't hear you come in.*
> *I am off to work.*
> *Another night where we don't*
> *see each other?*
> *Well, at least you took*
> *care of business last night.*
> *Love,*
> *That woman you sleep with occasionally.*

Eddie smiled as he read it, knowing that she was pulling his leg, but throwing in a little guilt as well. He needed to tell Marlowe, forcefully, that things were going to have to change once the new baby was here.

This filled Eddie with resolve to get the vampire drug dealer as soon as he could, as well as figure out a way to take out Drakula if he had to.

Why did the old vampire have such a desire to come to New York, anyway? Wasn't a decrepit old castle more his style?

And what about this world-ending papyrus? Marlowe seemed to know so little about it.

With a sigh, Eddie put the note into the pocket of his robe. He then headed downstairs to get some coffee.

In the kitchen, Eleanor turned around in surprise. "Eddie! I thought you went back on duty last night!"

"I did, but I got home about 1:00." Eddie smiled and kissed his mother's cheek.

He poured himself a cup of coffee and added cream, then sat at the table.

"You want some eggs or something?" Eleanor asked, pulling Eddie out of his reverie.

"Momma, I will eat anything you make! You know I love your breakfasts, and I haven't had one in weeks."

She waved her hand at him dismissively. "All right, I'll throw somethin' together. How long you gonna be working nights, Eddie?"

Eddie sighed. "Hopefully not too much longer. I gotta take down a drug dealer. Luis and I got his gang the other night."

"Is he pushing some bad shit?"

Eddie's eyebrows went up. "Momma, I'm surprised at your language."

Eleanor placed a frying pan on the stove and lit a fire under it. "Oh, the boys aren't here, and I'm the wife of a police officer. I know your terminology."

"Yes, Momma. It's some bad shit called Mind-Blo. It's a liquid, highly addictive, fills the user with a sense of euphoria and makes them think they have enhanced strength and energy. The crash when it wears off is harsh."

She sighed as she cooked. "Folks always comin' up with new ways to get high."

"The people who make it are pulling in a lot of money. We have to find the place they make the stuff, and I have a feeling we can only do that at night, and find the clubs where they sell it."

"That makes sense," Eleanor said, and slid the scrambled eggs onto a plate. "You want toast or grits?"

"This is fine, Momma." Eddie smiled.

She put the plate in front of him, and he took his fork and ate.

"So where did you get that ring?"

Eddie stopped mid-bite to see his mother examining the large silver adornment on his finger. He held up his hand. "It's Marlowe's, and it got stuck on my hand." He turned his hand over. "Then again, it turned out to be pretty useful."

"If you say so," Eleanor said. "You home for a while? I want to go shopping and it would be easier to use your car."

"That's fine, Momma. I want to relax until I go on duty at 4:00. I left my keys on the table near the front door."

Eleanor headed out to the front room as Eddie finished his eggs. He sat back in his chair and sipped his coffee.

Mind-Blo was more than just the hottest new thing. It was more than an incredibly addictive substance. It was something that Doctor Beverly Warren could not figure out.

He reflected on the confrontation at the airport. Why had the woman been so willing to concede? Could the attack by her companion, Lycius, have been a calculated move to see if the wizards could defeat them? According to her, the Drakula was now in New York.

Did the drug have anything to do with the Drakula?

Eddie drove his car into the city at about 2:30, after letting Marlowe know he wanted to stop by. He'd park in the police lot, then walk over and talk to the old man. That would give him about an hour before he went on duty.

He needed to get a handle on what it meant to have the Drakula in New York, and to see if Marlowe was any closer to finding this dangerous papyrus.

The dismal spirit face of Wraith, the house ghost, was the first thing that greeted Eddie when the door opened.

"Hey Wraith, is Marlowe around?" Eddie asked, attempting to be polite.

"Marlowe is in the living room, sir," the spirit told him with his sonorous voice and then stepped back to disappear into a wall.

"Do come in, Eddie," Marlowe acknowledged as Eddie stepped into the large room. The old man was in a burgundy dressing robe that appeared to be silk and ornately decorated with dragons and other fantastic beasts.

"I take it you checked to make sure everyone got home all right?" Eddie asked.

"Hm? Oh, yes, no trouble at all—although there were several vampires keeping watch on the townhouse." Marlowe shook his head. "It's to be expected, I presume."

"Things didn't go the way they'd planned last night."

"Not for anyone, from what Drusilicus told me," Marlowe said. "What intrigued me was this woman, Selene."

"Know anything about her?"

"Little and less. I have checked with several sources, and the only information I can glean is that she has been in Europe and involved with the family of Vlad the Impaler for centuries. Some even claim she was once a member of the royal family, when there was one."

"She claimed she's the Drak's consort."

Marlowe nodded. "She has represented the Drakula at many important gatherings. It is a pity I do not have a photograph of her. I could have researched her more."

"We were a little too busy last night for selfies."

"So I deduced. It was very astute of you to figure out that the coffin was empty."

"What do you think they filled it with, some of his native soil?"

Marlowe frowned. "I believe the need to be buried in one's native soil is a myth. I imagine if you have a comfortable coffin, you'd keep it when you travel."

"It's a pity we can't track the coffin."

The old man grinned. "Actually, we can."

"What? How?"

Marlowe's grin widened. "I had a member of the coven place a charm within the coffin while it was at the London airport."

"You sneaky old dude."

"I'll take that as a compliment."

"So you have a way to locate the coffin, wherever it is?"

Marlowe shrugged. "As long as they do not find the charm or remove it."

"Luis and I go on duty at 4:00. Sunset isn't until 7:00. What do you think about seeing if we can find old Drakky?"

"Oh dear," Marlowe worried, his hand going to his mouth. "Do you think that is the best course of action?"

"Look, if old man Drakula is in town, and he's out to find this papyrus that can destroy everything, and we can stop him—we should do it. We don't even have to kill him, just expose him to sunlight and let nature take its course."

"I doubt he will hide in a place where there will be windows," Marlowe considered.

"Too bad I haven't been able to get those UV lights," Eddie muttered.

"Oh yes, the ultraviolet lights you mentioned."

"I ordered a couple of UV flashlights online— they should be delivered to the precinct any time now."

Marlowe caressed his beard in thought. "Yes, I imagine that might have an effect on the vampires. I'm sorry, Eddie, but as you know, those of us who have walked the path as long as we have are not very knowledgeable about modern technology."

"Did you know anything about this Vasant lady?"

"Hm? Oh, yes, I actually have met her in the past. She hasn't been around—"

"I know," Eddie interrupted. "Not for a hundred years."

"Yes. But, to my recollection, she is a wise and fair wizard with a remarkable history. She left because of some social unpleasantness. But she is legit."

"Legit?" Eddie smiled. "I am really rubbing off on you, Marlowe. Are you going to get to work on that tracking spell for the coffin?"

"Yes, I shall. If you and Sergeant Vasquez will pick me up in your car, I will lead you to it."

With a nod, Eddie headed for the door. If they could track down the Drakula today, it would certainly make things easier for him.

It was a balmy spring day as he stepped out of the townhouse and headed down the transverse road into the park. The sun was bright and there wasn't a cloud in the sky. Once in the park, the light dappled through the leaves of the many trees that were now budding.

Eddie had split his life between his work as a detective and his after-hour endeavors as a wizard. It always seemed so easy for the guys in superhero movies. Eddie's life was much more complicated than what they showed on the big screen, and most issues were not merely black and white.

Like the confrontation at the airport last night. They could have fought the vampires and the four of them might have won, but at what cost? It was easier to call out the game for what it was and try to make the best of a bad hand.

Selene was interesting as well— obviously the Drakula had wisely placed her in charge of the operation. She realized how last night would be a loss for her and her companions. They needed Eddie and the wizards desperate to get the coffin, and that would allow them to be sloppy, make bad choices, and easy to defeat. If the wizards were a united front, focused on defending themselves from attackers, it would not go the way she wanted.

Eddie was also sure that the death of Lycius gave her pause. If Eddie had a weapon that so easily destroyed a young, strong vampire, what else might the wizards have at their disposal?

He went into the lobby of the twenty-second precinct and down the short hallway to the detectives' bullpen, where Luis was sitting at his desk and tapping away at the computer.

He sat across from his partner and murmured, "You want to go hunt a vampire?"

Luis raised his eyes excitedly. "Our bad guy from the other night?"

"Better. How about Dracula?"

Luis frowned. "Dracula is real?"

"Yeah, and we get to chase him down."

Luis considered this. "Right now?"

"You got it."

Luis rose and grabbed his sports coat off his chair.

"Dominic," Eddie called out to the detective typing away at his own desk.

Dominic turned his bulldog face to Eddie. "Yeah?"

"If anyone asks, we're following a lead on that drug ringleader," Eddie told him.

Dominic smiled. "Good hunting, LT."

A few short minutes later, they were in an unmarked police car provided by the City of New York and had picked up Marlowe, who wore a dark-gray velvet suit jacket and carried his ebony walking stick.

Marlowe got in the rear bench seat behind Eddie and Luis. Eddie opened the sliding glass in the divider so they could talk.

"Did you bring a weapon in case we find him?" Eddie asked Marlowe as he sat down.

"I thought you guys just used your staffs for everything," Luis questioned.

"Well, I brought this." Marlowe pulled a beautiful hand-carved wooden stake from his pocket and held it out through the open divider.

Luis whistled in approval as Eddie pulled into traffic. The stake wasn't square but rounded and came to a frighteningly sharp point. The wood was pale and had a good weight to it.

"Wow. This is beautiful."

"White oak," Marlowe told him. "And I have a wooden mallet in another pocket."

Luis gave him back the stake, and he put it away.

"I assume we're heading downtown?" Eddie asked.

"Why downtown?" Luis wondered.

Eddie shrugged. "Vampires live in the Village."

"That explains a lot," Luis grunted.

Eddie glanced at Marlowe in the rearview mirror. The old wizard had taken out his small crystal ball and stared at it as it filled with a purple mist.

"Yes," Marlowe said without looking up. "Down Fifth Avenue might be the fastest route."

"Is Fifth Avenue *ever* the fastest route?" Luis complained.

Eddie guided the car through the midtown traffic. Nothing was going very fast, and Eddie avoided getting clipped by a taxi or hitting a harried bicycle messenger.

Soon they were slogging their way down past 23rd Street, and Eddie had to get into the correct lane to stay on Fifth Avenue.

"How we doin', Marlowe?" Luis asked.

"We're still going the correct direction, sergeant," Marlowe replied, his eyes fixed on the sphere.

"Hopefully, we'll be there before dark," Eddie muttered as he swung around another double-parked car, only to be stopped at the next light.

"Any idea where we will end up?" Luis asked.

"Not as far south as the Battery," Marlowe assured them, still looking at the ball.

It was another fifteen minutes before they got past 14th Street. Lanes were shut off, people crossed the street whenever they liked, and buildings with scaffolding forcing people off the sidewalk and into the street.

"We're in Drusilicus' neighborhood now," Eddie commented.

"There are worse parts of town," Luis added wryly.

"It appears our goal is straight ahead," Marlowe promised.

Eddie chuckled. "There's nothing straight ahead but the—"

His voice fell away.

Straight ahead of them stood the huge arch, the entrance to Washington Square Park. The structure towered seventy-seven feet into the air and marked the official separation of Greenwich Village and downtown, where the streets ceased to be a simple grid and went off in odd directions.

"There!" Marlowe pointed at the huge arch through the open window in the divider. "That's where the coffin is."

They approached the arch as traffic allowed, and Eddie saw the two full-size statues of George Washington that faced Fifth Avenue. The one on the left was in full battle regalia with the Inverness cape that sported a short secondary cape and a tricorn hat he'd worn as general in the Continental Army. The right-hand statue showed Washington in presidential garb, with his wig and civilian clothes of the time.

Eddie turned the corner and parked the car in the first open space, blocking a fire hydrant. He pulled a printed sign from the sun visor that read "POLICE ON DUTY." He slipped it into the windshield and both he and Luis stepped out, with Luis opening the back door for Marlowe. The old man stepped out, using his cane to push himself along.

They strode toward the ornate structure, and it awed Eddie just how massive it was, rising many feet over their heads. He also noticed that on three sides of each supporting pillar there was a series of heavy metal gratings underfoot. They were strong enough to walk on, but they were open in an egg-crate design.

Underneath the grates were several feet of space, and openings in the concrete. This was for drainage, designed to carry rainwater away from the base of the huge monolith.

"The coffin is somewhere near this arch?" Eddie murmured to Marlowe.

"No, Eddie, it is *in* the arch," Marlowe whispered back.

Eddie gazed up at the vast marble monument. "This thing has an inside?"

"Of course, Eddie," Marlowe chatted excitedly. "In fact, it used to be the park office back in the day. They still need access to change lights and do repairs to maintain the structure."

As they studied the outside of the arch, Marlowe pointed to a short door on the western side that was only about five feet high and painted white to blend into the marble.

"Man," Luis muttered. "I can get through a door that small, but I won't like it."

Eddie scrutinized his massive partner. The door was less wide than Luis and not nearly as tall.

"How about you secure the perimeter?" Eddie suggested.

Luis shrugged. "That's fine with me. I don' like confined spaces."

The three approached the door, and Marlowe reached out for the knob.

It did not turn.

Marlowe leaned on his walking stick and closed his eyes for a moment. There was a click, and the door came open.

Luis leaned close to the old man. "Hey, let me ask you. Eddie needed his stick and now he's got these words to make things happen. But you just do magic stuff, with, like, a wave of your hand. How come?"

"Excellent question, sergeant," Marlowe beamed. "We accomplish the things we do through a combination of will and intention. He uses words at this point because he needs them to get himself in the correct mindset. However, I have done this for many years and can make things occur with but a thought."

"Handy," Luis marveled.

"Are we gonna stand out here all day, or are we going in and taking care of Drakula?" Eddie complained.

"Sorry," Marlowe nodded. "Fear not, Eddie, we still have the sunlight for a few hours."

Marlowe, though much shorter than Eddie, had to duck as he passed through the door. Eddie lowered his head and squeezed through after him. He glanced back at his partner, who nodded as if to say, "I got you covered."

The interior was narrow, with neat brick walls to his left and right. It was only then that Eddie realized they had not made the monument entirely of marble, just the exterior. It made sense that the structure had interior metal and masonry to support it.

There were several cardboard boxes filled with some kind of storage that lay under a masonry spiral staircase a few feet inside the door. Next to the staircase, a thick iron pole ran up and out of sight, offering additional support.

Marlowe stood on the bottom step.

As Eddie shut the door behind him, the small, cavernous room plunged into darkness, with the only light shining down the staircase.

"Where is that light coming from?" Eddie asked.

"There are skylights on the roof," Marlowe explained as he climbed. Eddie followed, his eyes adjusting to the limited light as he drew near. Each step was lined with old, but well maintained, terra-cotta tiles.

"When was all this built?" Eddie asked as he slowly ascended behind his mentor.

"Started in 1890, finished in 1895. I was there when they dedicated it."

"Of course you were," Eddie replied sardonically.

"The outer layer is Tuckahoe marble, brought to Manhattan from a quarry in Tuckahoe, New York. It's closed now."

The masonry staircase circled around the white-painted iron pole. Sturdy metal brackets angled from the iron pillar to shore up the rounded walls. The brick was set in a circular pattern, and made the interior round, concealing the square exterior.

There were a lot of steps and they ascended them slowly, Marlowe using his cane for support. They listened for any sound that could suggest a trap or an attack. Even though the vampires would not be awake at this hour, they had humans under their control who could venture out in the day and would have no problem killing for their masters.

They reached a landing that opened up to a narrow attic space. The circular steps continued up one more rise that Eddie assumed led to the roof.

The area between the supports opened to a seventeen-foot-high ceiling, lined with beautiful terra-cotta tiles that rose in majestic curves over their heads. The oddly shaped room was lit from several rectangular skylights on the ceiling that allowed the light to pour in, the height of the arch reaching beyond the shade of trees.

On the right side of the room was a white pipe, apparently to drain water from the roof down to the street below.

In the center of the room was an ebony coffin.

It wasn't the elaborate one from the airport, but a plain black box with wood that was covered with many layers of lacquer.

"That's not the coffin we saw last night," Eddie whispered, his voice echoing off the ceramic in the walls.

"Really? I was afraid of this." Marlowe sighed and bent to pick up a small piece of metal from the floor. It was golden and had a red ribbon hanging from it.

"This is what I was tracking. It is enchanted so I can find it anywhere."

Stamped into the metal, was the same coat of arms that was on the silver ring Eddie wore.

"Hey, that's the same design as on this ring," Eddie told Marlowe and held out his hand.

"It is the family crest of Kresnik, a famed vampire hunter," Marlowe told him quietly. "I had a wizard place this seal in that coffin that arrived last night while it was at the London airport. I can only guess that the vampires discovered it and placed it up here to waylay us."

"Why?"

"Well, there is one way to find out," Marlowe said. "We open the coffin and see if the inhabitant knows anything."

Eddie observed the sunlight that still shone into the room. "If it's a vampire, we would kill them by opening it in the sunlight."

Marlowe frowned. "Indeed. Odd they would lead us here."

"Maybe not. If I was a suspicious guy, I would say that this whole thing is a set-up."

"A set-up?"

"Yes. We open the coffin, accidentally kill a vampire, and then the Drakula can claim we attacked them while they slept."

Marlowe mulled this over as he stroked his long, white beard. "You think they led us to this coffin, on the chance that we would open it and kill the vampire inside?"

"Yeah, and then they can claim we started a war. I mean, last night I killed that vampire and they were ready to fight us because of it. But they all saw that he attacked me first, so we could get out of it."

"I see the logic in what you say, Eddie, and I have a solution," Marlowe answered, his eyes narrowed. "It might be best if we prepared ourselves for battle."

With a gesture, Marlowe's suit and pants vanished, his white robes took their place, and his cane grew into the tall blond wood staff in his hand. Eddie shifted his clothing to his red robes and tall boots as his staff slapped into his right hand.

"What's your solution?" Eddie insisted.

Marlowe smiled, and with a gesture, a mist formed on the ceiling. It was thin at first, nothing more than a cloud, but it soon thickened to become a black barrier that shut the sunlight out completely.

A white light appeared at the top of Marlowe's staff. "Do you like this idea?"

"I get it." Eddie said. "If we open the coffin, the vampire is safe. He tries something and you get rid of the mist, and he gets burned up."

"Should he attack and break my concentration, the mist will dissipate on its own," Marlowe assured him.

"Okay, let's just step back a bit," Eddie ordered as they made their way toward the stairs. He gestured with his staff and muttered, *"Patentibus!"*

The lid of the coffin shuddered, then slowly lifted on its hinges and opened. Inside was a raven-haired woman in a black dress that hugged every curve and showed off her impressive bosom. She had bright-red lips and appeared to be asleep.

Eddie and Marlowe approached when the woman did not awaken or even move.

"That's Selene," Eddie blurted.

"Is it?" Marlowe responded, surprised by this.

Eddie drew closer to the coffin and examined the face. "No, I'm wrong. That's Lysandra. She helped us last year with those FBI agents."

"Ah, yes," Marlowe recalled.

Eddie tapped on the side of the coffin with his staff. "Hey there, wake up. We have some questions."

The woman rose into a sitting position so fast that both Eddie and Marlowe stepped back in surprise. Her eyes were wide open, and she gazed up at the ceiling to see the mist that protected her from the dangerous sun.

Seeing she was safe, she exhaled heavily and lay back in the coffin.

"Wizards," she spoke in a husky tone. "You have spared my life."

"From what I understand, you're actually already dead," Eddie snorted.

"Yes, but they put me here to be sacrificed."

"What do you mean?" Eddie asked.

"A trusted friend brought me to a club, and a group overpowered me. They brought me to this coffin through the door in the roof."

"There's a door in the roof?" Eddie wondered, looking up at the masonry ceiling.

"Yes. They dragged me here, far too many to fight. They put me in the coffin, then sealed it with a spell."

"Wait," Marlowe pondered. "Who used a spell?"

"There was a woman with them, who appeared to have magickal abilities."

"Was her name Selene?" asked Eddie.

"Yes," Lysandra said, and a hard look crossed her face. "She looked a little like me. She said the wizards would think it was her and kill me. A real stone-cold bitch. Good dresser, though."

Eddie and Marlowe exchanged a look. "We're familiar with her. So they just left you here?"

"They left a charm that would bring wizards, that's what they said. I thought you would come, open the coffin, and burn whoever was inside," she confessed, and a single blood-red tear slipped down her face.

"Why did they do this to you, Madam?" Marlowe asked, always the gentleman.

"I helped wizards. That time in New Jersey was just a fluke, but I betrayed the fact that the Drakula was coming to New York to the Wizard Greywacke."

Eddie frowned. "So let me get this straight. You let Drew know the Lord of the Undead was making his New York appearance, and your own people stuck you here to be killed?"

"They have already killed Strix, the young vampire who had overheard the announcement."

"Wait, Strix? Thin guy, dressed in black, lots of piercings?" Eddie questioned.

She nodded.

"Is this as Drusilicus said, Eddie?" Marlowe inquired.

Eddie glanced at his mentor. "Yeah, that matches the guy with the stake through his heart."

"Wait, *you* are the Wizard Marlowe?" Lysandra asked.

"I am indeed," Marlowe confirmed.

"You were to find this once I burned," Lysandra continued, and reached into the coffin to pull out a small roll of parchment and held it out to the old man.

Eddie took the ragged, rolled-up paper. There was a bright circle of red sealing wax near the bottom, with some kind of design imprinted into the wax.

Marlowe stepped back in shock, his eyes wide, his hand trembling as he took it from Eddie.

All at once, the mist floating on the ceiling thinned. Lysandra gaped in terror and a moan escaped her lips. Without a second's delay, Eddie pushed Lysandra into the coffin and pulled the lid closed just as a ray of sunshine burst through the rapidly fading smoke.

"Marlowe!" Eddie yelled, "The mist, the mist!"

Marlowe's head snapped up, and instantly the clouds on the ceiling thickened once again.

Eddie carefully opened the lid of the coffin to find Lysandra wide-eyed with fear. "You okay?"

"I… am," she observed. "Thank you for your fast thinking, wizard."

"Well, I think your friends are probably going to come back to see if you're dead."

"I would expect them to."

"Look, if we hang around here until after dark, do you have someplace you can go to hide?"

"Indeed, I do."

"Okay— you lie back and I'll close the lid, and we'll watch over you. Then when night comes, we'll take you downstairs and you can leave."

She nodded. "You are most kind, wizard."

"You helped us. We can't let you get hurt because of that. Now, go on, get comfortable."

She lay back against the padded satin inside the box and nodded.

Eddie smiled and told her as he shut the lid. "See you in a couple of hours." He checked the seal and that the top was in place before he turned to Marlowe. "Okay, you can relax."

The mist disappeared, and the fading sunlight brightened the room again.

"What happened, why did you freak out?" Eddie asked.

"Forgive me, Eddie," Marlowe said, with the paper still clutched in his hand he leaned on a nearby wall, as if for support.

"You worried me. It takes a lot to throw you."

Marlowe nodded and held the paper aloft. "Yes, and because of this, I now know the identity of the Drakula and why he comes to destroy New York."

TEN

Despite numerous demands to explain, Marlowe insisted he would only speak once they were back at the townhouse, and only in front of the entire group. Eddie left Marlowe alone in the attic room as he went outside to relieve his partner and to call his captain to explain where they were.

He left Marlowe his small hand mirror to call the other wizards to bring them together for the revelation.

Now, on his phone with Captain Jacobs, he was going over his excuses for being out of his precinct area.

"That's right, captain, there was a rumor that the distribution was increasing downtown. That's why Sergeant Vasquez and I are down in Washington Square Park, to run down a lead."

"Okay, lieutenant, but please only observe. I don't want to hear from the Eighth Precinct that my detectives were stepping on toes."

"Just observing and gathering information, sir. We'll be back uptown after dark."

"Keep the pressure up, lieutenant. I got word of another OD from Mind-Blo here in Central Park."

Eddie shook his head. "Until we get an antidote, that is going to keep happening."

"We have the best scientific minds on it." Jacobs sighed. "I'm going home. Call me if you get anything we can use."

"Yes, sir," Eddie said, and ended the call.

The Mind-Blo epidemic was indeed getting worse, and it was one more thing that Eddie didn't want to worry about. Considering that six months ago no one had ever even heard of it, it was quickly making the rounds of all the clubs, starting as a simple street drug. Now, it was popping up in places where the more sophisticated New Yorkers went, making it harder to control.

"What was up there?" Luis said as he joined Eddie at the arch with a cup of coffee.

"It's kind of neat. There's a big open room up there. Marlowe said it was the park office once." He took a sip of coffee. "Oh yeah, and a coffin."

"Of course," Luis replied nonchalantly. "Anyone we know in it?"

"As a matter of fact, yes," Eddie said. "Remember that vampire lady who came on to you last year?"

Luis blanched. "You kiddin' me?"

"Not in the least. Marlowe blocked out the sun so she didn't get fried—"

"Wait, there are windows in there?" Luis said, and eyed the arch.

"Skylights, yes. So she pulls out this parchment with a seal or something, and Marlowe now says he knows who the Drakula is."

Luis took another sip, watching the people strolling around the park walkways. "So... who is it?"

"He wants to tell everyone all together, so he's arranging a meeting."

"You want me to sit in?"

"It might help."

"The vampire chick—you leavin' her in the arch?"

"No, they forced her in there and she's afraid for her life. We're going to escort her to a place where she'll be safe."

"Oh boy," Luis said, and wiped sweat from his head with the back of his hand. "Last time I saw her, she came on to me—made me feel weird."

"That was her glamour."

Luis frowned. "She's in a magazine?"

Eddie sighed with frustration. "It's a power that allows a vampire to attract a human. If she tries it again, I'll stop her."

"Gracias."

"De nada," Eddie said, and took another sip. "Anything suspicious out here?"

"People playing Frisbee. Oh yeah, and a drug deal under that tree over there." Luis gestured toward a small grove of trees.

"Think it was Mind-Blo?" Eddie worried.

Luis shook his head. "Probably just pot. They were pretty open about it. With Mind-Blo, pushers know the city has been putting out all those public safety announcements, so I think they'd be a little more secretive."

"Mind-Blo makes the most money," Eddie grumbled.

"That's the reason they sell it, but who wants to find out that someone died from your product? It's bad for business."

"Unless you don't care. A lot of dealers figure that they just sell the product. The user's the one responsible for what it does."

At that moment, the door in the arch opened, and Marlowe ducked to step out onto the tiled walkway at this entrance of the park.

Marlowe approached and handed Eddie the mirror. "I have to go. Please come to my house after dark as soon as you can."

"I'd like to bring Luis as well," Eddie said.

Marlowe frowned. "Very well, I suppose that is probably for the best. May I ask you to keep watch on Lysandra upstairs? I am concerned there might be an attack from the roof."

"On it," Eddie said, and then added, "You got a way uptown?"

"I believe I do," Marlowe said, just as a large yellow cab driven by Rusty Claremont turned the corner.

As Marlowe got into the car, Eddie nodded to his partner, then went back inside the arch and quickly went upstairs to the empty room to wait by the coffin until nightfall.

Eddie spent the last hour as the city progressed into twilight playing on his phone and sending text messages to his wife and mother.

The room grew darker, and Eddie manifested his staff to create a light on the crown of the stick. It had a reddish quality, but lit the room easily. Soon after sundown, Eddie heard the lid rise. Lysandra sat up and peered around the room. She held out her hand like a princess, and Eddie took it to assist her stepping out of the coffin.

She rose to her full height, almost as tall as Eddie. This was impressive since she was barefoot.

"What happened to your shoes?" Eddie asked.

"I lost them the last time I turned into a bat," she explained with a smile as she surveyed Eddie up and down.

"I thought they just changed with you."

She shrugged. "Not when they're Prada." She stuck her lip out in a pout. "I really liked those shoes." She glanced over at the staircase. "Anyone show up?"

"Not yet. If we move, we can get you to someplace safe before they find out that you didn't fry," Eddie said.

"I don't think that will be hard. There is a place I can hide out just a few blocks from here."

"Okay then, let's move."

Eddie's staff supplied light as they descended the stairs, and the interior of the monument was indeed much creepier at night.

She stopped at the outer door and stared at it. "Wow, what a short door."

"Didn't you see it when they brought you here?"

"I told you, I came in through the roof. There's an enormous door up there."

Eddie gestured at the doorway. "Ladies first."

She opened the short door and ducked through it. Eddie followed her after he hastily transformed his staff and returned it to his pocket. She stopped on the far side of the door as Eddie closed it, and with a whispered word he set the locks in place, securing it.

"You are here again!" Lysandra said and walked up to Luis. "Thank you for helping rescue me."

She pushed her lips to Luis', much to the big man's surprise.

"Lysandra," Eddie spoke forcefully, "let go of my partner!"

She pulled back from Luis and sighed. "Sorry. There is something about your friend that pulls me in. I will try to control myself."

Luis had an expression of a man smacked in the face with a shovel. His features were relaxed, and he stared, slack-jawed, at Lysandra.

Eddie grabbed Lysandra's arm and turned the tall vampire to face him. "What did you do to my partner?"

"Nothing!" She smiled. Her eyes had become an unnatural shade of red. "I just kissed him. Okay, he might have gotten a little of my venom."

"*Venom?*" Eddie hissed. "That stuff you guys use to *enslave* people?"

Lysandra leaned close and lowered her voice. "It is part of the process. When we drink from a host we inject them with a venom that increases blood flow and gives the host a feeling of euphoria. It makes humans desire us."

Eddie yanked her arm toward Fifth Avenue, annoyed. The last thing he needed was Luis not being at his best. "You said you had a safe house. Let's go now!"

"Okay, okay," she whined. "I didn't bite him. I wanted to…"

Eddie turned and gestured to his massive sidekick. "Come *on*, Luis."

Luis' expression was one of a man hit in the head a few too many times, but he trotted after them.

"There is just something about that man that is so yummy." Lysandra gazed at Luis with a lascivious stare. "I don't know what it is. He's just so... *big*."

Eddie turned Lysandra to face him. "He is my partner and you're lucky I didn't incinerate your ass with my fire-powers when you grabbed him."

"I wouldn't *hurt* him. I know he's with you, and I am grateful for the rescue," Lysandra said, and headed north in her bare feet. "Besides, I'm in a relationship these days."

Eddie walked quickly to keep up with her. "Then what was that greeting?"

"Wizard, I am a vampire, a creature of emotion, and your partner excites me on a primal level." Lysandra huffed, glancing back again.

"Go easy, girl. He has a wife and six kids," Eddie warned.

She glanced back at Luis. "I can see why. He just oozes *animal*."

"Not for you, he doesn't."

She inhaled deeply. "I will control myself in the future."

"Make sure you do," Eddie warned. He glanced behind them to see Luis follow, walking like a drunken man but keeping up. "Aw geez, I think I have to stay with him."

"It's close. I'll get there with no problem. Stay with your partner."

Before Eddie could argue, she continued up Fifth Avenue. Eddie headed back to Luis.

"You feelin' better?" Eddie asked.

"A little. That was one hell of a kiss," Luis said and leaned against the stone wall of a nearby building.

Eddie watched Lysandra as she strode away, but spoke to Luis. "She has some kind of poison in her kisses." He then turned to Luis and lowered his voice. "You think she did that on purpose?"

"What?" Luis said, still unsteady and confused. "Why?"

"So we wouldn't follow her." Eddie turned to see the retreating shape of Lysandra. "Head to the car. I'm going to go after her."

"Uh, okay," Luis said, and turned to head back to the car, still in a daze.

Eddie stepped forward and attempted a spell he'd only used once in practice. Marlowe had shown him the basics of a concealment charm, and Eddie seemed to have been able to do it. This would be the first time he'd tried it in real life.

He went up the street, staying close to the building, and set his will and murmured, *"Occultatum."*

A thin mist clouded Eddie's vision. If it worked right, no one could see him. He charged forward, being careful not to get into the path of anyone walking, as he knew they would run right into him.

He could still see Lysandra, though it was more difficult through the mists the spell created in his vision. She stopped in front of an ornate house on Fifth Avenue. It was an elaborate creation, built in another era—several stories high and painted white, with large marble columns out front.

Lysandra stepped to the door and knocked gently on it.

Eddie pressed himself against a nearby wall. This house was familiar. The door opened, and Drusilicus Greywacke stood there. Lysandra went into his arms, and he kissed her head.

Eddie drew a little closer, just in time to hear Drusilicus murmur, "I was worried."

The vampire pulled back. "One of your friends saved me."

"A wizard?" Drusilicus asked with a raised eyebrow.

"Yes, the black guy with the yummy partner. I made sure they didn't follow."

Drusilicus scanned the street. "How clever of you! Why don't you go inside? I am sure Howell will get you anything you might need."

"Okay," she gushed, and gave his cheek a peck. She went in and the door closed.

Drusilicus pulled out his pocket watch. *"Revelare,"* he stated in a clear voice.

Eddie felt something akin to electricity pass through him, and the surrounding mists vanished.

Drusilicus stepped away from the door and quickly closed the gap between himself and Eddie. "Really, lieutenant, did you think a clumsy hiding charm would fool me?"

Eddie tried to recover from the ease with which Drusilicus had broken his spell. "I wasn't trying to fool you. I was trying to find out where she was going."

"Well, you have your answer," Drusilicus said in a calm voice. "Thank you for escorting Lysandra here, lieutenant. Good night."

Eddie got right into his face. "You wanna tell me what's going on? Because in about fifteen minutes, I am going to be in

Marlowe's house, and I am sure he would be interested to know that you are making goo-goo eyes with a vampire."

Drusilicus kept his voice low. "Marlowe also has a vampire living at his house."

"I got a feeling the fringe benefits are different in your case."

Drusilicus reddened at this, even though he was only illuminated by the dim street lamps. "I do not have to explain myself to you."

"No, but you're gonna have to explain things to Marlowe," Eddie snapped, then turned to walk away.

"It just *happened*," Drusilicus barked.

Eddie slowly rotated and returned to stand next to Drusilicus, who stared down at the ground.

"Just one of those things?" Eddie surmised. "How do we know she isn't controlling you?"

"Because she would not do that," Drusilicus stated, unable to meet Eddie's eyes. "We have... affection for one another."

Eddie's face darkened. "She's a *vampire*, Drew. I may be new at this game, but I think everything she does is for one purpose: to feed."

Drusilicus gestured dismissively. "How can I expect you to understand? You're what, forty years old?"

"Forty-one."

"I am over one hundred and forty," Drusilicus said. "Everyone I grew up with or cared for is dead. They turned this woman in 1840. We share something more than feeding. We share a history few people can."

"What about the venom? She kissed my partner, messed with his mind."

"I have a potion for its influence, and we are... careful."

"Shit!" Eddie muttered as the realization sunk in. "So, you're having sex with her?"

"I am as human and vital as any other man, lieutenant. Yes, I have a woman I care for, and I make love to her. But we are careful, so that she does not lose control and I do not lose my mind."

Eddie shook his head. "I am going to have to tell Marlowe."

"Eddie, please!" Drusilicus beseeched him.

"There are just too many dangers. You know that better than I do, for crying out loud."

Drusilicus peered up and down the avenue, and went on. "I will tell Marlowe. But not tonight. Tonight a much more important story must be revealed."

"Involving Marlowe?"

Drusilicus nodded his head sadly. "I believe that to expose the Drakula, he is going to have to tell all of us his own history."

"That should be interesting," Eddie said. "You will tell him tomorrow or I will."

"I swear," Drusilicus vowed.

As Eddie drove uptown, Luis had his window open to let the cool spring air wash over his face as he tried to clear his head.

"What took you so long?" Luis asked. He pulled a bottle of water out of the glove box and sipped some. Then he poured some into his large palm and slapped it against his face.

Eddie kept his eyes fixed on the road. "That lady vampire is staying with Drusilicus."

"Oh?" Luis said. "You mean, like Daniel lives with Marlowe?"

"I think Drew and Lysandra have a much more... friendly relationship."

Luis's face flushed. "He is... with *her*?"

"That would be my guess."

"How dare he?" Luis bellowed and reached for the steering wheel. "We have to go back."

Eddie had to jam on the brakes for a traffic light, so his partner didn't have time to put the car into a spin.

"What are you doing? Have you gone crazy?" Eddie screeched.

Luis gripped the wheel with one hand. "She is *mine*. I must go back and fight for her!"

"Either you get your damn hand off the wheel or I will magic your sorry ass."

"No, I must fight for her."

Cars behind them blew their horns as the light had changed, and Eddie could not go forward because his partner held the wheel in a death grip.

Eddie tried another tack. "How about I phone Maria and tell her you're in love with a vampire?"

The reaction was stronger than any spell Eddie could have mustered, even with the full power of his staff. Luis let go of the wheel, hung his head, and whimpered, "Oh... yeah... Maria."

Eddie took control and got the car going forward, fists and middle fingers waving in his direction.

"Look, Luis, what you're feeling isn't real. It's that woman's venom. It's making you act crazy."

Luis shook his head. "Yeah. And it's weird, I feel like I'm comin' down off a drug."

"Once we're at Marlowe's, we'll get you a cup of coffee."

Luis nodded sadly, but after a moment, his face brightened. "You mean, from that coffee set he's got where everything moves on its own?"

"The same."

It was after dark, but only about 8:00 PM as Eddie pulled the unmarked into the police lot, and they headed over to Marlowe's townhouse on foot.

They reached the steps that led up to the front door, and Eddie glanced at his partner. "Are you better now?"

"Yeah, but I won't turn down coffee."

Eddie knocked on the door, and Daniel Kraft opened it, a serious look on his face. "Good, you're here. There's been a lot of vampire activity tonight. Glad to see you made it safely."

The chairs in the enormous living room were once again in a circle. Seated in the chairs were Bankrock, Dalehead, Willowdell, and much to Eddie's surprise, Vasant. The brown-skinned woman sat next to Marlowe, and the pair spoke in low tones.

Eddie pointed to a chair next to the tea trolley for Luis. He nodded and headed to it, talked to the trolley, and it magically poured him a cup of coffee.

Eddie approached Marlowe and Vasant and extended his hand. "Vasant. Glad you could make it."

Her smile was dazzling. "Ah yes, the wizard I met in my arch. Did you find the killer of that poor soul?"

"Not yet, but we're trying. I am happy to see you might help us."

"I have been a hermit for far too long," she told Eddie with a smile. "It is time I met with my fellows once again."

Marlowe said, "We shall start in just a few—"

There was a loud pounding at the door, and Wraith appeared through a wall to answer it.

"That's probably Drusilicus," Eddie said.

Vasant gasped. "Him? Here?" She then immediately controlled herself.

Without a look back, Eddie sat in the chair next to Luis and commanded the trolley to give him a cup of coffee with cream.

"I still would love, for one day, to have this over at the precinct," Luis said as the silver cream jug poured its contents into Eddie's cup.

"Ain't happenin'," Eddie replied.

Drusilicus stepped into the room, and his eyes went from person to person but stopped on Vasant.

The Indian woman stared at the floor for only a moment, then raised her eyes to meet his. His own eyes grew wide, and he slowly approached her chair.

"*You!*" Drusilicus gasped as he stared at the woman. In a flash, both were standing facing each other with their large wooden staffs in their hands, in attack positions.

Marlowe stepped between them with his arms raised. "Wizards, please. I suggest we bury any past animosity, at least for the evening."

Drusilicus stepped back and his staff shrank to become a pocket watch that went into his vest. Vasant also vanished her staff and placed a ring with a large amber stone onto her finger as she sat down, perfectly under control, her handsome face expressing nothing.

"Seems like there's trouble in wizard-land," Luis whispered to Eddie.

"You think?" Eddie responded, surprised by this turn of events.

Drusilicus sat in the chair farthest from Vasant and glared about in annoyance.

Marlowe stood in the center of the circle and cleared his throat. "Gentlemen," he began, and then nodded to Dalehead, Willowdell, and Vasant. "And ladies."

All three returned the acknowledgement.

"I asked you to come here because I have a clue to the identity of the person who currently carries the title of the Drakula. But to understand, I shall have to give you some of *my* history."

"This should be good," Luis whispered.

"In my long life, I have gone by many names, most of them would be unimportant and forgettable to you. However, one name I carried centuries ago was Merlin."

Eddie raised his arm. "Wait. Merlin? Like knights and Camelot and all that stuff?"

A titter ran through the group.

"Exactly, Eddie. The very same," Marlowe reported.

"But that was like a thousand years ago," Eddie pointed out.

"Yes, may I continue?" Marlowe insisted.

"Please go on," Drusilicus stated with annoyance. "And, lieutenant, please hold your observations until he finishes."

Bankrock chimed in, "Most of us knew this. I cannot see the significance such an old identity might have to our current dilemma."

Marlowe nodded wearily. "Of course. Let me go on."

He drew himself up to his full height and raised the walking stick he held. A mist appeared in the center of the room. From the fog, human shapes appeared as Marlowe went on.

"Centuries ago, I studied the path of the wise, where I earned a staff and the title of wizard."

As he spoke, the mist became an old man, who handed his gnarled wooden staff to the misty shape of a young Marlowe.

"This was in Britain, just as the Roman legions were leaving. The country was in an uproar with different tribes of Celts fighting for supremacy." The mist became a group of soldiers marching away, and then a battlefield with fighters only about six inches tall striking each other with bronze swords. "One man rose to power and put all of Britain under his rule—Uther Pendragon."

A majestic man rose from the mist and raised a sword over his head.

"I acted as his advisor, as I did for his son, Arthur."

The smoke became the shape of Marlowe as he stood beside a young man.

"Whoa," Luis said. "Like King Arthur? The Knights of the Round Table?"

Marlowe sighed heavily. "Yes. But Arthur had an illegitimate son, and he asked me to take him under my wing and train him on the path of the wise."

Eddie frowned. "You mean Mordred?"

"He was called Modredus then. He studied with me, as did a rather gifted young lady named Nimue."

Again, the fog formed into shapes that showed a younger Marlowe as he instructed a young woman and a young man.

"I taught them simple enchantments, all part of the process one must master on the path to being bequeathed a staff."

The fog became a woman who held a ring. She manifested a beam of light that struck and knocked the young man off his feet. All three of the shadow shapes laughed as the Marlowe character helped the young man to his feet.

"They studied with me for several years. Unknown to me, they eventually became lovers."

The Marlowe shape fell away in the fog, and the two young people leaned forward to kiss before they dissipated.

"I did not really know Modredus' genuine desires. I thought he was a student of the path, not a jealous interloper who sought a way to take the throne from his father. He believed that if he had a staff, he could become king."

The mist became the young man, older now, standing in the center of the room with his fists closed in anger.

"Despite all he had learned, he came to realize that it could be a long time before he would be worthy of a staff. So—he conspired to take my staff from me."

He couldn't meet the eyes of the listeners, the memories obviously painful to him. "He convinced Nimue that I would never allow them to come into their own power. Nimue sought power as much as her lover."

Marlowe watched the fog shape of Nimue.

"The pair of them, using incantations I had taught them, imprisoned me and strove to steal the power of my staff."

Misty shapes battled each other in the mist until the image of Marlowe fell.

"They could not take the staff from me, but they stole some of its power and placed it into several enchanted items."

The fog staff rose into the air and shot misty lines to a ring, a metal stamp, and a small locket.

"Then Modredus started a war with King Arthur."

A battlefield rose with men fighting. One side was using magic against the other, gesturing at knights and flinging them away with beams that shot from their hands.

"I was more powerful than they could imagine, and I broke free to defeat Modredus and Nimue, but not in time to save King Arthur. Not only was he killed, but his royal seal disappeared that day."

The Marlowe made of smoke arose and, with a staff in hand, easily defeated the smoke images, but the Mordred figure pulled a knife and stabbed King Arthur.

With a flick of Marlowe's hand, the mists disappeared, leaving only the old man standing in the middle of the circle of chairs. His eyes glanced about the group as he spoke in a low voice. "Nimue escaped, and I never saw her again. I stripped Modredus of his charms, and he cursed me as I sent him into exile. I heard rumors that Modredus went to Europe to learn the ways of dark magick that I would not teach him. I assumed that eventually he died… until today."

Marlowe pulled from a pocket in his robes the small piece of parchment Lysandra had given him with a faded wax seal in the corner.

"This paper contains a simple message in an ancient script," he said, and raised the paper to his eyes. "Rwy'n dod atoch chi, hen ddyn."

Eddie spoke up. "What does that mean?"

Marlowe nodded. "That is Welsh for: 'I come for you, old man.' This is a letter from Modredus to me, and it carries the seal of King Arthur. The one that went missing after his death."

All the wizards talked animatedly to each other. Only Drusilicus sat in his chair with his arms crossed and did not join in.

Drusilicus finally raised an arm and shouted to bring the room to silence. "Marlowe, what does any of this mean, and what does it have to do with the Drakula?"

Marlowe gathered his thoughts. "This scroll was left by vampires so that I would see it. I can only assume that it means that my apprentice from long ago at some point became a vampire. I am also afraid that he has achieved the title of the Lord of the Undead."

This started another round of excited chatter throughout the room as each wizard argued his concerns and the implications of this news.

Eddie stood and clapped his hands until it was quiet again. "What do you need from us, Marlowe?"

The old man stood, wide-eyed, as if he hadn't planned what to say or do after making this revelation.

Marlowe cleared his throat. "According to the prophecy, he has come here for a papyrus that will unleash chaos upon the world." Marlowe spun in a quick circle to take in all the wizards in the room. "I have reason to believe that this papyrus is in my possession."

"Your possession, Marlowe!" Bankrock raged. "This goes against the Agreement of Magickal Limitation in the New York City Boroughs—"

Marlowe cleared his throat and raised his hand for silence. "I held many ancient papyri in my workshop back those many years ago. If Modredus had seen it, it would explain why he comes to Manhattan now."

"But that is to our benefit," Drusilicus interjected, rising, so that everyone turned to him. "Being a vampire, he cannot enter your house without an invitation. If it is indeed here, the papyrus could not be in a safer location."

Eddie stood. "Hold on. Remember when the Great Evil almost destroyed Central Park last year?"

Luis and several wizards nodded.

"Well, he needed five talismans to make the spell work. He needed those powerful charms to do it. Doesn't it make sense that Mordred—or Modredus, or Drakula, or whatever the chump is calling himself —would need an enormous power supply to make this spell work, even if he could get his hands on the papyrus?"

The wizards nodded and turned to each other to agree.

"So the first thing we have to do is find out what this bad guy could use as a power source. If we can cut him off from what he's planning to use, we can stop him."

Marlowe rose. "Eddie speaks sooth!"

"Sooth?" Eddie repeated.

Marlowe went on. "The Drakula would need an enchanted object of significant power. Although he must have extensive magical knowledge after all these centuries, he will need to power the spell!"

Drusilicus spoke up. "Bankrock, can you scan for magical items and energies?"

Bankrock nodded, and instead of merely looking annoyed, he seemed lost in thought. "I can, but it depends how well-hidden it is. If they sealed a magical object in a container with the spells—"

"Wait!" Eddie barked. "Sealed in a container. You mean like a coffin?"

"Uh-oh," Drusilicus muttered.

Bankrock's eyes brightened. "Why, yes. If it had very strong magical enchantments, I would recommend a large coffin, and one probably inlaid with metal—"

"A metal like gold?" Eddie felt worried.

"That would be ideal!" Bankrock agreed.

Willowdell cleared her throat. "Something like the one we saw at the airport last night?"

Bankrock gaped at the woman, stunned. "What?"

"Was it inlaid with ze gold?" Dalehead asked. "That would be easy to find with an appropriate spell, *n'est-ce pas?* Zere is little gold in Manhattan."

"Except for 47th Street," Luis commented, mentioning the street where many jewelers sold their wares.

Eddie spoke up. "The Drakula's servants brought a large coffin to Manhattan last night. It might have contained something. We didn't examine it to avoid an incident."

"The lieutenant is correct," Drusilicus said and stood. "We all need to be aware of any place where magickal power levels are much higher than they should be."

"I can tell you that," Daniel Kraft said as he stepped into the room.

Drusilicus turned to him, incensed. "Have you been listening to our conversation?"

"I asked Daniel to remain nearby," Marlowe said forcefully. "For those of you who don't know, this is Daniel Kraft. He is a vampire and sometimes can get us useful information." Marlowe turned back to Daniel. "Please go on."

"They focused everything on Greenwich Village," Daniel said. "The vampires are being unusually bold, and they keep the police quite busy from all the nuisance complaints from the people who live there. I believe that some vampires have been feeding on the populace."

This information received shocked looks from the gathered group.

"Openly?" Bankrock fretted. "That is against the Vampire Control Act of—"

"Are you aware of any specific talisman or enchanted object in that part of town?" Eddie interrupted Bankrock.

Daniel shook his head. "No, but I can tell you that the center of the vampire activity is Washington Square Park. If you were to search for anything, I would recommend looking there."

"Or under it," Marlowe added.

Eddie turned to his mentor. "Under it? Are you saying there's, like, tunnels under the square?"

"Many," Marlowe sighed.

"Actually, that makes sense," offered Bankrock. "There are tombs under that park. I imagine a vampire would consider one of those tombs a very safe place to hide during the day."

"Tombs?" Eddie blurted. "Underneath the park?"

"Really, lieutenant, don't you know New York history at all?" Drusilicus rebuked him. "Washington Square Park used to be a potter's field. In fact, they used to have public hangings there."

Eddie paused for a moment and racked his memory. "'Multitudes who sleep in the dust of the earth will awake'. Isn't that what the prophecy told us, Marlowe?"

"Indeed, it did," Marlowe replied.

"Seems like a graveyard would be a good place for that to happen," Eddie speculated.

"Madre de Dios," Luis muttered and quickly crossed himself.

ELEVEN

There were discussions for over an hour, each wizard making suggestions and Bankrock quoting legalese. Finally, Drusilicus rose. "I live only a few blocks from Washington Square. My suggestion is that we use it as a launching site for any operations."

The group nodded and Bankrock added, "We would be close enough to take swift action when needed."

"Yes," Drusilicus declared. "We can even use my mirrors to teleport in or out quickly if necessary. I have full-body mirrors, and I enchanted them to help with the process. I also heavily protected my house from magickal interference."

"Depending on who's staying there," Eddie murmured to Luis, who nodded in agreement.

"I will try to discover any magickal source the vampires could have access to, talismans and the like," Bankrock confirmed.

"Seems like a wise choice," Marlowe said, looking at the little man. He stepped to the center of the room again and cleared his throat. "I must ask our other guests, Dalehead, Willowdell, and Vasant to reach out to other wizards—see what you can find out about vampire activity."

Vasant raised a hand. "I think it would be best if Dalehead and Willowdell were to do this. I am no longer familiar with the coven members in my part of the world."

Dalehead nodded. "I will talk to those I know in Europe. Since zis is from where ze Drakula has come, zey will tell us more."

Willowdell turned to Marlowe. "I can talk to t'ose in New Orleans and the voodoo community."

Marlowe nodded. "Very well, we have a plan."

Drusilicus declared, "It would be best if I were off."

He shot a withering look at Vasant and headed for the door.

Daniel stepped close to Eddie and murmured, "Stay until the others leave. I may have information for you."

Eddie nodded, just as Vasant rose from her chair. "It is best if I left as well. I will be residing in my arch to be available for you, Marlowe."

Eddie headed for the door with Vasant. "I'll let her out," he said in way of explanation. Once both of them were in the entrance hall, Eddie stopped the Indian woman as Drusilicus went outside and closed the door.

"What's with you and Drusilicus?" Eddie whispered. "I mean, not that I blame you."

"Oh?" Vasant responded.

"He and I haven't hit it off well," Eddie explained. "In fact, I think he's a stuck-up jerk."

This gleaned a small smile from the woman. "There are others who have said such a thing with more flowery speech."

"It looked like the two of you were going to start a duel right there in the living room."

Vasant gazed at the floor and sighed heavily. "I will only say this. There was a reason I have lived as a hermit the last one hundred years, and it is because of him. I thought it best to avoid contact with others for a while."

"You guys have a fight or something?"

She smiled knowingly. "Quite the opposite. Marlowe is not the only one who has had problems with an apprentice." Vasant bowed slightly, opened the door, and stepped out into the night.

Eddie closed the door and returned to the living room.

Dalehead and Willowdell were talking to Marlowe, and Eddie overheard some of what they were saying as he drew near.

Dalehead spoke quietly, "I will seek what I can, but zere can be no promises."

"Yes, and you know how tight-lipped the voodoo practitioners are," Willowdell explained. "Some of t'em might want to help the vampires."

"Do your best, ladies. I have endless faith in you," Marlowe told them.

The women nodded and headed off for the front door.

Bankrock rose and also made for the door. "Well, Marlowe, now that we know what we are dealing with—or should I say *who* we are dealing with—I am sure we can stop his plan. Especially if you can locate that papyrus."

"By Zoroaster, I hope you are right," Marlowe told him.

The little man tightened his rather short tie and went to the door, with a cursory nod to Eddie as he left.

Eddie returned to his seat, observing Marlowe and Daniel.

Daniel was watching the door, undoubtably reaching out with his heightened senses to make sure the others had left. He then sat in a chair near Luis and Eddie.

"I believe I know the identity of the vampire you are looking for, Eddie," Daniel began.

"It appears to be a most illuminating night," Marlowe said.

Luis spoke up. "Hopefully, it won't be a guy who's a thousand years old."

Marlowe sighed. "Vampires are unlike wizards. We age, but slowly. Vampires do not grow older once turned."

Eddie nodded to acknowledge Marlowe then turned back to Daniel. "Do you have a name?"

"He currently travels under the name Orfeo."

Luis grunted. "Well, that's better than the Flintstones names the wizards got."

"Now we need a location where we could find him," Eddie said.

"The word on the street is that he is looking for new sellers for the product," Daniel told him. "I have to say after what happened to you at the airport, my information might not be good."

Marlowe drew closer. "Now, now, Daniel. I don't see how anyone can blame you for that!"

"Except Drusilicus," Eddie added.

Luis joined in, confused. "What happened at what airport?"

"I'll tell you later," Eddie said. "Do you have any idea where we could start looking for this guy?"

"It appears he has been recently frequenting some clubs down in the Village. He has had a great deal of luck recruiting down there."

Luis exhaled heavily. "Just give us a place to start, okay?"

Daniel nodded. "I believe if you go to the club known as the Velvet Glove, you might have some luck."

Eddie checked with Marlowe. "Is Rusty out on the street? If so, we might want to get a ride."

"Why can't we drive?" Luis asked.

"Parking might be a problem," Eddie suggested. "If we have a cab at our disposal, I'd like to use it."

"You can contact him," Marlowe suggested. "He had to run an errand for me, but I am sure he is back by now."

Eddie drew close to the old man. "Do you think there really was something in that coffin? Did I guess wrong?"

Marlowe considered it. "It is hard to say. It certainly sounds like a trap, from what you have told me. With all those vampires guarding the box, as well as this Selene woman, who apparently has magickal training, perhaps there was something of value within."

"Like a talisman or something?"

Marlowe considered this. "If it contained significant power, sealing it in the coffin would keep us from detecting its true capabilities."

"Okay, well—Luis and I are going to focus on our case. Stay in touch."

"Truly indeed, Eddie."

Eddie headed over to Luis, who was still speaking quietly to Daniel. "Let's move out."

With a nod to Daniel, Eddie and Luis headed to the door and out onto the street.

As they reached the sidewalk, Eddie stopped, closed his eyes, then said aloud, "Rusty!"

"What are you doin'?" Luis wondered. "Conjuring up a cab?"

Instantly, a yellow cab pulled around the corner, going no less than sixty. It roared up the street and stopped next to Eddie and Luis with a screech of tires.

"Need a cab?" Rusty said through the open passenger window.

"No me digas!" Luis marveled as they descended the steps and approached the vehicle. "Ain't you the cab I followed the other day?"

"The same. Get in," Rusty bellowed.

As Luis got into the car, he admired the large back seat. "A Checker? I thought they didn't make these anymore."

"I've had this one a while."

Eddie spoke as he joined Luis in the back. "Hope I didn't pull you from wherever Marlowe sent you."

"Nah, I knew you'd want me. Besides, business is slow." Rusty gave a suspicious look at Luis in his rearview mirror. "A lotta... folks... left town."

"It's okay," Eddie muttered. "He's my apprentice and my partner."

"Oh, yeah? Now I remember! I met you da night of the Great Evil, da whole thing about da fifth talisman," Rusty gushed. "Welcome to da path of da wise."

"Uh, thanks," Luis said.

"So business is bad?" Eddie said.

"Bad ain't the word," Rusty went on as they headed downtown, again hitting all the lights perfectly. "You wouldn't believe what's goin' on. Everyone's upset there might be a war with the vamps. Some of us don't feel safe in our own arches in Central Park. What's New York comin' to if ya ain't safe in ya own arch?"

"People live in the arches?" Luis said with a surprised look at Eddie.

Eddie shrugged. "Didn't I tell you that? Yeah, Riftstone posed as a homeless guy, but he lived inside his arch."

"Yeah. I got one myself," Rusty boasted.

Both detectives stared at Rusty in shock. Finally, Eddie said, "I didn't know you had your own arch."

"Sure. I used to drive Greywacke around all da time. Of course, it was horse and buggy back den. He told me he'd never've been able to get Central Park built, if I hadn't been around to drive him to all the meetings with Vaux and Olmsted."

"Which arch is yours?" Luis wondered.

"Da one on 90th Street and Central Park West. It was built in 1890, twelve years after da park had opened. At first dey just called it 'Rustic Arch', but Greywacke eventually got it named 'Claremont Arch'."

"Is that why you have people call you Rusty?" Eddie said.

"That's right, since you need two names these days," Rusty said with a big grin. "Y'see, it's the only arch big enough to fit my cab, not dat you could see it in dere. I finally up and put bars on it a few years back."

Luis nodded. "Yeah, that arch has got bars that keep it closed. I thought they used it for storage."

"Nah, too many miscreants usin' my arch. Besides, I'm a New Yawker. I like to have bars on my windows."

Eddie smiled, as the cab pulled up across from a dilapidated warehouse below 14th Street that bore a small sign: THE VELVET GLOVE.

"What do I owe you, Rusty?" Eddie said and pulled out his wallet.

"On da house. It's wizard business," Rusty said. "I gotta tell you though, you guys don't look like dis club's regular clientele."

"What does that mean?" Luis demanded.

"Nuthin'," Rusty demurred. "But it's a big LGBTQ hangout."

"It's a gay club?" Luis sputtered.

"Calm down," Eddie said. "We're just looking for a perp."

"But I never... I mean ... how do I act?" Luis worried.

"Like you would anywhere else," Rusty advised. "It's just people out to have fun, and I gotta tell you dey got a show with drag queens—dere some of the sweetest people you ever met."

Eddie drew close to Luis' ear. "Our perp, he's looking for people he can hook and get to sell his shit."

Luis frowned. "Okay, but don't tell Maria I went in."

"I won't." Eddie smirked. "Unless you do something really stupid."

"You'll be fine. After all, dere all there to have fun. Dey ain't trying to convert you," Rusty said as they got out of the back of the cab.

"We just want to see if we can get a lead on this Orfeo guy. We tell anyone we talk to that he's pushing a dangerous drug. Just keep it simple."

"Right… simple…" Luis said.

"I'll stay close," Rusty told Eddie, "in case you gotta follow up on another lead."

The detectives approached an aisle of velvet ropes where a few people stood in line waiting. Two men were there, one bare-chested and wearing a dog collar around his neck. His partner was in leather pants, vest, and a biker hat with chains. Behind him was a woman in a fashionable men's suit, holding hands with a woman in a schoolgirl dress.

At the door, there were two men. They were both African-American and had shaved heads and a lot of muscles, obvious from the short sleeves of their formal wingtip shirts.

Eddie approached, and the taller man pointed to the line with an oversized hand and growled, "The line is there."

"Yeah, about that," Eddie said as he opened his billfold to show his shield and pulled his jacket aside to show his sidearm, as Luis did the same. "We just want to look around."

The first man glanced at the crowd and turned the detectives away so he could murmur. "You gotta warrant?"

"You gotta brain?" Luis countered.

Eddie raised a hand for Luis to be quiet. He spoke softly but in earnest. "We got a guy pushing that Mind-Blo crap, and he's recruiting. We got a tip he's here. Let us look around, and if he ain't here, we're gone."

The bouncer appeared hesitant.

"Or we make a phone call, get a warrant, and bring about twenty cops here to close the place down," Luis threatened.

Eddie again held up his hand. "Sergeant, this is a man who is loyal to his job and trying to do the right thing. No need to threaten anybody." He returned his gaze to the bouncer. "What do you say?"

The man opened the catch on the rope and indicated the door with a shake of his head. Eddie and Luis approached the door and went in. It opened to a stairway, and they headed upstairs, where they could hear the thumping rhythm of loud music over their heads.

"You do bad cop very well, Luis," Eddie said.

"It just comes naturally." Luis smiled.

They reached the top of the stairs and pulled the door open to deafening music that immediately gave Eddie a headache.

Lights flashed hypnotically around the large dance floor. At a booth was a bearded DJ wearing a silver lamé dress as he played the almost deafening track of his selection. The corners of the space hid in darkness, but Eddie saw that there were alcoves with curtains that could be closed to hide each alcove from the rest of the room and create a private space.

Couples of various genders and stages of undress were on the floor dancing together. The flashing lights made it hard to discern who was who or what they were wearing, although one guy wore a flesh-colored spandex bodysuit that gave the impression he was wearing nothing at all.

Eddie and Luis exchanged a look. Since attempting to talk would be impossible over the raucous music, Eddie gestured to the private alcoves, and Luis nodded. Eddie pointed to the curtained private area in the corner, and the two men circled towards it, walking past tables with couples. A male couple was watching the dancers, each with a stoned look on their faces. The next pair were women exchanging tiny kisses, totally focused on each other.

Luis fixated on the first curtained room. He drew close and only slid the curtain the tiniest amount to glance in, then released it and shook his head.

They went to the next curtained enclosure and Eddie pulled the curtain only enough to peek in. He immediately glimpsed the man who had bested them on their drug bust the other night and who was handing a small vial of blue liquid to a very handsome young man.

Eddie released the curtain and glanced at Luis, who pulled his weapon. Eddie did not pull his gun but gestured and his staff appeared in his hand. They both pulled the curtain aside, and Luis aimed his gun in a two-handed grip. The young man opened his mouth to cry out, but neither of the detectives heard anything over the thunderous music.

Farther inside the booth the drug ringleader actually seemed surprised, and that made Eddie smile.

Moving faster than one could imagine, he grabbed the table and flipped it up and through the parted curtains, flying toward an oblivious couple at a nearby table. At the same time, he ran.

With a gesture, Eddie froze the table in midair. He pointed his staff at the rat-faced man with the slicked-back hair, his legs suddenly tangled and he fell.

Eddie levitated the table rapidly back into place as Luis grabbed the vial away from the young man, who was cringing with fear.

With a whispered word, Eddie levitated their prisoner through the air, and smashed him through the nearby exit door.

Eddie and Luis ran to follow him into a back stairway reeking of old grease and rancid food, so it must have been near whatever passed for a kitchen in the nightclub.

The conjured force had hit the perp hard, but he sprang to his feet, his fingernails extending into pointed claws, and his canine teeth growing into vicious fangs. Eddie met his eyes. His irises were now a bright red.

The man leapt at Eddie with surprising speed, but Luis had come through the door with his pistol in a two-handed grip. Before Eddie could react, his partner fired two shots into Orfeo's chest that not only threw him back, but tumbled him down the flight of stairs to the bottom of the stairwell.

Carefully, the two detectives climbed down the slippery steps. Luis still held his gun, and Eddie carried his staff. The man lay at the bottom of the steps next to a metal exit door.

He raised his head and grumbled, "Was that really necessary?"

"I dunno," Eddie said. "You gonna come quietly, Orfeo?"

"You found out my name," the man grumbled. "So what?"

Eddie shrugged. "Don't be a problem, Orfeo. 'Cause I got a whole lotta hurt I can dish out."

"Yeah," Luis agreed. "And I gotta lotta bullets."

Orfeo's eyes were still red and his canine teeth extended past his lips. He held up his hands in surrender and rose painfully to his feet.

"I also may have packed some silver bullets," Eddie threatened.

Luis glanced to him and frowned. "I thought that was for werewolves."

Eddie shrugged. "Works on vampires too." He held his right fist up. "I killed a vampire with this ring the other night."

Luis kept his eyes on Orfeo as they stopped about two steps above the man. "I was wondering where you got that. *Me parece bien.*"

"We want to know where you get your supply," Eddie demanded as they continued slowly down. "Who is making the drug?"

"Of course, officer," Orfeo answered, his hands still up. There were two wounds on his torso, and the cloth was damp with a black substance that Eddie assumed was the vampire's blood. Although Eddie could see the hole in the clothing, the pale flesh underneath was closing rapidly. All at once, Orfeo's body expelled the pair of bullets from his wounds one at a time, each making a dull ping as they fell to the floor.

With a lightning fast move, Orfeo slammed the crash bar to open the door and instantly dissolved into mist.

Eddie raised his staff—too little, too late. The breeze caught the mist and Orfeo blew away before Eddie could conjure his powers.

Both detectives ran to the bottom of the stairs and gazed out into the empty alley, but there was no sign of the vampire.

"Damn," Luis cursed and holstered his weapon. "You can shoot that guy and he still gets away."

Eddie nodded as he put his staff away. "I knew bullets couldn't kill him, but did you see how he had to get the bullets out of his body before he could change? That's important to know."

"Hey, man?" a timid voice said behind them.

Eddie and Luis turned to see the pale young man at the doorway. He followed them down the back stairs.

"You took my vial, man," he said. He had blond hair and chiseled features and gave the suggestion of an actor from a television show.

Luis nodded. "Yeah, we call that evidence."

"We're with the police," Eddie said, and pulled out his billfold to show his badge.

"You don't understand—I need that," the young man said, and licked his lips.

"You're going to have to do without your fix, buddy," Luis said harshly.

"No, you don't understand," the blond man spoke more fiercely. "I need it!"

Eddie approached the blond carefully with his hands out. "That stuff will kill you. Do you know how many deaths have occurred from that shit?"

"I don't care," the man said. "I need it. Give it to me!"

Luis and Eddie exchanged a glance and Luis regarded the man, who was shorter and much thinner than he was. "I don't think so. I think you need to get into rehab, for your own good."

The man jumped at Luis and grabbed his arm with surprising strength, his eyes turning bright red as Eddie watched.

"Hey! Get off," Luis shouted and slammed the young man in the face with his free hand.

The man looked dazed, then fell to the ground, unconscious.

"Man," Luis muttered, "that one is *muy loco*."

Eddie checked the blond man's pulse and breathing, and they were normal. "Did you see his eyes?"

"No, I was too busy trying to smack his face," Luis said, and examined the hand he had used to flatten his assailant. "Nice to know I haven't lost my touch."

"His eyes turned red, like Orfeo's did," Eddie reported.

Luis was surprised. "Really? How did that happen?"

"I think I've got an idea. We need to get this guy to Marlowe. You still got the drug?"

Luis reached into his pocket and extracted the small vial.

"Let's get Rusty and bring this guy and the drug to Marlowe. I just got an idea."

About an hour later, Rusty, Eddie, and Luis sat in the breakfast room of Marlowe's townhouse. Rusty was having a cup of coffee while Eddie was bringing the cabdriver up to speed on the earlier meeting.

"Yeah, I know all about him being Merlin," Rusty said with a laugh. "But he said that the Drakula is Mordred? I thought that bastard was long dead."

"It appears he isn't," Eddie said, a cup of hot coffee floating to the space in front of him.

"Yeah, but that part about Nimue and Mordred fooling around. Did he mention *he* was in love with her as well?"

"It… um… didn't come up."

"That makes the story a lot more interesting," Luis said. "Old Merlin in love with a young woman who steals his powers?"

"It's probably a sore subject with Marlowe," Eddie considered.

Rusty held his cup out as the silver coffee pot flew over to give him a refill. "They say it's why he ain't trained no one for a thousand years." He took a thoughtful sip. "Except you, Eddie."

"Wow, that's a long time," Luis mused. "You gonna live that long, Eddie?"

"How do I know?" Eddie grumbled. "I'm still trying to get used to the fact that I'm going to be a father again."

"Really? Hey congrats," Rusty said.

"I wish this all weren't happening at the same time," Eddie confessed.

"Y'never know when dis stuff'll hit da fan," Rusty said. "I mean, we've done peace treaties with da vamps before. Back in 1793, because of events in Vermont. Den again, in 1854 because of things dat went down in Connecticut. We've had so few problems in de last few years. We leave dem alone, unless dere attacking people."

"If only I knew what we—" Eddie began.

A noise came from the hall as a door was closed, and Marlowe slowly ambled into the breakfast room.

"The guy I smacked all right?" Luis asked.

"Sleeping comfortably in a room upstairs. Daniel was kind enough to carry him up," Marlowe said and gazed at Eddie. "I finished the test you asked for, and I must ask—how did you know?"

Luis frowned. "Know what?"

"My experiments on the drug you've brought me have proven conclusively that the ingredient that produces the high in this— what is it you called it?"

"Mind-Blo," Eddie answered.

"Yes," Marlowe agreed. "The active substance is vampire venom."

Rusty stood up at the table, his mouth open in shock. "What?"

"There are other chemicals also—a stimulant and a dopamine reinforcing agent—but they merely speed up the effects of the venom. There was also Polypodium leucotomos, an herbal extract, but I am not sure of its function." Marlowe carefully pulled out a chair and sat at the table, his eyes never leaving Eddie. "How could you have known?"

Eddie exhaled heavily. "I saw a flash of the red eyes, like the vampires get when they attack. That and the fact that when a vampire kissed Luis, he acted like she had doped him."

Luis's face went a little red. "Only for a few minutes."

Marlowe sat back in the chair, steepled his fingers, and pressed them to his lips. "Go on."

"It makes sense. Why is this drug so addictive? The venom makes the victim return to the vampire again and again. Why is it killing people? Because ultimately, that's what the venom does, it either enslaves the victim or kills them."

"That's very good thinking, Eddie," Marlowe said after a long pause.

"It also could explain why the drug came from nowhere and is prevalent now. It could be part of the Drakula's plan. The question is, where are they getting this venom?" Eddie turned to Rusty and Luis. "What do you guys think?"

"I'm way out of my league," Luis stated. "But it explains why Doctor Beverly can't break down the chemicals that make up the stuff."

"And why she said there was something organic in it," Eddie added.

Marlowe nodded. "It would appear, Eddie, that we are seeing the fruition of a plan meant to not only destroy us, but all of New York as well."

TWELVE

T he four men sat in silence considering everything they had just learned.

Rusty finally broke the silence with an enormous yawn. "Well, I'd better get to my arch and park my car."

"Wizard Claremont," Marlowe said. "You have been such a help tonight. Please stay here."

Rusty brightened. "Well, if it ain't no inconvenience."

"Not at all," Marlowe replied, and turned to Eddie and Luis. "May I extend the offer to both of you as well?"

Eddie shook his head. "No, we've got to check in at the precinct, then get out of here."

"At least you can do that 'vanish into the trees' thing," Luis grumbled. "I gotta drive back up to the Bronx."

"You head home. I'll clock us both out and write up the incident," Eddie said wearily.

"Really?" Luis said. "LT, you're the best."

Eddie rose, and so did Luis.

"Do we report I discharged my weapon?" Luis said with concern.

Eddie faced his partner. "I'm sure that no one heard it over that music, and it certainly didn't hurt Orfeo."

"Barely slowed him down," Luis muttered.

"That's the truth," Eddie agreed, and turned to Marlowe. "Marlowe, if you can, do more tests on what we brought you and that guy while he's still here. Find out everything you can. If we can stop this drug, it might put a kink in whatever the Drakula is planning."

"Agreed, Eddie," Marlowe said. "I shall make it my top priority."

"Can you do that memory thing to the guy, so he doesn't remember being here?"

"Yes, I shall alter his memories and attempt to cure him of the venom. That is, if I can concoct the right potion."

Eddie recalled his talk with Drusilicus and his claim of a potion that protected him from Lysandra. "You should ask Drusilicus. I understand he knows a potion that can counteract the venom."

"Really?" Marlowe replied in surprise. "Why would Drusilicus have that?"

Eddie sighed. "You'll have to ask him. But I have it on good authority that he does."

"You constantly surprise me, Eddie," Marlowe marveled.

Eddie nodded in reply as he and Luis headed for the door.

They returned to the street, their way illuminated by streetlights shadowed by the budding leaves of a tree in front of the door. The air had grown chilly, and Eddie pulled his suit jacket close around him.

Luis, who seemed unaware of the chill, lumbered along next to his smaller partner up the transverse road toward the precinct house.

"Well," Luis finally broke the silence, "at least we probably saved that guy from overdosing on the stuff."

"There is that," Eddie said as they headed toward a tunnel for the road that ran overhead. "But this Orfeo, he's good at what he does. He's sure of his abilities and uses them without hesitation —"

Eddie stopped speaking and walking at the same time. He put up his arm to stop his partner, as if that could even slow Luis down if he wanted to keep going. Years of working together made the bigger man freeze.

"What?" Luis whispered, peering into the tunnel ahead of them.

"Just a feeling." Eddie held out his right hand as his staff slapped into it. He murmured, *"Inlumino."*

A red glow appeared on the crown of the staff, and Eddie filled the tunnel with a bright white light. It started small, like a flashlight, but increased in size and brightness. As it did, there was a loud chittering as a cloud of bats flew out of the tunnel.

Eddie conjured a dome of protection over them both as several of the winged mammals lunged for them, fangs extended for attack. It repelled the creatures and they bounced off the dome causing it to spark with red flashes.

The light under the tunnel now blazed like the sun. The remaining bats flew away into the night, and tunnel faded slowly to the shadowy enclosure it had been before.

Luis gulped. "Were those—?"

"Vampire bats, yes. Lying in wait for us." Eddie spoke calmly, but he was breathing hard.

Luis crossed himself clumsily. *"Madre de Dios."*

With his staff still in hand, Eddie led Luis cautiously through the tunnel, both of them looking up the entire time. The red light at the top of the staff bathed the brick and stonework the color of blood.

Once through, they continued to follow the sidewalk as they calmed down.

Luis gestured at the staff. "You can make light with that thing?"

"Pretty much. Marlowe says that since it is the Staff of Fire, I can control light in many forms, make colors and stuff. He made me do exercises where I could feel the vibration and the frequency of the light."

"Light has a frequency?"

"Colors do, each a little different. So far, I've only learned that illumination trick. There's a lot to learn."

"Pretty handy, in this case."

They were approaching the steps for the lot where he and Luis parked their cars. "Let me come with you to your car."

Luis seemed to straighten up and get taller. "You think I can't handle myself?"

"Luis, I've seen you punch a demon in the face," Eddie stated proudly. "But these vampires are sneaky and they have that glamour power."

Luis shook his head, deflated. "Yeah, right. That stupid broad kissed me and I was ready to leave Maria for her."

This made Eddie chuckle. "You wouldn't leave a real woman like Maria for a bit of fluff like Lysandra."

"As far as I'm concerned, she can stay with Drew-silly-ass," Luis retorted.

They reached Luis's car, and he unlocked the door with the key, as the vehicle was too old to have electronic locks.

"We gotta get you a new car," Eddie said, looking at the busted heap that was Luis' mode of transportation.

"With six kids and Catholic school payments?" Luis quipped. "I doubt it, man."

"Maybe we can get you a magickal one."

Luis nodded. "How about Rusty's cab? Then I can make some extra money after work."

"How are you guys pulling off Catholic school?"

"It ain't easy. Maria does volunteer stuff with the church and school, and we get some scholarships. In a few more years, I'm gonna hafta get a side job, once they're all in school." He looked toward his dirty windshield. "Eddie, I gotta go."

"Sure, partner. See you at the 4:00 PM shift tomorrow," Eddie said. With a roar, Luis started his car, and with a puff of smoke out of the exhaust he pulled it out of the parking space and pointed it toward home.

With a sigh, Eddie vanished his staff, returning it to his pocket, and made his way across the street to the bullpen in the 22nd precinct.

An hour later, he finished his preliminary report citing an anonymous informer that gave him the tip about the Velvet Glove. He recorded how they confronted the suspect, and his subsequent escape out the back exit.

He didn't like the fact that he had to suggest the drug pusher had outrun him, as Eddie was pretty fast on his feet, but he couldn't very well explain that the bad guy turned into mist and blew away.

He didn't report that he and Luis confiscated a small amount of the drug, as Marlowe was still analyzing it. If there was any left, he planned to take it to Doctor Beverly.

A uniformed man, Higgins, stuck his head in the bullpen. Eddie was hard to miss, as he was the only detective there at 1:00 AM. "Hey, LT, you gotta package."

Eddie frowned, hit the key on the computer to file his report, and got up and stretched. It pleased him that the magic from his staff had made so many of his aches and pains simply go away.

"Things calm tonight?" Eddie asked.

"They are in Central Park," Higgins told him. He was a brown-haired man and so thin, he gave the impression a breeze could knock him over. Yet, Eddie once saw him take down a suspect who resembled a wrestler.

He handed Eddie a small box. "Here you go, LT."

Eddie took a gander at it, and memory flooded back. "The flashlights! I've been waiting for these."

Eddie opened the box to extract two standard-looking flashlights. The lenses were a series of tiny dark-blue ultraviolet LEDs.

There were no batteries in the new arrivals, and Eddie slipped both of them into a drawer of his desk. He wished he could have given one to Luis, as it would have given him a viable weapon to protect himself against the vampires.

He would worry about the batteries tomorrow. In the meantime, he headed out, waving to Higgins as he went through the glass double doors.

He walked across the street and up the wooden stairs to the unlit parking lot, as if he were going to drive home. Instead, he went up a side pathway into the wooded area before he gestured to produce his staff.

Sometimes he could transport without even producing his staff, but he was tired and didn't want to risk his concentration being weak.

When he came through the trees, he wasn't in a tiny park in Teaneck, but on a hilltop, looking down upon open land with a valley below. The stars were bright over his head, and the streetlights of the city had disappeared.

He glanced at his staff, and then the woods behind him, trying to understand if he'd made a mistake. Was he not focused enough? Had he let his mind wander? Changing locations in the forest had been one of the first things Marlowe taught him, and he'd always done it well.

A dozen feet from him was a small campfire. With a glance at the trees behind him, Eddie made his way slowly to the fire, transforming his clothes to his wizard garb in case he needed to face something unexpected.

There was no one there as he approached, but several large rocks stood in a circle around it. Looking all about, Eddie went to sit.

"Welcome to my fire," came a deep voice.

Eddie jumped up in shock, but the voice came again in a soothing tone.

"You are safe here, Wizard Berman. Please sit and enjoy the warmth and the hospitality of my fire."

Although Eddie still could see no one, he carefully sat down as he ran through many attack and defensive spells he could use. The fire would make an excellent weapon if needed, as he could control the flames, making them as small as a match or as hot and bright as a blowtorch.

"No one will harm you, wizard," came the voice from everywhere and nowhere. "I thought it was time that we should meet."

"Okay then." Eddie rose to his feet, his staff aloft. "How about you come out and show yourself?"

An enormous shadow loomed on the other side of the fire, and at first, Eddie thought that there was another source of light projected behind a man, giving him an enormous silhouette. He slowly sat back down on the rock, using his staff for support.

A being lumbered into the firelight. Eddie certainly wouldn't call him a man. He had to be over eight feet tall and covered from head to foot in long reddish-brown hair. His shoulders were immense, probably as wide as Eddie was tall, and his arms hung much longer than a man's.

His face was not that of an animal, but distinctly that of a human with a long beard and no mustache. The center of his face was as brown as his fur, and his eyes were the most surprising. Although they had the shine of an animal in the firelight, they were clear and blue and reflected nothing but kindness.

Eddie gulped as the massive creature sat on the biggest rock around the fire and towered over Eddie, who at that moment didn't feel like an all-powerful wizard anymore.

"You... you're..." was all Eddie could manage.

"Misinghalikun," the giant replied helpfully.

"Yeah, him. Missing... Masing... uh... is there a better name I can call you?"

The giant pushed out his lips in thought. "You may call me Stone Face. That is what my name would be in your tongue."

"And you are—and I don't mean to be insulting if this name offends you—you're a Sasquatch?"

"That name troubles me little," he disclosed, and then leaned closer as if to impart a secret. "But I dislike the term 'Bigfoot'."

Eddie shook his head adamantly. "Then I ain't calling you that."

"Would you care to smoke?" offered Stone Face. "The *Pukwudgie* are kind enough to bring me tobacco."

Eddie met his host's eyes, seeing an element of excitement in them. Marlowe's admonitions about good manners when dealing with magickal beings flashed through his head.

"It... um... would honor me to smoke with my... uh... host."

This caused a huge smile to appear on Stone Face's countenance, and he laughed deeply and resoundingly. "You are wise beyond your years, Newling."

It surprised Eddie that the Sasquatch knew the term, and more so when the creature reached behind a rock and pulled out a buckskin bag. He loosened the top and put his enormous hand in to bring out an elaborate pipe covered with carvings: a bow, arrowheads, and other Native American symbols. He took a finger's worth of dried tobacco and placed it into the bowl of the pipe, using his giant pinky to press it into place.

He reached to the fire, extracted a thin burning branch and used it to light the pipe, puffing on it as he did so.

Stone Face took several large drags, blew the smoke into the air, and offered the pipe to Eddie. Eddie wasn't really a smoker, but he'd indulged in a few cigars during his life and knew not to inhale. Eddie took the pipe with a respectful bow and brought it to his lips. He puffed several times on it, the tobacco so strong that it made his eyes water. He blew out the smoke and returned the pipe to his host, trying not to cough, as he was afraid this might be rude.

The Sasquatch put the pipe to his mouth and spoke in his deep voice. "Forgive me for pulling you away, but I thought it was best if we talked."

"You can do that?" Eddie asked, surprised that he was no longer exhausted. The strong tobacco was giving him a real hit of nicotine.

Stone Face nodded. "It is within my abilities to do many things."

Eddie frowned, confused. "You have magickal powers?"

"I have magick far older than you might guess, young wizard." There was a twinkle in his eyes. "Why do you think I can always make sure no one gets a good photograph of me?"

"So, *that's* why." Eddie slapped his knee. "Man, don't that beat all."

"I have watched you, Eddie Berman. I see your heart and the type of man you are. That is why I told Skysoarer to seek you. I wanted to thank you for healing their Granny."

Eddie sighed and gazed at the ground. "Yeah, I'm glad that worked out, but I have to tell you, I got lucky. I just guessed at what to do the whole time."

"Your hand may have been guided a bit."

"What?" Eddie said, taken aback. "By who?"

"Me." Stone Face handed him the pipe again.

"Why didn't *you* just help Granny?" Eddie took another drag, and the tobacco didn't seem so harsh anymore.

"I choose not to interfere in the ways of others. That is why I sent Skysoarer to you. I knew you would try to help and, unlike many of your ilk, you would welcome… suggestions."

Eddie handed back the pipe as he blew the smoke out into the air. "It might make the world a better place if you got involved."

Stone Face sat and stared into the fire. "I can only do as I can."

"That's pretty lame," Eddie observed. "Your help could make a difference."

"That is why I have brought you here, Eddie Berman. I owe you a debt for your help. I will tell you why they attacked Granny."

Eddie stared at his host in amazement. "Does it have something to do with all of this?"

"It does, young wizard. The vampire attacked the Granny to steal a totem of significant power."

"How do you know that?"

"Because I gave it to the *Pukwudgie* for safe-keeping. It was the Mask of *Misignwah*."

"Is it like a talisman? An object imbued with magick?"

"Yes. The Mask of *Misignwah* has the power to change you into any shape you desire—from a man or a woman, to a deer or a hare. I used it, when I went forth among man. I could become any person I wished and only change back when I removed it."

"You do that a lot?"

The huge, hairy creature sighed. "Not for many a year, which is why I had the *Pukwudgie* hold it for me. I find I am truly happy when I am in the forest and in my natural state."

He took a large drag on the pipe and blew a smoke ring into the air.

"That's pretty good," Eddie said looking at the ring as it dissipated.

Stone Face shrugged. "I've got a lot of free time. And tobacco doesn't hurt me."

"You left the mask with the *Pukwudgie*. How did the vampires find out about it?"

"All I can discern is that one who wields a staff found it."

"A wizard?" Eddie gasped. "Do you know who, or how I can find him?"

"This wizard is using his powers to hide from me and all who seek him."

"Can you stop him?"

Stone Face took another inhale from his pipe and contemplated the starry night. "My blood has already killed one who attacked you."

Eddie glanced down at the large silver ring on his finger. "Your blood? You mean, that blood I put in the ring? That was your blood?"

Stone Face nodded his head as he smoked.

"You… uh… want it back?" Eddie asked, holding the ring out.

"I gave it to Marlowe many moons ago. I could feel it when it struck the monster down."

"Yeah, it did the job well, I can tell you that," Eddie said. "Do I have your permission to use your blood? I mean, it seems only right to ask."

Stone Face nodded. "I gave permission when Marlowe took it, but I give it to you also, Eddie Berman."

"I'm glad we got that all settled." Eddie stared into the fire, not knowing what else to say.

"My people are excellent at discerning patterns and upcoming events. I brought you here to tell you that you will face a challenge that will affect many others." Stone Face kept looking at the night sky. "You might not survive."

Eddie exhaled loudly. "Thanks for the encouragement."

Still looking up, Stone Face went on. "You must learn the true nature of your *kanshilësu*—your power—and embrace it."

"How do I do that?"

"That is for you to learn."

Eddie gritted his teeth. Why did magickal beings have to be so damn mysterious all the time? "That's not much help."

"Your enemy thirsts for vengeance and to rule over lesser beings while you do not. That is to your advantage, do not forget it."

Eddie rose cautiously from his place, and the giant stood up to look down upon him.

"By the way, I like your partner. The rest of you seem so tiny, but he does not."

"I'll be sure to tell him."

"It would be best to keep our meeting to yourself," Stone Face advised. "Not all are trustworthy."

"Um… okay," Eddie replied.

"Now, do you wish to go home?"

"Please."

Instantly, the giant disappeared, and Eddie was staring at the front door of his house. Like the magic of Skysoarer, Stone Face had transported him instantly to his home, without even a gesture.

Eddie looked around, but the neighborhood was dark, and he was sure no one had seen him. The ability to teleport from one set of trees to another had always been a useful skill, but what Stone Face and Skysoarer could do was on an entirely different level.

He instantly transformed his clothes and put away his staff in order to have his house keys to get in. Once he unlocked the door, he went over to a small cabinet in the living room and opened it. There were only about two or three bottles of wine and liquor, and Eddie grabbed the scotch. He poured himself a good belt, threw in a couple of ice cubes.

He still had the taste of the tobacco on his tongue, and the stinging flavor of the scotch was a delicious counterpoint.

He went to the living room, kicked off his shoes, sat in the one recliner, and leaned it back a bit as he sipped the fiery liquid.

He muttered to himself, "Vampires, little people, and now a Sasquatch. I'm beginning to understand why wizards become hermits."

Eddie finished his drink, leaned back, and fell into a dreamless sleep.

"Eddie."

Eddie groaned, "Momma, I don't wanna go to school today."

"Maybe not," Eleanor chuckled, "but you got two boys that do, and they gonna come down here like a herd of elephants. Go up and lie down with your wife. She ain't feelin' good."

Eddie sat up, wide awake. "Cerise? Is it the baby?"

"I don't know, but I gotta make breakfast. You head on upstairs."

Eddie got out of the chair and took the stairs two at a time to rush to his bedroom. She'd drawn the curtains, and Eddie could only see Cerise as a dark shape in the bed.

He went to the first curtain and pulled it open, allowing sunlight to come into the room. He knelt by the bed and watched his wife's face as she lay on her side.

She had her eyes tightly closed. "The light, that's so bright."

Eddie went back to the curtain and closed it halfway. "I heard you weren't feeling well."

"Tired," she said from the bed. "I've called work. I just don't have the energy to go in today."

Eddie returned to the bed and kissed Cerise's lips. "Are you sure you're all right?"

"I'm just tired," she said. "I *am* growing a human being in here, you know."

She rubbed her belly for emphasis, and Eddie put his hand on her, gently caressing her distended flesh. She rolled a bit to lie on her back, and Eddie froze.

On her neck were two tiny puncture marks evenly spaced apart.

Eddie tried to talk, and it took him a moment. "What happened here?" he asked as he gently touched the bite marks.

She put her hand under his to rub the spot. "Hmm? Oh, I dunno, feels like a bug bite or something."

"Let me take a better look," Eddie insisted.

She pushed his hand away. "It's nothing."

Eddie went to the window and opened the drapes again.

"Eddie, I said that was too bright! Can't I have a little subdued lighting in my own bedroom?"

"I wanna look at that bite, honey. Can you sit up?"

She shook her head, her hand firmly in place. "Just let me sleep."

As Eddie stood near the window, he noticed a small folded note he hadn't seen before. It was a brown paper, like parchment. He picked up and unfolded it.

A Warning

Join not the battle

or face the consequences.

The words were in a dark-brown ink that resembled blood. Cerise's blood.

THIRTEEN

"How could this happen!" Eddie railed at Marlowe a few hours later. They were in the living room of Marlowe's townhouse, and Eddie had asked Drusilicus to be there as well. He had just finished telling the tale of the bite on his wife's neck.

Eddie continued to shout at his mentor. "You told me there were magickal protections around my house. Hell, we did them together—"

"Eddie, I can only surmise that whoever did this is not merely a vampire, but one learned in our ways," Marlowe told him as he stroked his beard in thought. "Mordred has training and centuries of practice, and if he taught this Selene woman—"

Drusilicus cleared his throat. "I do not see how a vampire could have bridged your threshold."

"My threshold?" Eddie repeated, no less angry at him.

"Yes, a vampire cannot come into a house unless invited in," Drusilicus explained. "You need to ask your family if they invited any stranger who claimed to be a new neighbor or something."

"Would that do it?" Eddie worried.

Marlowe spoke up. "Once you invite a vampire into a house, they can return at their convenience. It is only the first time they need an invitation."

"Is there any other way?" Eddie demanded.

"If you carry them into a house," Drusilicus suggested.

"Great! So now my entire family is at risk!" Eddie exploded.

"The first thing you must do is remain calm," Drusilicus soothed. "This is a serious threat and we will face it with serious countermeasures."

"Says the man who's banging a vampire!" Eddie barked.

"What?" Marlowe gasped, as Drusilicus flushed.

"Yeah, you wanna know *why* he has an antidote for vampire venom? Because Lysandra is his house guest, with all the fringe benefits!"

"Is this true, Drusilicus?" Marlowe demanded.

By now, Drusilicus was a bright shade of red. "I know they frown upon this in the wizard community—as do the vampires— but we have a genuine affection for each other."

"Or she's got you wrapped around her finger and is making you do whatever she says," Eddie stormed. "How do I know *she* wasn't the one who attacked Cerise? She's been to my neighborhood, she knows where I live."

Drusilicus's chin went up. "I can assure you, she was with me the entire night—"

"How about when you were asleep?"

"The entire night!" Drusilicus repeated with anger. "I am an experienced wizard able to discern when someone leaves or enters my home, skills that you would be wise to learn."

"How about you and I going a few rounds?" Eddie threatened. "I'll show you exactly what I've mastered."

"Gentlemen," Marlowe said and rose from his chair. "This fighting will solve nothing. We need a plan to protect Eddie's family, and to make sure that his wife and her child are unharmed by this attack."

Drusilicus sat down warily and extracted several small vials from his jacket pocket. He placed them on a low coffee table.

"This potion will counter any effects caused by the venom. I brought these four for Marlowe to use in his tests against the drug. Take one home and have your wife drink it."

"Will it hurt the—"

Drusilicus lifted his hand to interrupt. "It shall in no way damage your unborn child. We must counter the venom. Under its influence, once night falls, your wife will do anything the vampire commands her."

Eddie shook his head. "This is like what happened the last time, when that warlock made her into a puppet. Why are they always picking on her?"

Marlowe observed Eddie sadly. "Because it is your weak spot, Eddie. You are powerful, but your family is mortal."

"You understand why we remain alone, lieutenant," Drusilicus added. "It should also be clear why being with someone who can defend themselves against dark forces might be a logical choice in a relationship."

Eddie glared at Drusilicus. "What are you gonna do if someone comes after her with a stake? Then what?"

Drusilicus appeared very calm. "Then I will lose her. People die every day, Eddie. It is tragic, but it is the way of the world. If you continue to walk the path, you will have many losses in your long life." Drusilicus reached down to pluck one of the small bottles and offered it to Eddie. "Make sure she drinks all of it and watch her to make sure she does."

"I trust my wife."

"Really?" Drusilicus stated as he leaned back in his chair. "Did she attempt to hide the vampire's mark?"

Eddie frowned at this. "Yeah, kinda…"

"The vampire can exert control from the first bite. This is the beginning of the process to enslave a victim."

Eddie shook his head, still mad but listening. "How does any of this work?"

Marlowe spoke up, "As early as the seventeenth century, there were men who suggested a pathogen caused vampirism."

"Never heard about this," Eddie said.

"Probably not. They were all burned at the stake for heresy," Marlowe concluded.

"The point is, lieutenant," Drusilicus said, "we do not want the venom to remain unchecked in your wife's system. I would recommend that you rebuild the charms around your threshold."

Eddie nodded. "I can do that."

Drusilicus sighed. "But you must tell the members of your family not to invite anyone into the house. A normal mortal can step in without an invitation, but it will keep a vampire out." He turned again to Marlowe. "Can we spare anyone to keep watch?"

Marlowe shook his head. "I don't see how. Many of the coven are away preparing for the Vernal Equinox."

"What's so important they have to prepare?" Eddie bickered. "I mean, we might have a war with the Lord of the Undead! Don't they realize some backup would be a good idea?"

"There are four major holidays for the coven, Eddie—the two equinoxes and the two solstices, called by many names. It is the time when magickal powers ebb and flow."

"For once, I must agree with the lieutenant," Drusilicus pointed out. "We must call our forces together. Do you think Ahbay or Eugenia might assist?"

"I will reach out to them," Marlowe said. "I think the best choice would be for you to go with Eddie and secure his house. I can stay here and see if your potion can free those under the influence of the drug."

Drusilicus's lips were a tight line. "Very well, but we must do so quickly. I do have appointments today."

Eddie stood up, and Drusilicus rose as well. "Shall we go?"

The pair headed to the door, and with a wave to Marlowe, they headed out into the bright, sunlit street.

"Does your wife like to tan?" Drusilicus asked as they crossed Central Park West.

Eddie frowned. "You've met my wife. She's pretty dark already."

"My apologies, that was badly put. Does she enjoy sunbathing?"

"What are you getting at?"

They stepped off the path and into the woods, both of them drawing their staffs as they did.

"I would recommend she sit outside in the sun for at least an hour. Combined with the potion, it will burn any of the venom from her body. It should be good for her Vitamin D production as well."

They stepped out from between a pair of trees in Teaneck, both vanishing the large sticks with a simple gesture.

"I'd like to invite you for lunch. I mean, if you got the time," Eddie said. He felt sheepish after almost coming to blows, and here Drusilicus was helping cure his wife and protect his family.

"That is very kind," Drusilicus said graciously. "As I recall, your mother's cooking is quite excellent."

"Yeah, she's got the touch." Eddie beamed as they stepped toward the tall white fence that backed the property, and the large tree where a demon had made threats while holding his son hostage the previous year.

We got through that then, and we'll get through this now.

He brought Drusilicus in the back door, right to the Berman's kitchen. The smell of homemade chicken soup wafted in the air, and Eddie saw a large pot of it heating on the stove.

Hearing the noise, Eleanor came in, dressed in a simple top and comfortable pants. She stopped, surprised to see Drusilicus.

"Oh! Mr. Grey!" Eleanor exclaimed.

"It's Greywacke, Madam, but please just call me Drew."

"Oh... yes!" Eleanor said, and drew close to Eddie. "I'm glad you're here. Cerise still isn't out of bed!"

"We got some medicine," Eddie disclosed. "That's why Drew came out with me."

She went to Drusilicus and took his hand, much to his surprise. "You know I never thanked you properly for helping me the way you did."

It surprised Eddie to see Drusilicus actually smile at his mother and say, "Seeing you looking so radiant is all the thanks I need."

Eleanor chuckled in reply.

Okay, now that was class.

"I have brought something for your daughter-in-law that should help."

"Yeah, let me take it up to her," Eddie suggested.

Drusilicus pulled the vial from his pocket and drew closer to whisper, "Watch her carefully and make sure she drinks it all." He stepped back and announced loudly, "I'll start on that request of yours." He nodded, tilted his head towards the outside, and headed for the door with a final, "We shall meet in the kitchen to discuss the precautions you need to take."

"What-all is he gonna do?" Eleanor wondered.

"He's going to do some protective spells."

She grimaced. "Why?"

"To protect the house from strangers."

"Ain't no strangers in this house," Eleanor stated. "And the only one acting weird is you, like when you came home last night."

Eddie frowned. "Momma, I got home at about 2:00 AM last night and fell asleep in the chair in the living room."

"Not that," she said, and patted his arm. "When you showed up about 8:00 and said you forgot your phone, and stood outside the back door."

Fear crossed Eddie's face. "I did *what?*"

She folded her arms in front of her chest. "You stood outside the back door and said you forgot your phone, your voice sounding all funny."

"Funny?"

"Yeah you were talkin' all gravelly. I finally told you to come on in and get your phone."

Eddie blinked. "And did I?"

"Yeah, you came in, went upstairs, then ran down and out without even a kiss to your wife who was watching television in the living room! Honestly, Eddie, if you are going to come all the way back home, the least you can do is give a minute of your time to your pregnant wife."

Eddie stood stock still, feeling as if a hole had opened up under his feet, his brain no longer working. Finally, he went into the backyard.

Drusilicus was in his blue robes with his staff in his hand. "That was quick. Did she drink all of it?"

Eddie stepped up to the blue-clad wizard and glanced around to make sure they were alone.

"My momma said I was at the house last night at 8:00 PM, just standing around outside saying I had forgotten my phone."

Drusilicus eyed him with suspicion, also looking around and keeping his voice low. "And were you?"

"No, I most definitely was not. My momma finally told me to get inside and get my phone."

Realization dawned on Drusilicus' face. "Thus making an invitation to enter to whoever it was."

"You think it was our vampire? Disguised as me?"

"At about 8:00 PM last night we were all meeting at Marlowe's for his grand confession. You and the sergeant joined us at about 8:10. I assume you didn't come home?"

"Damn straight."

Drusilicus nodded. "It was definitely our vampire. It would appear he can create illusions—"

"I thought only a wizard could do that…"

"Agreed, unless the vampire possessed a talisman that could help with such a transformation."

"That might be possible. Damn, I was so upset about Cerise, I forgot to tell Marlowe."

"Could you at least tell me what you are talking about?"

"A stolen Native-American magickal mask. One that can allow the user to appear to be anyone. The Mask of Missing-link or something," Eddie fumed.

Drusilicus frowned. "How do you know this?"

"I'd rather not reveal my sources," Eddie replied.

Drusilicus shook his head. "Even so, it would still require someone with magickal training. Even with a potent talisman, there are few who could use such a mask."

"Which points to Mordred?"

Drusilicus exhaled loudly. "Mordred had magickal training. If he could find an enchanted object or a talisman, it is quite possible he would know how to use it."

"I don't think the attack occurred when the fake me went inside, because my Momma said Cerise was in the living room."

"Small matter. Once the vampire is allowed inside the house, he may return any time he wishes."

"What should we do?"

"Did you give the potion to your wife?"

"Not yet," Eddie replied.

Drusilicus's jaw tightened. "I suggest you do that first. Then we need to instruct everyone in your house that no one is to be invited in, for any reason."

Eddie headed back into the house, up the stairs, and into the darkened bedroom. He threw open the curtain and let in the sun. This elicited another moan from Cerise, who pulled the sheets up over her eyes.

"Nooooo, let the expectant mother sleep," she begged.

"Honey, you gotta get up and come outside into the sun."

"I don't have to do anything!" she groaned from under the sheet.

"Honey, please. Someone attacked you last night."

She pulled down the sheet and her eyes bore into him. "Attacked me? Who would do that?"

He sat next to her on the bed. "A vampire."

She scrutinized him carefully.

"I have a potion that should help," Eddie said, and pulled the small vial from his pocket.

"Is that from your Mr. Marlowe?" she asked.

"Actually, Drusilicus made it. He promised it has no ill effects for you or the baby."

"How did a vampire get in?"

"Apparently, Momma invited me into the house last night."

She frowned, obviously confused by this statement.

"Momma invited someone in that she thought was me, but wasn't. It was a vampire. Once invited into a house, it can return any time it wishes."

Her expression grew very serious. She reached out and took the vial from Eddie, unscrewed the top, and drank the contents without hesitation. She handed back the empty bottle and told him, "Ugh, that tastes terrible."

Eddie exhaled with relief as he retrieved the vial, sealed it, and put it away. "Sorry, baby. What made you decide I was right?"

"I went to sleep with the window open last night. It was closed when you came here this morning, but the outer screen was up."

Eddie grew concerned. "As if it were closed from the outside?"

She nodded, fear etched on her face. "Are we safe here?"

"Drusilicus is reinforcing our threshold right now. I'm going to help him. We'll stick some serious vampire repellant into it."

"That's good. What should I do?"

"If you could come out back, get some sun, it should remove any of the remaining venom in your system."

She nodded. "I want to take a shower. I'll be down soon."

Eddie offered a hand to help his wife out of the bed. She toddled off to the bathroom, and he returned to the kitchen.

Eddie glanced out the window to see Drusilicus gesturing with his staff and mouthing words he could not hear.

"Is he okay out there?" Eleanor worried as she stirred the soup on the stove.

"He's just doin' what he can," Eddie stated. "Momma, I gotta talk to you."

She took the large spoon and placed it onto a porcelain holder on the stovetop, and turned to face her son.

"The guy you saw last night? He wasn't me."

She frowned at this. "Very funny. I saw that movie *Gaslight*. I ain't crazy."

Eddie put out his hand in a consoling gesture. "No, you aren't, Momma. You were fooled to think it was me, but he wasn't."

She eyed him suspiciously, but said nothing.

"You know the people I deal with, what they can do, Momma. One of them might have something that allows them to look like anyone they want."

"Why would anyone do that?" Eleanor wondered as she stared up at Eddie.

"To get invited into our home."

Eleanor considered this. "That's why you—or whoever that was—stood outside."

"They couldn't come in without an invitation."

She shook her head. "And that's what I did, when I told—whoever that was—to come in."

Eddie nodded seriously. "We have to be careful not to invite people into the house. A regular person and even a wizard can walk right in without an invitation, but a vampire can't."

"Why do this, hon?"

"A vampire bit Cerise last night."

Eleanor jumped at this. "What?"

"It's okay," Eddie soothed. "We gave her a potion, and she needs to get some sun, but she'll be okay."

"Oh, Eddie, the baby—"

"The baby's fine, too. You gotta tell the boys not to invite anyone into the house. Even if it is someone they know."

Drusilicus stepped into the kitchen. He was wearing his suit again, and held the pocket watch that was his staff as he returned it to his pocket.

"Any problems?" Eddie asked, moving to him.

"None. I also added to your threshold. Now, anyone who is not in their correct form will glow."

"Glow?"

"Yes, a lovely green color that should be quite obvious."

"We can do that?" Eddie wondered.

"Lieutenant," Drusilicus said with annoyance, "you have been a wizard for less than a year. Did you think you had mastered all the skills that sages have studied for multiple lifetimes?"

Eleanor piped up. "Mr. Greywacke, you talk nice to my Eddie. You don't have to hold down a job and learn this stuff in your spare time. So, you just back off."

Eddie folded his arms and peered smugly at Drusilicus.

"Forgive my lack of manners, Mrs. Berman," he said to Eleanor.

"Thass all right, but I don't want no one talkin' down to my Eddie."

Drusilicus took a deep breath and plastered on a smile, then turned to Eddie. "How did it go with the potion?"

"She drank it. I watched her."

"Good. If she can come out into the sun, I will take my leave."

Eddie glanced up the stairs with concern. "Let me check on her."

He bounded up the stairs and went into the bedroom where he could hear the shower running. He opened the door to the bathroom and peeked in.

Cerise lay unmoving on the floor of the glass-enclosed shower. In one step, Eddie was in the shower, staff in hand, and his robes in place. A dome of protective light flashed around the room. He knelt next to her, his staff clattered to the floor and he rolled her onto her back.

"Cerise, Cerise, baby," he shouted.

Her eyes fluttered open. "Eddie?"

He breathed a sigh of relief. "Baby, what happened?"

"I felt faint, I guess," she said weakly.

He reached over and shut off the water that had soaked his robes. "Can you stand?"

She nodded, and he carefully got up and helped her to her feet. He helped her back into the bedroom, and once she was sitting on the bed, he held out his hand. His staff lifted off the floor and flew to him. He made a small circle, and a dress flew to his wife and covered her like a second skin.

"Wait right here," Eddie told her. He went to the back stairs and yelled down, "Drusilicus!"

The dark-haired man took the stairs two at a time. "What is it?"

"She fainted. It might be the potion," Eddie snapped. He led Drusilicus into the bedroom and his houseguest fell to one knee in front of Cerise.

"Madam, are you all right?" Drusilicus asked.

"I felt a little faint, that's all," she said, holding her belly with both hands.

Drusilicus held out his pocket watch, and it transformed into his staff. There was a blue light at the top of it that bathed Cerise with its glow. This made Cerise lie back as the beams of light lifted her prone body into the air.

"What is it?" Eddie demanded.

"I am not sure. It appears my potion did not purge the venom from her blood!"

"Could your *girlfriend* have switched it?" Eddie snapped.

"She is not my girlfriend—but I am a bit surprised."

Eddie stared at the floor, trying to keep his panic in check. "What should we do?"

Drusilicus' jaw went hard. "I would suggest you call for an ambulance."

FOURTEEN

Eddie accompanied the ambulance to the hospital. Drusilicus headed out before the EMTs arrived, claiming that he needed to work on his venom antidote.

It was a brief ride to Holy Name Hospital, a huge, sprawling facility with a multi-level parking lot built up on top of a hill near the center of town.

Eddie felt reassured as they went inside, as the logo for the medical center was a stylized cross. He figured if there was one place, other than a church, that might keep vampires away, this was it.

The orderlies wheeled Cerise in. She had regained consciousness after Drusilicus released his spell. Eddie was in a daze as he went into the waiting room, unsure of what he should do.

He sat, picked up a magazine, opened it, and saw nothing on the page as questions kept running around his mind.

Had a vampire used the stolen Native American mask? It could explain why Strix got staked in the Springbanks Arch—his attacker could have appeared as someone he knew. Daniel sent the team into a trap, but swore the information had come from a trusted source. Could his source have been the shape-shifting vampire? Lysandra mentioned a trusted friend led her into a trap of her own. Again, this suggested a shape-shifter. And finally, his momma saw someone she was sure was Eddie and invited him in, and that gave the vampire the opportunity to attack Cerise.

His head was swimming. He couldn't quite figure out what any of it had to do with Mordred. Was Mordred using the mask? He could have been in New York since this began, sending the wizards in all the wrong directions.

Eddie heard a muffled voice repeating his name. He reached into his pocket to extract the small round mirror he kept on him at all times.

Marlowe's face was in the mirror and he called out, "Eddie Berman," over and over.

Eddie stood and noticed the stares. "New kind of phone," he said in way of explanation. "Really small."

The nurse behind the desk cleared her throat loudly. "No cell phones in the waiting room."

Eddie nodded and headed outside through the glass doors. He made sure no one was close, then waved his hand over the mirror. Using his will, he reached out to his mentor.

"Eddie! By Zoroaster, Drusilicus just told me about your wife. Will she be all right?"

"I dunno, they're running tests on her right now," Eddie said. "Did Drusilicus tell you that a fake me showed up last night?"

"Yes, and that would explain how the vampire gained entrance. Do you think that was when your wife was bitten?"

"No, the guy was only in the house for a minute or two, and Cerise was downstairs at the time. I think the attack was later, using our bedroom window. Whoever it was left that warning note I told you about."

"So you think the attack was later in the night?"

Eddie shook his head. "Yes. I fell asleep in the chair downstairs, spent the night there."

"Then I must point out another theory. Perhaps the vampire was seeking to attack *you*, Eddie."

Eddie frowned. He had not considered this at all, as he'd been so worried about Cerise. "Then why bite my wife?"

"It was a second best decision, but the only choice after the vampire gained access to your house. Think about it Eddie, the warning note would have much more meaning, if you had woken with bites on your neck."

Eddie paused, taking this in. If Eddie had been bitten, he would be the one controlled by a vampire. That would have made things much worse. Eddie shook his head, collecting his thoughts. "I forgot to tell you—a vampire has a Native American mask that allows him to change into anyone."

"Yes, the Mask of *Misignwah*. Drusilicus mentioned such an artifact, and I am aware of it. I thought it was in the possession of Stone Face."

"He's the one who told me about it."

Marlowe stared through the mirror. "You met *Misinghalikun*?"

"Met him? I smoked with him," Eddie explained. "He pulled me to his mountaintop while I was trying to get home."

"That sounds like something he could do. Eddie, why didn't you tell me this?"

"He asked me not to mention our meeting."

"Ah!" Marlowe replied, and nodded his head. "I see. Well, this does indeed change the situation."

"How so?"

"Although vampires can change form, to bats and mist, they cannot alter their faces or create complex magickal illusions. Even with an enchanted item, physical transformation takes a lot of energy, despite wizard skills or a talisman like the mask. As you know, creating illusions is much easier."

Eddie considered this. He had seen Marlowe create very involved illusions, like making himself appear as a doctor, bringing a patient out of a hospital to an ambulance. In reality, he had merely levitated one of their wounded associates to the back seat of Eddie's car. But to all who watched, the powerful projection Marlowe created had deceived them.

"Could the Drakula, or Mordred, have been here in New York longer than we thought? I mean, if he could disguise himself so well?"

"We know someone who is adept with many talismans. Drusilicus' former apprentice, Caleb."

Eddie sighed in frustration. "That whack job? He was nothing but trouble."

Marlowe shrugged. "Still, if you wish answers, he might be the correct one to speak with."

"I'm staying here until I know about Cerise, then I'll get into New York and see about questioning Caleb."

"As you wish! I hope she will be well, Eddie."

"You and me both," Eddie said. The glass on the mirror silvered over as Marlowe faded away. He returned it to his pocket, extracted his cell phone, and hit the number for his partner.

"Vasquez."

"Luis, some things have happened and I need to bring you up to speed."

Eddie went into the full story, ending with the trip to the hospital.

"*Madre de Dios*," Luis muttered several times as Eddie unfolded the tale. At the end, his partner inquired, "What can I do to help?"

"I'm glad you asked. You remember when the Great Evil thing went down, that Caleb guy, the one with the talismans?"

"Sure do. Caleb Heinz, like the ketchup."

"I need you to find out if he's still in town, and if so, where."

"I can do that."

"Good. Last time we checked he was working at Magickal Cherub, that magic supply store downtown."

"Yeah, the place with all the incense. The one time we questioned him, he had an apartment down in Alphabet City," Luis said, referring to a neighborhood in downtown Manhattan in the East Village. "I'll see what comes up. He had a rap sheet, so I should be able to locate him."

"Thanks, Luis."

"The vampires are gettin' personal now. I mean, attacking your wife like that."

"So it would seem," Eddie said, feeling the anger he had barely contained. "Which means that I am going to kick their pale asses."

"That should make it very personal for them as well."

"Catch you later, Luis."

"Adios, mi compadre."

Eddie hung up the phone and went back inside to the waiting room, feeling more frustrated than he believed possible. Here he was, a wizard with amazing abilities he was finally getting confident using, and he was helpless to protect his wife or his home. He truly understood why Marlowe and many other wizards he met were so solitary.

This was the second time he'd put his family in danger because he had embraced the path of the wise. If he had no powers, the evil forces wouldn't bother with him, and his family would be safe. Wouldn't it make more sense to just give it up, pass his staff to someone more worthy? An unmarried person could devote themselves totally to the calling of the wizard.

When Drusilicus gained the staff of the element of water, he had passed his former staff to Caleb, his apprentice, who rejected it in the end. That staff was waiting for a new master, and neither Drusilicus nor Marlowe had chosen a worthy recipient.

Eddie bolted up out of his seat with superhuman speed, startling the people in the waiting room.

He muttered apologies and headed for the door.

He had believed that the Drakula started all of this a short time ago, but the search for the ancient papyrus and the planning to find it had to have taken more time: months, even possibly years.

He pulled out the mirror and chanted 'Drusilicus' over and over.

It took a minute, but the glass silvered over and Drusilicus' face appeared, dressed in his blue robes and with his staff in hand. He appeared to be looking into a much larger mirror than the one Eddie held.

"Do you know anything, Eddie? Is she all right?" the man said, concern written on his face.

Eddie considered that although Drusilicus could be a pompous pain, he always treated Eddie's family with respect and now, genuine concern.

"I don't know anything yet, but I need to know about your staff."

Drusilicus was surprised. "My staff? Whatever for?"

He rotated the stick in his hand, looking it up and down.

"Not that staff."

"You're not making sense, lieutenant."

"Your old staff, where is it?"

"Whatever do you mean?"

"Where is your former staff now? I know Caleb rejected it, but what happened to it? Does Marlowe have it?"

"No, I do," Drusilicus responded haughtily. "Stored in a closet."

Eddie set his jaw. "Get it."

Drusilicus looked as if he was going to say something snippy, but seeing the look on Eddie's face, thought better of it. "Very well. I will call you back."

The image faded, and Eddie was staring at himself again. He slipped the mirror into his pocket and paced, again thinking through the timeline.

Mind-Blo had only been a problem for about six months, and Orfeo had used Central Park as his base of operations. Why? Eddie knew it was a place of power, and if there was a wizard involved, could they be hiding in one of the wizard's arches?

Then again, there was the surprising appearance of Vasant within the Springbanks Arch. She just showed up with an excuse that she'd been a hermit for a hundred years?

There were far too many possibilities, and it was all a tangled mess.

Eddie stepped back into the waiting area but remained near the door in case Drusilicus called back.

A doctor entered, dressed in scrubs and a white lab coat. He was a short Indian man with straight hair and brown skin. He gazed through horned-rimmed glasses and called out, "Berman?"

Eddie ran over. "I'm Eddie Berman, doctor."

He glanced up at Eddie and led him to a corner for privacy. "Ah, yes. I am Doctor Ramsen."

Eddie offered his hand to shake. "I appreciate your help, doctor. What's the story?"

He smiled as he shook Eddie's hand. "I am the staff gynecologist. There is nothing to worry about. Your wife simply has a case of pregnancy anemia."

"Anemia?" Eddie repeated.

"This is not uncommon with a pregnancy after the age of thirty-five. Your wife's body is just having a little trouble producing enough blood for herself and the baby. We have her on an IV of vitamins and iron that should help her along."

"And the baby?"

He considered the chart a second time. "She is fine."

"She?" Eddie gasped as unexpected tears stung his eyes.

"Yes, definitely a she. We did an ultrasound, which she didn't like. She kicked up a storm."

"I'm having a little girl," Eddie spoke in awe.

"Yes, congratulations," he said very matter-of-factly. "Now, we will keep her overnight for observation, just in case we might have to consider a transfusion. I was told your wife works in this hospital, is that correct?"

"Yes, doctor, she's a surgical nurse," Eddie said.

"That would explain why I have not met her. She is going to have to rest for the remainder of the pregnancy, get off her feet—"

The man went on, but Eddie didn't hear. They were going to have a little girl, and his heart swelled almost to the bursting point. How had he thought anything was more important than this? New York City could go to hell, he didn't care. He could throw away his staff, and it wouldn't matter.

The only important thing was this new life he and Cerise were bringing into the world.

"Can I see my wife?" Eddie blurted, interrupting the doctor mid-sentence.

The man considered it for only a moment. "She is awake, I don't see why not."

He quickly led Eddie into a large emergency room ward. Curtains set individual areas off, creating personalized alcoves in the large space. Apparently, they had not yet assigned Cerise a room.

The doctor nodded and went back outside the curtain as Eddie stepped to his wife.

Cerise smiled up at him from the bed. "Did he tell you?"

Eddie couldn't stop smiling. "A little girl."

"So much for the surprise. Are you disappointed?"

"Of course not," Eddie gushed. "But you need to take care of yourself."

"I'm feeling better. I guess it took a little while for that potion of Mr. Greywacke's to take effect."

I hope that's all it was.

"My only concern is you. We have to be careful. I'm fighting some bad people now."

Cerise sighed. "I thought after what happened months ago we would have some peace."

"I hoped so, too." Eddie replied. "But the vampires had a different idea."

"Are the boys safe?" Cerise worried.

"I think so. Drusilicus put up barriers around our house to protect them and Momma."

She nodded sadly. "Is this the way of things now? Every few months you have to risk your life to fight against some dark creature?"

Eddie met her eyes. "You say the word, and I give all of this up tomorrow."

She touched his face. "I wish I could, Eddie. Just to have a normal life for us and our kids." Her eyes were wet. "But you make a difference for so many other people."

Eddie took her hands again. "Baby, you are always my first commitment."

She exhaled heavily. "Then go. Stop this bad guy and bring my big, black man home safe to me."

Eddie smiled. That phrase was their own private joke, as Eddie was not all that big, and his skin was a much lighter shade than his wife's. "Get some rest." He leaned forward and kissed her head.

"I will," she said and rubbed her belly. "I'll take care of our little girl. Go make sure there is a world to bring her up in."

Eddie rose, and with only a quick look back, headed out of the curtained area into the lobby and out the door.

He had made up his mind.

As he stepped outside, he heard a voice calling to him. He quickly retrieved the mirror and saw Drusilicus. "Drusilicus, do you have it?"

Drusilicus gave the impression he had tasted something unpleasant. "No, lieutenant. It would appear my former staff is missing."

"Can you track it? Are you still the master of it?"

"It would seem it has a new master, and I have lost my connection."

Eddie shook his head.

Drusilicus went on. "I am sure you have every call for recriminations, but I want to assure you—"

"That won't help," Eddie interrupted. "Tell me, who could give it to a new wizard?"

Drusilicus frowned in thought. "Well me, of course. Then I suppose Marlowe as coven master…"

"How about Caleb?"

Drusilicus was aghast. "It… might be possible."

"Seems the best place to start. I'm coming into Manhattan to have a talk with your former apprentice. I want you to think about something."

"What is it?"

"Who's been in your house who could've stolen that staff?"

A muscle in his jaw twitched, but Drusilicus said nothing as they both knew the answer.

"I'll catch you later," Eddie said, and with a gesture the image in the glass disappeared.

Eddie made his way down the hill and wandered a few short blocks to the Teaneck Creek Conservatory which supplied a tree-filled enclosure where Eddie could transport himself instantly to Central Park.

Once in New York, Eddie headed for the precinct with a new sense of urgency. He needed to talk to Caleb, who was skilled as an enchanter, a person who could use talismans to create magick. Caleb could craft talismans himself with the skill of a trained jeweler. He had once created a talisman of invisibility to follow Eddie around. When he ran into a protective spell of Marlowe's, the charm had ceased to work.

The young man had a serious love of money and would probably design talismans for anyone who offered him enough. When he rejected the staff, had he kept the ability to gift it to another? If so, he was the prime suspect on the magickal side of the entire endeavor. A vampire like Mordred with mystical knowledge only needed a staff to do anything a wizard could, and Lysandra had said that the vampire woman, Selene, also possessed a working knowledge of magick.

He went into the precinct and entered the bullpen. It surprised him to see his partner at his desk, leaning back in his chair and staring at the computer screen.

Luis lifted his eyes from the screen. "How's Cerise?"

"Okay," Eddie said as he sat in the chair next to Luis' desk. "Doctor says it's pregnancy anemia."

Luis nodded. "Anemia? Isn't that what you get when a vampire attacks you?"

"Exactly. They're keeping her overnight, but she's going to be okay. They did an ultrasound, and the doctor didn't know not to tell me."

"And?"

"It's a girl."

"Oh, man, that is such good news!" Luis gushed, with a huge grin. "You're gonna love it. Little girls are the best! They ain't always punching each other like boys."

"I'm still trying to get my head around it," Eddie said.

"You gonna love it, man. But—is Cerise safe in the hospital?"

"I hope so."

"Might be a good idea to send one of the wizard posse to look out for her once it gets dark."

Eddie nodded but couldn't think of anyone he could trust to send other than Marlowe or Drusilicus.

Luis turned to his computer. "I think I got your man."

"Caleb?" Eddie replied as he peeked over Luis's shoulder.

"Yup, he got a business license and rented a space downtown on Sullivan Street in the Village."

"Rented a space? Does he sell those talismans he makes?"

Luis shrugged. "He's listed as a 'Reader and Advisor' and the license claims that it is for entertainment purposes only."

"That's an out that phony psychics have been using for years."

Luis shrugged. "Yeah, but with those toys of his, maybe he can really see the future."

"The question is, where did he get the money to rent the space? How long has it been open?"

"Two months."

"If he made a large financial score, that fits into my timeline."

"How could that *idiota* make a big score?" Luis wondered.

Eddie leaned close to his partner's ear. "By selling his staff to a vampire."

Luis straightened his chair upright and stared at Eddie. "You kiddin' me? You think he would do that?"

"Now you know why I want to talk to him."

"His place doesn't open until 4:00 PM."

"You got a home address?"

"Same as last time."

"Then we go now," Eddie said.

"I'll drive," Luis responded, and stood up.

"We need to bring these," Eddie said, pulling the UV light flashlights out of his desk drawer. "We need to get batteries."

"What do they take?" Luis asked as Eddie handed him the light, and he gazed at the circle of tiny LEDs behind the glass.

"Three triple As."

"I got plenty of those," Luis said, and opened his own desk drawer to reveal a box of about fifty of the small batteries.

Eddie popped the batteries into the flashlight and flicked it on. In the bright sunlight coming through the windows, he couldn't really see anything. He flipped it over to see that the bulbs had all lit up.

Luis spoke in low tones. "I don't think this is strong enough to smoke one of them."

"It certainly isn't the output of the one Beverly had. But it should surprise the hell out of them."

Luis grinned. "I'll take that. Something to make it a fair fight."

"Next time we're at Marlowe's, we'll get you something like this ring," Eddie said, holding up the large silver ring in a clenched fist.

"Any ideas what would work?" Luis asked.

"Rusty has a water gun full of garlic and holy water."

Luis considered this as they headed out and across the street to pick up their usual unmarked police vehicle.

They parked on Eighth Street and Avenue C and headed down the block. They went into a tenement building, catching the door as someone came out. The stairs reflected a more auspicious past.

The landings had beautiful tile work in delicate patterns that were now dark with grime and dirt.

Upon reaching the fifth floor, Luis was panting like a racehorse, but Eddie had the energy of a wizard and wasn't even breaking a sweat. He pounded on the appropriate door, recalling it from their previous visit months earlier.

"Who's there?" a voice responded.

"NYPD," Eddie announced.

The glass eye of the peephole glinted in the light. The occupant had seen them.

"Go away," the male voice insisted.

Luis stepped forward, still panting. "You wanna play it this way, my man? You know my partner can just blow your door off its hinges, right?"

The door made several clicks and rattles and slowly opened to reveal Caleb, dressed all in black. He had shiny metal piercings around his eyebrows, ears, nose, and even his lower lip. He wore a black shirt with long sleeves. His hair reached to his shoulders and was unpleasantly black and oily.

"I thought I never had to see you again," he complained, glancing at Luis. "Any of you!"

Eddie pushed his way through the door and into the apartment. "Yeah, I'd prefer that too, but you keep doing stupid."

"Real stupid, man," Luis agreed.

Caleb's face turned red. "What the hell do you want?"

Eddie turned and stared at the young man. "Where is the staff?"

Caleb blanched for a moment. "Is that all? Man, you guys are really barking up the wrong tree."

"Why don't you enlighten us?" Luis growled.

"We know about your new business reading tarot cards, or whatever," Eddie snapped. "Where did you get the money to start it?"

Caleb appeared honestly confused. "What are you talking about? I started it with the cash that lady gave me for surrendering the staff."

Luis glanced at Eddie, confused as well. "What?"

"I would think you guys would know this shit! I mean, I didn't, but I was a freakin' apprentice with a master who had a stick up his ass."

Luis leaned close to Eddie. "If he's talking about Drusilicus, I can't argue with that."

"Sh!" Eddie replied. "Go on."

"Look, this lady—tall, nice rack— shows up here, right? She shows up one night, claims Marlowe sent her, and she's holding the staff. Then, she tells me this whole story about money owed to me as an apprentice and wants to give it to me but I gotta give her the staff for safekeeping or inventory, or some damn thing. I agree, she speaks some weird words, and I repeat them after her. Then, she takes off and gives me a paper bag. The friggin' bag had twenty G's in it."

Eddie's jaw dropped open. "The bag had twenty-thousand dollars in it?"

"Yeah," Caleb gushed. "Can you beat that? She says it's a consolation prize given to apprentices who return their staff. So, I take the money and set up a little place on Sullivan Street. It makes me legit. I can still sell talismans to my high-end customers, but I also do readings. I got an emerald imbued with ancient runes that gives me peeks into people's future. Man, I am *so* good. I put out the stupid tarot cards, and while the mark—I mean customer—looks them over, I rub this emerald and I can see what will happen to them *every* time."

"Describe the woman," Eddie ordered.

Caleb stared at Eddie in confusion. "What are you talking about? The tall babe with the full lips and the nice tits. Come on, you must have seen her."

"Give us a little more to go on," Luis insisted.

Caleb shut his eyes, trying to remember. "Okay, okay. She had dark hair down past her shoulders. An expensive dress with pretty high-end jewelry, no tats or piercings. Dark eyes and an air about her, y'know, like Drusilicus, where he thinks his shit doesn't stink."

"Keep goin'," Eddie cajoled.

"That's about it. Look, I gotta take a shower and go open my place. Are we done?"

"Yeah, we got it," Eddie said, and turned for the door, then stopped. "Do you still have a talisman for protection?"

Caleb frowned. "I got a sixth pentacle of Jupiter, to protect the wearer from all earthly danger. I got one I could let go for a thousand."

"I just need to borrow it for a few days," Eddie explained.

"Okay, so five hundred."

Luis stepped forward. "How about you loan it for free, and I don't rearrange your face?"

"Okay, okay!" Caleb whined. "I gotta find it."

Caleb went through a curtain into the bedroom, and Luis drew close to Eddie. "Whaddya want this for?"

"I want something to protect Cerise."

"From earthly danger?"

"Or vampires," Eddie asserted.

Caleb came back into the room and held out a chain. On the end of it was a bright-silver disk. The amulet had crossed lines in the center, Hebrew words within those lines and letters from a mystical alphabet along a circle on the outside.

Caleb held it out, and as Eddie reached for it, he pulled it back. "Since they didn't train you with talismans, I'll give you the rundown."

"Very kind of you," Eddie said sarcastically.

"You can carry it around, like in your pocket, and it won't do anything. It only works when you put it on over your head. And, like any magick, you gotta focus your mind—"

"Will and intent," Eddie responded.

"Yeah, that. Once you do, it'll work."

"Got it."

Caleb handed the chain and the amulet to Eddie, who pocketed them.

"When will you bring it back?" Caleb demanded.

"As soon as I can."

"Make sure you do," he grumbled.

"I will. Don't leave town."

"Where the hell would I go?" Caleb responded.

Eddie and Luis stepped into the hall, and Caleb slammed the door behind them.

"Do you think the woman was Lysandra?" Luis asked. "This lady that got the staff?"

"The woman he described could be Selene. She's a vampire and Mordred's consort. But it would mean she got to NYC months ago, and then flew back to London to ride over with the coffin."

"Either way, it don't sound good," Luis lamented.

FIFTEEN

Luis drove back uptown as Eddie pulled out his small mirror to communicate with Marlowe.

He only had to call the old wizard's name a few times before his face appeared in the looking glass.

"What is it, Eddie?"

"They tricked Caleb into transferring the power of his staff to either Selene or Lysandra."

"What? That is outrageous!"

"It might not be the kid's fault. She gave him a cock-and-bull story about how she was doing it for you and she offered him money."

Marlowe's face reddened. "To think that wizards would resort to bribes for someone to relinquish a staff!"

Eddie used a calming tone. "Look, the kid is young—a pretty woman offered him cash, and I am sure she used her vampire glamour on him."

"If what you say is correct, a vampire now has a wizard's staff." Marlowe sounded worried.

"The scary part is that once she received the staff, she can transfer its power to Mordred or anyone she wanted."

"And Mordred has the training to know how to use it. I am afraid I may have an inkling as to when Mordred might strike. According to my reading of the signs—"

"What did you use, tea leaves?"

Marlowe sighed, flustered. "Eddie, you know I am well versed in several forms of divination."

"Okay, when?"

"I believe he shall use the power of the equinox, when the balance between light and darkness—"

Eddie interrupted, "Yeah, I know, when good and evil are equal and the world could slip into chaos, and yadda-yadda-yadda."

"You do not seem to take this seriously."

"Marlowe, the equinox is on March twenty-first. That's two days from now, right?"

"Yes, Eddie, I believe you are correct."

"Then you gotta call every wizard you know, contact the coven, and get them to pull a force together to help if he unleashes something."

"I will get right on it, Eddie," Marlowe said and faded away.

Eddie stared at his own reflection in the mirror, then put it away. He pulled out his cell phone and called Drusilicus.

"Really, lieutenant," Drusilicus grumbled as he answered. "I hope you realize I prefer a mirror."

"From what you guys have told me in the past, some wizards can listen in on mirrors," Eddie said. "I have a question. Is there a potion that can undo a shapeshifter, even one using a talisman?"

"Undo?"

"Yes, force them back to their authentic form?"

Drusilicus paused as he contemplated this idea. "It might be possible, lieutenant. I assume you wouldn't want one that had to be ingested?"

"No, something sprayed into the air would be best. Marlowe is going to have a meeting tonight. Can you have something by then?"

There was another pause, and then a sharp intake of breath. "By tonight? You must be joking, lieutenant!"

Eddie tried to be conciliatory. "Please, Drusilicus. We might have a spy in our midst. Caleb relinquished your old staff to a female vampire, and she has a talisman that allows her to appear to be anyone she wants."

"Caleb did what?" Drusilicus bellowed.

"Look, that isn't important now. I can tell you about it later. If you have anything that can disrupt a shape-changing spell, we might catch the spy tonight!"

Annoyance crept into his voice. "I shall have to look at my Grimoire to see what I can find."

"Thanks, Drew."

"You always ask the impossible, lieutenant," he added indignantly as he ended the phone call.

Eddie wanted to say something snide in return, but since Drusilicus had ended the call anyway, he thought better of it.

Luis had been quiet during both conversations. There was little he could add and less that he could recommend. "This whole thing's gonna go down in two days?"

"Looks like it," Eddie said as they turned up Central Park West.

"You think this lady can become other people and is spying on you?"

"As well as Marlowe and the other wizards. They had to have someone in Drusilicus's house. How else did the woman steal the staff and take it to Caleb?"

"Wait, if they had the staff, why did they need Caleb at all?"

"Because a spell was needed to assign the power of the staff to the vampire. Anyone might get ahold of a staff, but there are magickal spells needed to grant the user its power."

"That was what Caleb was talking about when he said the woman had him repeat a bunch of strange words."

"Exactly. That was the spell that gave her the use of the staff's magick."

Luis turned the car down the transverse road and soon pulled into the lot across from the precinct.

Eddie sat staring out the front windshield. "Two days, and I don't know what to do."

"You seem pretty good with your own staff these days."

"Apparently, not good enough. I don't have any idea how we stop these vampires or what they are working on behind the scenes. Hell, we haven't even seen this Mordred guy yet."

"What's gonna happen in two days?"

Eddie contemplated this. "I don't know. End of the world, dead rising—bad stuff."

"I ain't no wizard, but I *am* a detective, and I think that is the first thing you need to find out."

Eddie drew a deep breath. "Then we have to talk to Marlowe."

The pair of them exited the unmarked police car and started up the sidewalk of the transverse road toward Marlowe's townhouse.

As they passed under the tunnel for the west roadway that ran overhead, Luis held up his UV flashlight.

"It's still daylight, Luis. There are no vampires under here right now."

"You can't be too careful," he responded, but slipped the flashlight back into the pocket of his sports coat.

They crossed Central Park West and down one block to 85th Street and soon were knocking on Marlowe's door.

Marlowe waved them in, a hand mirror in his grip. He was in the middle of an animated conversation with a gray-haired and bearded wizard.

"He looks busy," Luis muttered to Eddie.

"Let's get some coffee. He'll talk to us once he's off the mirror."

As they strode to the breakfast room, he could hear Marlowe's voice rise in frustration as he spat out a flurry of odd words.

The breakfast room table was covered with different papers, parchment, several large moldy books, and a collection of pendulums, crystal balls of various sizes, an open box of hand-carved runes, and several decks of tarot cards.

The magickal tea trolley was empty.

"Now what do we do?" Luis moaned.

"I got this," Eddie said and looked up at the ceiling to yell. "Wraith?"

"Yes, sir," a voice said from behind them.

Luis started, his hand going to his chest. "Don' do that, man. You scared the shit out of me."

Wraith—Marlowe's ghostly major-domo— was mostly transparent, dressed in his morning suit and striped pants from a bygone era. He stared grimly at the two detectives.

"Sorry to bother you, Wraith," Eddie told him.

"I am happy to serve, Wizard Riftstone," Wraith replied, sounding as if having Eddie bother him was the saddest part of his afterlife.

Eddie went on. "We were hoping to get some coffee. Could you refill the trolley?"

"Of course, sir. Will that be all?"

Luis was still eying the ghost with annoyance. "You got any of those little cakes? I really like those."

"Very well," Wraith lamented and pushed the cart to a nearby doorway. The door opened and the trolley and Wraith went through it.

"Man, that guy creeps me out," Luis said as he examined the table and all the paraphernalia laid out over it. "Looks like Marlowe's been busy."

"Yeah, he's trying to find a papyrus," Eddie said.

The door opened and the trolley, now laden with its usual coffee and tea pots, a creamer and sugar bowl, rolled into the room. There were now several plates of different pastries as well.

It rolled to a stop, and the door closed with no sign of Wraith.

"So sorry." Marlowe entered, obviously flustered. "It's just wizards can be so... difficult. Makes me wonder why I agreed to be coven master at all. Let some other poor fool have the job! Tea, please."

A pot flew up to pour a cup, and it hovered delicately over to Marlowe, who took a sip.

Eddie noted the collection of items on the table, with barely any room to place their cups. "You've been working on finding the papyrus that Mordred might be looking for?"

Marlowe brightened. "Indeed, I have—and I can claim success."

"Success?"

Marlowe slid papers aside on the table and lifted a folded pack. It was brown and had lines of crisscrossing fibers woven together, looking more like cloth than paper. "I found it."

Marlowe carefully unfolded the bundle. Although old and brown, it appeared to still be flexible and seemed undamaged. Elaborate lines and symbols in both black and red ink covered the page. "I was in possession of the papyrus the entire time!"

Luis frowned. "When you said a papyrus, I thought it was— like—rolled up on sticks. How old is that thing?"

"Almost three thousand years. This is one of the best-preserved papyri from the Middle Kingdom." Marlowe sipped his tea thoughtfully.

"What is that writing? It certainly isn't hiro... hero... um... those pictures like on the pyramids," Luis attempted.

"I believe hieroglyphics is the word you are struggling for, sergeant," Marlowe explained. "Yes, this is hieratic writing, a hieroglyphic script. The priests and holy men used it. They also imbued this papyrus with magickal energies that allow it to remain undamaged until it was destined to be used."

Eddie acknowledged the clutter on the table. "I'm surprised you didn't know you had it."

"I can only surmise that it was in my possession when Mordred was my apprentice, and only recently did he realize its true power."

Eddie nodded. "Which is what led to this whole 'come to New York and fulfill the 'prophecy' thing?"

"Yes," Marlowe agreed. "But why now, I wonder?"

"How did you get it? I mean, you were in England when you were Merlin. When were you in Egypt?"

"Eddie, I traveled the world for years before and after I met Uther Pendragon. I collected artifacts from many civilizations, but I was unaware that this was the original Papyrus of Sekhmet until I saw it again tonight."

Luis spoke up, "You'd better get that in a safe or something."

"The papyrus is perfectly secure in my home. No vampire, except Daniel, could come in without my permission."

"Can we hide it in that inter-dimensional room where you keep your potions?" Eddie questioned.

"That was where I found it, Eddie."

"Why don't you burn it or something?" Luis suggested. "Then the vampires got nothing to come for."

"They imbued it with great magick, sergeant. Look at it. It is in perfect condition for an ancient papyrus. Until it performs its grim purpose, it is quite indestructible."

"Then what can we do?" Eddie insisted.

"I believe I can put several magical spells on it that will make it unable to be touched by a vampire, even one who might possess the power of a staff."

"Getting a staff was necessary to activate it?" Luis wondered.

Eddie considered this. "How did they find out there was a staff without an owner? That has to be rare, right?"

Marlowe stroked his beard. "Usually, when a wizard passes on, his apprentice is initiated by the coven fairly quickly. In fact, you were there when Caleb acquired the Staff of Greywacke. Since Caleb rejected it and we brought no apprentice forward, Drusilicus kept the staff. I can only surmise that someone saw it in his house, or that Drusilicus told them it was there."

"Or maybe Drew-silly-ass just gave it to them," Luis snorted.

Eddie spoke up. "Look, Drew can be a pain, but I don't think he'd do that. I'm more concerned that he's sleeping with Lysandra. I wouldn't put it past her to go skulking around the house when Drew's asleep."

"I am still not happy about such an arrangement," Marlowe said. "Do you think she has used her glamour on Drusilicus?"

"Who knows?" Eddie noted. "So, how did you find the papyrus?"

"I located it by wearing the Hat of Remembrance."

Marlowe was speaking of a strange hat that he kept in his room full of ingredients he used in his potions. The extra-dimensional storage room was the size of a football field, with shelf after shelf of jars, vials, and containers of arcane items. This room only appeared in Marlowe's basement when conjured by the old wizard. The hat allowed him to remember the location of each item, and Eddie had used it to help with his own recollections when he had fought a warlock months earlier.

Luis nodded. "Did you guys find that big-ass box?"

"Box?"

"That big coffin you tol' me about," Luis reported.

"I am afraid with that task, I have had little luck," Marlowe lamented. "It could be almost anywhere, as New York is a nexus with portals that traverse dimensions into alternate realities that reside next to our own."

Luis regarded Marlowe and Eddie. "Do I need to understand what he just said?"

"I never have," Eddie exclaimed, "and he took me to one of them."

"Good," the big man said, as he folded his arms stubbornly.

"Are there any other places that it might be possible to hide something?" Eddie asked. "I mean, other than those tunnels under the park where you and I almost got lost."

Marlowe considered this. "Well, there are the arches."

"The arches?" Luis pondered. "Yeah, Eddie tol' me they named the arches after wizards and that you guys have, like, apartments or somethin' in them."

"That is… mostly correct," Marlowe replied.

Eddie held a finger up to his mouth as he thought about this. "Each wizard has a space in the arch that bears their name and only that wizard can use it, right?"

Marlowe put the papyrus onto the pile of parchments on the table. "Yes, every wizard may enter the hidden chamber within his or her arch."

"Does Eddie got one of those?" Luis said, his face brightening.

"Oh yes, Riftstone used to reside in his arch," Marlowe reassured.

Eddie nodded. "Is this chamber protected from someone trying to find it, y'know, through divination?"

Marlowe sat up straighter. "Indeed, it would be. Such a place is a *Sanctum Sanctorum* for the wizard. Soon after they built the park, many of the wizards lived within their arch."

"So why ain't there a Marlowe Arch?" Luis asked.

"I agreed to always remain an outsider and have a residence where wizards could congregate."

Eddie went on. "My point is that the staff taken was the Staff of Greywacke. Drusilicus now carries the Staff of Water, allowing him access to the Trefoil Arch. What if the person who took the staff wanted to use Greywacke's hidey-hole?"

"By Zoroaster," Marlowe muttered. "It would be the perfect hiding place, undetectable by either wizard or mortal eyes."

"Or any kind of divination," Eddie added.

"Okay," Luis approved. "If that's true, how do we get into it? Don't you need, like, that specific staff to open it?"

Marlowe smiled. "No, as coven master, I am bequeathed with the power to open any of the hidden rooms within the arches. Also, Bankrock has the authority to open them as well."

"Bankrock?" Eddie asked.

Marlowe sighed. "It is part of his abilities to locate any member of the coven. Since he cannot look into an arch through divination, we granted him the authority to enter them."

Eddie rose from his chair. "Well, he ain't here, so it is up to you. While it's still daylight, I suggest we take a walk over to the Greywacke Arch and see if we find anything."

The three men crossed Central Park West and wound their way past a low wall with the words "MARINER'S GATE" chiseled into the stone.

They went up a short hill, following the pathways that led toward the East Side, knowing that the arch they sought was downtown and near Fifth Avenue.

Along the way were people walking dogs or pushing children in strollers. They passed over bridges where they needed to be careful of bicyclists. Food vendors sold hot dogs and a multitude of drinks, and another cart had ice cream and other frozen delights.

The park was fairly busy, even though it was still early spring. The trio strode past rock formations, some that rose ten or twenty feet in height.

They passed the Great Lawn where men and women were readying the baseball diamonds for summer play, and the new grass was growing. They walked across custom-made tiles used on many of the pathways through the seven-hundred and seventy-eight acres.

They approached a flight of stone stairs that led to a giant monolith pointed up at the sky. The ancient obelisk was thousands of years old and brought to this park by a team of dedicated builders.

"Does anyone know what happened here that night?" Eddie said as he gazed up at Cleopatra's Needle.

"I do," Luis answered. "But, to be honest, I'm still trying to forget."

"We are almost there Eddie, come!" Marlowe chided, and they continued down the path.

At their next left turn, they stopped. Greywacke Arch stood there, waiting for them. The center of the arch rose into a point as the Museum of Natural History loomed beyond it, the glass of one of the museum's buildings glimmering in the sun.

They drew close to where they could see the ornate carvings in the stone. Chiseled into the rock were vines of small plants on every other stone. Further up the keystone, the group of vines appeared to form a face.

"You want me to be lookout?" Luis asked.

"That might be the best choice, Luis," Eddie agreed. "Watch where we go in and try to keep people away from that section."

"How long you gonna be?" Luis worried.

"Not long. I mean, how much can be in there?" Eddie told him.

Marlowe walked along the inside of the tunnel. His hands touched the red brick and stopped at the little patterns of yellow bricks that were used for decoration in the passageway. He poked and prodded as he went, and Eddie and Luis watched a few pedestrians as they went through the archway.

"Should I shut it off?" Luis whispered. "Stop people from going in?"

"We'd need several cops, and the last thing we want is more people to explain this to," Eddie brooded.

"What else can we do?" Luis said with a glance around at the people coming and going.

"Just monitor where we go in because it will be where we—"

"Ah-ha!" Marlowe announced, his voice echoing in the tunnel. He was about halfway down the brick-lined passage, and he held up a hand to wave Eddie over.

"Do the best you can," Eddie recommended, then headed into the tunnel to join Marlowe as Luis surveyed the scene.

"Do we need an illusion?" Eddie murmured as he drew close to the old man.

"Oh no, I doubt it. I think it will be quick." Marlowe glanced one way and then the other, and touched the tip of his ebony walking stick to the three-brick pattern in front of him and whispered something in Latin.

Eddie expected the wall to open up as it had for Vasant in the Springbanks Arch.

Instead, he felt himself pulled forward into the brick of the arch, and he and Marlowe instantly passed through the wall into a room beyond.

The change was sudden, and Eddie was now in a lightless room. He reached out to the wall and felt bricks under his hands. A light appeared at the top of Marlowe's staff, manifested from his walking stick in the dark. Eddie glimpsed back to see a red-brick wall behind them, and it also had the yellow bricks in the same pattern as within the arch. They were in a large white room with a domed ceiling.

There was simple furniture, several chairs, a table, and even a bed in one corner, also white.

In the middle of the room a large, ornate, black-and-gold coffin rose from the floor.

"That's the coffin from the airport," Eddie gasped.

Marlowe stared down at the large wooden box, noting the carvings and the precious metal decorations. "Are you sure?"

"Absolutely. Do you think there's a vampire in it?"

Marlowe considered this. "It could even be the Drakula. If Mordred had received the staff—"

Eddie lifted the ring he still wore and hit the secret catch so the silver needle extended. "If so, I can take him out with Sasquatch blood." He paused for a moment. "I mean, do you think it's still good? I used it once, but I figured it had enough—"

"It's fine; it's a magical substance, and the ring has enchantments to keep the blood fresh, but I may have a better weapon." The old man reached into his pocket and pulled out a large wooden stake and a small mallet.

"You carried that here with you?"

He shrugged. "I prefer to be prepared. Shall we see if there is an occupant?"

"Can he attack us? I mean, vampires are pretty fast."

"He won't have his full powers until after sundown. I would, however, still advise caution."

Eddie held out his hand as his staff appeared in it and his clothes shifted to his red fighting garb. "Okay, I'm ready."

"Very well, we lift the lid on three. One. Two. Three!"

The two men threw the heavy lid open and jumped back. Eddie held out the silver ring with one hand and his staff with the other as Marlowe pointed the stake like a knife.

Nothing leaped out of the large wooden case, and Eddie and Marlowe peered into the casket. Inside were hundreds of tiny bottles filled with a liquid with a slight bluish hue under the light of Marlowe's staff.

Eddie reached in, lifted a bottle, and held it up to the light.

"What is that?" Marlowe wondered.

Eddie nodded. "Mind-Blo, the stuff I gave you to analyze." Eddie examined the numerous bottles. "This amount could addict the entire city. There must be hundreds of bottles here."

"Whoever is using this lair is storing the drug here," Marlowe concluded. "It makes sense—direct sunlight would destroy the vampire venom that causes the effect."

"Mind-Blo has something to do with all of this. Is it how they're funding what they are doing? Like paying off Caleb?"

"That is a possibility."

"And where are they getting all the vampire venom? Is it given willingly or have they imprisoned vampires and forced them to produce it?"

Marlowe stared at Eddie in shock. "I hadn't considered that."

"Well, maybe we should. If we want to avoid a war with the vampires, maybe we need to convince them we have a common enemy— whoever is creating this drug."

"It might be a hard thing to persuade them of, Eddie."

"Well, we can't just leave this here."

Marlowe's eyebrows raised. "It's not the sort of thing we can just levitate out of the park."

Eddie smiled. "That depends on how it appears to the outside world. Here's my idea…"

Luis paced near the spot where Eddie and Marlowe disappeared. Luis hadn't noticed a woman standing nearby as the two men vanished into the wall, and she gasped.

"Did you see that? Those two people, they just—"

"Sh!" Luis said, then drew closer to her and whispered. "Didn't you recognize that guy? He's that magician from TV."

"Oh?" the woman gushed as she stared at Luis through her thick glasses. "Was he the one from *America's Got Talent?*"

"Yeah, he's practicing a trick for his next special. Don't tell anyone, okay?" Luis tried a genuine smile, but it felt forced.

The woman put her finger to her lips and winked conspiratorially. She wandered off, only looking back two or three times.

How long would they be? What if there was a vampire, and it got the drop on them? How could he help?

He continued pacing and looking up and down the walkway, but fortunately, no one was coming in either direction.

There was a quick flash of light in the tunnel, and Luis looked in. There was Eddie, but instead of his suit he wore only a white shirt with a tie, black pants, and had a white captain's hat on his head.

Also, he was holding a trumpet.

Luis had never seen Eddie with a trumpet or any other musical instrument. He also noticed that behind Eddie was a group of men, mostly African-American, who wore the same white shirt and dark pants, and they all held musical instruments. One large man had a tuba that wrapped around his body, so he had to duck a little in the tunnel.

With a glance behind him, Luis ran over to Eddie. "Were all these guys inside there?"

"Hit the side of your head with the flat of your hand," Eddie answered.

"What?"

"You heard me."

Luis shrugged his massive shoulders and smacked the side of his head. The group of men, and Eddie's uniform, vanished. Behind him, where the musicians had stood, were Marlowe and an enormous coffin floating in the air in front of him.

Luis started, and a second later, Marlowe and the coffin were gone, and the jazz musicians had returned.

"It's an illusion," Eddie hissed. "Just go with the flow."

The musicians put their instruments to their lips and began a mournful jazz tune as they exited the tunnel toward the park.

People who were approaching the tunnel all got out of the way as the musicians stepped to either side of the walkway, and a hand-drawn caisson, resembling an old-time stagecoach with large wooden wheels, rolled out to the walkway. It had a flat wagon and metal brackets on both sides supporting the elaborate coffin. In the front, a cross beam steered the first pair of wheels, and a handsome white man was pulling it. Pushing the cart from the back was Marlowe, dressed in a somber black suit.

Luis shook his head and could see the truth: Eddie stood to the side and Marlowe walked behind a floating coffin.

A moment later, the illusion reappeared, just as the nonexistent musicians played their instruments and lead the procession through the park.

With a shrug, Luis joined the group and followed along behind, eyes sharp, in case it failed to deceive someone.

To the contrary, people saw the procession and stepped out of the way as the musicians and coffin headed slowly down the walkways. Some people even bowed their heads in respect.

Luis grinned and exchanged a look with Eddie, who pretended to play his illusory trumpet and march along with the group.

It took them a half-hour to return to the Mariner's Gate and the jazz band escorted them across Central Park West, but the phantom musicians turned and headed uptown.

Marlowe created a new illusion of the front of the townhouse, and using it as cover, got the coffin in through the front door. Luis and Eddie went up the stairs and shut the door, and the illusions faded away.

The two detectives leaned against the outer door, tired from the walk and the anxiety of discovery.

Luis smiled. "That was pretty neat."

Eddie, who was now back in his suit, the projected uniform gone, smiled as well. "I hope Marlowe didn't wear himself out. That was a long way to levitate an object."

"Is that the coffin you told me about? The one from the airport?"

"The same. It's full of Mind-Blo."

"What?"

"That's why we had to bring it. I think it could be Orfeo's entire stash."

Eddie and Luis headed to the living room where Marlowe placed the coffin. Eddie lifted the lid and revealed the many bottles to his partner.

"Jeez!" Luis blurted. "Have you tested it?"

"I will do so, sergeant," Marlowe said and grabbed a bottle.

"When are the wizards coming?" Eddie asked.

Marlowe's eyebrows rose. "Hm? Oh, not until later."

"We can't leave the coffin here," Eddie said.

"I'll move it after I've tested this sample," the old man said and proceeded to the downstairs door. "There is much to do! "

Luis had seen the basement room and knew it was where Marlowe trained Eddie. It also served as the old man's lab, though he wasn't sure how that worked.

As Marlowe walked away, Luis grabbed a bottle and took a seat, his eyes going from the bottle to the coffin. "That's a lot of the stuff."

Eddie nodded. "We may have effectively shut Orfeo and his guys down."

Luis held his bottle to the light. "If so, how do we write this up?"

Eddie shrugged. "I guess we transport the drug to the precinct."

"You could take it over in the coffin." Luis grinned.

"Yeah, that won't look weird at all."

"It could explain how they kept hiding the stuff," Luis suggested. "It's a pretty good cover."

"There's no way we can say we found it in one of the park's outbuildings."

Luis returned his gaze to the large coffin. "Claremont Arch gets locked up. We could say we found it there." He frowned. "I dunno, man, that seems like it's a lot bigger than what you need for one body."

Eddie shrugged. "They built it for the Drakula. Maybe he's claustrophobic."

"Maybe."

Eddie checked his watch. "Sunset is coming. We should get to the precinct and write up what we can. I'll get a bag and we can bring some bottles for analysis."

"I'd rather get through that tunnel when there is still some daylight," Luis said and shuddered involuntarily.

"If you want, we can take the paths and go over the bridge instead of under it."

"I'll want to do that at night," Luis conceded.

Luis watched as Eddie went over to the basement door and pulled it open. Hanging inside the door were several cloth bags, and he grabbed one.

"Marlowe!" he yelled down the stairs. "We're going!"

A voice called back, far below in the basement, "Oh? Very well, the meeting will be at 9:00 PM."

"I'll be here," Eddie called back and shut the door.

He returned to Luis and handed him the bag. The pair of them loaded twenty of the tiny bottles.

"That should be enough," Eddie stated.

"Where do we say this came from?"

"We reexamined the outbuilding that we raided and located a hidden stash."

"So, we didn't look around enough the first time? What kind of sorry-ass detectives are we?"

"You got a better story?"

Luis thought for a moment. "Not really."

"Then let's go with that. The important thing is that it is off the streets, and Orfeo can't keep poisoning people with it."

Eddie and Luis headed for the door, leaving the huge coffin in the large open room.

As Eddie stepped outside, Luis thought he heard a click and the sound of a door opening on rusty hinges. When he glanced back, he saw nothing, and followed Eddie out the door, closing it as he went.

SIXTEEN

Luis and Eddie spent the next few hours doing what detectives do in New York City: catch up on reports and paperwork. The NYPD gave them a lot of latitude when investigating a case, as long as there was paperwork to cover their actions.

Eddie and Luis did not take advantage. They were both honest cops who believed in putting in a full day's work and not slacking off.

But Eddie had to admit —this was an extraordinary circumstance.

Showing up with multiple bottles of the drug they were trying to take off the street was sure to count in their favor. With the hundreds of bottles locked up in the coffin in Marlowe's house, he felt they'd effectively taken a great deal of it out of the hands of the dealers.

He and Luis turned in the cloth bag of the drug to the evidence clerk, filling out paperwork there as well. Eddie then sent Captain Jacobs an email to inform him of the find and asked Jacobs to have it analyzed. Based in vampire venom, Eddie was sure they wouldn't be able to come up with an antidote if a person OD'd, but there was always the possibility.

He called his mother to check on the boys and the house, and anything she heard about Cerise.

"We're all fine, Eddie," Eleanor said over the phone. "The boys are worried about their momma, but I got them dinner and they did their homework. I figure I'll take them to see Cerise in the morning."

"Wake me up and I'll go with them."

"Eddie, you ain't been gettin' enough sleep," Eleanor worried.

"I need less sleep these days," Eddie confessed. "Besides it's good practice for our new daughter."

"It's a girl?" Eleanor shrieked, excited by the news.

Eddie had the pull the phone away from his ear due to her volume. "They did an ultrasound, and it is definitely a girl."

Eleanor shrieked again. "Thank you, Jesus! I got me a granddaughter at long last! I'd given up hope, but thank you, Jesus."

Eddie thought perhaps the magickal infusion of energy he'd received with his staff was more likely the thing to thank, but why ruin his mother's celebration?

Suddenly, Eleanor became serious. "You sure she's safe in that hospital?"

"I am about to make sure she is, Momma, don't worry."

"All right, see you in the morning."

Eddie hung up and turned to Luis, who was using his two-finger typing style on the report.

"I have to do something in the woods for a few minutes. Can you cover?"

"Should I ask?" Luis coaxed, staring at the computer screen.

"Probably not."

"Then you got it, bro."

Eddie nodded and headed out of the precinct. Twilight was falling, and the streetlights were snapping on. Eddie quietly crossed the street and took the wooden stairs to the parking lot, and through it to a small clearing just off the bridle path. He reached into his pocket to extract the wooden whistle he'd carried since the day he'd met the *Pukwudgie*. Although that was only a few days earlier, he felt as if it were a lifetime ago.

He raised the wooden implement to his lips and blew into the tube. He heard nothing with his ears, but he felt like there was a high-pitched whine that pierced through his head.

He lowered the tube and closed his eyes to shake his head and recover from the strange noise. When he opened his eyes, the eighteen-inch tall man with gray skin and pointed ears stood before him in his buckskin pants.

Eddie lowered to one knee. "Wow, that worked well."

"Walker of the Wise, you have called upon me," Skysoarer stated plainly.

"Yeah... um... how's your Granny?"

"She is well, and we have increased the protection of our home to repel any other *Skadegamutc* who wish to do us harm."

"That's good," Eddie said. He weighed his next words. "I... would request your help, if I may."

Skysoarer nodded. "We are indebted to you."

Eddie rubbed the back of his head. "I was just wondering if you could guard my wife."

Skysoarer frowned. "She is in danger?"

Eddie nodded. "The same sort of creature that bit your Granny attacked her."

"The *Skadegamutc*?"

"Yeah… um… that. Could you, or one of your tribe, keep watch over her? She's in the hospital."

"She is within a *palsëwikaon*? Do you wish us to free her?"

"No, just protect her, guard her, so none of the Skad-e-whatevers can get to her."

"This is a small request for the great service you did for our people."

Eddie sighed. "She is great with child and I must fight… um… evildoers."

His entire request felt pretty lame and the correct formal speech was difficult for him.

He pulled out the Seal of Jupiter on the chain he had taken from Caleb hours earlier. "I have a charm. I would like you to place it upon her."

Eddie held it out to the *Pukwudgie* on its chain. Skysoarer took the medallion, as large as a frisbee in his tiny hands.

"This is an impressive totem. I shall place it over her head so she is protected."

Skysoarer beckoned Eddie closer, and Eddie leaned in on both knees.

"Think of her, and the place where she is," Skysoarer said, then placed one hand on Eddie's temple.

Eddie thought of Cerise and the hospital as best he could. Skysoarer closed his eyes for a moment, then released Eddie's head and took a step back.

"I shall place the totem and watch over her, Walker of the Wise."

Eddie bowed his head. "I am most grateful." He offered the wooden whistle to Skysoarer.

"You may still have need of that, Walker. We shall meet again."

Eddie blinked at the little man, but in the moment of that blink, Skysoarer had disappeared.

Eddie stood and dusted the dirt off his knees. "Man, I gotta learn how to do that."

He checked his watch and saw that it was already past 8:00. The meeting at Marlowe's was at 9:00, and it would be best to get there early.

He headed back into the precinct and the bullpen to find Luis still pecking away at the computer, exactly as he'd left him.

"What were you doing?" Luis whispered as Eddie sat at his desk across from his partner.

"Arranging some protection for Cerise."

Luis frowned. "You can do that?"

Eddie nodded. "Come on, we gotta get to Marlowe's."

"I'm just finishing up," Luis said, and impaled several more keys.

Eddie sighed as Luis finished the report.

At 8:30, he and Luis left, taking the cement paths overland, instead of the transverse road under the tunnel, because of Luis' fear of an ambush. It wasn't a bad choice— no point pushing their luck with the vampires out to get them.

They climbed the steps to Marlowe's townhouse, and as they drew close to knock on the door, it was opened abruptly by Daniel Kraft.

Daniel stepped back, his eyes wide, obviously surprised to see Eddie and Luis.

"Hey, Daniel," Eddie said. "Did we startle you?"

Daniel cleared his throat. "A bit, yes," he answered, his voice sounding odd.

"Hey, man, you got a cold or something?" Luis asked.

"Vampires don't get colds," Eddie said, and eyed Daniel with suspicion. "You okay?"

Daniel nodded curtly and pushed his way past Eddie and Luis, muttering, "Gotta go," again with his voice sounding odd.

Luis shook his head and pushed his way through the open door as Eddie watched Daniel as he headed down the street.

"Sometimes that guy is *mucho loco*," Luis grumbled as Eddie followed him into the townhouse.

"It isn't just me? He was acting strange, right?"

"Who can tell? Your entire group is pretty strange most of the time."

They arrived in the living room, where the large coffin still stood. "I'd better tell Marlowe to move that out of here."

"Yeah, not exactly a good icebreaker at parties," Luis said and opened the lid.

The coffin was empty.

"What the hell?" Luis sputtered. "Eddie, the drugs are gone."

Eddie strode to his partner's side and reached out to touch the blood-red satin that lined the elaborate box. He felt padding and cushioning under his fingers, but the multiple vials of the drug were gone. "Where did they go?"

"I don't know, maybe your wizard-guru-guy hid them or something."

"Excuse me, have either of you seen Marlowe?" a deep, resonant voice spoke up.

Luis and Eddie turned to see Daniel Kraft, just as he reached the bottom of the circular stairs from the second floor.

Luis' mouth fell open. "How did you get back inside the house?"

Daniel glared at them as if they had gone insane. "I woke up a little while ago and just came downstairs. I haven't left the house at all."

"The shapeshifter!" Eddie bellowed and ran out into the street. He flew down the stairs, and took off in the direction the fake Daniel had gone.

Eddie was a runner, working out on the Shuman Running Track around the reservoir in Central Park ever since he'd been there. Since gaining his staff, he needed very little exercise, yet he had gained speed and strength.

This explained why Daniel had sounded funny. The stolen Mask of *Misignwah* allowed the wearer to look like anyone, but the user still possessed his own voice.

Eddie almost plowed into Rusty, who was walking and talking with Dalehead on their way to the townhouse.

"Hey, Eddie, what's the rush?" Rusty responded amiably.

"Did you see Daniel?" Eddie panted.

"No, I was heading for the meeting and saw Dalehead about a block ago," Rusty told him.

Eddie listened carefully, but Rusty sounded perfectly normal.

"I... believe I zaw Daniel," Dalehead told Eddie, and she sounded like herself as well with her French accent still coloring her words. "He went across ze street and into ze park."

She pointed vaguely toward the park. Eddie stared across the street, and even in the streetlights, he saw the four foot high cut-stone wall and the huge rock formation beyond.

"There's no entrance there," Eddie reflected. "The last pathway into the park was at 85th Street."

Rusty and Dalehead exchanged a glance, and the cabdriver shrugged and said, "Maybe he turned into a bat or something."

The pair went past him as Eddie stared across the street at the small wall and the rock formation that towered behind it. It was all part of Summit Rock, the highest elevation in the park, with grass and trees growing from the soil on the top, and steps carved into the stone to allow access to visitors. The side that faced Central Park West was tall with nothing but barren stone rising one hundred and forty-one feet, more suited for a mountain climber than a leisurely stroll.

If it was a vampire that had the Mask of *Misignwah*, he or she could have changed into a bat, but what would it do with the mask? Carry it in one of its clawed feet? Not unless it was a large bat, but he would have noticed a creature that big flying across the street.

He turned back to the townhouse and followed Rusty and Dalehead up the stairs.

Once inside, Eddie went to Luis who watched the newcomers. Eddie shook his head, and his partner knew without a word that the suspect had gotten away.

"My goodness," Dalehead chirped, as she noted the enormous coffin in the middle of the living room. "Zis certainly does not add to ze ambience."

Marlowe came up from the basement as Dalehead and Rusty spoke. With a glance at the guests, he went straight to Eddie.

"Eddie, I tried to analyze that sample of the drug."

"What about it?" Eddie murmured, his eyes on the coffin.

"It wasn't the drug at all. As I studied it, it *disappeared*."

Luis, who stood close to listen, spoke quietly. "Yeah, and all the little bottles in the coffin disappeared, too."

"Were they merely an illusion?" Eddie asked.

Marlowe shook his head. "No, more like a magickal construct. Something woven together from elements in the air into a temporary solid form."

"How long would a thing like that last?"

Marlowe shrugged. "Since they all vanished, I would have to say the construct lasted until nightfall."

"Eddie, we just put a twenty of those bottles into evidence," Luis fretted.

"They probably disappeared as well. Damn, that's going to trigger an internal investigation."

Luis exhaled heavily. "Oh man! All we need is Internal Affairs looking into everything we do, and right now with all this craziness—"

"But why?" Marlowe interrupted. "It takes a great deal of magickal energy to generate and maintain such a creation. It would tire even an experienced wizard. Why go to all that trouble?"

Eddie looked at the coffin, an idea beginning to form. "Marlowe, someone got in here."

The old man's eyes grew wide. "What are you talking about?"

"When Luis and I arrived, Daniel was leaving—"

Luis continued the tale. "Only when we got inside, Daniel was coming down the stairs."

"You think the first Daniel was a vampire using the Mask of *Misignwah*?" Marlowe sputtered. "But, why would he…"

Without finishing his sentence, the old man was on the move, going fast for a man of his advanced years. Luis and Eddie followed as he led them into the breakfast room and the pile of parchments that covered the table.

Marlowe ran his hands through the papers, moving them aside and folding up some of the larger ones.

"Don't tell me he got the papyrus!" Eddie exclaimed.

"He did indeed," Marlowe grunted. "Stolen!"

"I thought you were going to protect it," Luis accused. "Put a spell on it or something."

"I was waiting until the others were here to use our combined powers," Marlowe blurted. "That would have made it impossible for anyone to remove it from the townhouse."

"How did this guy get in here to steal it?" Luis bellowed. "You said a vampire can't just walk into your house, right?"

Marlowe was still going through the papers and trying to organize them. "There are magickal safeguards. No vampire could get into this building."

Eddie groaned, his idea finally fully formed. "We carried them in!"

"What?" Luis said. "How could we have carried a vampire in here?"

Eddie's jaw grew tight. "In the coffin."

Marlowe turned to Eddie. "It might be possible, if the coffin had its own magickal defenses."

Now it was Eddie's turn to be on the move, heading out to the living room. Several more people had arrived, Bankrock and Drusilicus, as well as Willowdell and a tall, gray-bearded man Eddie had not yet met. They were milling around and chatting, some staying near the enchanted tea trolley, which had been moved to the living room.

Eddie went directly to the coffin, examining the sides as he circled it. The guests watched him as he did so. Finally, Eddie went on one knee at one of the side panels and whispered, *"Patentibus."*

The side panel fell open to reveal a space in the base of the large coffin that easily could have fit two people if necessary. The panel was so well-designed and hidden by the carvings of cherubim and gargoyles that it would have been all but impossible to see without a careful examination.

Marlowe wore an expression of fear and concern.

Eddie spoke first. "That's why the fake drugs were in there. So we would bring the coffin *here*."

Marlowe nodded. "And the many bottles would make us choose to transport the entire coffin instead of just removing the drugs."

Drusilicus examined the large open space built into the coffin. "Clever. They made the coffin overlarge so the user could hide in the bottom compartment. Undoubtably to confuse any vampire-hunter."

"That's why they flew it over from England," Eddie fumed. "Hell, both the vampires who came off the plane could have been inside it, in separate sections."

"That could explain why it was empty," Drusilicus agreed. "Again, your instincts were correct, even if the actual circumstances were wrong."

"Do you have that potion I asked you to make?" Eddie whispered.

Drusilicus drew close. "Yes, I have constructed a simple container that will explode it into a fine mist. I merely throw it into the air and the entire room is affected."

"Hold on to it. We might want to use it soon."

Drusilicus became quite serious and glanced about. "Do you think the vampire is here, in this room?"

Eddie peered at the doorway, as Vasant came into the room. The female wizard was in a striking dark-blue sari that would look proper at almost any event. Elegant, yet stylish. He wondered if she was the disguised vampire arriving now. Having once brought the vampire into the room, they'd essentially invited her or him into the house. That person could come and go anytime they desired, despite Marlowe's magickal protections.

"I'll let you know," Eddie told Drusilicus and headed straight to Marlowe.

The old wizard was shaking his head, trying to get his mind around the problem.

"Marlowe," Eddie said, "is it possible to strengthen the protections you have around the townhouse?"

Marlowe frowned. "Yes, I will have to make it so the vampire cannot reenter."

Eddie gazed around at the many guests. "He could be here, now."

Marlowe pivoted his head. "What? You think he ran off, then doubled back to join our group?"

"If I could appear to be anyone I wanted, that's what I would do," Eddie said. "Think about it, you could hear everything your enemy is planning."

Marlowe stared at the floor, as if to think this through. He was usually decisive, but he seemed dazed and confused.

Eddie pressed on. "Look, if he came back, maybe he still has the papyrus. We can stop him."

Marlowe nodded. "What would you advise, Eddie?"

"Drusilicus has something that might reveal our unwanted guest. How about we get this coffin out of the way and act like we're starting the meeting, introduce people, that sort of thing?"

Marlowe nodded, stepped away from Eddie, and spoke in a loud, clear voice. "Everyone, move away from the fireplace. I shall move this... um... box aside."

The guests got out of the path as Marlowe raised his walking stick, and the heavy coffin rose a few feet into the air and easily levitated over to block the opening of the fireplace, where it lowered to the floor.

"Everyone find a chair. There should be enough," Marlowe said.

The guests immediately headed to the padded chairs. Some guests gestured, and the chairs came to them to help form an overlarge circle.

Marlowe sat in a very large chair Eddie had never seen before. It was like the other wingback cushioned chairs, but the back was higher, and it gave the impression of a throne. Eddie thought it must signify that he was the coven master.

Instead of sitting in a chair next to Luis, Eddie chose a seat next to Drusilicus, exchanging a nod with him as he sat.

"You all set?"

Drusilicus lifted an eyebrow. "Just say the word, lieutenant."

As everyone quieted down, Eddie noticed no one was wearing wizard robes or carrying their staffs.

Marlowe gazed around the room. "We have many who have not been introduced, and it would be best if we knew who our companions were. Each person should stand and announce themselves. Inscope, shall you start?"

He pointed at a man two chairs away from Eddie, who rose and spoke. He was the tall, bearded man Eddie had noted before. Dressed in a faded shirt, stained pants, and a jacket far too small for his lanky frame, he appeared quite disheveled. Wizards often disguised themselves as homeless people and sometimes added a foul odor to keep people away.

Inscope rose and spoke with an odd accent that made him sound like a pirate. "I be long time in Europe, made me path to America, and now I keep to the park and stay at mine own arch…"

He went on as Eddie scrutinized the group. It certainly was an odd mix—some people came across as being well off, like Drusilicus, and then the others who appeared homeless. Then there were people like himself and Rusty, just plain working-class guys.

Inscope finally finished, and Drusilicus rose next. "I am Drusilicus Greywacke apprenticed by the Wizard Greywacke." He gave a telling look to Vasant. "And others."

The Indian woman set her jaw in annoyance and flushed a bit.

"I carry the staff of the element water and am one of the Five," he finished and sat down abruptly.

Eddie rose. "I'm Eddie Berman. I'm with NYPD and I carry the staff of the element fire."

This caused some people to whisper to themselves. They all seemed to have heard of Eddie, and he wasn't sure how he felt about that.

"I think all of us coming together is a great opportunity."

Eddie caught Drusilicus' eye and nodded. The well-heeled wizard stood, threw a small ball into the air, and struck it with a beam of blue light, conjured from his pocket watch, just as Eddie conjured his staff.

There was a *pffft*, and a thin white vapor descended onto the many guests like a cloud, making the room hazy. The others rose to their feet in protest.

Eddie was in full wizard garb, with his staff raised as he scanned the group through the artificial fog that was rapidly fading.

He turned to see Dalehead as she coughed. Her hands flew to her face, as if in pain.

There was a sound like ripping cloth, and suddenly, Dalehead's body twisted and shoulders seemed to dislocate with a loud crack. Instead of her face, there was a two-colored oval wooden mask that was taller than her head. It had holes for the eyes and mouth and it fell away to the floor. The woman who stood was taller with dark raven hair and before everyone stood Selene, the vampire consort to Drakula.

She picked up the mask in one hand, as a staff instantly appeared in her other hand.

Before anyone could react, she bellowed, *"Oppressio!"*

No one was prepared for the attack except Eddie, who had formed a dome of protection when he conjured his staff. The other wizards and Luis all fell back as a powerful wall of force rammed into them with the skill of an experienced user of magic, but Eddie held his place. His protective dome lit up in bright flashes of red as the energy bounced off it.

Not all the wizards had fallen. Marlowe stood with a protective white wall around him. He faced Selene and bellowed, "Who dares?"

With a withering look to Marlowe and a gesture, Selene created an illusion. Instead of the long raven locks, she appeared for a moment to have short blond hair, cut in a pageboy style. Although the change in hair was dramatic, her features remained the same. She looked at Marlowe and said with a bell-like voice, "Have you missed me, my old love?"

This froze Marlowe to the spot, his eyes wide in disbelief.

Selene's hair returned to her dark tresses, the illusion broken, and she turned to run for the door, the staff in one hand and the magical mask in the other. It had revealed her true clothes as well — a black jumpsuit and sneakers, a logical choice for someone who had been hiding inside a chamber in a coffin.

Eddie cried, "*Coligo*," attempting a binding spell against the fast-moving vampire.

She put up a gray dome of light that deflected the spell, still heading for the door, as Eddie attempted several others in his repertoire.

Her vampiric abilities made her faster than a normal human, and in seconds she was at the door and through it.

Eddie ran for the door, albeit at a slower speed, and yanked it open to an empty street. There were no passersby on the sidewalk or across the street, and he slammed the door in frustration.

"We *had* her!" Eddie gasped, tired from the amount of energy he'd used in his attempt to stop her. Although she'd only possessed Caleb's staff for a few short weeks, she obviously was well-practiced in the arts and probably a better wizard than Eddie.

He marched over to Marlowe, who slowly lowered into his chair as the others began to get back on their feet, trying to understand what happened.

Marlowe stared at the floor and didn't look up until Eddie got in his face.

"Marlowe, why didn't you stop her?" Eddie demanded, but kept his voice low.

Marlowe raised his head, and he seemed far away. "What?"

"That was *Selene*," Eddie insisted quietly, with a gesture to the door. "If you had helped me, we could have stopped her. She was the one who had hidden in coffin and used the mask to become Daniel. Then she doubled back disguised as Dalehead. Marlowe, she has the Papyrus of Sekhmet!"

"Papyrus?" Marlowe repeated in a dull monotone.

"Didn't you hear me? Selene—she works for Mordred!" Eddie stood up straight, his hands clenched into fists.

"No, that wasn't Selene," Marlowe replied.

"Of course it was! I met her at the airport."

"I am sure you did, but her name is actually Nimue," Marlowe croaked.

"Nimue? You mean the girl who stole your powers, like, a thousand years ago?"

Marlowe nodded wearily. "She is more than Mordred's helper. She is his lover, and only now do I realize that she has also joined him in becoming a vampire."

"Then what do we do?"

Marlowe's face was full of uncertainty. "I have no idea."

SEVENTEEN

They attempted to get the meeting back to order, but Marlowe was in no condition to lead it.

Eddie drew close to Drusilicus and said, "You're going to have to take over."

"Me?" Drusilicus objected.

"Yes, you're one of the Five, and Marlowe is a mess."

"A vampire invaded his home. I am sure any of us would be a mess," Drusilicus stated.

"He says that Selene is actually Nimue, that woman he was in love with a thousand years ago."

"Really?" Drusilicus raised an eyebrow. "She looks good for her age."

"Will you stop being a pain and take over? I am going to take Marlowe up to his bedroom. You try to get the wizards working together."

Drusilicus surveyed the room. Furniture had been knocked over by the wall of force Selene used against the wizards. Several of them had shifted their clothing into robes and held their staffs, while others remained in normal clothes. All of them looked disoriented.

"Once again, lieutenant, you ask the impossible," Drusilicus said observing the crowd.

"You've always wanted to be coven master—this is your chance," Eddie said.

"More like herding cats, in this case," Drusilicus murmured and gave Eddie a dirty look. He went to the center of the large circle of chairs and spoke. "Attention please, we must all remain calm. You can now all see the enemy we are up against. We need to discuss ways we can prepare…"

He went on, but Eddie, with a signal to Luis, helped Marlowe up, and they gently led the befuddled wizard to the circular elevator at the other end of the large room.

"I thought she was dead," Marlowe babbled, mostly to himself. "If I had known, if I had *known*…"

Luis shut the grillwork door of the elevator. "You know we almost got killed the last time we got in this thing, right?" he muttered to Eddie.

"I remember," Eddie snapped, as he pushed a button and the elevator rose. "You want to carry him up the five hundred or whatever steps?"

"No, *gracias*, I'll pass." The elevator ascended and they gazed down on the seated wizards as Drusilicus tried to get the conversation started among the motley group.

"Where are we going?" Marlowe said as the elevator reached the second floor, and Eddie pulled the gate open for them to step out.

"To your room. Maybe you should take a sleeping potion or something," Eddie suggested.

"I'm a big fan of aspirin," Luis said as he helped Eddie escort Marlowe in the correct direction.

"I cannot believe it," Marlowe said, shaking his head. "I was convinced she was dead. All these centuries, and she is as fresh as the last time I saw her."

"Yeah, she looks good for an ancient dead broad," Luis quipped.

Eddie gave him a dirty look.

As they escorted Marlowe down the hall, suddenly and silently Daniel Kraft appeared, startling Luis.

"Is everything all right?" Daniel said, worried to see Marlowe being led by Eddie and Luis.

"He had a shock," Eddie told him. "We need to get him to his room."

"What happened?" Daniel said and rushed forward to assist Marlowe.

Luis shook his head. "His old flame disguised herself as a wizard and stole the world-ending piece of paper."

Daniel frowned. "Sometimes I believe you say things just to confuse me, sergeant."

"Now you know how I feel," Luis responded.

"Can you get him to bed, help him lie down?" Eddie said and peered over the balcony at the seated wizards far below. "We need to get back to the meeting."

"I can take it from here," Daniel said, and escorted Marlowe to his room.

Eddie and Luis headed back to the elevator.

Luis asked, "This Selene—or whoever she is—was she disguised as Dalehead the entire time?"

Eddie shook his head as they entered the elevator. "I don't think so. I first met her at Marlowe's during the day, and she left in sunlight. I believe she left the townhouse as Daniel, then doubled-back using the mask to become Dalehead."

"So what happened to Dalehead?"

Eddie shook his head. "I have no idea."

"So we got the open case on the stake guy—" Luis began.

"Strix," Eddie said.

"Whatever. And the open case of the drug lord, Orfeo, who is a vampire. And a bag of evidence has disappeared."

"That sums it up."

Luis shook his head. "We better make some headway on these cases or the captain is going to be very unhappy with us."

The elevator reached the first floor, and they headed for the group, hearing voices raised in disagreement and arguing with Drusilicus. A skinny African man in a black and purple Dashiki with a long beard spoke English with a heavy accent and kept slipping into a dialect that Eddie didn't recognize.

"We have let these *ramanga* have too much freedom to feast upon the innocent. It is time to strike them down."

This received nods and voices of support throughout the group, and Drusilicus waved his hands to calm the assembled wizards.

"There are more immediate concerns," Drusilicus said loudly. "Not all the vampires attack the innocent and kill for pleasure. Some do not wish harm to the mortal world or us. We believe an attempt to bring forth an ancient prophecy will happen in one day's time. I must ask all of you to be available to help stop this event."

This made the group quiet down and listen.

"It would be best if you stayed near Manhattan. I can offer you lodgings here at Marlowe's townhouse, but those of you who possess an arch in Central Park, please remain there. You saw tonight, our enemy has a way to make themselves look like people we might know, so do not invite anyone into your abode, either by word or gesture."

There were murmurs of assent.

"We shall make this townhouse the center of our activities until tomorrow night," Drusilicus went on. "I would like anyone with a prophetic ability to speak to me or Bankrock."

"So you don't know what they will do?" Exclaimed the man in the Dashiki.

"We are convinced that they will use Washington Square Park. But, we are unsure how they will attack and in what way. Bankrock and I will assign you positions down in Greenwich Village when the attack is imminent. Since we are dealing with vampires, I suggest you sleep during the day to prepare yourselves. Thank you all."

Drusilicus stepped away as Bankrock stood and held up a clipboard. In a clear voice, he began to organize the various wizards.

Drusilicus approached Luis and Eddie. "How is Marlowe?"

"In shock, I guess," Eddie said, watching Bankrock as he spoke to the group.

"Nimue was Marlowe's greatest love," Drusilicus explained. "From rumors, I know that her involvement with Mordred was— difficult for him."

Luis spoke up. "Since she's helpin' Mordred, I guess they're still involved."

"So it would appear, sergeant," Drusilicus sighed.

"I'm worried about Dalehead. If Selene could masquerade as her, she must have put her out of commission."

"Bankrock can locate any wizard in the coven. We shall speak to him once the meeting breaks up."

"Aren't we kinda screwed?" Luis pointed out. "I mean, if Mordred's got the papyrus now, and Selene's got a staff, it's kinda game over."

Drusilicus threw his shoulders back. "We have a full day of sunlight tomorrow, and the vampires will be asleep. We shall have to make that time count."

"At least we're aware of the impending situation," Eddie said as he observed the various wizards. It was maybe ten people— far more than the group he had when they'd taken on the Great Evil.

He wondered if it would be enough.

"I wanna check on Dalehead tonight, and tomorrow I have to visit my wife in the hospital before I can come to NYC and go vampire hunting," Eddie turned to his partner. "Luis you look tired. Why don't you call it a night?"

Luis nodded. "I'm nervous about getting my car, y'know, by myself."

Eddie and Drusilicus exchanged a look. Luis was right. All of them were in danger, and Luis was the one with the least protection.

"Ask Rusty if he'll escort you. He's got his squirt gun," Eddie said.

Luis nodded. "Oh yeah, the one filled with holy water and garlic. That might work."

Luis stepped away and approached Rusty as Eddie watched. After a moment, they headed for the door, with Luis waving at his partner as he left. Eddie turned to Drusilicus, but the other man's eyes were on Vasant.

"What's the story with you and Vasant?" Eddie asked.

Drusilicus kept watching the dark woman. "Are we intimates, now? I believe that is none of your business, lieutenant."

Eddie sighed. "Come on, Drew, I gotta know if there is a problem with the two of you that might imperil the mission."

Drusilicus turned to look at Eddie, a slight smile on his lips. "My, you can use big words when it suits you."

"Cut the crap, Drew. I need to know."

Drusilicus stared at Eddie, then shook his head. "Very well." He turned and stepped toward the outer hall. "When I was an apprentice, Vasant was my first teacher."

"This was more than a hundred years ago, right?"

"Close enough," Drusilicus said, and glanced over at the woman who was now speaking to Bankrock. "It was a different time, Eddie. Many in my class considered people of color— especially a woman of color—inferior. She was like a goddess to me. We had to meet in secret as upper-class white men couldn't be seen with an unmarried Indian woman."

"But she trained you. Obviously you two got along."

"Far too well. She was older than me, and her morals were not exactly the Victorian norms of the day."

"Cut to the chase, Drew."

He sighed. "To use the vernacular, she took me to her bed."

"Drew, that ain't the way they say it nowadays. But, wait, are wizards allowed to… uh… *fraternize* with their apprentices?"

"It was against the code and still is. Vasant had not had a physical relationship in centuries, and smitten as I was, we acted foolishly. I was living with my parents at the time and one morning, my father's servants discovered us together in my bed."

"Whoa! You go, dawg."

"Really?" Drusilicus considered Eddie with a lifted eyebrow. "It was quite the scandal. My parents, who knew nothing of my wizardly ambitions, told me I must give her up and never see her again."

"And that was that?"

"On the contrary. I told them I wanted to marry her."

"That probably made your dad blow a gasket."

"I stormed from the house and swore that we would live together in sin if necessary. I headed to her arch to confess my love and ask her to be my bride."

"I take it that did not go well?"

"She rejected me and admitted it had been foolish to take me as her consort. She told me I was immature and knew nothing of love."

"Ouch."

"She believed that our romantic feelings had kept her from being the teacher she should be, and told me I was to apprentice under Greywacke."

"Double ouch."

"She intended to return to India and become a hermit to better understand her own desires. With that, she disappeared, and I didn't see her again until a few days ago."

"I guess you were pretty mad."

"It devastated me. I returned to my parents and sheepishly told them I had ended the relationship at their request."

"You fixed that situation at least."

"My parents tried to find me an appropriate match, but I focused on mastering the abilities of a wizard under Greywacke's tutelage. I rejected their choices and never married."

"You've been alone all this time?"

"Yes," Drusilicus muttered. "In part because of Vasant, and in part, I suppose, because of my own stubborn nature."

"And now you're with Lysandra," Eddie stressed. "Another relationship that the wizards find unacceptable."

Drusilicus paused as he thought about this. "I suppose you are right. I had not considered that."

"Looks like you're quite the rebel."

"So it would appear," Drusilicus replied, no humor on his face. "You have nothing to fear over Vasant and I working together. Now that the initial shock has worn off, I shall do what needs to be done with whomever I need to work with. I am sure she feels the same."

"Good to know, Drew."

"I'd best talk to Bankrock to know where he plans to assign me," Drusilicus said as he stepped away.

"Do that. Then, Banky and I have to find Dalehead."

There was suddenly a pounding on the front door, and since Eddie was the closest one, he peeked out through the small lens, where he saw a frantic Rusty.

Eddie yanked the door open. "What happened?"

"Come with me right now!" Rusty gasped. "The vampires have abducted your friend!"

EIGHTEEN

E ddie glanced over his shoulder at the others. "I need to get help."

"No time, come right now!" Rusty insisted.

Drusilicus arrived and regarded Rusty over Eddie's shoulder. "What's going on?"

"Rusty says vampires jumped him and Luis," Eddie said frantically.

Rusty nodded. "Eddie, if you come along, I think you can stop 'em."

Drusilicus put up a restraining arm in front of Eddie.

"I've got to help my partner," Eddie hissed.

"I am sure of that, lieutenant," Drusilicus said and turned to Rusty. "I wonder if Rusty should come inside first?"

Eddie started. There was a warning in Drusilicus' tone.

"If I may," Rusty said and eyed the doorway.

"The question is, can you?" Drusilicus said and stepped back to leave an opening.

Rusty appeared annoyed.

"I mean," Drusilicus went on, "I am sure that you are here to warn all the wizards and not merely to trick the lieutenant into coming with you?"

Rusty turned and dashed down the stairs, as Drusilicus placed his hand on his pocket watch and gestured. Rusty stumbled and he fell down the last few stairs.

Eddie called forth his staff, and with a glance up to the trees, followed Drusilicus down the stairs.

Drusilicus pulled Rusty up by his hair and tossed him back against the stone steps with surprising strength, as his staff appeared in his hands.

"This is not the Wizard Claremont, but a vampire imposter," Drusilicus stated, his staff at the ready as Rusty stared daggers at him.

To all appearances, he was Rusty, from the hair on his head to the clothes he wore.

"Are you sure?" Eddie asked.

"He couldn't come through the door without an invitation," Drusilicus clarified. "No doubt he was trying to entrap you, lieutenant."

Eddie leaned close to Rusty again. "How does this work? I mean, is he wearing that mask? Is it an illusion or what?"

Drusilicus considered this. "The mask is a talisman of significant power and it alters your outward appearance into the person you wish to become. This obviously is not the same vampire who impersonated Dalehead."

The fake Rusty sneered, "Get bent, wizard."

"I believe they chose him because he has a voice and intonation similar to Rusty. You had best tell us what this is about or the lieutenant and I shall have to make things… unpleasant."

Eddie twisted the silver ring on his finger. "Were you at the airport the other night?"

"Yeah, you got lucky," the prisoner spat.

Eddie raised his hand. "This ring contains enough Sasquatch blood to do the same thing to you as it did to Selene's boyfriend."

"That would be one way to recover the mask," Drusilicus said, his jaw set. "If we reduced the host to dust, the mask would simply fall away."

"Or —you could take it off," Eddie suggested. He held out the ring and pressed the hidden button, and the small needle unfolded, gleaming in the streetlights.

"I thought you was a cop!" the prisoner protested.

"Yeah, but you're already dead," Eddie stated. "This would merely complete the process."

"I gotta stand to take da mask off."

Eddie closed the needle on the ring and stepped back, glad that his bluff had worked. He had no intention of stabbing an unarmed prisoner with something that would kill them.

Drusilicus grabbed the phony Rusty by the arms and set him upright and with a dirty look at each wizard, the phony Rusty reached to his face and pulled.

The person before them changed as he pulled at his face. The body got shorter and plumper, and the clothing became dark and simple.

Before them, holding the bicolor mask, was a short, squat vampire Eddie immediately recognized. "You're Tuck, aren't you? You're a friend of Lysandra."

Drusilicus snatched the mask away from the man who was only about five feet tall.

"Yeah," Tuck sneered, "and you're the wizards the Drakula is about to destroy."

"Show us where you were going to take the lieutenant," Drusilicus snapped.

"Drew, that must be a trap," Eddie warned.

"When they see Tuck in his natural state, they will realize we spoiled the trap. Then we can ascertain if they abducted the sergeant, or if this was merely a diversion."

"Should we get the others?"

"I think we can handle whatever we're walking into, since the element of surprise is gone." He prodded the short man with his staff. "Lead us."

With a nasty look to Drusilicus, Tuck led them toward the 86th Street Transverse Road.

As they walked, Eddie pulled his cell and called Luis. It immediately went to voicemail.

As they strode toward the tunnel that crossed over the road, Drusilicus studied the mask. "Fairly simple. It appears to be carved from wood, not the usual material for a talisman."

"Why not?" Eddie asked, his eyes focused on Tuck.

"Wood doesn't hold the charge like metal or crystals would." He turned it over and inspected the unexpressive face. "There are several gems on the front. That's what probably contains the magickal properties."

They were about ten feet from the tunnel, and Drusilicus easily stepped ahead and put his staff in front of Tuck. "Far enough."

"We grabbed your guy beyond the tunnel," Tuck insisted.

"Lieutenant, since it is simple for you to control many types of light, would you be so kind as to illuminate the tunnel?"

Eddie nodded and held his staff aloft. Inside the tunnel a dazzling effulgence flared and became almost blinding.

Nothing came out of the tunnel, but Eddie noted something on the sidewalk near the center of the covered space.

It was a UV flashlight.

Eddie entered the tunnel and picked it up. The glass was smashed and the batteries had fallen from the handle.

Drusilicus joined him, shoving Tuck in front of him.

Eddie handed Drusilicus the broken device. "This is where Luis had made his stand."

Drusilicus turned it over in his hand. "I am no expert, but I doubt this would have enough power to injure a vampire."

Eddie pulled out his own flashlight and aimed it at Tuck. "We could find out—unless you have any information, Tuck."

Tuck held up his arms and flinched. "The big guy had one. It blinded a couple of guys, but the wizard's right, it ain't got enough juice to kill."

"Blinded them?" Eddie marveled. "Permanently?"

"How the hell do I know?" Tuck spat indignantly. "Probably temporary. Anything that don't kill a vamp, we can heal from pretty quick."

"Except for burns and wounds caused by silver implements," Drusilicus intoned. "Then they heal no faster than a human."

Eddie stepped menacingly toward the small vampire. "How about if someone rips their head off? If you don't tell me where my partner is, I'm going to do exactly that!"

Tuck swallowed. "Look, I was told we snatch da guy. I wasn't told nuthin' else."

"Perhaps I can answer that for you, wizard," a female voice interrupted them.

Eddie and Drusilicus scrutinized the far end of the tunnel to see Selene in her dark jumpsuit. She had one hand on her hip, the other held a six-foot-tall staff with a grayish light glowing at the top of it.

A halo of red fire appeared at the top of Eddie's staff, as his clothes shifted to his battle robes and boots. "What did you do with my partner?"

Drusilicus put his own staff in Eddie's path. He spoke firmly but quietly, "Do not attack. This is the trap."

"Ah, Wizard Greywacke, I was told you were crafty," she mocked, and then her eyes turned to Eddie. "Perhaps you should listen to him."

Several figures landed beside Selene.

Drusilicus sighed as they watched several more vampires leap down the walls from both sides of the transverse road to close off both ends of the tunnel.

"Give us the papyrus," Drusilicus shouted, his voice echoing in the tunnel. "Or we shall take it."

Selene curtsied politely. "I am afraid I don't have it. By now, my minions have delivered it to my master." She straightened and threw back her shoulders.

As Eddie watched the opposite end of the tunnel, more vampires joined the first group.

"More company," Eddie murmured.

"I am aware, lieutenant," Drusilicus responded without taking his eyes away from Selene. "The sergeant is a mortal and an innocent. Return him to us."

"Or what?" Selene countered. "You'll fight us? What if I assure you on my oath that the big man will remain unharmed?"

"Then why'd you take him?" Eddie demanded.

"To keep you away from the ritual my master wishes to perform. If you, Wizard Berman, stay out of it, we shall return him."

"While you destroy Manhattan? Not a good deal," Eddie told her.

"Selene, you have Mordred's ear. Is there anything we can do to prevent this?" Drusilicus attempted. "A war between our two groups or the use of the spell on that papyrus will benefit none of us."

A howling collection of catcalls and yells from the vampires on both ends of the tunnel put Eddie's teeth on edge.

Selene raised her hand, and the noise stopped. She cleared her throat. "Perhaps there is a peaceful solution to this conflict. First, return the mask and Tuck to me."

Eddie and Drusilicus exchanged a glance, but Drusilicus handed the mask to the diminutive man, who grabbed it and spat

on the ground in front of Eddie's feet. He strode out of the tunnel
with the mask firmly in his hand.

He brought it to Selene and gave it to her with a quick bow.
She took the mask and glared at the wizards. "If you wish to spare
New York, then send us Marlowe."

"What?" Drusilicus frowned.

"If the old man comes to my master—alone, tomorrow night
—we shall spare the city."

Drusilicus considered this. "Is that what this is all about?
Simple revenge for something that happened a thousand years
ago?"

Selene's jaw set. "Mordred and I have not forgotten what
Merlinus did to us. If you wish to save this city, he must surrender
himself to us."

She stepped back, and the vampires gave a mighty roar. The
night air was tainted with the coppery smell of blood as the
vampires shrieked. They poured into the tunnel, fangs glinting in
the dim light as they charged. Eddie and Drusilicus thrust
themselves back-to-back to face both ends of the confined space
as the horde advanced.

"*Oppressio!*" Eddie yelled, and the ring of fire on the top of his
staff grew amazingly bright. A wall of force pushed against the
attackers, bowling them over with the strength of his spell. Eddie
was still not good at the intricacies of subtle magick, but when it
came to pure power, he had plenty of punch.

Drusilicus was knocking over the attackers at his end of the
tunnel, a bright blue light on top of his staff.

However, the monsters were hardly dazed and rose to their feet, fangs extended, and drool dripping from their mouths. Their eyes glinted in the light from Eddie's staff with the reflected light of a predator.

"Ring of fire," Eddie yelled as fire, waist-high and hot, rose from the pavement in a circle around the two wizards. With a gesture, the fire moved away from them and toward the army of attacking vampires, scorching the ground as it went.

One quick vampire, a young male, leapt over the flames to get Eddie. Eddie took a step toward him and punched him with the hand that bore the silver ring. Even without the needle and the Sasquatch blood, it was remarkably effective. The vampire fell back and his face wore an impression in the shape of the ring's design.

Drusilicus levitated a vampire to smash him into the masonry roof of the tunnel, then threw him beyond the fire about ten feet away from the two wizards, hoping to keep the mob of bloodsuckers at bay.

"We need to end this," Drusilicus told him.

"I could create higher walls of fire that move out and burn everything."

"Not bad," Drusilicus said, "except in this tunnel, we would run out of oxygen. Also, they have your partner, so incinerating them would be an act of out-and-out war."

"And this isn't?" Eddie said as, with a minor effort of will, he swatted a vampire out of the air as it jumped over the flames in attack.

There was an odd sound, like an animal call. With a roar, the vampires rose into the air, shrinking and transforming. Their bodies twisted and shifted into bats that rose into the sky with high-pitched squawks and squeals.

Eddie and Drusilicus were alone.

With a gesture, the ring of fire died away, and they slowly came out of the tunnel.

"Why did they run?" Eddie wondered, as he stared into the night sky.

"Their function was to keep us from following Selene," Drusilicus explained. "I assume once she was safe, someone gave them a signal to flee."

"What time is it?" Eddie asked.

"Almost midnight, but you should be able to feel it."

"I do. I just wanted to make sure."

"To what end, lieutenant?"

"To the end that we only got twenty-four hours to stop these vampires or they're going to destroy New York."

"This is terrible," Marlowe complained.

The only wizards who remained at the townhouse were Bankrock and Vasant, and the four of them were sitting around the table after rousing Marlowe from his bed. Marlowe wore bright blue silk pajamas with electric stripes of pink going up and down the garment. He had also thrown on a robe with a paisley pattern that appeared like multiple amoebas mating.

Eddie let Drusilicus tell the tale, watching the reaction of the assembled wizards.

"Do you think they were attempting to capture you, Wizard Berman?" Vasant asked.

"Probably," Eddie said, "but for what purpose, I don't know."

"You do not know what happened to Wizard Claremont?" Bankrock piped up.

Eddie shook his head. "Not at all."

Marlowe cleared his throat. "Then I must insist that you remain here tonight, Eddie."

"Who's gonna protect my house, my kids?" Eddie said as he rose.

Drusilicus put a hand on Eddie's shoulder. "Lieutenant, I have strengthened the protections on your home, and without your presence, they have no reason to attack."

Eddie pushed Drusilicus' hand away. "Except for revenge. They could kill my entire family, just for spite."

Marlowe turned worried eyes to Eddie. "If they have captured Rusty and somehow incapacitated Dalehead, the risk is too great. We are not just dealing with a vampire—we are dealing with an experienced sorceress who gained the power of a staff!"

"You didn't even know she was still alive," Eddie bellowed, his anger getting the best of him. "What kind of wizard are you?"

"There is no need to disrespect the coven master," Bankrock admonished him.

"Why don't we all sit and talk?" Drusilicus suggested, trying to calm the group. "Flying off the handle and yelling will accomplish nothing."

Eddie glared at Drusilicus, and then returned to his seat, fighting to steady himself. The fear for his family and his partner felt like a weight on his heart.

"We cannot do anything more this night," Marlowe said. "If they are attempting to reduce our numbers, it is best to stay in a safe place."

"Selene, or whatever her name is, can walk right in here."

"Not through that door," Drusilicus spoke calmly. "Someone would have to open it."

"Couldn't she just knock it down?"

"There are many layers of protective spells," Marlowe explained. "And even if she could get through it, none of her vampire cohorts could follow."

"Besides, to what purpose?" Bankrock said. "She has given Mordred the papyrus, and she has the power to help him activate it. Right now they have the upper hand."

"Unless we give them Marlowe," Eddie said. "And we are *not* doing that."

"Actually," Marlowe offered with a twinkle in his eye, "I may have a plan to make that work."

"Is it better than how we have fared so far?" Drusilicus asked.

"It might give us the edge we need," Marlowe looked them each in the eye. "Let me tell you my idea."

NINETEEN

E ddie awoke the next morning in the overdone bedroom that he stayed in when he was at Marlowe's. The light was dim, only a little coming in through a crack in the heavy crimson drapes that covered the window. His staff was lying in bed next to him.

Marlowe designed the bedroom in what Eddie called "Victorian Bordello" with overstuffed chairs and large wooden dressers and furnishings, and all the cloth on each piece was a deep scarlet.

Dressed in a pair of pajamas transformed from his suit, Eddie grabbed his staff and headed to the bathroom just down the hall from his room, passing the small brass plate on the door that was engraved in fancy letters with his name:

Eddie Berman

Each bedroom had a similar brass plate, and the occupant's name would appear on it for the length of the guest's stay.

Eddie turned into the spacious bathroom, the walls and floor covered to the ceiling with tiny white and black tiles. In the room stood a huge claw-foot bathtub designed to accommodate an elephant, surrounded by a shower curtain.

It was only about 6:00 AM as he stepped into the shower. As always, the hot water was the exact right temperature the moment he turned it on.

Once shaved and dressed, he shrank down his staff into the wooden credit card and put it in his wallet as he headed for the elevator to the ground floor.

Eddie felt something vibrate in his pocket and pulled out his phone, but it was not quivering. He returned the phone to his breast pocket and reached into the outer pocket of his sports jacket to extract the wooden whistle given to him by the *Pukwudgie*.

It vibrated in his pocket.

Eddie reached the first floor and headed for the outer door. If Skysoarer was trying to get in touch, he could not get past Marlowe's magickal protections.

He stepped outside, and held the whistle aloft. It was early morning in spring, but already New Yorkers were moving from place to place.

"Walker, I am down here!" a small voice said.

Eddie gazed down to see Skysoarer. The eighteen-inch-tall man was transparent, more like a collection of lines drawn in the air in his shape than an actual body.

"What happened?" Eddie said, wanting to reach out to the little man.

"Speak softly. I am invisible to all but you," the little man explained.

Eddie bent to lean a little closer so he could speak quietly. "How did it go last night?"

"You were correct, Walker of the Wise. One of the *Skadegamutc* attempted to go into the room of the mother of your children."

Eddie frowned. "Were you able to stop him?"

"I stopped her."

"Her? It was a woman?"

"Yes, a tall one."

"What was her hair like?"

"Long, and as black as the crow."

That description fit the two female vampires Eddie knew: Selene or Lysandra. "How did you defeat her?"

The Native-American sprite crossed his arms and regarded Eddie with a smug look. "I made it so she could not open the window."

"Really? That's all?"

"She came to the window as a *pisilunkòn*, a bat, and then stood on a ledge to become a woman. She tried the window for quite a while but could not open it."

Eddie couldn't stop smiling. "Good work."

"I knew she would not enter through a door without an invitation, so when I sealed the window, she finally went away. I have guarded your woman all night."

"I thank you for your service, Skysoarer." Eddie bowed in a way that he hoped suggested respect.

"I will rest now. If you need me or any of the *Pukwudgie*, use the whistle."

The little man's outline faded, and he disappeared.

"Man, he's good," Eddie marveled. He pulled his cell phone and hit the number for his home. His mother picked up on the first ring.

"Eddie?"

"Momma, how are you?"

"Annoyed you didn't come home last night and didn't call."

"I had to stay in the city for work. I'll be home soon, and we can all visit Cerise in the hospital. Any problems I should know about?"

"No one showed up at our doorstep and pretended they were you, if that's what you mean."

Eddie smiled. "Okay, I'll be home in a few minutes."

He hung up the phone, and then another thought hit him. He quickly hit the number for his partner's wife, Maria.

"Hola?"

"Maria, it's Eddie."

Her voice turned into a wailing moan. "Was he shot? Is he hurt—"

"Maria calm down. His phone battery died."

"Battery? Hold on." It sounded like Maria covered the mouthpiece and chattered off to someone in Spanish. Then she was back. "He couldn't call me from the precinct?"

"Maria, we're on a stake-out. An undercover one. Both of us can't get away, so he told me to call you."

She gave a tremendous sigh. "But he is all right?"

"Good as gold. Now look, Maria, we're gonna be on this assignment for about the next twenty-four hours, but I promise we will be home soon. I only got a few hours off to go check on Cerise, and Luis is covering for me."

"That is so like him," Maria said, and Eddie could almost hear tears in her voice. "My big husband. Thank you, Eddie. I was so worried."

"It's fine, Maria. We'll talk soon."

Eddie ended the call. He hated to lie to Maria, but telling her Luis had been kidnapped by vampires seemed worse. Besides, he would get Luis back.

Wouldn't he?

He secured the door and headed to the breakfast room to find only Marlowe was awake.

He was organizing the many papers on the desk, moving them into piles and in some specific order that only he understood.

"How did you sleep, Eddie?" Marlowe asked without looking up.

"Good," Eddie watched as Marlowe put the papers into piles as an idea occurred to him. "How did she know it was here?"

"Pardon?"

"I mean, I look at all these old scrolls and stuff you have. I wouldn't recognize one from the other—how did Selene know that specific papyrus was right here?"

Marlowe considered this. "I don't know... and to add to the mystery, I didn't know I had it until I put on the Hat of Remembrance. It was in my extra-dimensional storage, so technically, the papyrus wasn't *here* at all."

Eddie considered it. "Marlowe, I'm thinking we got played."

"Played?"

"Yes, that original prophecy made you go looking for the papyrus. Once you found it and brought it here, they could steal it."

Marlowe slowly shook his head. "Nimue knew I possessed it. I have kept it since the days of Arthur."

"If she and Mordred were bent on revenge, why did they wait so long? I mean, *centuries?*"

Marlowe sighed. "It must have taken centuries to earn their place of power. There is no vampire that would disobey the word of the Drakula. Then they had to find an opportunity to gain the power of a staff."

"I think that's when all this started. Somehow word got out that there was a staff without a master."

Marlowe nodded. "There were vampires watching us the night we fought the Great Evil."

"Waiting to see who won." Eddie nodded.

"Probably. But I was not aware of a vampire presence when Caleb told us he didn't wish to have a staff."

"As I recall, we were both pretty busy," Eddie said, and ordered coffee from the magickal tea set that quickly jumped to his service. "How did she find the papyrus among all these other papers?"

"She possessed a staff, Eddie, and knew what she was after. Will and intent, as always. She probably set up that entire scenario for us to find the coffin after she knew the papyrus was on this plane of existence."

"I gotta go see my wife."

"Is she better, Eddie?"

"She should be fine. I had her watched last night."

Marlowe frowned. "Really?"

"I'll be back in a few hours. We can search for Dalehead and Rusty, and you can get out that table of weapons for tonight."

"That is an excellent suggestion."

Eddie headed for the door. He hated to leave the old man so upset that his onetime apprentice had gone to such lengths to bring him down—but he had other responsibilities.

He crossed the street into the wooded section of the park and instantly transported to the small grove near his home. He let himself in the back door, where his sons and his mother were sitting at the table.

Eleanor glanced up as Eddie came into the room. "You hungry? There's eggs."

"Not really."

"You should eat, keep your strength up," Eleanor told him.

Eddie pulled a plate from a cabinet and dished some eggs from the pan on the stove. He sat down at the table and ate.

"Is Mom all right?" William, the elder son, asked. He shot up to his father's height in just the last six months.

"Yeah," Eddie said, trying to sound casual. "But, she's almost forty, and that complicates pregnancy." He smiled at his sons. "You two are going to have a little sister."

"A girl? That's great, Dad," William cheered.

"Man, is she gonna be crying all night and stuff?" Douglas frowned with all the exaggerated annoyance of a twelve-year-old.

"Probably, she's a baby," Eddie said. "But we'll manage."

"We got a baby sister, while we're in high school," William complained.

"Looks like it." Eddie grinned at his son.

"Old people havin' babies." Doug shook his head in disgust. "Yuck!"

"Don't say that when you see your mom," Eddie told him calmly. "She has enough to worry about."

"I know better'n that," Doug answered, offended.

Eddie smiled at this. "Finish up. We gotta visit your mom, and then I gotta get back to work."

"Another long day, dearie?" Eleanor worried.

"Hopefully the last one," Eddie said, and stared at the eggs for a moment. It would be a long day, and if Marlowe's plan didn't work, things would get very bad for New York.

When they were brainstorming the previous night, the plan seemed like a good one but there were so many things that could go wrong.

If he didn't succeed, the vampires would hunt down not only Eddie, but each member of his family. What would he do then?

"Eddie, you all right, honey?" Eleanor touched his arm.

Eddie started. "Sorry. Yeah, I'm good. Okay, guys, let's go. Momma, are you coming?"

"I'll visit her later in the day, Eddie. This is just you and the boys right now."

"Shotgun," bellowed William.

"Not so loud, son," Eddie said, feeling jumpy and ready to hit the ground in fear of a weapon. "Also, please don't yell *shotgun*.... it means something different to a cop, okay?"

William nodded. "Sorry, Dad. Next time, I'll just yell 'front seat.'"

"Then your old man can avoid a heart attack," Eddie said.

Doug got in the back without complaint, and soon Eddie was pulling into the multi-level parking lot of the Holy Name Hospital.

Cerise was sitting upright as they came in, and delight showed on her face. "There are my men!"

Eddie held back while the boys hugged her first. He smiled to see them fawn over their mother. "How are you feeling?"

"Better, stronger. They can release me today. They just want to do a few more—"

She sucked in a breath with a surprised look on her face.

Eddie grabbed her hand. "What is it?"

She held her breath for a moment and then let it out slowly. "Just a contraction. It was nothing. It's going away."

"A contraction, you say?" a voice came from the door.

Doctor Ramsen, the gynecologist that he had spoken with the previous day, stepped into the room. "Are these your sons, Mr. Berman?"

"Yes, this is William and Doug," Eddie said.

"And you had a contraction, Mrs. Berman?" the doctor asked again.

"Just a small one, doctor," she answered.

"Gentlemen, I must ask all of you to leave the room," Ramsen said, and touched a button on the wall that summoned a nurse.

"Is everything okay?" Eddie worried.

"Perfectly normal, but there are things I wish to check."

A nurse stepped into the room as the doctor put on a pair of rubber gloves and said, "Just give us a minute."

Eddie and the boys stepped into the hall and the nurse closed the curtain that shielded the bed from view. Eddie heard low voices: the doctor, then the nurse, then Cerise as they spoke in quiet tones.

Finally, after a few brief minutes, the nurse pulled open the curtain as the doctor removed his gloves, grabbed a clipboard, and approached Eddie.

"Go sit with your mom," Eddie said to the boys and stepped away with the doctor. "What's up?"

The doctor led Eddie into the hall. "Your wife seems much better, but I would advise against releasing her."

"Why?" Eddie asked with concern.

The doctor smiled. "Her cervix is dilated beyond three centimeters."

"What?" Eddie replied, shocked by this. "She's in labor?"

The man nodded. "Probably started in her sleep. This happens in cases of pregnancy anemia. The mother sometimes gives birth a bit early. There's nothing to worry about, but I believe she is having this child today."

Eddie's mouth was dry. "Today? I've gotta be in New York... my job..."

"It is not my place to tell you what to do, but this baby will be born within the next twenty-four hours, Mr. Berman, whether or not it fits your schedule." He made a quick note on his clipboard. "I will check on her in a few hours, and I advise you to call your personal obstetrician."

With that, the man strode away, leaving Eddie with his mouth gaping.

With unfeeling fingers, he struggled to take out his phone and call his mother.

"What is it, honey?" Eleanor said upon answering.

"Momma, Cerise is gonna have the baby today!" Eddie hissed.

"How wonderful!"

"You don't understand. I gotta go to New York!"

This took Eleanor by surprise. "You gonna run out on Cerise while she's in labor?"

"I don't have a choice. Can you get a cab over here and drive the boys home?"

Eleanor was silent for a long moment. "You'd better explain it to your wife, Edward."

His mother called him Edward. She wasn't happy.

"I'll tell her. Can you call the cab?"

"I will."

Eddie walked back into the hospital room. He pulled out his car keys and handed them to William. "Your gramma's coming to pick you up. You give her my keys."

"Sure, Dad. Ain't you stayin'?" William asked.

"You guys let me talk to your momma, alone, please?" Eddie said.

The two boys exchanged a glance and headed out of the room. Eddie knelt at the bedside and focused on his wife.

"You have to go," she said with a sad look in her eyes.

He had to tell the truth. "I don't want to, Cerise. But these bad folks, these vampires? They've got Luis."

"What?" Cerise said, her eyes wide. "Does Maria know?"

"I gave her some cock-and-bull story about his phone battery bein' dead and that we're on surveillance, and I got off for a couple hours to visit you."

"And you have to be there to save him," Cerise said, her jaw firm.

"I really want to be here," Eddie told her and cradled her hand. "I wanted to coach you through this."

She brought his hand to her lips to kiss it. "Luis needs you more. After all, he's fighting vampires, and I'm just having a baby. I've already done it two times."

"I'll call our obstetrician on my way to New York. Momma will pick up the boys."

"I will be fine, sugar. You just take care of my big, black man."

Eddie stood, bent, and kissed his wife's head. Then he turned to join his sons in the hall.

"Momma gonna come home?" Doug asked.

"No, Doug. She's staying here. She's in labor."

"Really?" William gulped.

"Dang," Doug added.

"Your gramma will come by and pick you two up. But I need you guys to be on the alert. Don't invite anyone into the house, you got that?"

"Does this have something to do with all the weird stuff, like last year?" Doug asked.

"A bit. And the bad guys cannot walk into the house unless you invite them," Eddie reassured them.

"Good to know," William declared.

"I gotta go," Eddie said and headed down the hall.

As he walked away, he heard William ask his brother, "You think it's gonna get crazy like it did that last time?"

"I got no idea," replied Doug.

TWENTY

Eddie was soon standing in front of the townhouse on 85th Street looking up at the stone steps with renewed anger. His wife was in labor and here he was, trying to stop vampires.

He knocked on the door and Bankrock opened it, dressed in a suit with a bow tie and quite agitated. "It's about time. We have much to prepare."

"If you got something negative to say, keep it to yourself, Banky."

"There's no need to be rude, Wizard Berman."

Eddie turned on Bankrock, his temper flaring. "Oh yeah? The vampires abducted my partner, we don't know what happened to Rusty or Dalehead, and my wife is having a baby right now!"

Bankrock blanched. "Oh my! Really?"

"Yes," Eddie said, and leaned against the closed outer door as if his strength had left him. "I should be there."

Bankrock nodded and stood up as straight as he could. "I understand."

"Do you?"

"I have been a father… more than once, in fact." He turned away, lost in memory. "But I had duties to perform. I had no wish for my children to be at risk." His jaw grew tight. "Is it any wonder why I have focused on the more mundane duties available for me in the coven? I am not cut out to be an adventurer like men such as you."

Eddie suddenly felt bad. "Bankrock, you do your job really well. And I've seen you in a fight—you're a big help."

"That is kind of you, Wizard Berman, but we both know that I am not an imposing figure."

"You can be when the need arises," Eddie said. "Look, I didn't mean to yell at you. What's happening isn't your fault."

"Hopefully, we can defeat this adversary," Bankrock said, straightened up, and quickly wiped his face with a pocket handkerchief. "Now come, they await us."

Eddie followed Bankrock into the cavernous living room. Once again the large table was in the middle of the space, overloaded with weapons one might use on a vampire. Around the table stood Drusilicus, Marlowe, and Vasant.

"The five of us, then?" Eddie said.

"Yes," Marlowe told him. "The others are following the plan. We must first find Dalehead and Rusty. I have sent Inscope to seek the lair of our foes."

"Why Inscope?" Eddie asked, unimpressed from the short time he'd met the tall, gray-bearded wizard.

"Wizard Inscope has several unique prophetic abilities," Bankrock told him.

"Really?"

Bankrock continued. "Yes. He can peer through walls with his mind's eye."

Eddie shook his head. "Man, that would come in handy on a bust." He leaned toward Marlowe. "You gotta teach me that."

Marlowe smiled. "In due time, Eddie. Meanwhile, if Inscope succeeds in his task, we must go confront the enemy in his lair in Greenwich Village. If we can, we must finish before nightfall."

Eddie raised an arm to attract the other's attention. "Everyone, my wife is in labor. So, if we could end this quickly, I would appreciate it."

"Once again, lieutenant, you put undo pressure on us all," Drusilicus stated with a stern face. Then a small smile appeared. "But I know you wish you were there."

Drusilicus held out his hand, and Eddie shook it. "Thanks, Drew."

Vasant sighed. "Being the only person in the room who has given birth, I must say that this desire for the men to be in the birthing chamber is a modern contrivance. Unless the husband is helping with the delivery, they are very much in the way."

"She has our hopes and prayers, Eddie," Marlowe told him.

Vasant cleared her throat. "We can't change the direction of the wind, but we can adjust the sails."

"That sounds wise," Eddie said.

Vasant lifted her eyebrows. "I hope so. I wrote it."

Marlowe announced, "Take what you need, and we must be off. Bankrock, have you had any luck with the location spell for either Rusty or Dalehead?"

Bankrock reached into his suit jacket and pulled out a small crystal ball. "No, neither. Do you still think looking within their arches to be a good choice, or just a waste of time?"

Marlowe sighed. "So far it is the only decision I can see. We must give Inscope another hour or so to finish his task."

"Very well," Bankrock said and returned the ball to his pocket. He turned to the table to pick up a finely carved pointed stake.

Eddie inspected the table until he located the bottle marked "Sasquatch Blood." He hit the button that opened the ring and, using the eyedropper, filled the small reservoir to the top. He resealed the bottle and shut the compartment on the ring, then he closed his eyes and thought of Stone Face and their meeting in front of the fire.

"Give me your strength, brother," he murmured.

In a few minutes, the wizards had selected their choices from the assorted weapons. Vasant surprised Eddie by taking a bright-silver knife. She was wearing an Edwardian outfit, consisting of a skirt that went past her knees with a long-sleeve white blouse and double-breasted vest. She slipped the knife into the waistband of the skirt and covered the hilt with the vest.

Drusilicus slipped a pair of stakes into his suit jacket. Meanwhile, Bankrock and Marlowe were on the side of the table away from Eddie, so he didn't see what they prepared.

"Ready, then?" Marlowe asked.

Nods and grunts went around the table, and the five wizards stepped away and headed for the door as one unit.

In a flash, they were outside, down the stairs, across the street and in Central Park.

Marlowe held up his hand to stop the group. They certainly were an unconventional group with him in his inexpensive suit, Drusilicus in a suit that was the epitome of a successful businessman, Vasant in her Victorian lady-of-action garb, Bankrock with his bow tie and tweed suit, and Marlowe, who for some reason wore a jacket that was a purple paisley, and carried his elaborate walking stick.

Marlowe spoke simply and quickly. "We need to get to Dalehead's arch on 65th Street, so instead of walking twenty blocks, let us use the grove of trees. Agreed?"

Everyone else nodded and followed Marlowe into a wooded area as he lifted his walking stick above their heads. Instantly, they had to push their way through the greenery to see several asphalt paths in front of them and a clearing with only a few trees.

"Sorry," Marlowe apologized. "This part of the park does not have a lot of coverage."

He pointed down the path that took a sharp left turn, and using his cane, headed toward it as the others followed.

"It has been a long time since we wandered together in the park, good lady," Drusilicus murmured to Vasant, but Eddie overheard them.

"My goodness, sir, are you flirting with me?" Vasant whispered back, teasing him.

"It is merely a recollection. When we were last together in public, you wore a similar outfit."

"As I recall, it was quite the scandal. A dark woman walking side by side with a white man."

"Things have changed."

They passed a man, who although it was only spring, wore only a tattered pair of shorts as he lay on a blanket on the lawn, snoring loudly.

Vasant glanced over at the man, who was all but exposing himself. "Some changes are not for the better."

The huge open archway appeared before them on the path. It was a magnificent structure with a quatrefoil design upon the top of the bridge that spanned it. There were accents carved into the stone resembling four leaves, each facing a different point of the compass.

Protruding from the arch were decorative abutments of carved stone that bordered the path on both sides. The opening was carved stone, but inside were alternating rows of brick and stone on the soffit and down the walls of the structure.

Drusilicus stopped before the arch and scanned the area as Bankrock closed the distance and checked the other side.

Eddie stepped near Drusilicus. "I don't think there are any vampires out during the day."

"I am more concerned about their human spies." Drusilicus said and turned his head to Marlowe. "Marlowe, I think we can begin. Bankrock and I will keep watch."

Marlowe nodded, and Eddie and Vasant joined him. Marlowe raised his walking stick as he mumbled a few words. After only a moment, the bricks opened up to a section and the three people stepped in. The wall immediately reassembled behind them as they passed through.

They were in a simple room, a neutral beige color, with all the appearances of a comfortable European apartment, with a small living room and three doorways for what Eddie assumed was a bathroom, kitchen, and bedroom. The place was neat, but antiseptic, as if the owner didn't visit very often. Marlowe opened the middle door that revealed a small hallway with a bedroom at the end.

The three headed down the hall, and Marlowe held his wizard's staff aloft, a white light on top to illuminate their way.

In the darkened bedroom was a large bed, and in the middle lay Dalehead in white bedroom attire that seemed to consist of many layers of gauzy fabric.

Vasant and Marlowe went to her. The old man touched her neck, feeling for her pulse, as Vasant lay her hand on her forehead.

"What is it?" Eddie asked. "Is she dead?"

Marlowe lowered his head and exhaled. "No, it is the Dark Sleep."

Eddie was familiar with the term. He was told that it was a place between life and death, like a coma. Only two or more wizards could rouse someone from this state.

"There's three of us," Eddie suggested. "We can bring her back, right?"

"There is something else," Vasant said. She waved her hands up and down a few inches above Dalehead's still form. "I believe they have given her a drug, as well as the sorcery."

"Then we dare not wake her without knowing about the drug," Marlowe warned.

Vasant stood up straight. "It could be a drug that our powers would activate, with unknown consequences to Dalehead."

"Or us," Marlowe murmured.

Eddie sighed and nodded, familiar with a similar occurrence that had happened the previous year. "We can't just leave her like this!"

"I am afraid—of our choices—it is the best one," Vasant persisted.

"She is correct, Eddie," Marlowe agreed. "By the time we analyze the drug and come up with an antidote, the day will be past. We have far too much to accomplish this day."

"Could they have dosed her with Mind-Blo?" Eddie asked. "One of the major ingredients of the drug is vampire venom."

Marlowe nodded. "I hardly see what that has to do with—"

"The Drakula is going to make his move, tonight," Eddie interrupted. "Somehow, Mind-Blo has something to do with all of it, but I don't know how. The timing of when it showed up on the street is just too much of a coincidence."

"What are your wishes, Marlowe?" Vasant asked.

"Let us go to Claremont's arch. I fear we may find him in a similar condition."

Marlowe waved his walking stick and he, Vasant, and Eddie passed through the conjured opening.

Drusilicus and Bankrock joined them in the tunnel.

"Is she there?" Bankrock asked.

"Yes, and in the Dark Sleep," Marlowe told him.

Bankrock gasped. "Who did this, when did—"

Vasant put up her hands to calm him. "We know not, other than she is there. She is unconscious and was given some kind of drug."

Drusilicus moved near. "This does not bode well."

"Great insight, Drew," Eddie muttered.

"Let us head off to Claremont Arch," Marlowe ordered. "It is near 90th Street, so I suggest we go back to the small grove we used to get here. Unless you two would prefer your tradition of exchanging insults."

He headed away at a fast pace, and the others moved quickly to keep up. No one spoke as they went into the small covering of trees and bushes and pushed their way out onto another asphalt walkway in a different section of the park.

Marlowe led them uptown on a path that led to Central Park West, but kept moving and pointed with his walking stick. "There."

Hidden by a tree and numerous bushes was a stone arch with metal bars along the front.

"Is there a path to it?" Eddie asked, not seeing a break in the greenery that led to the arch.

"No, there used to be a pedestrian path that went under the roadway," Marlowe said. "But they changed the location of the path over the years, so the arch was closed."

"How does Rusty get in it?" Eddie wondered.

"From above," Marlowe offered. "He drives his cab into the 90th Street entrance road, then comes to a stop above the arch and sinks right into it."

"Very convenient," Bankrock said.

"But not much help for us," Drusilicus noted. "How do we access it?"

Marlowe considered it for a moment. "I believe we have to climb down to the barred door and go in that way."

"Not I," Drusilicus huffed. "This suit is Armani. And I believe the lady is not dressed for such an adventure."

"I will go, if you need me," Vasant corrected with a glare at Drusilicus.

"No, I think Eddie, Bankrock, and I will do," Marlowe stated. He pointed back down the pathway. "I think if we go this way, the slope will be more gentle."

"We shall keep watch," Drusilicus offered.

The three men went down the slope. There was a pathway, worn by foot traffic, but the original stone walkway was long gone. Bankrock led the way, making bushes and vegetation fly out of their path with a mere gesture.

They reached the barred entrance, and with a simple lifting of Marlowe's walking stick, the door creaked open on old hinges.

Looking at the metal bars, Eddie said, "Now I know why he calls himself, 'Rusty'."

The entire arch had tables and storage of all sorts in the cramped location, but it appeared these items were left years earlier.

Bankrock said, "Can we go into his room now? This place is quite foreboding."

Marlowe gestured at the one section of the wall not obstructed by storage, and an opening appeared that they quickly went through.

The room they stepped into differed greatly from Dalehead's. Instead of a quaint apartment, there was a garage that looked like it came out of a dream. There was a floor of rubberized material that was in alternating squares of black and gray. Bolted on the wall were multiple cabinets and a workbench, all painted red metal. In one spot on the wall were shelves with containers of oil and different car fluids, as well as cleaners, polishes, and waxes.

A toolbox as tall as Eddie stood on huge wheels and probably contained every tool known to man or wizard. There was a compressor and a lift, and in the middle of the room was Rusty's cab.

Rusty sat in the front seat, apparently asleep, as they could hear his wracking snores throughout the room.

Marlowe went to the driver's door and opened it carefully, and Eddie caught Rusty as he fell from the seat, since he had been leaning against the door in his slumbers. Eddie sat him upright but he did not wake.

Marlowe waved his stick over the sleeping man. "He appears to be in the Dark Sleep as well."

Bankrock drew near. "Was he also drugged?"

Marlowe passed his stick over the sleeping cabbie a second time. "Yes, I am sensing the strange drug within him as well."

Bankrock shook his head. "We have lost two of our best fighters. This is terrible."

Eddie raised an eyebrow. "What's worse is wondering what happens after sundown."

There was a tiny voice, and Marlowe quickly pulled out a small mirror from his paisley jacket. A tiny image of the Wizard Inscope was inside the glass.

"What is it, Inscope?"

The man's gravelly voice resounded with that odd accent of his. "Ye were quite right, Marlowe. I have indeed located the underground hideaway ye spoke of, right where you said it would be."

"What can you tell us?" requested Marlowe loudly.

"It t'would be best if ye came here. The things I have uncovered are most... unexpected."

"Very well," Marlowe sighed. "We shall make haste."

He put the mirror away and turned to Eddie and Bankrock. "There is nothing more to see here. I believe Inscope has located a place that may provide many answers for us."

TWENTY-ONE

They stepped away from Claremont Arch after Marlowe had secured the door, and made their way up the slope. At the tree near the top, Drusilicus and Vasant were talking animatedly, and both were all smiles.

"Everything okay?" Eddie said, and both Drusilicus and Vasant faced Eddie with looks of embarrassment.

"Quite... fine, lieutenant," Drusilicus stated, a bit red. "Any sign of Rusty?"

Eddie considered them both. Vasant was observing the ground, a flush on her cheeks, as Drusilicus focused on a nearby tree. "Yes, he was in his cab, but in the Dark Sleep, just like Dalehead."

"Shouldn't we try to awaken him?" Vasant suggested.

By now, Marlowe and Bankrock had reached the summit. "We cannot; we must away. Drusilicus, are you familiar with Washington Square Park?"

Drusilicus was all business. "Quite."

"Good, you must lead us to a place to materialize that will be out of sight," Marlowe insisted.

"During the daytime, on a Saturday?" Drusilicus frowned.

"Time is of the essence."

Bankrock spoke up. "Marlowe, I do not advise we move about the city like this. One person might pass through groves without attracting undue attention, but surely a group of five people—"

Marlowe sighed. "What would you have me do?" He gestured at the barred arch. "Our cabdriver is in a coma."

"You could call an Uber," Eddie suggested.

The others gaped at him, and finally Vasant said, "What is an Uber?"

"Very well," Drusilicus said and placed his palm against the pocket that held his watch. "I shall use a simple diversion spell, so that people will not notice our sudden appearance."

He led the group to the nearby copse of trees and they all stepped out in a corner of Washington Square Park. The usually sedate park was overflowing with people, as it was a warm day for March. People were milling about, watching several street entertainers who were doing juggling and magic. Tourists were taking photos near the Washington Square Arch or the giant fountain in the middle of the park.

"Where to?" Eddie said, pleased to note that most of the people hadn't noticed their sudden appearance. There was a young man who sat on a bench that stared right at them, but then he merely got up and wandered away.

"We need to get to the catacombs," Marlowe said.

Eddie got in front of the group with his hands raised. "Wait a minute. *Catacombs?*" He glared at Marlowe. "Like the ones you and I went through that last time?"

"Those were extra-dimensional, Eddie," Marlowe pointed out. "These are on this plane of existence."

"How do we get to them?" Eddie worried. "I mean, we have an entire park full of people."

Bankrock turned to Marlowe. "The fastest way would be the drains around the arch, if memory serves me."

Eddie recalled the openings covered with the heavy metal grating he'd noted on his previous visit. He really didn't want to go crawling around in those.

"Nonsense, I have a much better choice," Marlowe said. "Follow me."

Marlowe led the group toward the center fountain. Eddie couldn't help but wonder how this was any better. Disappearing into a fountain would attract more attention than simply going inside the door of the Washington Square Arch.

Marlowe went to the fountain and headed directly toward the arch. He stopped a good ten feet from it and turned toward a flagpole in a slight alcove behind a short black chain. The flagpole rose out of a large metal cylinder that had an enormous base at least five feet high with a small doorway in its side and a hole for a key.

"Here we are," Marlowe said, and gingerly stepped over the chain.

"That's a flagpole," Eddie hissed.

Marlowe nodded. "Yes, it is. And I am sure the people who raise the flag every day are unaware of its other uses."

Marlowe stepped to the small door on the side of the pole, waved his stick, and pulled it open. He touched his stick to it again, ducked, stepped inside the metal cylinder and quickly disappeared from view.

Bankrock went to the chain and followed. Several onlookers, curious about the strange people going into the small space, came over to watch.

As Vasant headed to the small door, Eddie faced the gathering crowd and held up his badge. "Nothing going on, folks. This is a semiannual... um... flagpole inspection."

Drusilicus followed Vasant and ducked very low to place his leg into the small doorway. He soon headed in, and the people in the crowd murmured with amazement about four people fitting into a container that could not possibly fit even one.

"Move along, folks, nothing to see here," Eddie said and stepped over the chain and backed his way to the open doorway. "I mean it, nothing to see!"

People shrugged and moved away as Eddie held the door open and stood behind it. "The NYPD appreciates your cooperation. Have a nice day."

He quickly ducked into the doorway and down a stone, circular staircase that burrowed into the ground. He stepped within and pulled the door closed behind him.

It opened back up.

Eddie gestured and his staff zoomed into his hand. He waved it, and the door slammed closed.

It was now completely dark, and Eddie produced a light on the top of his staff.

He descended the steps and noticed several lights ahead of him, the other wizards using their own staffs to light their way. He saw the slightly different shades of glowing circles as he stepped down carefully.

The descent was precarious, as the steps were only wide enough for him to fit. Though once he was underground, the old stone walls spread back a bit to give him more space than the flagpole container at the top. As far as Eddie could tell, the staircase had been carved into a tube that went straight down into the earth.

He finally reached the bottom of the circular stairs, where the other wizards waited in a small room. The ceiling was only seven feet tall, except for the shaft of the staircase, and Eddie ducked as he joined his four companions.

They were all in their wizard robes, though Vasant, once again in yellow silk, was in an outfit much like Drusilicus'. She was resplendent in a short tunic with leggings and tall boots, showing off her slim figure.

Eddie shifted his clothes into his red fighting tunic and noted what Vasant wore. "A little different from the other night."

She smiled. "A bit, yes. Ladies in this time have a little more freedom in their clothing choices. I saw one woman in a pair of pants that were ripped in many places."

"That's the style nowadays," Drusilicus assured her.

"Seems like it would be chilly," Vasant replied.

There was an open archway that was now filled by the tall, bearded wizard Eddie met the previous night. He was in dark-magenta robes and his staff was in hand.

"Inscope, thank you for meeting us," Marlowe greeted him.

The man stared down his large nose and arched his impressive eyebrows as he peered from person to person. "This is all ye bring? Two wizards, a Newling, and a woman?"

Apparently, misogyny was as much a part of wizard culture as anywhere else. Eddie saw anger flare in Vasant's eyes, but she said nothing.

"Most of the coven are resting now," Marlowe said. "We expect the conflict to be tonight. This is a scouting mission, nothing more."

"Thou will see much, I assure ye," Inscope said, and then headed into the next chamber.

"Great, another guy speaking 'Oldspeak,'" Eddie grumbled.

"Forgive his lack of manners, Vasant," Drusilicus said to the woman.

She sighed. "Some things are still prevalent, I am afraid."

They went one at a time through the archway. The walls were solid stone, as if each room was carved into the very bedrock under the city. The next chamber was round, more like a tunnel than a room. There was a clear center path, but on both sides of the walkway lay broken wood and human skeletal remains.

A skull stared up at Eddie, hollow-eyed and disconcerting.

"What is this?" Eddie said, as they made their way carefully through the tunnel.

"One of the old tombs," Bankrock whispered. "The wood you see are the remains of the coffins. The rest, well, I believe you can figure it out."

"I guess there are no vampires in here," Eddie murmured.

"No," Inscope said as he reached the next archway. "That wouldst be the next chamber."

Eddie paused. "So you can see through walls? What is it, X-ray vision?"

Inscope stood up straighter. "I hast no idea of an 'X-ray' but I use me prophetic vision to reveal what lies within each chamber."

They stepped into another round tunnel-like room with metal brackets attached to the walls. In several rows, metal arms held fairly new coffins, stacked three high. There was a bottom grouping on the floor, with just enough room to open the lid, then another set of coffins at waist height, and finally a set of coffins that just cleared the ceiling.

"Whoa," Eddie said. "How do the vampires get down here?"

"Honestly, Wizard Berman." Bankrock rolled his eyes. "How little you have studied our foe…"

"You may not have noticed, but we've all been a little busy," Eddie snapped. "I haven't been able to catch up on my reading."

Drusilicus spoke up. "The vampires can access these catacombs as bats and transform into their human shape once they are here."

"The beasts canna change once the sun be risen," Inscope said as he reached an old wooden door at the end of the chamber. "If they are a bat when the sun comes up, they remain a bat until nightfall. It is the same if they are mist."

Marlowe spoke at this point. "Stories tell of vampires caught in mist form and blown apart, unable to regain their bodies."

"Silence now!" Inscope interrupted. "Lower the light of thy staffs. We ha'e no wish to disturb the denizens of yonder room past this door."

The group exchanged glances, and with a thought, the lights became less bright so that each wizard's feet were in darkness. Inscope carefully pulled the door toward them, and the next room was as black as pitch. He stepped in, disappearing into the gloom instantly.

Marlowe shrugged and entered next, followed by the others. Eddie was last and scanned the coffin room carefully. Although vampires slept during the day, he knew they could come out of the coffins if the need arose, as long as it did not expose them to sunlight.

Eddie stepped through the doorway into a much larger room than the tunnel-shaped one he'd just left, and a more traditional square shape. Again there was a cleared walkway through the room, leading to the next doorway. Oddly, outside the walkway were drips of what appeared to be cement everywhere. Little droplets discolored the floor in multiple places. There was a noise, and Eddie glanced up at the ceiling.

It was covered with bats.

A huge black-winged mass of the small creatures, all huddled into groups that left almost no bare spot on the ceiling of the concrete room. Eddie could see wrought-iron wires attached to form a crisscrossing grid on the ceiling that allowed the creatures to hang upside down easily. The mammals appeared to be sleeping, their wings folded and their eyes closed.

A shiver went down Eddie's spine, and he swallowed repeatedly to keep from throwing up.

As they approached the next archway, Eddie ducked. Even though he wasn't tall enough for his head to touch the bats, they creeped him out.

Marlowe pointed up at a square opening in the ceiling where the iron grid was open. "Ah, a vent. That is how the vampires get down into this place."

"Yeah, I'm thrilled," Eddie hissed, with a glance at the many small bodies hanging from the ceiling. "Can we get into the next room, please?"

"Really, lieutenant," Drusilicus smirked, "a few winged mice and your courage takes flight?"

"No, a room full of vampires and no way out makes me nervous," Eddie muttered.

Inscope opened the door, and the wizards stepped through, moving as quietly as they could. Eddie only relaxed once the door to the bat cave was closed.

Marlowe brightened the light on his staff, illuminating another square concrete room. This one had a dozen chairs that suggested they came from a school. Each chair had an attached arm that formed a desk in front of the chair. On each desktop were several jars with rubber pulled tightly over the lid.

"This t'was the place I found most curious," Inscope said.

Eddie picked up one of the sealed jars. "What on earth are these for?"

The others did not seem to know. Marlowe picked up one jar and examined it carefully. He studied the jar from the outside and pressed his finger on the rubber membrane on the top.

"Eddie, do you know how they make anti-venom?" Marlowe asked.

Eddie turned to the others, but they just stared back. "No."

Marlowe went on. "They collect the venom of a snake and then inject small amounts into an animal. Over time, the animal produces antibodies in their bloodstream. They harvest the antibodies and concentrate them into the product given to snakebite victims."

Drusilicus spoke up. "Fascinating, Marlowe, but what does this have to do with this room or these jars?" He picked up one of the rubber-coated containers to illustrate his point.

Marlowe raised one eyebrow with a gleam in his eyes. "To get the venom, a brave soul must milk the snake."

"How do you milk a snake?" Eddie asked.

"By having it bite a container similar to this," Marlowe explained and held the jar up for all to see. "Some people just hook the snake's fangs on a container, and then press on the venom glands, but with some species, the snake can only eject the venom when it actually bites something."

"You mean, like vampires do?" Bankrock speculated.

"That is true," Vasant pointed out. "They only inject their venom once they have broken the skin of their victim."

Marlowe nodded. "I believe they used these as a substitute for a victim. If a vampire pierces the rubber top with his fangs, he would instinctually release his venom."

Eddie's face contorted in disgust. "This is how they've been collecting the vampire spit to make Mind-Blo?"

"Doesn't seem very sanitary," Bankrock fussed.

"I don't know." Drusilicus turned the jar over in his hand. "Sterilize the jars, seal them with the rubber. It makes a rather enclosed collection process."

"But why would the vampires agree to do it?" Vasant observed. "Vampires are individual hunters. Why would they give up venom they might need for a hunt?"

"If commanded by the Drakula, would they not?" Marlowe said.

"That means the place where they mix the drug is nearby." Eddie faced Inscope. "Have you seen a room where people are working with lab equipment?"

Inscope frowned. "Beyond this room is a hallway. At the far end be a white room with a windowed door. When I last went through, there were people dressed in odd white garb, with strange masks o'er their faces. Might that be what ye seek?"

Eddie nodded his head. "Sounds like a meth lab. They would need something like that to add the other ingredients in the drug."

Drusilicus asked Inscope. "What else is down that hallway?"

"Several rooms with coffins, like the one we passed," Inscope informed the others.

"Great, a freakin' vampire hotel," Eddie grumbled.

The gray-bearded man went on. "And there be one room that contains only one coffin."

This got everyone's attention. Marlowe quickly asked, "A single coffin?"

"Aye, with a large man who keeps watch o'er it."

Eddie could feel himself getting excited. "That could be Luis."

"If it is the good sergeant," Drusilicus warned, "he might not be himself."

"I know," Eddie said. "I saw how he reacted from just one kiss by Lysandra."

Drusilicus' eyebrows went up. "Lysandra kissed... your partner?"

Eddie shrugged. "She said she couldn't resist him."

"It appears your playmate might wish to play with others," Vasant said softly.

Drusilicus flushed.

"What do you think is our best line of attack, Eddie?" Marlowe said.

"You're asking our least experienced wizard?" Bankrock argued.

"I am asking the person most experienced at taking down criminals," Marlowe said. "Unless you have an expertise I was unaware of, Bankrock?"

Drusilicus spoke up. "I must agree with Marlowe. The lieutenant has often had the calmest head in tense situations."

Eddie nodded. "As much as I want to see if the person guarding the solo coffin is my partner, I have to say that we go for the drug room. If those are humans making the drug, they could attack us. We eliminate that threat first."

"How do we do it?" Vasant asked, excitement flashing in her eyes.

"We hit it full-bore wizard. Drew, you conjure a shield spell as we go in. Marlowe, see if you can contain any dangerous chemicals that might be in there. Vasant, you be ready to stun anyone you see. Can you do that?"

"That I can, Wizard Berman." She smiled.

"Good. We want something to incapacitate the people, but be ready with something strong, in case they're vampires."

Everyone nodded in agreement, except Inscope.

"What do ye wish of me, Newling?"

Eddie whispered to the tall man. "You stay in the hall and watch our backs. And call me lieutenant, Eddie, or Wizard Berman and cut the Newling shit, ok?"

The big man seemed flustered. "I meant no disrespect... um... Wizard Berman."

"Let's move," Eddie ordered. He pushed past Inscope and through the door into the hall beyond, his staff before him and his own protection spell ready.

They went to the last door in the hall. This doorway didn't appear ancient like the other doors in the underground area. It came across as brand new, with a double pane of glass in the upper half. Eddie crouched, ducked under the window, and went to the far side of the door and pointed for Drusilicus to frame the other side.

Eddie peeked in and saw a first-rate lab. The concrete walls were painted white. On the far wall was a series of shelves at eye-level, holding beakers, test tubes, and other containers.

There were two large Formica covered tables in the middle of the room with more lab equipment: a microscope, ring stands, Bunsen burners, and a supply of tongs and forceps.

In the corner were multiple racks that contained vials of the blue liquid that could only be Mind-Blo.

Eddie waited until everyone was in place, and then he reached for the knob of the door and silently rotated it.

He put his weight behind the door, and it slammed open."NYPD, hands in the air!"

The room reeked of acetone and ether, striking Eddie's nose with its pungent scent.

Drusilicus had the protective dome of blue light in place, and Eddie was grateful, because two men in white coveralls leapt at him like a pair of wolves.

When they hit the dome of blue light, it knocked the masks with the breathing apparatuses off their faces, and Eddie shook his head. Who attacks someone face-first?

As the masks fell away, Eddie saw the assailants were merely men, not vampires. Their faces were angry and vicious, like junkyard dogs commanded to tear apart any stranger who invaded their space.

Vasant merely gestured, and the two men fought the spell as they went to the ground, clawing the air, until they fell unconscious.

Marlowe stepped into the room, and a gentle breeze sucked the stink of chemicals out the open door.

Eddie went to the table that held the racks with vials of Mind-Blo. This would be more than enough to replace the phony stuff he and Luis had handed into evidence, but how could he get it out of there?

"Marlowe, any way to teleport this stuff to your place?" Eddie said, keeping his voice low.

"Hm?" Marlowe said. "I am afraid not. Since it contains vampire venom, I have no way to know how it would affect a teleportation spell. Also, the enchantments on my threshold would probably not allow vampire venom through."

Eddie exhaled in exasperation. "Damn, you got too many rules."

Marlowe met Eddie's eyes and shrugged.

"Any way we could carry this stuff out of here?"

Marlowe stroked his beard. "There are other possibilities."

Eddie nodded. "Please get to work on that!"

Eddie strode past his comrades and the fallen men, who Drusilicus and Bankrock had slid away from the door to lean against the wall. He stepped into the hall to Inscope.

"Anything?" Eddie asked.

"Nay," Inscope said in an undertone. "The monsters do not stir."

"Which room did you say had the one coffin with the guard?" Eddie asked.

Inscope pointed solemnly to a door across the hall. It was made of thick, old wood planks fastened with iron supports. "There."

Eddie glanced back at the others and saw that Marlowe was busy in front of the vials of Mind-Blo, and Vasant was capping bottles by having the tops fly up and onto them. Drusilicus and Bankrock were watching the unconscious men.

Eddie went to the door and opened the heavy metal hasp.

He eased the door open a crack as it creaked loudly on ancient hinges. The room was in utter darkness, so Eddie needed to slip his staff into the opening to see.

"Luis?" he attempted in a loud whisper.

The light slid past the solid door and revealed a coffin in the middle of the floor. It was a dark, shiny black box, the wood having been coated with layer upon layer of lacquer. It was fairly large, though not as big as the one they saw at the airport that now lay within Marlowe's townhouse.

The light fell upon a large man standing in the farthest corner of the room, hidden in the shadows.

Luis.

Eddie had expected his partner to be in a hypnotized state—staring blankly as he awaited orders—but the big man glared malevolently directly at Eddie, alert and angry.

Eddie opened the door a little more. "Luis? It's Eddie."

Luis opened his mouth, roared a battle cry, and charged straight at his partner.

TWENTY-TWO

Eddie fell back into the wide hallway, pulling the door closed even as he fully expected Luis to smash his way through.

With a whispered word and a quick gesture a small burst of fire hit the old lock mechanism and welded it together. The door reverberated as Luis smashed into it, but it held.

"Ye have roused the man," Inscope hissed after Eddie.

"I know." Eddie ran through the laboratory door. "Marlowe, do we have another way out of here?"

Marlowe stood in front of the empty table where the racks of Mind-Blo had been. "Can't we leave the way we came?"

"I have a feeling we won't be able to." A horrible racket came from the locked door, and they heard Luis's voice shouting incoherently.

The hall was suddenly filled with the susurration of wings flapping and the squeals of disturbed bats woken from their sleep by the loud banging.

Eddie grabbed Inscope's arm and pulled him into the lab, slamming the door closed.

"Secure the entrance," Eddie rasped to Drusilicus, who raised his staff and made a series of passes before the fragile door. The clear glass turned black.

The sound of flying bats echoed in the hall they just abandoned, and there came the sound of the flying mammals hitting agains the glass of the door, thumping and banging as they squealed , which made Eddie's skin crawl with the arhythmic pounding of the small bodies against the glass.

"Can they get through?" Vasant snapped.

Drusilicus still held his staff toward the door. "I have increased the strength of the glass, but if the vampires are indeed being awakened, it might not be enough."

Eddie turned back to Marlowe. "We need a way out of here."

"I… am at a loss, Eddie." Marlowe gulped.

The bats' screeching intensified as a much larger body pounded the door.

"T'would appear the human monsters ha' been roused from their coffins," Inscope concluded.

"Can you hold it?" Bankrock shouted to Drusilicus.

"So far." Drusilicus nodded tersely. "I must concur with the lieutenant. Marlowe, can you get us out of here?"

The door shuddered in the frame. Vasant held up her staff and yellow light flashed toward the door reinforcing Drusilicus' power.

Eddie checked the empty table. "Marlowe, where did you send the drugs?"

Marlowe glanced at the table. "I sent them into a pocket dimension."

"Can you take us there?" Eddie insisted.

"What? No!" Marlowe gasped.

"He's right, Wizard Berman," Bankrock said. "One only uses a pocket dimension for storage. There might be no air, no gravity, or even creatures worse than what is outside this door."

Bankrock gestured at the door, shaking with the force of the assault.

"Look," Eddie stormed, "there are vampires on the other side of that door—they have fangs, and they want us dead. We might be good, but they vastly outnumber us."

Drusilicus and Vasant focused on keeping the door in one piece, sweat breaking out on their faces.

"Can you use this... pocket dimension... or whatever the hell it is, to get us out of here and let us out somewhere else?" Eddie tried.

"I would not be sure where we would end up!" Marlowe said. "As I have often told you, teleportation is a difficult and delicate procedure. You must consider—"

"Enough of yer foolishness," Inscope bellowed. "Each of thee take a deep breath and follow!"

Inscope, with a gesture of his staff, tore a hole in reality.

It was a black, crooked line floating in space with a slight glow around it. Energy crackled and air whipped around it, causing loose objects to be buffeted on the different tables and shelves. Inscope took a deep breath, ducked his head, and stepped in. His body disappeared into the space.

Bankrock shrugged, inhaled deeply, and followed the taller wizard, disappearing into the jagged black line standing vertically in the room.

"You're next," Drusilicus shouted to Vasant above the whistling wind.

"Why don't you go? I can hold this," she responded.

"Madam, please," Drusilicus insisted.

"Well, while you two figure it out," Marlowe said, as he took a deep breath and stepped into the tear.

Lightning flashed around the black line.

"You two go. I got this," Eddie yelled.

"Do you think that is the best choice, Wizard Berman?" Vasant shouted back.

"I'm the cop. Leave now," Eddie responded and lifted his staff to support the door just as another resounding crash came from it, and the blackened window cracked.

Drusilicus took Vasant's arm, and they both inhaled and stepped into the portal.

Eddie watched them disappear and shook his head. Wherever this pocket dimension went to, at least they would all be in the same place.

Eddie kept the energy on the door as he backed his way to the rip in reality that was rapidly growing smaller. He put his hand in and felt an odd tingle on his flesh.

Eddie glanced back at the door and thought of Luis. As long as the creatures held him in sway, they wouldn't kill him. And he could think of no way to save his partner.

"I'll be back for you, buddy," Eddie hissed, sucked in a large lungful of air, and stepped through as he heard the door break behind him.

He was in perfect darkness. His skin tingled like a low-voltage current was running up and down his body. He had no idea where to go, what was up and what was down. He wasn't really standing on anything, but floating in the darkness. The surrounding void seemed to have a bit of resistance, and he found he could move through it.

He would not last long in this space without air.

A light shimmered over his head. Not having any solid object to push against, Eddie moved as if he were in water, making swimming motions upward. The light grew brighter as he headed up, refracting and sparkling as he drew closer.

He pushed his way up, and suddenly he *was* in water. Actual water flowed around him. It was such a shock, he almost breathed in, but he fought the urge and pressed upward.

Then, all at once, there was something under his feet he could stand against, and he pushed himself up and through the liquid and into the sunlight.

He felt concrete under his feet; the light dazzling his eyes as he rose out of a mere twelve inches of water. Dripping, he blinked several times, and as his vision cleared, he saw Marlowe and the others.

They stood near the center of the Washington Square Fountain.

A crowd had formed, and they were looking at the soaked wizards in their wet robes, with staffs in hand, having literally appeared from the middle of a fountain.

Several people had phones held high, undoubtably taking video of the unusual appearance, and shocked that six people had risen out of twelve inches of water.

Drusilicus regarded the crowd and cleared his throat. "What do we do? A memory charm?"

"Too many people," Marlowe asserted. "Plus, they are holding cameras."

Eddie thought fast and turned to the others. "I got this. Follow my lead."

Inscope frowned. "Where wouldst thou lead us?"

Eddie stepped in front of the others, splashing through the water, and raised his hands to get everyone's attention. "Ladies and gentlemen, if you enjoyed this effect, come see the new Broadway show, 'Magic, Live!' next month!"

With a gesture, fire danced on the palm of one of his outstretched hands. Marlowe gestured and several pyrotechnics like tiny fireworks went off over the drenched wizards.

After a moment of shock, the crowd applauded, and Eddie took a bow. Haltingly, the other wizards bowed behind him as well. The crowd dispersed as Eddie led the others to the steps that were part of the structure, and they climbed out.

Drusilicus offered a hand to Vasant, who pushed it away and said, "I can do it!"

As the team got to dry land, one of the crowd, a young man of about twelve said, "I think Criss Angel did it better."

Drusilicus raised his staff, but Eddie gestured him to stop.

The young man strode away unscathed.

"Shall we go to my abode?" Drusilicus suggested. "I am merely a few blocks from here."

Marlowe seemed weary as he squeezed water from his sleeve. "If it would not be any trouble."

"What possible trouble could we have?" Inscope asked.

"What trouble have we not had!" huffed Bankrock.

Dry and in their original clothes, they sat in a very nice room on the first floor of Drusilicus' townhouse. The rooms were much smaller than Marlowe's but a little more grand, with fine wallpaper and impressive furniture and artwork.

Once out of public view, it was simple for each wizard to use their abilities to dry themselves and transform their robes back to what they had been wearing. Marlowe, Drusilicus, Bankrock, and Eddie were back in their suits, and Eddie had even removed some wrinkles from his clothes. Vasant was back in her "Edwardian-lady-adventurer" outfit, and Inscope was dressed in what appeared to be rags.

Howell, the ever-efficient manservant, brought tea and coffee and a trolley laden with snacks for the guests.

"Marlowe, you got that supply of drugs somewhere we can access, right?" Eddie said as he sipped coffee, grateful for the heat of the beverage.

"Hm?" Marlowe said, and he seemed a bit flustered. "Oh, yes, I can access them anytime you need them, Eddie, and from almost any location."

Eddie turned to Inscope. "How were you able to get us someplace safe? I mean, everyone said that the risks of traveling through… whatever it was… were too dangerous."

Inscope faced Eddie. "Aye. I possess prophetic abilities, though they be limited. I canst know what be in rooms I have not been in, and inter-dimensional travel be much the same thing. I simply foresaw what space wouldst bring us unto a safe location."

"Though a rather wet one," Drusilicus grumbled.

"It still was a risky endeavor," Bankrock chirped. "But I admit we had little choice."

"I thought your solution for dealing with the onlookers was most clever, Wizard Berman," Vasant praised him. "And they accepted it so readily!"

"Lots of stage magicians do street stuff these days." Eddie smiled.

"Before my—sabbatical— the public would not so willingly accept that a conjuror could accomplish such a feat," Vasant went on. "Do the conjurors do such demonstrations these days?"

"Yeah, all over TV," Eddie told her with a shrug.

"Really?" she inquired. "And what is TV?"

"I would indulge you, good lady," Drusilicus said, "but it would only rot your brain."

Vasant frowned. "That seems a most unpleasant side effect."

Marlowe rose from his chair. "There is one last thing important I must do if we are to be ready this night."

"Do tell?" Eddie said.

"No, it is best that I do this alone. Drusilicus, you have a mirror I can use to transport myself to my townhouse?"

Drusilicus stood as well. "Yes, Marlowe, several full-length mirrors. But you seem tired. Is it wise to use so much energy?"

"In this case, it might be vital," Marlowe said.

"Very well," Drusilicus said as he picked up a small bell on a table and rang it.

The ever-ready Howell appeared at the door. "Yes, sir?"

"Howell, please show Marlowe to the room of mirrors."

"Very good, sir. Mr. Marlowe, if you will follow me."

Marlowe rose and left out of the room behind Howell.

"There is much of this age I do not understand," Vasant sighed.

Inscope waved his hand as if to shoo away a tiny insect. "It is for naught, all these foolish inventions of the mortals. Computers, portable telephones, they be distractions that cause them not to see the world around them. They cover up their ears with music, their eyes with images. T'would be better for them to see the beauty of this world."

"New Yorkers are not known for that," Eddie pointed out.

"Pity," Vasant added.

Drusilicus spoke up. "Marlowe is using a mirror to travel, if any of you would prefer—"

Eddie stood. "I only have one question, Drew. Is Lysandra here?"

Drusilicus leaned back in his chair, and his eyes glanced guiltily to Vasant. "I beg your pardon?"

"Drew, I ain't playin'. If Lysandra is here, I want to wake her up and speak with her."

Drusilicus turned scarlet as the others exchanged glances.

"Thou hast one of those *fiends* within thy house?" Inscope bellowed.

"This is most unusual," Bankrock responded.

Drusilicus was flustered for a moment, then shot back, "Marlowe has Daniel Kraft staying with him. No one has said anything about it."

Vasant smiled knowingly. "I am sure the situation is different, if you are harboring a female vampire, is it not, Wizard Greywacke?"

Drusilicus turned a darker shade of red.

"Look, I don't care about who is sleeping with who... uh... whom," Eddie told them all. "I need some information, and she is going to give it to me."

Drusilicus rose from his chair and gestured at Eddie angrily. "Or what? You'll stab her with that ring and turn her to dust? Is that your technique now, lieutenant? Since she's a vampire, you can kill with impunity?"

Eddie stepped eye to eye with Drusilicus. "I think she has compromised you. And they have my partner under their control. Lysandra might know something. I'm a cop. I know how to question a witness, and I know where to stop. Now, either you show me where she is sleeping or I will search your stupid house room by room."

"That will not be necessary, lieutenant," Drusilicus answered. "I shall lead you there myself."

"Good."

"And watch you question her."

Bankrock spoke up. "If he is under her sway that might not be —"

Eddie raised his hand and cut off the little man's argument with the gesture. "I'm okay with that."

Bankrock pushed himself to his feet. "Well, there is still much to be prepared."

"Be available tonight," Eddie told him without taking his eyes from Drusilicus.

"I will be, you can rest assured," Bankrock said, as the ever-helpful Howell appeared and escorted him to the door.

"I'd appreciate it if the two of you can remain, just in case I need help," Eddie said to Vasant and Inscope.

Inscope shrugged. "I ha'e no pressing engagements."

"We shall be at the ready, Wizard Berman," Vasant offered.

Drusilicus turned and walked to a staircase, and Eddie followed. The banister was a fine oak with exacting workmanship and glowed under layers of lacquer. The carpeted steps allowed both men to walk silently to the next floor. Drusilicus went down the hall, and at the second doorway, quietly opened it.

The room was in total darkness, but as Eddie opened the door, light poured in from the hall to reveal a plain pale-wood coffin in the middle of the floor. It was unusual for its complete lack of ornamentation of any kind.

With a gesture, Drusilicus lit a pair of candles. Illuminating a large four-poster bed with bedding and a blanket as the light brightened the room.

"Why can't she just sleep in the bed?" Eddie asked.

"She can't risk any sunlight peeking through a curtain," Drusilicus explained, as he stepped to the heavy drapes and made sure they were tightly closed. "Plus, I couldn't conjure a box for her. It had to be built from wood. This was available to me quickly."

"You wanna knock, or shall I?" Eddie proposed.

"You are the one who wishes to wake her. You knock."

Eddie bent and rapped several times on the simple unstained pine of the box. He waited with his arms folded. He knocked a second time. Then he lifted the lid.

The coffin, lined in red satin, was quite empty.

"Seems like your girl has flown the coop."

Drusilicus stood over the unoccupied box and frowned. He met Eddie's eyes. "I do not know how she could leave—not during the day!"

"Was she in the coffin when you came to meet us this morning?"

"Yes, I saw her go into this very room. I mean, I didn't see her get into the coffin—"

Eddie was already heading for the stairs, and Drusilicus gestured to extinguish the candles as he followed.

Eddie came into the downstairs room and approached Inscope as he sat. "Wizard Inscope, can your prophetic abilities allow you to see inside all rooms?"

The gray-bearded man pursed his lips thoughtfully. "Mostly, aye. Unless they be enchanted."

"How about a hidden room, or a hidden door?"

The wizard considered it and nodded.

"What are you thinking, Wizard Berman?" Vasant asked.

"Drew's vampire guest left, we assume, of her own volition." Eddie turned to Drusilicus. "You have a basement in this place?"

"Of course I do, but we use it for storage," Drusilicus responded in an annoyed tone.

"Let's find out, shall we?" Eddie suggested, gesturing for Drusilicus to take the lead.

With an angry sigh, Drusilicus led the others toward the stairway, but he went beyond it and opened a thin door built almost imperceptibly into the woodwork.

"It's this way," he said.

The others headed for the door, and Eddie took Inscope's arm. "Look for anything and everything if you can," he whispered.

"I knew this door be here," he replied before he started down the stairs.

They descended two landings before they reached the bottom of the stairs. The basement was dark and the walls built from carved stone. There were simple shelves along the wall full of boxes of different sizes. One entire rack was nothing but wine bottles stacked to the ceiling.

The wizards retrieved their hidden staffs, and each had a light atop of it to break through the gloom.

"Is there a reason you insisted I bring you down here, lieutenant, or do you just enjoy being underground?" Drusilicus snapped.

"You said that Lysandra couldn't risk even a bit of sun," Eddie explained. "So, what way could she travel? The only option I see during the day is underground."

Eddie noticed a large steel door that resembled a bank vault in one corner. It boasted an impressive lock on the outside, with some kind of strange timer.

"What's this?" Eddie asked as he stepped over to it. Finding it unlocked, he pulled the heavy door open.

"That is of no interest to you, lieutenant," Drusilicus blurted as he strode over.

Eddie peeked in the room, the light from his staff illuminating the total darkness. There was a cage in the center of the room. It was large and extremely sturdy, as if to hold a lion or something far more dangerous. All around the cage, hundreds of scratch marks were carved deeply into the floor.

"What's it for?" Eddie demanded.

Drusilicus pulled Eddie out of the door. "It is a… necessity. For the full moon."

"This is for Howell?" Eddie whispered.

Drusilicus nodded solemnly.

Eddie shut the door and returned to the group to ask Inscope, "Getting anything?"

"There be a passageway yonder," Inscope said and pointed.

"Don't be ridiculous, I have owned the house for decades," Drusilicus spat. "Don't you think I would know if there was an underground passage?"

"Oh, so this is a place where you hang out?" Eddie gestured at the wine rack on the wall. "Maybe come get a nice bottle of wine? Be honest, Drew, you only send Howell down here."

Drusilicus glowered at Eddie, as Vasant came over and touched Drusilicus' arm. "It certainly does no harm to look."

They made their way past the shelves of storage and into an adjacent chamber through an archway of cut stone.

Inscope drew ahead of them and pointed at a large, empty bookcase. "There it be," he announced.

"Yeah, an empty bookcase that doesn't belong down here isn't in any way suspicious," Eddie declared, and advanced to the wooden structure. He ran his hands on the shelves, looking for a way to open it.

"Really, Wizard Berman, that is unnecessary," Vasant said, with a slight motion of her staff.

The bookcase swung open on creaking hinges.

There was a tunnel lined with bricks and cut stone that ventured into darkness.

"Where does this go?" Eddie wondered.

Inscope closed his eyes and held out his hand. "It joins with other tunnels that lead back to the park."

Eddie faced the older man. "Wait, this tunnel goes to where we were? I mean, the vampires and all that?"

Inscope nodded. "Aye."

"Do you think the vampires know this passage exists?" Vasant mused.

"One did," Eddie said. "And if she did, it would suggest that they all know."

"That is not necessarily the situation, lieutenant," Drusilicus stated. "We are not even sure that she left my home. For all we know, she is sleeping in one of my many guest rooms."

"Do you hear that?" Vasant said, holding up one finger.

"Hear what?" Drusilicus inquired.

"Aye, they be coming," Inscope intoned with a nod of his bearded face.

Eddie stared down the black tunnel. In the distance he heard a sound like a great wind of hundreds of tiny wings as they flapped. The noise grew in volume, squeaks and squeals of thousands of bats as they approached like a wave. Eddie's skin went cold as groping fingers of wind rose from the darkness of the tunnel—a shrieking wind stirred by hundreds of flapping wings.

TWENTY-THREE

"**S**hut the damn bookcase!" Eddie yelled as he dashed behind the wooden impediment to slam it closed.

Drusilicus held up his arm. "No, wait. We must see what happens!"

"What's going to happen is about a thousand bats with fangs are going to kill us all!" Eddie stormed.

"No," Vasant said. "His threshold should hold them back."

"I must see if the magickal protections of my house have been compromised," Drusilicus said, a stern look on his face.

Eddie regarded the tunnel with wide eyes. "You picked a terrible time for a test, Drew."

The sound grew in volume as the bats drew closer.

Eddie faced the doorway, and put up a dome of protection around himself. "What're you gonna do if this doesn't work?"

The sound grew to almost a deafening pitch, and now the movement of the wings as the creatures flew up the tunnel. As the bats drew closer, Eddie's heart pounded, but as he watched the other three, they seemed calm and very focused.

A wave of flying vermin collided with the barrier, their dripping fangs screeching like nails on a chalkboard against the invisible wall. Their eyes, bulging red and manic, rapidly registered terror as wave after wave of their brethren smashed against them, smearing the transparent barricade with gore. Eddie shuddered, his jaw clenched as he reminded himself that they were already dead—and he wasn't.

Drusilicus grunted and with a movement of his staff, the bookcase slowly closed, effectively sealing out the carnage in the tunnel. He turned and faced the others. "I may not have known about this passageway, but the magickal safeguards of my home are still quite effective."

Eddie lowered his staff, and his protective dome disappeared. "You know what this means, right?"

Drusilicus thought about it. "That I could use an exterminator?"

"Only someone invited into your house could have stolen your old staff. The one that Selene or Nimue is now using."

"Wizard Berman is correct," Vasant put in. "And now we see the way she could have come into your house and left with it, at any time she wished."

"Ye have dallied with forces beyond your ken," Inscope accused.

"Yeah, what he just said," Eddie added. "Now, Lysandra has left to rejoin her vampire friends, and we don't know if she influenced you or not. Drew, she could have compromised you. What happens tonight if she can make you her puppet?"

"That will not happen," Drusilicus insisted, his jaw tight.

"But you understand our concerns," Vasant told him calmly.

"Standing around your basement will do nothing," Eddie said, his arms folded. "I have to get uptown and get ready if Marlowe's plan is going to work. We only have a few hours until nightfall and the whole thing hits the fan."

Eddie made his way toward the stairs up to the main house as the others followed him.

"Would you care to use one of my mirrors?" Drusilicus offered as he trudged up the stairs behind him.

"The subway is fine for me, Drew," Eddie snapped.

As the four of them arrived on the first floor, the room was dark from closed curtains, and a few lamps were lit. Howell waited for them, and next to him stood a sleepy-eyed Lysandra.

The tall vampire saw the looks Inscope and Vasant gave her, so she remained in one place and didn't approach.

"I heard you were looking for me," Lysandra said, looking warily at the others.

Drusilicus frowned. "Where—?"

Howell cleared his throat. "Forgive me, sir, I took it upon myself to check the other rooms for Miss Lysandra. Imagine my surprise when I located her in your bedroom, sir."

Lysandra seemed embarrassed. "I was planning to surprise you."

"You surprised me all right," Drusilicus blurted.

Eddie didn't let the tableau slow him down. He strode up to Lysandra until he stood right in front of her. "They took my partner."

She nodded shyly. "I know, Drusilicus told me last night."

Eddie glared at Drusilicus. "Nice that you two have no secrets."

"I was seeing if she knew anything that might help, lieutenant. We all are as upset about the abduction of your partner as you are."

Eddie glared at Drusilicus."You do not know how upset I am, or how upset I will be."

Lysandra spoke, "My people have rejected me, and I am afraid I knew nothing of this."

"Selene is following the orders of the Drakula," Eddie said. "I think only he knows what the overall plan is." He stepped away from Lysandra and paced as the others stood and watched him.

"What be he doin'?" Inscope asked Vasant.

"Thinking, I hope," Vasant offered.

Eddie stopped pacing and pointed his finger at Lysandra. "What do you know about tonight, the solstice, or whatever it is?"

"It is the Spring Equinox," offered Vasant.

Lysandra shrugged. "All I have been told are rumors. Tonight, the Drakula will reveal himself in New York and rain down destruction on the wizards and mortals."

"We have been over this, lieutenant," Drusilicus huffed.

Eddie went on. "Yeah, we've been told the Drakula is in New York—but has anybody *seen* him?"

Lysandra frowned. "I do not understand your question."

Eddie shook his head. "I guess I'm just grasping at straws. I gotta head uptown."

"May I accompany you?" Vasant asked. "I have never ridden a subway before."

"Sure," Eddie said, and headed for the door with Vasant following.

He heard Drusilicus speaking, "Go back to sleep, Lysandra, but perhaps your own coffin would be the best choice."

Eddie and Vasant quickly made their way to the nearby subway station at West 4th Street. Eddie used his Metrocard to swipe Vasant through the turnstile and led her to the uptown side of the station.

Vasant observed the scene, surprised by the clutter and the discolored walls with the bright advertisements as they headed for the train platform. As they drew to the concrete island with tracks on both sides, she stopped and grabbed Eddie's shoulder.

"I hear music," she stated simply.

"Yeah, there is a musician playing a keyboard," Eddie said, indicating a man seated at a bench with a small keyboard on top of a battery-powered speaker. He was playing something classical and doing so very well. He had a bucket littered with dollar bills.

"People pay him to do this?" Vasant asked as she drew close to Eddie and continued walking.

"He's a busker," Eddie shrugged.

"I am not familiar with that term," Vasant brooded.

"He's a street performer. He's got a license to play down here."

"They must get a *license*?" Vasant asked, amazed.

"Yeah," Eddie said as a subway rattled into the station and silenced him because of the noise. Vasant placed her hands over her ears at the sound.

"Come on, this is our train," Eddie said as the subway cars slowed and stopped.

They stepped into the car, and then Eddie grabbed one of the metal straps.

Vasant, not sure what to do, grabbed the one next to him. She leaned her head close to him. "This is all rather exciting."

"Just life in New York for most of us," Eddie told her, as the train lurched and headed uptown.

They got off at the 86th Street stop and climbed the stairs into the sunlight. Vasant was giddy from the experience and wore a big smile.

Eddie was surprised, he had grown used to the wizards being serious and somewhat dour.

The pair reached the block in front of Marlowe's townhouse.

"I gotta call home," Eddie explained, as he pulled his phone from his pocket. "I'll be there in a few minutes."

His mother picked up on the first ring. "Yes, Eddie?"

"How is she doing?"

"As well as she can. They gave her a shot, but it's slow and they're worried because of her age."

"She isn't that old," Eddie grumbled.

"She ain't that young either, Eddie. But she's a trooper. The wife of your partner showed up to help."

"Maria? That's good. She knows a lot about having babies."

"So she told me. Now you get your work done, and get here to meet your daughter."

"As soon as I can, Momma. I love you."

He ended the call and walked up the steps to find Vasant still outside.

"Anything wrong?" Eddie asked.

"I knocked, but no one came to answer the door," Vasant said.

Eddie frowned and pulled out the small mirror from his pocket. He concentrated until the reflective surface went dark, then he called out, "Marlowe? Marlowe are you there?"

The glass simply showed a dark pool that shifted like water under his gaze, but with no response.

"Damn!" Eddie muttered. "Daniel, are you awake? Daniel Kraft, something is wrong with Marlowe."

The mirror changed, and a dark, empty room appeared in the small circle. As Daniel was a vampire, he could speak in a mirror, but since he cast no reflection in the glass, his face didn't appear. There was a groan and a mutter of, "Can't I ever get a good day's sleep?"

"Daniel, it's Eddie. Something's wrong with Marlowe. Can you let us in?"

"Hmm?" a voice from the empty room replied. "Eddie, you're at the front door? I can't help you. Sunlight has filled the foyer, and I would have to have the curtains shut to even go down there." He then yelled, "Wraith!"

Another voice came from the mirror, but Eddie still saw no one. "Yes, Mr. Kraft?"

"Please open the front door for Eddie," Daniel ordered.

"Very good, sir."

Almost instantly the front door lock clicked and the morose, semi-transparent face of Wraith appeared at the opening.

Eddie slipped the mirror into his pocket and held up his arm to stop Vasant from going in. "Wraith, is anything wrong? Why didn't you open the door when we knocked?"

Wraith peered down his spectral nose at them. "Marlowe asked not to be disturbed, sir."

Eddie stepped in, looking around with caution with Vasant right behind him. The foyer and the vast living room beyond seemed perfectly normal. Daniel had been correct, the light from the setting sun blazed through the windows, which would be fatal for him.

There was no sign of Marlowe.

"Where is he?" Eddie asked the spirit, who was closing the door and securing it.

"He is in the basement, sir, but he requested to be left alone and undisturbed," Wraith insisted.

Eddie headed for the door to the enormous basement, only to find that Wraith moved in front him and blocked his path.

"I said that Marlowe requested to be left alone, sir," Wraith announced with a threatening tone in his voice.

Eddie stopped. Marlowe's spiritual major-domo had only ever treated Eddie with respect, but now Eddie could see that Wraith might fight to obey his master.

Eddie held up his hands. "Marlowe said he was going to do something, and I am worried about him. I will leave him alone, if you will make sure he's all right."

The ghostly figured considered this. "Very well, sir."

Wraith melted into the floor.

"Why did you let him stop you?" Vasant asked. "You could have pushed him aside with a thought."

"Until now, Wraith has always done anything I ask. Maybe Marlowe was protecting us, and I—"

The basement door burst open. Wraith was at the top of the stairs, his ghostly eyes wide. "It's Marlowe, he's hurt!"

Without a pause, Eddie and Vasant started down the stairs.

Wraith was babbling. "I'm so sorry, sir, but Marlowe made me swear to let no one disturb him. Now he could be dead and it's my fault."

"Never mind that," Eddie yelled. "Marlowe!"

The large room was completely different from the last time Eddie was there. The space was where Marlowe had trained Eddie in his magickal fighting skills against conjured monsters. It was also where his warehouse of potion ingredients would appear, filling the room with shelves and bookcases of supplies by the hundreds. It also was where the old man had conjured a cauldron and received a demonic message on one occasion.

This time, there was indeed a cauldron in the center of the floor, an overlarge pot that Eddie could have used to take a bath. It was on a raised platform in the middle of the room, and a haze of light-green smoke issued from it in a dense fog.

Lying on the floor in front of the smoldering cauldron was Marlowe.

Eddie rushed to him as Vasant shifted her ensemble into her robes and made her staff appear at her fingertips, the yellow light flashing about her hands.

"You must help him, good wizards," Wraith moaned. "You must."

Eddie checked for Marlowe's pulse and made sure he was breathing, then knelt down and lifted the old man a bit.

"You know any healing spells?" Eddie asked Vasant. "I've only done it once, and I have a feeling I got lucky."

Vasant made a small circle with her staff, and Marlowe drew a deep breath.

"Is he alive?" Wraith whimpered.

"Yes," Vasant reassured. "He'll be all right. You need to get ahold of yourself, Wraith."

"Thank you, thank you," the ghost gushed. "I shall go prepare him a healing tea."

He flew up to the ceiling and passed through it. Eddie focused on Marlowe who was blinking and opening his eyes. "Are you okay, Marlowe? It's Eddie and Vasant."

Marlowe sat up, rather quickly considering he'd been unconscious. "Am I too late? Has darkness fallen?"

"Relax," Eddie soothed. "We still have a couple of hours before sunset."

Hearing this, the old man relaxed and attempted to stand with Eddie's help.

"Go easy, there. What happened to you?" Eddie asked.

"I made a conjuration, using my abilities as a necromancer," Marlowe said, seeming remarkably frail.

"You were talking to dead folk?" Eddie asked.

This statement received an eye roll from Vasant. "That is what a necromancer does, Wizard Berman."

"Like I said, I might not know your fancy words, but I get the idea, okay?"

"Please, no arguing," Marlowe requested. "I have a headache. I also attempted to look into the future, and I am afraid that is what might have overwhelmed me."

Eddie frowned. "I thought you gave up being a prophet. You said it was too hard."

"When one can see numerous futures, depending upon many slight variations, it is a bit much."

"Let's get you upstairs. Wraith is making you some of your nasty tea."

Eddie picked up Marlowe's staff from the floor and handed it to Marlowe who leaned heavily on it.

"Tea would be nice," Marlowe said as they began to slowly climb the stairs. "But I have seen the truth. I will face the Drakula alone, and do as the vampires suggested. I have seen that it is the only way they will release your partner."

"Is that wise?" added Vasant.

Eddie spoke up. "The plan was that I would be nearby."

"I have a change to the plan, but you might not like it, Eddie," Marlowe said.

Eddie sighed. "Why should today be any different?"

"Get me upstairs, and all of us must use mirrors and contact the other wizards."

Vasant looked over at Eddie. "Like I told you, this is all very exciting."

Eddie shook his head and helped Marlowe up the stairs. "I could do with a little less excitement right now."

TWENTY-FOUR

A s darkness fell across Manhattan, deep in a tunnel underneath Washington Square Park, a coffin creaked open.

Selene sat up in the box and acknowledged the big man lighting a lamp on a nearby table.

"What may I get you?" asked Luis Vasquez, a faraway look in his eyes.

He held out his hand, and Selene took it and pulled herself gracefully out of the coffin. Other coffins on shelves were creaking open, but Luis's focus was totally on Selene.

"There was a disturbance. What has happened?"

"Wizards were here in the lab," Luis replied simply. "I kept them away from the master's coffin."

"What of the other vampires?"

"Some attacked them as bats, and some in human form. By the time they breached the lab, the wizards were gone."

"I must go see to the master," she exclaimed.

She strode from the coffin room into the next chamber, where numerous bats hung from the ceiling. One bat hopped to the ground, wrapped its wings about itself, and grew into the shape of a small, chubby man.

"What are your orders, mistress?" Tuck asked with a bow.

"Tell them to fly and post themselves on the buildings around the square, and send out scouts. Our enemies are aware and they have already attempted to stop us. I shall awaken the master, but do not trouble him—bring any information only to me."

Tuck bowed. "It shall be done, mistress."

Selene strode into the next hallway and saw the smashed laboratory door at the end. Across from it, the huge door of the master's chamber hung open with a broken, fused lock. She walked faster with Luis at her heels and studied the shattered door and the destroyed research room.

"They did this, the wizards?" Selene asked.

"Yes, mistress," Luis said, and crossed his powerful arms. "They tried to enter the master's room, but I stopped them. They have taken the drug and destroyed the lab."

She shook her head. "That part of the mission was almost finished. Stay here. I must wake the master."

She went into the hall across from the broken lab, and quietly slipped in through the damaged door as Luis stood guard.

Outside in the fading twilight, on Fifth Avenue a block from Washington Square Park, Drusilicus stood with Willowdell, holding a small hand mirror.

In the glass was Vasant. "Any signs yet?"

"No, just make sure everyone is in position. We must create the magickal barricade to keep out any unsuspecting mortals."

"It is a chilly night," Willowdell mentioned brightly. "T'at should keep most people inside."

"We shall take whatever good fortune we can," Drusilicus said and looked at the mirror. "You will see my signal, and then we shall begin."

"Fair thee well," Vasant said.

"And you as well," Drusilicus answered.

The mirror silvered over and he slipped it back into his pocket.

"I must get to my location," Willowdell said. "Do you t'ink this plan will actually work?"

Drusilicus stood stone-faced. "The lieutenant assured me he has backup coming."

A question appeared on her dark face. "What would that be?"

"We shall see when he accomplishes it. I personally have my doubts. But let us focus on our part of the plan. A spell to keep any mortals out, and the vampires contained within."

Willowdell nodded and strode out in front of him, heading into the park.

Drusilicus saw several bats fly from the roof of a small building in the park. In preparation, he sought the vent they saw while in the underground tunnels. It was a simple vent for the underground tombs the vampires were using, with an exit point in one of the small buildings used as offices by the park staff. He assumed the bats were the vampires, coming out now that night had fallen.

With a gesture, he changed into his blue robes, and his staff sent a thin blue light into the sky above him.

It was not uncommon for wizards to combine their powers to achieve a needed result, and Drusilicus knew this well, but to combine their abilities from a distance to create a protective barrier this large was a stretch for him.

When they'd come up with this part of the plan with Marlowe, the lesson the old wizard suggested was to focus on only each person's part of the spell.

Drusilicus took a deep breath and in his mind envisioned the protective wall about a block from the park. His mental image was a circle around the park, but his focus was the one-quarter that he was to create.

Invisible strands of will reached out, and he felt the other wizards as they touched his mind. Vasant was on the eastern point and Willowdell on the western. Bankrock added to the southern flank, Drusilicus could feel the barrier link and power vibrate through it like a live electrical cable.

Their combined energy was more than Drusilicus could have managed on his own and he felt the protections fall into place, as more bats flew out of the hidden vent. They circled in the air around the park, aware of the wall of energy that now trapped them. Several returned to the vent, undoubtably to report this to their master.

"It won't be long now," Drusilicus muttered to himself.

The night was suddenly pierced with sound. Large metal grates around the base of the Washington Square Arch screeched in complaint as they were pushed out of place. Male and female vampires leaped out of the holes in the ground with superhuman agility.

They came out with their eyes searching for their foes and formed a wall of bodies. Their eyes blazed with the baleful light of the undead as they formed a phalanx, barely visible in the dim light. Selene stepped out, her staff in hand, looking up Fifth Avenue to see Drusilicus as he stood on the sidewalk.

Wind swirled leaves and dust, and lifted the skirts of the red silk gown Selene wore. Her eyes roved over the chaos of vampires and bats until she glared, unblinking, at Drusilicus.

Behind her, a tall man levitated with no indication of effort, which was far more chilling than the violent eruptions of the other vampires as they leapt from the ground. He landed next to Selene, seeming to draw the darkness around him.

He was a handsome man, with sleek black hair and an immaculate beard, a square jaw and a noble face. He wore an expensive black suit with a black silk shirt.

Modredus, the Drakula.

He and Selene marched to the center of the arch as the wind came up and blew Selene's hair across her face as they stared at Drusilicus, and he saw their eyes flash red.

Vampires continued to come out of the grates and thronged into the park—hundreds of them.

The Drakula spoke a few words into Selene's ear. She nodded —and vanished.

She suddenly appeared about ten feet away from Drusilicus and planted her stolen wizard's staff in front of her. Her blood-red dress exposed her pale shoulders, looking like she was on her way to a night at the theatre instead of a battle.

"I told you that Marlowe must come alone," she spoke, her voice ringing with challenge. "Shall I kill the hostage? Shall my lord destroy your city now?"

"Marlowe has agreed to honor your wishes," Drusilicus offered with a bow of his head. "But we have no desire for mortal interference. The other wizards and I are here to keep mortals away—and to see that you honor your word."

"Where is Merlinus?"

"On his way, by himself. You neglected to tell him where you wished him to meet you."

She turned to Mordred, and he nodded, then she faced Drusilicus. "Have him come to the Arch. We shall be inside. What assurance do I have that he will be by himself and unaided?"

"By my power and oath, I assure you that Marlowe shall enter the arch alone," Drusilicus vowed. "I shall not move from this spot to aid him."

She considered his words. Breaking his oath would affect his powers greatly, and a wizard never made such an affirmation lightly.

She cleared her throat. "Nor your other wizards who surround the park?"

"You know I cannot make such a promise for them. But for this barrier to hold, we must remain where we stand."

"Very well. The papyrus, the spell, and if necessary, the sacrifice stands ready. We expect Marlowe within the hour. The Drakula cannot wait all night for him."

Drusilicus bowed his head in deference. "He could have arrived much sooner if you had not put his cab driver into the Dark Sleep."

"Is that what you think we did?" Her chuckle was like ice dripping down his spine. She turned her back to Drusilicus and gracefully moved toward Mordred. Several of the vampires framed the door on the side of the arch, and it stood unlocked and opened.

Selene took Mordred's arm, and they strolled to the doorway, then one at a time, ducked and went inside.

Drusilicus pulled the small hand mirror from his robes. "Marlowe," he whispered.

Marlowe's face immediately appeared. "Yes?"

"You were correct. They wish you to come to the Arch."

"I will be there shortly," Marlowe said, as the glass silvered over.

Drusilicus put the mirror away and faced the tall arch that rose above him, as the lights that illuminated it at night flashed on all at once.

From the south, a white glow drew closer. Vampires parted to move out of the way of the light. In the center of the illumination was Marlowe as he swaggered into the park. He was in bright-white robes that flowed to the ground, and he had the hood of his over-robe pulled over his face. His staff was in his hand and he used it effortlessly to help guide him and project power that crackled around him.

"Nice entrance," Drusilicus whispered with respect.

Marlowe headed to the doorway of the arch, and the light faded away. One vampire pulled the door open for him, and he stepped inside.

"Godspeed, Marlowe," Drusilicus whispered as the door shut behind him.

"Your stick stays here."

The vampire guard was over six feet and muscular, though the dark suit he wore hid it well. He was clean-shaven, including his hair and eyebrows, giving him an alien look.

Marlowe handed the creature his staff. He stepped aside and Marlowe headed for the circular stairs, lifting the hem of his robes as he pulled himself up by the small wall that circled the stairs.

Once up the many steps, he made his way into the upper chamber of the arch. Wrought iron candleholders stood at each end of the chamber, and the candle flames cast many shadows as they flickered. Some light poured in from the skylights above, from the powerful lights that lit up the monument at night.

Mordred sat in an elaborate throne-like chair of fine wood inlaid with precious stones, so large Marlowe wondered how they could have conjured it up there. Selene graced a smaller version of the throne, the staff in her right hand. The only other seat was a short stool that had seen better days. It was dull, the varnish faded and cracked.

Marlowe's eyes focused on Mordred. "Amazing. You look the same as at our last meeting."

Mordred gazed at Marlowe with contempt as Selene rose from her chair, a pair of shackles in her free hand. Although they appeared ancient, they were a bright and shiny metal that seemed to have a light of their own.

"Ah!" Marlowe barked. "The very shackles you imprisoned me with all those years ago, Nimue. Tonight is truly a visit down memory lane."

She stepped up to Marlowe and leaned the staff against her ample chest as she held out the shackles. "I am sure you recall, Merlinus, that these shackles—given to my master by Morgan Le Fay—make you unable to use your powers."

Marlowe smiled. "I recall that quite well, Nimue."

"Stop calling me that. I am Selene, the consort of the Drakula."

Marlowe pushed his lips out in a pout. "Really, calling Modredus your master does not sound like a healthy relationship."

"Give me your hands," Selene demanded.

Marlowe didn't move. "Not until you release the good sergeant. You have me as a hostage now and no longer need the mortal."

Selene looked to Mordred, not moving until he nodded.

Selene sighed and placed the shackles on the stool, then went over to the stairway and yelled down. "Vincenzo! Tell them to release the mortal."

"*Release* him, did you say?" the deep voice called back.

Marlowe called out. "Make sure he goes to one of the wizards surrounding the park. I am sure you know where those four are standing."

"Do as the old fool says," Selene shouted down.

"At once, mistress," Vincenzo called back.

She strutted back to the stool to retrieve the shackles. "I am being generous. I need do nothing you demand. We have your staff."

Marlowe smiled. "You know better than anyone that I can do much without my staff."

She stared at him, anger behind her eyes. "Pity there isn't a window to watch them release him."

"There is a way to watch," Marlowe said and glanced up at the roof over their heads. "In fact, we would have a panoramic view. Isn't that where you are taking me, anyway?"

"Look, old man, I am in charge here. I decide where we go and when," Selene fumed.

"Oh?" Marlowe said and peered past her at the seated Mordred. "I thought *you* were in charge."

Mordred moved at the speed of light, crossing the room and slapping Marlowe in the time it took to blink. The blow snapped his head back, and he grunted in surprise.

"We shall go up to the roof, but you will put on the shackles first," Selene said.

Without raising his head, Marlowe held out his hands, and Selene put the first bracelet on his wrist. It closed with a clack that reverberated in the small room. When the second one was closed and locked, the bright metal glowed. Marlowe stumbled forward, apparently weakened.

Selene helped him up. "Forgotten how weak they make you, haven't you?" She smirked.

"It is a bit of a surprise, I must agree," Marlowe groaned as he got his feet under him and stood. He appeared bent and weary.

"Now go up the stairs, old man. If you have to, drag yourself up there."

Marlowe made his way to the stairs and hauled his way up using the curling wall. With a gesture of her staff, the door at the top of the stairs flew open, and Marlowe, Selene, and Mordred climbed out onto the roof.

Marlowe gazed down at the street beneath them, looking north to see Drusilicus. Luis Vasquez was walking toward him. Drusilicus made a gesture and the big man leaned against the wall and slid down to a sitting position.

Even from the distance, Marlowe could see bruises on the detective's face, and Drusilicus checked him carefully then signaled up to Marlowe. Drusilicus' major-domo, Howell arrived in moments, and helped Luis to his feet, the pair of them headed towards Drusilicus' townhouse.

"It would appear you were not gentle with the good sergeant," Marlowe said.

"He was a fighter," Selene said. "Most of that damage was from your attempt to get to the master's coffin this very day."

"While under your influence, no doubt," Marlowe said.

"Indeed," Selene said under her breath. "Now hush, old man."

With a gesture of her staff, lights lit up on top of the arch, illuminating the three of them in a spotlight that Marlowe felt was visible for miles.

Selene grabbed Mordred's hand and held it up in the air as if he just won a prize fight. She called out in a loud voice that boomed and echoed off the surrounding buildings.

"My brothers and sisters, the Drakula is here!"

Cheers rang out from the throng on the street, and there was the chirping of thousands of bats from the surrounding buildings.

"He brings you the leader of our foes, without his cursed staff and in chains!"

This caused another cheer from the crowd, longer and louder than the first.

"Your lord—the Drakula—will bring an end to the wizards and this mortal city."

Marlowe's head snapped up.

"This night we shall break free and feed!" she screamed in ecstasy.

Marlowe put his head down and dragged himself past the open doors that led to the stairs, closer to Selene. "You said you would spare the city if I surrendered."

She faced Marlowe. "You think I need to keep my word to the likes of you?"

She handed her staff to Mordred—then she pushed Marlowe down the steps. As he fell, blood-curdling shrieks and cheers erupted from the brood of lurking vampires.

Mordred cleared his throat quietly. "You have a problem."

Selene shuddered, raising shaking hands now magically bound by the gleaming shackles. She opened her mouth to scream, her fangs like daggers against the ruby red of her lips—but she fell writhing to her knees, her power depleted.

"Get the key," she gasped. "It's on my throne."

Mordred, his face betraying no emotion, hurled himself off the edge of the roof, plummeting to the ground at breakneck speed. Barely slowing down, he landed gracefully and dashed toward the doorway back into the arch.

Marlowe levitated himself to a soft landing after Selene threw him down the stairs, and now his staff flew to him from where the guard kept it. He stepped into the throne room, glancing once at the elaborate chairs lurking in the middle of the room.

Moving as quickly as he could, he pulled out a vial filled with a red mist and poured out a smoking line across the floor.

The mist spread out and thickened, then shaped itself into the rough outline of a body as it roiled across the floor. The mist coalesced into—Eddie Berman in his red fighting robes.

Eddie drew a deep breath, panting as if he'd run a marathon. "I am *never* doing that again, you hear me?"

"Of course, Eddie," Marlowe soothed. "How do you feel?"

"Like I got turned into mist and shoved into a test tube," Eddie said. His staff appeared in his hand and he used it to help himself up. "Did you get Luis free?"

"He is with Howell. I was right— she put me in the shackles."

Eddie smiled. "Really? She had to know you got out of those things the last time she put you in them, right?"

"In her defense, it used to take a lot longer," Marlowe explained. "But I have perfected my ability to pick locks since then."

"How about the papyrus?"

Marlowe pulled the folded document from his pocket. "I fell into her, and it was right there."

"Remind me to watch those hands of yours," Eddie marveled. "You are one world-class pickpocket."

Marlowe put the papyrus into one of the pockets within his white robes, as the large guard, Vincenzo flew up the stairs and into the room with surprising speed.

He was repelled back against the wall by Eddie with a simple gesture of his staff.

A familiar figure shot past the fallen giant and headed up the second set of stairs to the roof.

"Orfeo!" Eddied grunted, and took a step toward the stairs himself, as Vincenzo rose to his feet to stop him. "Marlowe, take care of this guy."

Marlowe waved his staff and white rings of light wrapped the huge vampire like a mummy. He struggled against the bonds and fell to the floor, unable to move.

Eddie observed the fallen man. "Can you do that to Selene?"

Marlowe shook his head. "It won't work on one who carries a staff."

Eddie shook his head. "You guys have too many rules."

A rustling in the doorway drew their attention. There stood Mordred, his handsome face cast in shadow, blocking their path. He slowly moved toward them.

"Is he the Drakula?" Eddie whispered.

"So Selene says," Marlowe replied and stroked his beard. "He *is* the spitting image of Mordred."

Mordred glared from Eddie to Marlowe seeming to consider his options. Selene stumbled down the stairs, Orfeo helping her down.

"Orfeo, my man," Eddie said, raising the hand that didn't hold his staff. "Nice to see you. You're usually mist, or fleeing, or something."

"I will eat your heart, human," Orfeo spat.

"Release me," Selene demanded, shaking the manacles on her hands. "Or face the wrath of the Drakula!"

Mordred folded his arms and faced them, power crackling around him.

Eddie and Marlowe took a step back, staffs at the ready.

"He's really the strong, silent type, isn't he?" Eddie asked.

"You noted that as well?" Marlowe said.

"Yeah, she makes the speeches and demands, and he just stands there looking all 'romance novel'."

"You dare!" Selene shouted, as Orfeo bared his fangs.

Marlowe went on. "Give it up, Selene. I spoke to the spirit of Mordred this very afternoon."

Mordred sighed and rolled his eyes at Selene, and in a very feminine voice said, "I told you it wouldn't work."

His hands went to his face, grabbed under the chin line, and pulled. With the sound of tin foil being crumpled, his body altered, shrank, and developed graceful curves as Lysandra pulled off the Mask of *Misignwah*.

She was still in the masculine dark suit, but her long hair cascaded away from her face as she glared about the room. The two women were almost twins with their long dark tresses and strong features.

Orfeo was confused. "The Drakula is not here?"

"Fool," Selene snapped, "*I* am the Drakula!"

"Mordred is dead, so you played both roles," Marlowe announced. "You created the myth in Europe that the Drakula was Mordred. As his consort, you relayed his wishes, but you knew that to pull off your stunt here, you would need an actual person for the vampires to look upon and obey. That is why you required the mask."

Eddie shook his head. "You attacked the little people's Granny to get it? That's evil."

"You brought a young vampire with you to play the role once you had the mask, but Eddie slew him," Marlowe pointed out.

"Lycius," Eddie said. "Sorry about that. I didn't know he would be the star of your little show." Eddie regarded Lysandra. "So you had to get the person you'd been working with the entire time to step in."

With a screech, Selene leapt forward, but Marlowe merely raised a hand and pushed her aside with a thought. She fell onto her throne with a crash.

Eddie glared at Lysandra, his staff at the ready in case she attacked. "She had to get you involved so that you could get into Drew's house and steal that staff."

"I was happy to." Lysandra smiled smugly. "Once I knew that there was a staff without a master, I let Selene know. She came to New York months ago so we could create Mind-Blo. I seduced the wizard and got her the staff."

"Which Caleb was happy to bequeath to her," Eddie said. "I get it. Then she flew back to London and came over with the coffin like she just got here."

"It fooled you," Lysandra bragged.

"It did. As did your performance here in the arch. Making us feel sorry for you, claiming the other vampires left you to die because you helped us."

"I knew you wizards would find me in the coffin and I was sure you would spare me."

"Nice touch."

"I have the papyrus," Marlowe announced. "Shall we bring this to an end?"

"Wrong once again," Lysandra smirked. "You have *a* papyrus—not *the* papyrus."

Marlowe frowned. "What?"

Selene staggered to her feet, her back to the room. "You are not the only one with a means to escape these shackles."

There was a clatter of metal as Selene turned, a bright shiny key in her left hand. She held out her freed right hand and her staff flew into it.

"Damn," Eddie said, and both he and Marlowe were knocked off their feet before they could get a protective dome in place.

Eddie was lying on the concrete floor as he heard Selene shout, "Give me the mask and the papyrus. The Drakula *will* raise the bones of the dead."

"You are so sexy when you're angry," Lysandra gushed, and handed Selene the mask.

Selene put it on, and the wooden creation seemed to disappear into her flesh. She writhed in spasms as her lush curves filled out and her hair disappeared into her scalp with the sound of tearing Velcro. The room was filled with the sharp cracks of bone as she grew taller, her shoulders expanding to fill the stylish black suit that materialized over her newly masculine body. There was a smell in the air that reminded Eddie of hospital rooms and morgues.

A moment later, Modred stood in the room, holding the staff. He said in Selene's voice, "Let's go."

Orfeo looked back and forth frantically at the women as they headed for the stairs. "What do I do?"

"You wanted to eat his heart? Do it!" Mordred shouted and headed up the stairs, followed by Lysandra.

Orfeo sniffed at the two fallen wizards, and his eyes turned red as his fangs extended. He ran over to grab the fallen shackles, planning to use them on Eddie.

"Oh, hell no," Eddie shouted. *"Oppressio!"*

Orfeo lifted into the air and slammed against the wall, the shackles with him. He crumpled to the floor, stunned.

Eddie helped Marlowe to his feet. "Is she tellin' the truth? Did you get the wrong papyrus?"

Marlowe reached into his pocket and retrieved the papyrus, opening it to gaze at the inscription. "I am afraid she was correct."

"You know what that means," Eddie said, heading for the stairs. "You get the reinforcements." He stopped and pointed at Orfeo. "And bind up this guy."

Marlowe nodded as Eddie pulled out his small mirror. "Inscope?"

The gray-bearded man appeared in the glass. "Are ye ready for us?"

"Just as we planned, please."

Eddie took the stairs two at a time to the roof and stopped at the open doors at the top, his staff at the ready. He glanced at the sky overhead where dark clouds were forming, and flashed with luminescence from distant lightning.

Mordred stood at the edge of the roof holding a glowing staff and chanting odd words in a very womanly voice. Lysandra stood next to him, looking enough like Selene that the crowd probably didn't notice the difference, except that Lysandra was in the same dark suit as Mordred.

Lysandra, gripping a small wand made of crystal, fired a blast of pink light at him.

Eddie ducked back into the stairway and the small amount of protection the open doors offered.

"Some help up here?" Eddie yelled down to Marlowe. "Lysandra's got herself some kind of talisman."

"What is it?"

"Looks like a magic wand," Eddie said. "Man, do people actually use wands?"

"Sometimes," Marlowe answered as the sound of rushing wind came from the room below Eddie.

Another blast of light struck near where Eddie crouched and a roofing tile exploded. "Well, she's going all 'young wizard' on my ass."

Eddie raised his staff and with a whoosh, a blast of fire shot back at Lysandra and the disguised Selene. Without even a break in chanting, Mordred gestured with the upraised staff, and a protective dome rose up around them. The fire passed over them with no damage.

"Eddie, do not use fire—this is a national monument!" Marlowe yelled.

"What can I use against vampires?" Eddie shouted back.

"Your fire energy can do all forms of light. Try a laser."

Eddie ducked as another blast shot past him, and his protective dome flashed red to repel it. "I gotta learn new shit in the middle of a fight?"

"We practiced using different light," Marlowe shouted up to him.

"I remember," Eddie shouted. "I need more practice."

Eddie raised his own protective dome, and came out onto the rooftop, deflecting the blasts from Lysandra's wand as he planted himself on the roof.

"*Expelliatro!*" Eddie yelled, and the wand flew from Lysandra's hand as Mordred continued to chant. "Ha! I always wanted to do that."

A burst of energy shot up from the ground and knocked Eddie off his feet.

"What the hell…"

He stepped to the edge of the roof and gazed down. Dalehead was walking toward the arch, her staff at the ready, the top still glowing from her recent blast of energy.

He rose, dome in place. "Hey, Dalehead, it's me!"

She stared up with unblinking eyes to let loose another burst from her staff at him.

Eddie ducked and jumped back into the stairwell for protection. "What did I do to piss her off?"

Lysandra retrieved her wand and fired at Eddie again. "Fool, she is ours now! It was not the Dark Sleep as you thought. I drugged her with the vampire venom. She obeys us now, as does your cabbie."

Eddie ran down the circular stairs. Getting into the room was difficult because of the unconscious bodies of Orfeo and Vincenzo, both restrained by rings of light that wrapped around them.

Next to Marlowe stood Inscope as a dark crack in reality shrank and faded away behind them.

"Reinforcements be here!" bellowed Inscope. "What did we miss?"

"They used vampire venom on Dalehead and Claremont," Eddie panted. "Both of them are under the vampire's control, and that's not good for the guys holding the barrier."

Marlowe was alarmed. "If they bring down the barrier, the vampires are free to attack the populace."

"What do we do?" Inscope asked.

"Selene is still chanting the spell up there, which will activate the prophecy."

Marlowe hissed, "The dead will rise?"

Eddie nodded. "You and Inscope stop her. I have to help our guys on the street."

The arch quivered as if a slight earthquake rocked its foundations.

"What be that?" cried Inscope.

"The spell from the Papyrus of Sekhmet is working," Marlowe intoned. "I fear we may be too late."

TWENTY-FIVE

E ddie headed for the stairs and vaulted over the fallen body of Vincenzo. He was down the steps in seconds and paused at the closed outer door. Then, he pushed the door open and shot two blasts of fire at the guards who had been watching the doorway, and they fell back.

The light from the arch projected up onto a sky now completely filled with heavy clouds. High above their heads the black clouds were spinning into a dark funnel that churned angrily.

Eddie hit the ground as a blast of light came from Dalehead as she circled towards him. He did his best to repel it with a parry of his own. Then yelled *"Oppressio!"*

This sent his invisible wall of force slamming against Dalehead and a group of vampires that were just getting the courage to approach. They all flew back and to the ground.

He ran to Drusilicus, who was still focused on the barrier he was creating with the other wizards. "Why did Dalehead attack you?"

"She's under the influence of the vampire venom," Eddie explained. "It wasn't the Dark Sleep at all."

Drusilicus considered it. "That was why they kept her in her arch. Sunlight would have dissipated the effect."

"Drew, there are people who have been taking Mind-Blo, and it has the venom in it. Do you think it could do the same thing?"

"You mean, put them under the control of the vampires?" Drusilicus said, catching on.

"Marlowe said that there was another substance in the drug, *Polypodium leucotomos* extract. I found it online—it's an ingestible sun block."

Drusilicus gaped at Eddie, fear in his eyes. "So—sunlight would not easily cleanse the venom?"

"Which means a lot of regular people—mortals—are going to come here to fight for the vampires!"

"Or be a feast for the bloodsuckers," Drusilicus said and stared up Fifth Avenue. "I fear we may be too late."

He pointed a long finger to a crowd of people approaching with an ungainly gait, as if not completely under their own will. There were hundreds of them, and they carried a variety of weapons: knives, baseball bats, heavy chains, even sticks. Luis Vasquez was pushing his way to the front of the crowd.

"Oh shit," Eddie said, as he saw his partner. "What can we do? The barrier ain't going to do much against—"

There was a rumble, and the ground heaved and buckled as if a wave passed underneath cracking sidewalks, opening asphalt in large gaping holes and throwing Eddie and Drusilicus off their feet. As Drusilicus fell, his concentration and his spell were broken. The protective barrier around the park wavered and vanished, knocking the oncoming crowd over in a wave.

"Now what?" Eddie said as he raised his head.

"Didn't you stop the Drakula?" Drusilicus bellowed.

"We've had a setback or two."

"It's the spell; it's gaining power." Drusilicus pointed at a gaping hole in the road, as a bony arm reached up and grabbed the macadam to pull itself up and out. Rags hung from skeletal arms, as it struggled to pull up the rotted skull that was its head. It was stained by dirt and decayed flesh as it rose into view. The skull's canine teeth were pointed and long, and a red glow sat in the empty eye sockets.

"What the hell is that?" Eddie gasped, feeling sick.

"Vampire skeletons," Drusilicus said, terror in his voice. "I imagine if they feed on blood, they will grow flesh."

There was a small voice from a pocket in Drusilicus' robes. "The barrier is down!"

Drusilicus pulled out the mirror to see Vasant's face.

"Vasant!" Eddie yelled. "Dalehead and Rusty are under the control of the vampires. So are all the people that used Mind-Blo."

"What should we do?" the woman asked.

"Marlowe is trying to stop the Drakula. We all have to surround the arch and protect it so that he and Inscope can do it."

"We'd better get in there," said Drusilicus and pointed at the arch. Near the door to the arch stood Dalehead fully recovered, and now Rusty Claremont, in his taxi uniform, had also joined the fray.

Eddie stopped. "Can you take on those two? I'll get help."

"What sort of help?" Drusilicus demanded.

"It's hard to explain."

Drusilicus glanced up Fifth Avenue at the crowd who were getting up to their feet, Luis at the front. "Our choice appears to be vampires or possessed New Yorkers."

"Then I'll take the vampires." Eddie shouted, and moved into the park as Drusilicus deftly took on both Dalehead and Rusty at the same time.

Holes had opened all around the park, on the paved walkways, and in the playgrounds, even on the roadways that surrounded the park on all four sides. More of the dirty fanged skeletons were dragging themselves out of the ground. They lurched clumsily, as if it had been so long since they used legs and arms that it took getting used to.

"Oppressio!" Eddie shouted to throw back a group of vampires advancing upon him and reached into his pocket to find the UV flashlight. He'd forgotten it was there. He slid past it to the wooden whistle given him by Skysoarer.

He gave a hard and steady blow that made an ultrasonic sound buzz through his head.

"How may I help, Walker?" came a small voice.

Eddie saw the small Native-American figure in his buckskins. Eddie held out his hand to the fighting all about them. "We need help."

Skysoarer observed the scene. "I thought this is how your people usually act."

"No, this isn't! These are vampires, and look... there are skeletons rising out of the ground, in search of blood."

"I see, Walker of the Wise. I shall speak with the tribe about this."

"The tribe—" Eddie began. He had been looking right at the little man, who was suddenly not there anymore. There was no puff of smoke or change of any kind. He was there and then he wasn't.

"What does that mean— the tribe?" Eddie yelled at the sky.

Vasant, Bankrock, and Willowdell had entered the park from different sides and were pushing back vampires with blasts of their own power. A skeleton leaped up to attack, but Vasant smashed it into powder with a backhand gesture.

All around the park, wizards were attacking vampires, except for the wizards who were attacking each other. Fanged skeletons were reaching out blindly for anything that passed by them, and huge bats with dripping fangs were dive-bombing out of the sky.

Up on the top of the arch, Mordred continued to chant in Selene's voice. Her words boomed through the park as the funnel in the clouds overhead grew darker and spun more rapidly.

A vampire leapt up next to Eddie and caught him, knocking him to the ground. Eddie pulled out the UV flashlight and shone it into his eyes. The vampire covered its face and fell backward, then stumbled away through the crowd.

Vampires suddenly surrounded him. They were no longer beautiful with their pale skin and aristocratic style, but were nothing more than base animals: their eyes fiery red, their fangs extended and their features twisted in the horrible glee of the hunt, the prey and the feeding.

Eddie held them back with a conjured dome of protection as they growled and snapped their jaws at him, trying to reach past the barrier and take him, taste his blood.

As he stood, he peered past the drooling mob to see hundreds of small *Pukwudgie* as they flew into the park like an invading army. They fired small bows and arrows that not only made vampires fall to the ground, but several simply turned to dust as they were struck.

From all four sides of the park, Vasant, Bankrock, and Willowdell pushed past the crowd with walls of force and struck attackers down with beams of light.

A large hand fell on Eddie's shoulder and he froze in terror.

Someone or something had penetrated his magickal dome of protection. He had allowed his mind to wander to the battle and had not paid attention to his surroundings. He tried to move, but the hand had a grip of iron, and Eddie was sure he was about to feel the pinch as a pair of fangs wedged into his throat, and his last view of life would be the glowing red eyes of a vampire.

He glanced at the hand. It was hairy. It was *very* hairy, with a light-brown fur covering it.

He stared up into the face of a gigantic creature covered in long brown hair.

"Stone Face!" Eddie exulted, relieved, as he knew the Sasquatch could easily pass through any magickal construct Eddie might create. "I am so glad to see you."

"I understand you need help, my friend," the Sasquatch said as three vampires leaped upon him, and with his free arm he swatted them away like flies.

"I thought you didn't get involved in the human world."

Stone Face shrugged his massive shoulders. "I figured, what the hell."

Eddie smiled despite himself. He pointed up at the arch. "I need to get on top of that arch. Can you use magick to get me there?"

Stone Face looked up at the arch, then down at Eddie, and finally up at the arch again. "Can you give yourself a soft landing?"

"Say what?" Eddie worried.

"I will take that as a yes," Stone Face replied.

With that, the huge beast grabbed Eddie by the collar of his robes and the seat of his pants and, in one mighty effort, threw him in the air toward the arch. Eddie screamed as he rose like a missile to the top. He thought fast to remember his levitation spells as he reached the roof, but he was going so fast that he fell and rolled, and his staff went flying. He landed on his back directly in front of both Lysandra and Mordred.

Lysandra had kept Inscope and Marlowe at bay on the stairway, and she backed up a step when the hurtling body of Eddie ended up at her feet.

Selene, still wearing the guise of Mordred, kept reading and chanting, but Lysandra smiled and raised her wand at Eddie. "At last we can be rid of you, Newling."

The UV flashlight had fallen out of his pocket and he grabbed it, lifted and aimed it at the two vampires, and hit the switch.

Lysandra flinched away and covered her eyes. Mordred also turned away from the light, which made him stop chanting.

A blast of light from the stairway hit Lysandra and knocked her off her feet. Mordred opened his eyes, but they were now pure white, as if the flashlight had burned the color from them.

"I can't see," said Mordred with Selene's voice as he blinked repeatedly and held the papyrus in front of dazzled eyes.

Eddie held out his hand, and his staff flew into it. He inserted the wooden rod between Mordred's feet, and with a simple twist, tripped him.

He hit the rooftop and Eddie yanked the papyrus and the wizard staff away. Eddie rose and pressed his own staff to the chest of his adversary. "You make a move I don't like and a fireball is going right through you."

Marlowe moved up to Eddie's side, the shackles in his hands as Inscope stood over Lysandra, picked up the crystal wand she had been using, and snapped it in half in his big hands.

Marlowe leaned over Mordred and fastened the bright silver metal fetters to his wrists. When the second one clicked into place, Mordred let out a howl of anguish, as his body shook and twisted, the hair growing longer, breasts springing up as the body bent out of the male shape and returned to its female form. A wooden mask lay on the roof next to her as Selene sat there, panting, and her wizard staff was nothing more than a metal broom handle. Eddie grabbed her arm and pulled her to her feet.

"Hear me!" he yelled as he held the mask aloft. "The Drakula is a fraud! This woman has deceived you all!"

The combatants didn't even pause in their attack. Drusilicus was still in a struggle with Dalehead and Rusty, light flashing between them as they each parried and thrust. Vasant,

Willowdell, and Bankrock were surrounded by domes of light, but the vampires were climbing on top, trying to get past their defenses. Eddie saw Stone Face as he slapped vampires out of his way. One skeleton jumped up on the Sasquatch's shoulder and bit into his neck, only to dissolve to dust as the blood touched its fangs. The *Pukwudgie* still fought on, and although the little people were quick and had magick, the vampire's speed and strength was giving them the advantage.

The drugged humans also had entered the fray, and one of the risen skeletons had jumped on a man and set his fangs into him. As the bony monster drew blood, muscles and veins appeared on the body over the bones.

"They will not stop," Selene hissed.

Eddie turned to Selene to see that her eyes were dark again. Her vampiric powers had healed the temporary effect of the UV flashlight.

Selene faced Marlowe. "Even if I do not complete the spell, they will tear apart your city this night and there is naught you can do. Now I take my revenge for my long dead Mordred."

"I did not kill Mordred," Marlowe said as he observed the battlefield. "All I did was cast you out."

She also inspected the carnage, but with a smile. "You took our magick from us, but we heard of a way to have eternal life. The pair of us traveled all over Europe until we found a vampire. We beseeched him to turn us, and for centuries we served a new lord and worked our way up the lineage. Even so, a crowd of mortals slaughtered Mordred in the eighteenth century."

"I know," Marlowe said wearily, "his spirit told me."

"I swore on his dead body I would finish you and destroy the things you love. You love this city, and this night there shall be havoc. Many mortals will die, and wizards as well."

Eddie shook his head and tightly held the flashlight in his hand. He had an overwhelming desire to shine the UV light in her eyes and blind Selene again, just for spite.

It was at that moment that he recalled the words of the prophecy Marlowe mentioned from the Book of Daniel: *And they that be wise shall shine as the brightness of the firmament.*

Eddie cleared his throat. "Marlowe, the bearer of the Staff of Fire can do light, right?"

"Any shade or color," Marlowe said, scrutinizing the battle below with a stern face.

"Then I can end this," Eddie concluded in a somber tone.

"If ye can, then do so," Inscope demanded.

"It will kill the vampires, maybe all of them," Eddie brooded, and met his mentor's eyes. "Do I have the right to do that?"

Selene laughed. "One wizard, a Newling no less, and you think you can destroy all my people?" She sneered at Eddie. "You have not the power."

Marlowe faced Eddie, his face incredibly sad. "People are dying, Eddie, mortals and innocents. I am afraid we have little choice."

"It's all about vibration and wavelength, right, Marlowe?" Eddie said as he took a step away. He held out the UV flashlight and clicked it on, then pressed the light against his chest.

Feel the light... feel the frequency... the subtle difference of the wavelength...

He sensed the energy, the particular type of photons that made up that specific light. He felt it vibrate within him, and he allowed himself to vibrate with it.

I am one with the light.

There was a pulsing surge building under his skin. He felt both hot and cold, the burn of ice and the cold of space, as if he were both combusting and shrinking simultaneously. He had to use the cold, let that energy end this battle, once and for all.

He distantly heard Selene mock him. "He is a fool! Soon, my minions will come up here and kill you all!"

Eddie focused on the light, nothing but the light. He held up his staff, opened his eyes, and with a cry he pushed the energy he held within out through his arm, into the wood of his staff. It rose like a living thing and his staff crackled with a dark-blue ball of energy that sent out the mostly invisible light in all directions.

Anything white—the bones of the animated skeletons, and especially Marlowe in his white robes—glowed a bright blue. The light made the battle below stop for a moment, and all the combatants gazed up at the unnatural illuminance at the top of Eddie's staff.

At first, nothing happened, and the world seemed to hold its breath.

Did I get the frequency right? What if I missed it?

A sound, a cacophony of pain and fear, swept through the battlefield. Bats fell from the sky to smash lifelessly to the ground. Smoke came out of the vampires as the hundreds in the park all smoldered. They held their heads in agony as the light washed over them and through them, burning as it went.

Selene and Lysandra were at the epicenter of the release, and each shrieked horribly. They fell to the rooftop, their bodies smoking, as their flesh dissolved away. Their screams turned to croaks as the skin peeled from their skulls and then the bones themselves fell apart. The scent of burnt hair filled the night, pungent and sickening.

In moments, their empty clothing lay on the roof with nothing left but a fine ash that once was their flesh and bones.

The powerful light on the top of Eddie's staff faded as he gazed out over the park.

The remains of the vampires, whether bat, beast or man, lay about in smoldering heaps throughout the paved walkways and grassy knolls of the park. The burnt remains of bats continued to fall off buildings and trees. The corpses of the vampires were merely dust, that no longer filled empty clothing. The fanged skeletons were gone as well.

The entire park filled with a charnel smoke that formed a heavy, choking fog from the light that had destroyed the nightmare creatures.

In different places were the wizards, their protective domes came down as they gaped about in shock. Dalehead and Rusty no longer were fighting, but blinking their eyes and shaking their heads, as Drusilicus approached them cautiously.

The humans filling the park all appeared to be coming awake. The light pulled them out of their trances. Whatever chemical prevented the sunlight from cleansing the vampire venom could not withstand the power of the pure ultraviolet light.

Eddie regarded Marlowe and noticed the side of the old wizard's face had the slight red of a sunburn.

Eddie held out the flashlight, but the small device fell apart in his hands.

"Well, thass one way to end it, t'aint it?" Inscope said , and Eddie saw that one side of Inscope's face was tanned as well.

Eddie felt a tapping on his leg and looked down to see Skysoarer standing next to him. "Are we victorious?"

"I think so," Eddie said and knelt to speak to the tiny man. "Thank you, Skysoarer, and many thanks to your tribe, as well. They are mighty warriors."

"We shall tend to our folk. I may call upon you to heal any of our wounded."

Eddie bowed his head. "I would be honored."

In an instant, Skysoarer and all the *Pukwudgie* disappeared. Eddie glanced at the street below and saw Stone Face wave to him, and he waved back.

Eddie yelled down, "I've got something of yours!"

Stone Face frowned, but Eddie picked up the Mask of *Misignwah* and held it high for the Sasquatch to see. A smile broke out on the giant's face. Eddie lifted his staff and levitated the mask down to Stone Face, who put it on.

Suddenly, the hairy creature grunted, twisted and shrunk, and in his place was an average-height man with brown hair and chiseled features, wearing a finely tailored brown suit. He waved at Eddie again and strode away.

"Was that Stone Face?" Marlowe asked only seeing the man wave to Eddie.

"Yes," Eddie replied.

"Where do you suppose he's off to?"

"I don't know, going sightseeing, having a night on the town?" Eddie shrugged. "He doesn't get into New York much."

Marlowe frowned and examined the place where Selene and Lysandra had stood, using his staff to push aside the empty clothing. He picked up the fallen papyrus.

As Marlowe lifted it, the ancient papyrus fell apart in his hands.

Eddie stepped over to watch as the paper crumbled in his mentor's hands. "What's happening? I thought until it achieved its goal, magick protected it."

Marlowe held up the few remaining scraps. "I think the magickal energies that had sustained it have dissipated. It would appear its dark purpose is ended."

Inscope spoke up. "The mortals be awakening. What dare we tell them?"

"I've got an idea for that," Eddie answered, and turned back to Marlowe. "Can you help me create an illusion? This one won't be too difficult."

Marlowe stuck out his lips in thought. "What do you have in mind?"

TWENTY-SIX

L uis rubbed his head. It felt like he was waking up in the morning after a long night of drinking.

He was in Washington Square Park, but the last thing he could remember was being on his way to his car with that weird wizard, Rusty.

He touched a sore spot on his neck and felt two small indentations. What the hell had happened to him?

Some kind of bad-smelling smoke filled the park, but a breeze was clearing it slowly away. Luis saw dozens of people milling about the square. Some of them held bats, chains, and other weapons.

There was a bright light on the top of the Washington Square Arch, and he peered up to see a man on top. He wore a Safari outfit—khaki pants and a many-pocketed shirt with tall boots. On his head he wore one of those silly French hats—what were they called? A beret?

The khaki-dressed man was standing next to two men with large cameras on wooden tripods, and he held a megaphone to his mouth. On the top of the arch was a woman who held stapled pages, and two other men who appeared to be assisting.

"And—cut!" the man shouted. He was handsome, with a full head of hair and a mustache. "Ladies and gentlemen, give me your attention, please. That was an excellent take!"

Luis shook his head and studied the park to see several other men with large cameras on tripods hidden behind trees and bushes.

The man on the arch went on, "We think that take got all the footage we need. You all did a great job! Give yourselves a hand."

The director began to clap his hands, as did the cameramen and the entourage of people on top of the arch. After a moment, people in the crowd clapped their hands as well, and soon everyone was applauding.

This can't be real, Luis thought, and then he realized— it might *not* be real. He checked to make sure no one was watching him, then lifted his hand and slapped himself on the side of his head with an open hand.

In a flash, he saw Eddie, Marlowe, and a couple of people he wasn't sure of on top of the arch, each holding their big sticks. Then it changed back, and it was the director, cameramen, and assistants again.

He smiled. "It's an illusion," he said out loud and headed for the doorway that would take him into the arch.

Eddie was wrapping up his 'director' speech, even though all the people in the park saw a white guy in an outfit Eddie considered pretty weird, but Marlowe assured him was authentic.

"You are all released. With our thanks, please collect your release paperwork from our production assistants as you exit the park. We have to get things cleaned up and back to normal by tomorrow. And from all of us at Monumental Studios, thank you. New York is the best!"

He whispered to Marlowe, "Have the camera crew leave the top of the arch, and we should go inside, too."

Marlowe held his staff aloft, creating the illusion. "Should I have production assistants hand them forms? If we do, the paperwork will disappear once they are a certain distance away."

"Don't worry, they're New Yorkers, and they'll forget about the papers by the time they get home," Eddie told him in a low voice. "Also, if you can send a spell to help them believe they were all movie extras, it would help."

"I can do that." Marlowe assured.

The crowds of people shuffled slowly toward the exits, where projected assistants handed them nonexistent papers.

Eddie grabbed the shackles and Marlowe retrieved the broomstick, which was the disguised wizard staff Selene had used. Eddie handed the mystical handcuffs to Marlowe, who hid them away in a pocket of his robes.

Eddie closed the roof doors as Marlowe and Inscope went down into the large, open room in the middle of the monument. Vincenzo and Orfeo were sitting up, Marlowe removed the binding spell. They were groggy, but got to their feet.

"The Drakula is dead," Marlowe announced as he came down the stairs.

"You lie," growled Vincenzo.

"No, he doesn't," Eddie declared calmly. "In fact, I destroyed every vampire who was out there. You were spared because you two were in here."

"That is impossible," Orfeo uttered, unsure.

Eddie stared icily at the two vampires. "Look, I'll give you a chance. Leave New York—now, tonight. Never come back, and I swear we will not harm you. But raise your hand against any wizards or mortals here, and I will hunt you down and end you. Got it?"

Vincenzo and Orfeo glanced at each other and hung their heads. "I agree," they said in unison.

Luis came up the steps into the open space, eyeing the big Vincenzo as he did so.

"Luis," Eddie beamed. "Are you all right?"

"Yeah, just confused. What just happened? And why do you have suntans on one half of your faces?"

"Eddie defeated the Drakula," Marlowe said, his staff in one hand and the metal broom handle in the other. "And saved New York."

"It be quite the tale, I gi'e ye that," Inscope said, almost giddy.

Vincenzo and Orfeo headed down the stairs and out as Eddie and Luis talked.

"How long... I mean... what happened?" Luis asked.

"The vampires abducted you," explained Eddie. "One of them bit you and put you under their control."

Luis touched his neck again. "Yeah? I'm not going to become a vampire, am I?"

"Calm down, sergeant," Marlowe assured. "You were merely under their sway. They did not convert you. Plus, the light Eddie used was sure to purge any lingering effect of the venom."

"But Maria is worried," Eddie admitted. "I told her the battery on your phone died, and that we were on a stakeout."

"I need to call her. She gets nervous and then the kids get scared—"

"Kids!" Eddie slapped his forehead. "My wife is in labor! Guys, I gotta get outta here."

Marlowe smiled. "We have a half-dozen wizards here, Eddie. We can put the park back together before morning without you."

Inscope nodded. "It t'will look as if nothing happened at all."

"Come on, Luis," Eddie said, and headed for the circular staircase. "You can teleport with me. Maria is at the hospital coaching Cerise."

"Oh, man." Luis brightened as he followed Eddie down the stairs. "You got a place near the hospital we can, y'know, walk out of?"

"Yeah, just down the street."

Eddie ducked to get through the outer door, then assisted his partner as he pushed his large frame through the small opening.

Drusilicus was standing with Vasant, Bankrock, and Willowdell, who were helping the confused Rusty and Dalehead near the fountain. He turned and approached Luis and Eddie, with Vasant following him.

"Rusty and Dalehead are back to normal," Drusilicus explained, "though we will do some healing spells on them later."

Vasant came up beside him and casually placed an arm around his waist.

Eddie surveyed the damaged battlefield. There were vast holes in the ground, torn up walkways, bent wrought iron fences, and playground equipment leaned in precarious ways. "Marlowe is coming down to help you guys restore the park. Do you really think you can fix all this by morning?"

"Oh yes," Vasant said brightly, and her eyes met Drusilicus', both of them smiling.

"Eddie, it was a brilliant idea to tell the mortals it was all part of a movie. That way if any video should surface…"

"It can be dismissed," Eddie said. "How do you feel, Drew? Seems like Lysandra was using you the entire time."

"It would appear you were correct, Lieutenant," Drusilicus agreed. "I was indeed under Lysandra's sway. When you made that light, I found that any affection I had for her, any desire, was purged in that moment."

"That's good," Eddie said. "Now I have to get to my wife."

"Of course, your child!" Vasant said. "Go, be with her. Childbirth is difficult, even if you have done it repeatedly."

"Just how many children have you had, Vasant?" Eddie asked.

"Eddie," Drusilicus chided, "that is not a thing to ask a lady."

"Oh, posh," Vasant said dismissively. "I worry not of such things, especially not in this new age we are in. I have had…" she paused and observed the night sky. "I believe… about one hundred children in my lifetime."

Luis's mouth fell open. "A hundred!"

Vasant shrugged. "But please don't ask how many times I have been married."

"But you've been a hermit for the last one hundred years?"

She put her arm around Drusilicus' waist and slipped under his arm. Drusilicus smiled and placed his arm around her shoulders.

"Yes," she cooed. "But I believe it is time for me to be with people again." She glanced at Drusilicus. "Perhaps even one special person."

"Good luck, you two," Eddie said. "Luis and I have to go."

Drusilicus and Vasant headed back to the wizards, holding hands, and Luis smiled back at them. "Nice to see."

"Yeah, it might just mellow ol' Drew out." Eddie raised his staff, and he changed back into his clothes, and he returned his staff to his wallet. "Now we can use those trees right there—"

Before he could finish the sentence, a figure swooped out of the air, threw Luis aside like a rag doll, and clamped Eddie by the shoulder in a grip of iron.

"You shall not live past this night!" shouted Orfeo, lifting Eddie up in the air, his eyes fiery red and his fangs fully extended.

The vampire lunged for Eddie's throat and clamped his lips onto him, his teeth impaling him. Eddie tried to struggle, but as the teeth pierced his flesh, he was overcome with a wave of relaxed pleasure. It was as if he had slipped into a hot tub, and Eddie felt every muscle relax, the desire to escape or fight back gone.

There was a strange noise and the stench of burning flesh, and all at once Eddie dropped to the ground, Orfeo's teeth releasing from his neck.

Eddie blinked to see that the vampire was smoldering and screaming. A few feet away Rusty Claremont was standing with a water gun pointed at the monster.

"Holy water and garlic," Rusty yelled at the vampire. "How's dat feel?"

Orfeo, writhing in pain, rose as if to leap upon Rusty, but before he could, Eddie hit the catch on the ring and stabbed the small needle into Orfeo's leg.

The scream of pain and frustration was loud enough to echo off the nearby buildings, and the drug dealer's body twitched and shook, and then fell apart, bending at odd angles as it writhed on the ground and dissolved away to nothing.

Luis helped him to his feet. "You okay, man?"

"Yeah, yeah," Eddie said, trying to get to his feet and rubbing the wound on his neck that had sealed up once the vampire released him. "We gotta get out to New Jersey."

"I'll drive you!" Rusty suggested. "My cab is only a block away."

"No, no, I can do the walk in the woods thing," Eddie muttered.

"You ain't in no condition. Let the man drive us," Luis said. "Thanks, Rusty, we'd appreciate it."

The cabdriver headed off as Luis helped Eddie to a bench.

"Okay, okay," Eddie said, as he sat on the bench. His throat hurt and his head was still swimming.

"What was in that ring that did that?"

"Sasquatch blood."

"I guess it works. He won't be pushing any more drugs."

"I let him go," Eddie croaked and stared at the empty pile of clothes. "I told him I wouldn't hurt him if he left town."

"You had no choice, man. He was gonna kill you."

Eddie shook his head as waves of grief washed over him. "I killed them all, Luis."

"What are you talking about?"

"I killed all the vampires. I burned them up with ultraviolet light."

"Like Doctor Beverly did?"

Eddie nodded, his eyes filled with tears. "What kind of monster am I?"

"You just saved every human being in that park, man. You ain't no monster."

"I did it so easily," Eddie lamented. "So easily…"

The yellow cab pulled onto the street just beyond the broken wrought-iron fence.

"Come on, Eddie. Let's go see our wives."

Luis helped Eddie through the twisted fence, and the two men got into the back of the cab before it sped off.

As Eddie leaned his head back with his eyes closed in the cab, Luis called Maria with Eddie's phone.

"Luis!" she squealed. "I been so worried."

"Just a stakeout," Luis lied. "It's all cleared up. The drug dealer is… um… under arrest."

Even though Maria had experienced some of the strange events surrounding Eddie since he became a wizard, he didn't want to say that Eddie turned the guy into a pile of dust.

"How's Cerise doing?" Luis went on.

"She's a champ. The baby is here, a beautiful little girl."

Luis lowered the phone. "Eddie, your daughter is born!"

Eddie nodded. "That's good."

"We're on our way, Eddie and me," Luis said. "Be there in about twenty minutes. Thanks for helping, Maria."

"Get Eddie here! Eleanor is home with the boys, and I got to get home to our kids."

"What time is it?"

"Almost midnight. My momma is watchin' the kids, but we gotta get home. Tomorrow is church."

"Okay, we'll be there soon, *Amante*."

Luis handed Eddie the phone. "You okay? You don't look good."

"I fought vampires and got bit, and you're worried about how I look?" Eddie said without opening his eyes.

"Good point. So, are *you* gonna turn into a vampire?"

"No, the vampire has to give you his blood to make you turn. So, even though you and I were bit, we have nothing to worry about. Just get some sun to purge the venom."

"Well, there's that at least."

The cab pulled in front of the Sacred Heart Hospital, and Eddie and Luis stepped out. Luis leaned down and said. "What do we owe you, Rusty?"

"My treat. Least I can do, right? See ya."

The yellow cab sped off as the two detectives headed inside. They were a sight as they made their way to the security desk. Luis had sunburn on one half of his face, Eddie had blood on his neck, and both of them had been in their clothes far too long.

The security guard eyed them with suspicion and observed the blood on Eddie's neck. "This ain't the entrance for the Emergency Room."

"No, man," Luis said. "We are going to Maternity. My friend here just became a father."

Again the security man appeared quizzical. "Looks like you two have been out celebrating for the last few hours."

"Yeah, I guess it does," Luis chuckled, and pulled out his shield and opened it for the security officer. "Actually, we are detectives, and we just got off a bust, so lighten up, okay?"

He shrugged and gave them visitor badges and instructions on how to get to Maternity.

Eddie was walking better and followed Luis into the elevator. "How do I look?"

"Like crap, man," Luis said.

"Good, then Cerise will know everything is normal," Eddie sighed.

They got out of the elevator and walked to the nurse's station. The nurse on duty watched them, unimpressed as they drew near.

"Hi there, I'm Eddie Berman."

"Oh? Nice of you to show up, Mr. Berman."

"We're cops. We were on a stakeout."

"Well, good thing she had friends. I'm sorry, but you ain't seeing your wife or daughter until you clean yourself up." She pointed at the door of a nearby men's room. "You get washed, then we'll put you in a hospital gown and get some gloves on you."

"Yes, ma'am," both men said, and they followed her finger into the restroom.

A few minutes later, the two men returned and were washed and even had their clothes cleaned and pressed, since Eddie used magick to accomplish the task.

The woman watched them return to her desk and shook her head. "Well, don't you two clean up good?"

She winked at Eddie and came out from behind the desk with a hospital gown and helped him put it on over his clothes. Eddie put on a pair of gloves and a surgical mask, and she then escorted Eddie into a side room.

The lights were subdued, but bright enough to see. The nurse put on a pair of gloves and mask herself and walked to the end bassinet. In the center of the small bed was a tiny little girl. Her skin was a dark caramel, and she was tiny and wrinkled, and had a small covering of black curly hair on her head.

She was the most beautiful thing Eddie had ever seen.

The nurse lifted the sleeping child to Eddie, whose eyes filled with tears of joy.

"Hello, you," he whispered.

"Not such a tough police officer now, are you?" the nurse said with a smile behind her mask.

"I guess not," Eddie said, and joy ran through his heart as the tiny person yawned and shifted closer to him.

Luis and Maria stood on the other side of the glass and Luis gave him a "thumbs up" gesture. Luis put his arm around his wife and she pulled in under his arm. Luis' eyes were wet as well.

"What's her name?" the nurse asked.

"What?" Eddie asked.

"Her name? It beats calling her, 'Hey, you!'"

Eddie looked down at the tiny child in his arms. "I... don't... know. We never really chose a name."

The nurse sighed behind her mask. "Just like a man. Give her to me. She had a busy day. You got your whole life to be with her."

He handed the tiny bundle to the nurse, who returned her to the bassinet.

Eddie pulled down his mask as he approached Luis and Maria. "That's my daughter."

"She's beautiful, Eddie," Maria said. "Now you go see Cerise. Luis and I gotta get home."

Maria led them down the hall. "So you guys gonna stop doing nights now?"

"Yes, ma'am," Eddie said. "We are officially back on days."

"Hey, boss, can I have the day off tomorrow?" Luis asked.

"It's Sunday. We're already off, Luis."

"Then I guess it's okay."

"But Monday we have to go in and clean up the loose ends and write the reports. Then I am going on leave for a couple weeks."

"Vacation time!" Luis said.

Eddie went into the room, and Cerise lay in the bed. Around her neck was the silver amulet that Caleb made and Skysoarer had placed there. Her drawn face turned to him, and she smiled as Eddie approached.

"I missed the show," Eddie said.

Cerise sighed tiredly. "There was a lot of screaming and cursing, and you know how I hate it when people use bad language."

"Especially if it's you," Eddie said, and ran his fingers through her hair. "I saw her. She has your hair."

Her smile grew wider. "That was a surprise. The boys were bald as a baseball when they were born."

"She's beautiful, Mrs. Berman." Eddie kissed her hand.

"I agree, Mr. Berman." She touched the disk on the chain around her neck. "Where did this come from?"

"I had it delivered," Eddie said. "It protects you from harm."

She shook her head. "Just like a man."

"What?" Eddie frowned.

"You get a magickal talisman, and you don't get me one to make childbirth easy," she chuckled.

"Sorry, I didn't think of that," Eddie apologized, and then frowned. "Did we think of a name? The nurse asked, and I drew a blank."

"We discussed some names, but not recently. We talked about Louise after Luis, and Maria, but once I saw her, I knew what it had to be."

"That's good," Eddie smiled. "What?"

"Ellie," she said simply. "Short for Eleanor."

"After Momma?" Eddie said, his voice breaking.

"Do you think she'll mind?"

"I think she'll be thrilled," Eddie said, as his eyes filled with tears one last time that night.

EPILOGUE

Bright and early Monday morning, with Eleanor getting the boys off to school and calling everyone she knew to announce her namesake, Eddie drove into New York.

He had requested the vacation days, but he had to finish up the paperwork and write an acceptable report of the incidents of the last few days.

He couldn't very well tell the captain that he'd ended a drug epidemic by frying the creators as well as the distributors of the drug.

Luis was already there. His big partner pulled him aside. "Took care of the drugs that disappeared from evidence. Marlowe came over and pulled them out of— I don't know—thin air, and I turned them in, and Marlowe was able to make my signature appear on the form to say I signed them out for a recount. Turns out we have more of the vials than the original estimate, so the recount made sense."

"That's great, Luis."

They both started on reports and checked things with each other, sometimes in inaudible whispers, as they wrote up the incidents of the last few days.

Eddie also called Beverly Warren at the ME's office and told her they were dropping the case of the John Doe who had shown up in Springbanks Arch with the stake through his chest. The official conclusion would be listed as "accidental death."

"Accidental death?" Beverly repeated. "Even with a stake through his heart?"

"My report speculates that the victim was obsessed with vampires, which is why he had the wooden stake. While searching the tunnel carrying the sharpened stake, he tripped and fell on to it, impaling himself. Does the Assistant Medical Examiner disagree with that assessment?"

"I believe the Medical Examiner's office will agree with your theory based on my examination of the body on site," Beverly said over the phone. "That will keep my record on the up and up."

"You're welcome."

"Congrats on your new kid. I hope she has your wife's looks."

"Not fair to pick on a newborn."

"See you at the next crime scene, Berman. And seriously, congratulations—and thanks."

Eddie was writing up a full explanation of Saturday night. His story was that he and Luis pursued the drug dealer, described as Orfeo, and they crashed a movie set down in Washington Square Park. In the confusion, Orfeo had escaped, but Eddie was sure that he had left town and folded up operations.

It all seemed pretty lame, but Eddie needed to include the important elements without going into depth. What he wrote would be close enough to what witnesses might report.

He also wrote that he and Luis had found the drugs in Claremont Arch as that location was locked and filled with storage for the park. It made more sense than a coffin full of drugs in a magic, hidden room in Greywacke Arch.

Finally, once he'd written and rewritten the report, he stood and put on his jacket.

"You heading out for parental leave?" Luis asked.

"I can take up to twelve weeks. I figure I'll take two," Eddie said.

"Good thing," Luis grinned. "NYC might fall apart without us."

"You never know." Eddie smiled.

"I gotta bone to pick with you, man."

Eddie opened his arms in innocence. "What did I do this time?"

"You weren't there for Ellie's birth. Maria was."

"I know, I was busy rescuing you."

"Now she's going on and on about having another baby. Man, I already got six kids!"

"So go for lucky seven, Luis. That's between you and Maria. I am staying out of it. *Adios.*"

He roamed the transverse road back toward Central Park West and made his way to 85th Street and Marlowe's townhouse. He knocked on the door and Willowdell answered it.

"Good morning, Wizard Berman," she effused with a cheerful smile. "I was just about to leave for New Orleans."

"Oh?" Eddie asked. "Have a pleasant trip."

"I wanted to t'ank you. Word in New Orleans is the vampires are all scared of the wizards now."

Eddie frowned. "Scared?"

"Now t'at we got a wizard who can turn them to ash. I t'ink we will have less trouble with them in the Big Easy, I will tell you that."

Eddie studied the ground in thought.

"You should be happy!" she gushed. "T'is will make things much easier for wizards around the world."

She patted Eddie's shoulder and headed down the stairs as Eddie stepped into the foyer and ran into Drusilicus, who stood there with a relaxed smile.

"Beautiful day, isn't it?"

Eddie glared at the man. "What got into you?"

"Hmm?" Drusilicus said almost dreamily. "Only spring. In the spring, a young man's fancy lightly turns to thoughts of love."

"If only you knew a young man," Eddie told him as he pushed past him and into the foyer. "How's Vasant?"

"She has taken up residence in my townhouse."

"No more problems about you two seeing each other?"

"At our last encounter she was a wizard, and I, her apprentice. Now I am a wizard and one of the Five, there is no longer anything to separate us."

Eddie smiled. "I'm happy for you, Drew, as well as Vasant. It's nice for her to be with someone after a hundred years of solitude. No further longings for Lysandra?"

His expression turned grim. "You had been quite right, Lysandra had infected me with her venom. Your ultraviolet light burned any desire for her completely out of my system."

"That's one of the things I'm here to talk about with Marlowe..."

"Did someone mention my name?" Marlowe said as he came into the room. "Eddie, will you join us for breakfast? I have all of your favorites."

"I can't stay," Eddie said, and turned to his mentor. "I just wanted to thank you for getting the drugs to Luis this morning."

The elder wizard's eyes sparkled. "You'll be glad to know I have the staff Selene used safely locked up until we can find an apprentice who is worthy to be given it."

"I understand your daughter is doing well, lieutenant?" Drusilicus interjected.

"Ellie's fine. She and Cerise are coming home today."

"Ellie Berman," Marlowe said. "A fine name. I am sure your mother is most pleased."

"She's through the roof." Eddie couldn't help but smile. Then he grew serious. "I needed to tell you I have to focus on my family."

"As you've told us repeatedly for months, Eddie," Marlowe said. "I figure in a few months we can start your next level of training—"

"No, we can't," Eddie said.

"Lieutenant, we were all impressed with your skills," Drusilicus insisted. "But there is still much for you to learn. I am sure you realize that."

"There is a lot to learn, but maybe not by me," Eddie said.

Marlowe frowned. "What do you mean, Eddie? You are a gifted wizard, a *magus* to be sure."

"You've saved New York twice in less than a year," Drusilicus agreed. "Doesn't that show your value to the world?"

"When I met Stone Face he told me that my enemy thirsts for vengeance and to rule over lesser beings while I don't. Even so, I killed hundreds of vampires the other night."

"And saved countless mortals," Marlowe shot back.

"But it's not okay," Eddie said, staring at his hands. "This whole magick thing, I see how the other wizards, the ones that have been around for centuries, have lost a lot of their humanity, making them no better than the vampires."

"That's hardly fair, Eddie," Marlowe said.

"Also, as long as I am a wizard, it makes my family a target. I have to reevaluate all of it. This might not be the right choice for me."

Marlowe and Drusilicus exchanged a look. Finally, Marlowe implored, "What do you want to do, Eddie?"

"I am taking time off. Six months, maybe a year with no magick of any kind. If I feel I want to continue, I'll contact you. If not, I'll surrender my staff and you can find someone more worthy."

Drusilicus' mouth became a tight line. "There is no one more worthy than you, Eddie."

Eddie faced his former opponent. "Thanks, Drew, that means a lot. But I have to decide that. Right now, I want to go home and be with my family."

Eddie headed out into the spring day as the sun beat down through the trees. He avoided the copse of trees and headed to his car to drive home, just like anyone else.

As he walked, he glanced back to see Drusilicus and Marlowe gazing sadly at him from the doorway of the townhouse.

FREE PREVIEW

THE **WEREWOLVES** OF **WASHINGTON SQUARE**

NYPD WIZARD DETECTIVE BOOK 3

ARJAY LEWIS

MIND
BENDER
PRESS

THE WEREWOLVES OF WASHINGTON SQUARE

T he full moon crested over Greenwich Village, far outshining the glow from the huge marble arch that was the centerpiece of Washington Square Park. Bright lights illuminated the large open plaza as the glow of windows seemed to float in the air from the many high-rise buildings encircling the monument.

The nearby benches and permanent cement chessboards abounded with shadows, lending those usually joyful areas a sinister air.

It was a chilly spring night, and the few New Yorkers walking through the park seemed to sense the strangeness of the hour. They stayed in the well-lit central area, avoiding the murky walkways snaking through the trees.

A tall man with shoulder-length dark hair and a pointed nose stepped out of a grove, holding a pocket watch. He was followed by a shorter man with a white beard and an ebony walking stick in his hand. Finally, a black-haired, tall woman with a tawny cast to her features appeared. The moon glinted off the large stone in the ring on her right hand.

"Marlowe, are you certain this is where Willowdell said we would find the lycanthrope?"

Marlowe nodded his head wearily. "The prophetess was quite sure."

Drusilicus shoved the watch in the pocket of his expensive three-piece suit. "We have had little success pursuing the creature."

"Are you sure it is the beast that killed that man?" the woman asked. "We've only known it was a werewolf since yesterday."

"It killed in Central Park the first night of the full moon. This is the third and final night," Drusilicus replied, an eyebrow raised. "It is unfortunate we didn't realize the danger sooner."

"Oh, don't nag, Drusilicus," Marlowe grumbled.

The woman smiled. "He is right. It does not become you." She looked over at Marlowe with concern. "Are you sure you are up to this? You appear tired."

Marlowe sighed. "Vasant, let us find the beast and be done."

A scream ripped through the night air.

With hardly a thought, the trio ran toward the disturbance, the taller man's stride much longer and faster than the other two. As they ran, their clothes underwent a surprising transformation. Their formal clothing shimmered and became tunics, leggings, and tall boots—Drusilicus in blue, Vasant in golden yellow, and Marlowe in white. All three of them suddenly held tall wooden staffs and raw power seemed to crackle around them.

Drusilicus arrived in a clearing where a woman crouched in fear behind a park bench, breathing hard, her eyes wide with terror.

Before her was an animal. It was a wolf with thick reddish fur, gray around its eyes and ears, and a white belly. Its fur bristled as it growled at the woman. Drool oozed from its muzzle and its eyes were a fiery red.

The monster turned to Drusilicus, staring at the tall man. The air reeked of the animal's strong musk, and Drusilicus saw malice in its eyes. He paused for a moment, then a blue light appeared at the top of his wooden staff. With a gesture, a beam of blue light lashed out at the creature, striking empty pavement, cracking the sidewalk on impact.

The monster leapt into the air, sailing over the stunned wizard.

With heightened reflexes and a century of training, he enveloped himself in a protective dome of magickal light.

The flying wolf landed upon the dome with such force, it knocked Drusilicus to the ground. The dome held, and the creature leapt only to fly straight at Vasant, mouth open and fangs gleaming. A dome of yellow light appeared over her as she dropped to one knee, enveloped under the protective sphere.

The wolf merely bounded off the top of her shield, lunging at Marlowe as he stumbled into the clearing and directly into its path.

"Marlowe!" Drusilicus tried to warn him, but it was all happening too fast as the canine fell upon the older wizard and knocked him to the ground.

Drusilicus and Vasant both jumped to their feet to see a second wolf— this one with a thick gray pelt—leap upon the attacker and shove it off the older man.

The two canines fought, biting and wrestling as they growled and tumbled over the open ground. They were about the same size, but the reddish wolf seemed to have the upper hand. Eventually the gray wolf pushed it off and faced it.

With a glance at the wizards, the red wolf vanished down another pathway, the gray wolf in pursuit.

Vasant moved toward Marlowe, but he was already getting up and gesturing to Drusilicus. "The woman, see to the woman."

Drusilicus approached the terrified woman still cowering behind the bench, her face white with fear.

"What was that?" she stammered. "Who are you?"

"Madam, were you bitten?"

"I don't see how a dog could be that big—"

"Madam," Drusilicus interrupted. "Were you bitten? Tell me."

"No, no," she gulped. "What was that… that… thing?"

"Where were you going?" he asked quietly.

"To my apartment," the woman said. "I was just out for a run, and that creature…"

Drusilicus made a small circle with his staff. "It was nothing. You saw a big dog that scared you, but you ran past it and headed home."

The woman's eyes glazed over. "Yes, I got scared and ran home."

"You saw two men from animal control and they pursued the dog," he told her.

Still spellbound, the woman replied. "Yes, animal control. I recognized the uniforms."

"You are going right home and to bed," Drusilicus told her.

She rose and without another word, she ran off without a look back.

Drusilicus let his shoulders relax and walked back to his companions. "Now we see the problem. There are two of the creatures. Let us pursue them at once."

Vasant looked up at Drusilicus, her eyes hard. "We cannot."

"What? But the night is still—"

"I am bitten," Marlowe confessed.

Drusilicus' eyes grew wide in alarm as Marlowe held out his hand, where a drop of blood dripped from a single wound.

"Which one?"

"The gray one," Marlowe said.

"But it looked like it was trying to save you," Vasant said.

"In the werewolf's defense, it might not have meant to bite me," Marlowe agreed. "But during the full moon, it cannot control itself."

"Marlowe, you know what this means." Drusilicus looked worried. "If it infected you, at the full moon next month you will —"

Marlowe sighed. "I am no good for you. I cannot fight the one that bit me—I am now part of its pack."

Vasant nodded. "Return to the townhouse quickly. Perhaps your vampire friend Daniel can remove the infection from your blood."

"Yes, that's good thinking," Marlowe said.

"I dislike the idea of you going there alone," Drusilicus said.

"I will be fine," Marlowe said. "We can worry about me on the morrow. You two pursue the werewolves. Do not let them strike again."

Marlowe headed into a grove of trees and disappeared.

"This does not bode well," Vasant said, watching Marlowe as he disappeared.

Drusilicus could only nod, his mouth a tight line.

To be continued

in

The WEREWOLVES of
WASHINGTON SQUARE

ABOUT THE AUTHOR

K nown as the "Wizard Of Odd", Arjay Lewis is an actor, magician, and multi-award-winning author.

I write tales of the strange and the horrifying.

I have spent my life as an entertainer, amusing people as a street-performer in the 1970s; a Broadway and casino artist in the 1980s; a party performer in the 1990s and 2000s; a cruise ship performer in the 2010s.

Stories have always been in my mind, and I have been writing since the 1990s. My reason to write is simple: to entertain. I write the type of books that I like to read: murder mysteries, strange tales of unnatural gifts, odd happenings and horror.

Please visit my web site and sign up for my mailing list to be "in the know" for upcoming books. Visit me on Facebook, Twitter, or my Amazon Author page.

And thank you for reading. You are the reason I write.

www.arjaylewis.com
www.facebook.com/arjaylewis
www.twitter.com/arjaylewiswrite
www.amazon.com/Arjay-Lewis

ALSO BY ARJAY LEWIS

Doctor Wise Series
Fire In The Mind
Seduction In The Mind
Reunion In The Mind
Haunted In The Mind
Devotion In The Mind
Asylum In The Mind
Specter In The Mind
Vengeance In The Mind
Echoes In The Mind
Infection In The Mind
Justice In The Mind
Ritual In The Mind
Vanished In The Mind

Horror
The Muse
Kept In The Dark
The Vanishing
Digger

Romantic Suspense
(with Debra Snow)
A Study In Murder

NYPD Wizard Detective
The Wizards Of Central Park West
The Vampires Of Greenwich Village
The Werewolves of Washington Square

FREE NOVELLA

VOWS

AND OTHER TALES OF THE MACABRE

For those who enjoy a good scare, here is a collection of stories designed to give you nightmares. These stories that have been published in *Weird Tales, H.P.. Lovecraft Magazine Of Horror, The Ultimate Halloween,* and *Sherlock Holmes Mystery Magazine.* If you tried to get them from their original source they would cost over $20.00. But you get them for FREE by signing up for Arjay's Newsletter

VOWS: A story of devotion that extends beyond death itself.
SIREN: A Sci-Fi fantasy of a condemned prisoner lost in space.
THE DARK: A guard sees creatures in the night...are they really there?
DREAMCATCHER: A walk in the woods...but you are not alone.
THE TRAVELER: What do you do if your flight is delayed...forever?
INTO THE ABYSS: A makeup artist gets the dream job...at a price.

www.arjaylewis.com/free-stuff.html